INDIGO DONUT

PATRICE LAWRENCE

Hodder
Children's
Books

HODDER CHILDREN'S BOOKS

First published in Great Britain in 2017 by Hodder Children's Books

1 3 5 7 9 10 8 6 4 2

Text copyright © Patrice Lawrence, 2017

'Praise Song for My Mother' by Grace Nichols. Copyright © Grace Nichols.
Reprinted by permission of Grace Nichols

A CIP catalogue record for this book is available from the British Library

ISBN 978 1 444 92718 4

Typeset in Berkeley Oldstyle by Avon DataSet Ltd,
Bidford-on-Avon, Warwickshire

Printed and bound in Great Britain by Clays Ltd, St Ives plc

The paper and board used in this book are made from wood from
responsible sources.

MIX
Paper from
responsible sources
FSC
www.fsc.org   FSC® C104740

Hodder Children's Books
An imprint of
Hachette Children's Group
Part of Hodder and Stoughton
Carmelite House
50 Victoria Embankment
London EC4Y 0DZ

An Hachette UK Company
www.hachette.co.uk

www.hachettechildrens.co.uk

To Patrick Edward Singh
I wish we'd had a chance to know each other better

You were
water to me
deep and bold and fathoming

You were
moon's eye to me
pull and grained and mantling

You were
sunrise to me
rise and warm and streaming

You were
the fishes red gill to me
the flame tree's spread to me
the crab's leg/the fried plantain smell
replenishing replenishing

Go to your wide futures, you said

'Praise Song For My Mother' by Grace Nichols

1

It was coming back again, like a film on slow stream, except someone had hit the mute button. The silence made it worse – it meant everything else was turned up to full. There was the smell: old tea mugs and burnt toast and smeared plastic takeaway boxes. The taste in her mouth: sugar so harsh it made her head hurt, like she'd breathed it in and it had stuck in clumps behind her eyeballs. She remembered how the last few jelly beans had rolled out on to the floor in front of her, stabs of colour between the ashtrays and crumpled cigarette papers. Or had they been M&Ms? A silver mobile phone was balanced on the magazines on the sofa next to a tangled pile of clothes. They were for her, her mum had said. She could try them on later.

Where are you, Nanna?

She was fully in the memory now. She looked down at her feet. Her bare toes in her sandals were still crusty from the sand pit at the park. She hunched over, hooking her hands around her knees, bracing her back against the door. It stayed shut. And everything behind it stayed silent.

Maybe she should knock. But Daddy had said she could

only come in if there was an emergency, something like a fire. He'd checked the cooker was turned off and smiled at her mum.

'See, Mahalia. It's okay. We won't be long.'

He'd pulled her out of her mum's arms and planted her on the floor. Her mum had bent over and kissed her on the nose.

'That's a magic kiss, sweetheart. You'll be all right.'

Then her mum had followed her dad into the bedroom and closed the door.

But she wasn't all right. She'd been all right where she was before. In Mummy's arms. She closed her eyes and screwed up her face, turning so her ear pressed against the door. Suddenly, her head was full of sounds. Different sounds, from before she was brought here. Her fingers squeaking across the wet sand pit as she gouged out a long, windy river. The wooden elephant, the giraffe, the lion, the zebra – all lined up. She was going to bury the crocodile deep in the sand, ready to nip the elephant's trunk when it bent over to drink in the river. Or was it the giraffe's neck . . . ?

She could hear the slosh and thud of water filling the buckets and the shrieking as the other kids soaked each other. And Nanna's voice cutting through it all, telling her they had to go soon, after one more ride on the twirly slide.

Then the thump as the boy dropped from the swing,

screaming for his mummy, and Nanna fading away as she ran over to help him.

And the man, over by the bench, calling her name. She hadn't known who he was. He'd promised to take her on an adventure, but he'd left her in this room.

Nanna?

She opened her eyes. The sound stayed turned up. Two bird puppets were arguing on CBeebies. An ambulance – or was it a fire engine? – howled in the distance, getting louder, like it was charging towards her. And the banging, hammering on the front door, so hard it made her cry out for Mummy.

And her name. Someone was shouting through the letterbox.

But she didn't want to open that door. She wanted to open the one that would lead to her mum.

Something shifted behind her. She twisted round as the bedroom door opened. Grey trainers. Jeans. A pillow lying in the middle of the dark floor, like it was floating. Feet on the bed, toes shiny with nail polish. A hand dangling down, like it was waiting to be held.

She touched her nose. The kiss had sunk away. The magic was gone. She wasn't all right. She wasn't all right at all.

2

The spider was big. Indigo reckoned that if an elephant and a tarantula could get it together, this mutant would be their baby. She swatted it into an empty mug and chucked the beast out of the window. It scuttled over the ledge and disappeared.

'It's okay, Kee. It's gone!'

Keely opened the door slowly. 'Did you close the window?'

'Yeah.'

Felix's long face appeared over Keely's shoulder. 'The thing was so damn big it could probably smash its way back in.'

Indigo hooked the mug on the stand. 'Well, if you don't move your bloody boxes out of my way, you're going to find its badass giant brother in your bed.'

Felix swaggered into the kitchen and yanked the Chart off the side of the fridge. 'It says here you lose points if you bad-mouth your bro.'

Indigo faked a big yawn. 'That's your handwriting, you idiot. And you are not my "bro".'

Felix nudged Keely. 'See how she treats me? But we

know it's all show. She's going to miss me, really.'

Indigo looked up. 'Dream on!' All her spare stuff was going into his room and she was buying the biggest jar of Nutella she could find and leaving it bang in the middle of the kitchen table, spoon stuck in it and all, because she'd know it was still going to be there when she came back.

He *had* to go. That way he'd be safe from her. Didn't he understand?

She wanted to tell him, but it felt like the words were tied on a string to her stomach and just thinking them made the string pull tight.

He was waving the Chart at her, like she didn't know it by heart already. 'Let me see. Indigo Bankes. You have successfully stacked the dishwasher and been granted three ticks. *Bedroom tidy?* A bit of a fail there. No ticks. *Not losing keys*. That's five ticks. How come you get ticks just for not doing stuff? Kee, that's not fair! You never did that for me.'

Keely laughed. 'You were my learning curve, Felix.'

'Your practice model! Great! You should have given social services a discount.'

'Believe me, Felix, they get me cheap. How many ticks have I got?'

'You're doing pretty crap, to be honest, Kee. *Lay off the chocolate Hobnobs*. No ticks. *Keep up the pilates*. Kee?'

'It's seven o'clock on a Tuesday morning in a room

full of skinny minnies.' Keely shook her head. 'Not happening.'

'That means you're well out of this month's competition.' Felix held the Chart close to his face and squinted hard at it. 'And so, indeed, is Indigo. This month's treat goes to Yours Truly.'

Indigo swiped the Chart off him. 'See that?' She underlined the column with her finger. '*Do One Big Special Thing*. I just did that. Extra points – right, Keely?'

Keely nodded. 'That dinosaur spider was definitely One Big Special Thing, Indigo.'

Indigo flipped a V to Felix.

He shook his head. 'You're so definitely going to miss me.'

Keely had turned her back to them, buttering bread. 'Of course we will, won't we, Indi?'

Indigo dug her teeth into her bottom lip. Keely didn't get it, neither. The three years with Felix had been all right. When the thing had sparked off in her, it hadn't been bad enough that Felix and Keely were in proper danger. But it was only a matter of time. When he finally got his arse out of that door, she had to let him go, crumple him up and shove him into the back of her head, in the darkest, most faraway corner. And it would have to be the same for Keely – push her even further back, past every other foster carer she'd known, so not a single memory could leak through.

Indigo raised her voice. 'So, you going to get me those Atomic Blondie tickets, Kee?'

'Send me the link, hun.' Keely opened the fridge door. 'Sorry, Indigo, we're out of yoghurts. I'll stick some money on your dinner account if you want to grab something in the canteen, okay?'

'Yeah. All right.'

'Or I can make you a sandwich. Though I haven't got much to put in it.'

'You could always go to the fried-rat place,' Felix said.

He was standing by the sink, speed texting. Keely was trying to dodge her way around him. He always managed to prop himself in the wrong place. Indigo wasn't going to miss that. Or when he blasted bloody Grace Jones without his bloody headphones and it was *doof, doof, doof,* through the walls until Keely got him to turn it down. Or when Indigo had to step over his scummy pants on the bathroom floor.

Pulling out the bad things made it easier. She could already feel him curling round the edges and getting smaller.

Keely was still big and solid, though. She made the world around Indigo feel solid too. But that didn't matter. Indigo couldn't risk it. She knew what was inside her and what it could do.

Right now, Keely had her hands on her hips. 'Chicken

shops are the devil's work, Felix. Don't encourage her, unless you want her to end up like me.'

Felix slipped his phone in his pocket and went and flung his arm round Keely's shoulders. 'There's nothing wrong with you.'

Keely shrugged him off. 'I wish my knees agreed. They are definitely wrong.' She kissed Felix's cheek. 'Go on, or you'll be late.'

'Who cares?'

'Felix . . .'

'Joking!'

'And let me know if you're staying at Wade's. Just so I don't call the police.'

'Ah.' Felix's voice from the hallway. 'Those were the days.'

The front door banged shut behind him.

Keely wrapped her sandwiches in cling film and stashed them in her lunchbox.

'You okay, Indigo? You've gone all quiet.'

'I'm all right.' Though her stomach felt like it was tugged right up to the top of her head.

Keely leaned over and kissed Indigo's forehead. Indigo breathed in her scent – cucumber and posh Gaultier perfume. Social services should scrape off this smell and put it in bottles so they could spray it on all foster carers, because that's how real mothers were supposed to smell.

Indigo knew she should be a real daughter back, putting her arms round Keely, maybe kissing her too, because Keely deserved it.

But she held her breath and did her statue thing until Keely moved away.

Keely's lips twitched like they were giving Indigo a little shrug and then she smiled. Her sparkly nail tapped the Chart. '*Be on time*. We all need ticks for that one. You're in double English first thing, aren't you?'

'Yeah, with Queen Crapheads Saskia and Mona. Do I have to go?'

'You promised.' Keely squeezed her shoulder.

Statue! Statue! But it was too late. Indigo had let herself sink into the squeeze. She *had* to do better.

'It's only been three weeks, Indigo. Not long enough to give it a proper go. It's probably your last chance, remember?'

Yeah, she remembered. It didn't mean she agreed.

'*And* you made me fork out for that Topshop jacket. It's not exactly Pitt Academy's dress code, is it?'

'It looks good, though, Kee.'

'It's beautiful, my darling! So put it on. Go to school. Feel great and be good.'

'Is that your new catchphrase?'

'Yup. And I'm off to light up the lives of Tottenham's happy shoppers. I'll see you later, hun.'

9

A swish of bag, footsteps down the hall and the front door, quieter this time. Keely always caught it before the wind did.

Indigo rinsed her bowl and spoon. She'd better get sorted. She slid her timetable out from under the fridge magnets. Every day at Pitt was pretty crap, but Thursdays were extra shite. Saskia, Mona, the grinning slimeball Levy, and that stupid seat she had to sit in, right up front under the teacher's nose. And then there was that weird-looking boy, Bailey, right behind her, trying to pretend he wasn't having a good old gawk. Typical. The tall, skinny one with the mad hair *had* to be the one that was into her . . .

She dropped her timetable next to the Chart, went into her bedroom and plugged in the hair straighteners. She should have wiped them down first because yesterday's anti-frizz serum was not smelling good.

God. She was supposed to read that poem for English. Mr Godalming had given her a little sideways look when he handed out the worksheet. She'd seen the title and shoved it straight in her bag.

'Praise Song For My Mother'.

Godalming must know. Most likely all the teachers did. They'd probably tossed a coin in the staff room. *Last one left gets her*. Then, when Godalming realised he was the loser, he'd have asked more questions. And it was always someone else they asked, not Indigo, because it was easier to talk about her than to her. He'd have seen the list of schools she'd been chucked out of. Maybe he knew how many foster homes she'd passed through. And he'd read about her mum and her dad and how they'd found Indigo curled up by the bedroom door.

At least Godalming didn't put on the usual performance – that look, his head to the side, a bit embarrassed and a bit sorry, not sure if he should really say something.

He hadn't said, *If you ever want to talk about your mum, Indigo . . .*

So, she hadn't had to say, *No, I don't.* Then watch his head tilt to the other side.

She stretched out a strand of hair and ran the straighteners down. It smelled like she'd been standing too close to bonfires.

All the teachers probably got strict instructions not to mention her dad. Adults never did. It was only other kids who wanted to know every detail about what happened in that stinking flat in south London, like they hadn't Googled it already. Maybe the adults thought you could catch murder off her, like the vomit bug. Or they didn't really want to know what it looked like. A pillow. Sparkly nails.

Breathe.

See? It was easy for the thing to wake up, scrabbling and hooking her insides, heaving itself through her. All those counsellors and key workers and social workers tried to tell her it was something else. It was only that care worker in Medway who'd nearly got it right, when she yelled at Indigo that the apple didn't fall far from the tree. The apple didn't fall at all. It was the same apple. Same seeds. Same thing inside her that her dad had. It was always alert, always waiting. It made him pick up a pillow and hold it and hold it until . . .

BREATHE!

And again!

It loosened and dropped back down inside her. Not all the way, but enough.

Breathe.

Easier now.

She checked the mirror. She looked like she'd been standing under a helicopter. No way was she facing Pitt Academy like this.

The letterbox banged. Crap. It was nearly nine. Indigo uncoiled another clump of hair and clamped it between the straighteners.

The letterbox crashed again. For God's sake! She was not going out on the street with a head full of greasy frizz. She propped the straightener on her hair-clips tin and went into the hallway. A few letters and a pizza menu were scattered on the mat and a package was jammed in the letterbox. She scooped up the letters and dropped them on the radiator shelf. The package was a small padded envelope, with Keely's name and address scrawled in Biro, though half the writing was lost on the other side of the letterbox. Indigo tugged at it. Jesus, the postman must have used a hammer to bang it in. It was well stuck. Keely needed to have a word next time she saw him. Indigo gripped the envelope tight, feeling the plastic bubble wrap inside pop beneath her fingers. She pulled again. One sodding centimetre. Indigo did not have time for this. Her straighteners were probably going to set fire to her room soon. One hard yank and . . . the stupid thing was free.

Great. Keely's delivery looked like it had picked a fight with all the other letters in the sack. The sticky brown paper had peeled away from the bubble wrap and the flap had come half-unstuck.

Indigo gave the envelope a little shake. There was something small and solid inside. She squeezed it. Hard edges. Maybe Keely had been on eBay again and forgotten to check the size – like the time she swore the hand-carved rocking chair was such a bargain and when it came, it just about fit in her palm.

Indigo sniffed. Shit – she was right about her straighteners! She dropped the package on top of the other letters. It had a council postmark. She should have noticed that before. It could be anything. It could be from anywhere in the whole of the council, but these sorts of packages usually came from social services. Last time, it was a couple of old photos of Scarlet and Coral for Keely to give to her. But that was last year. There couldn't be anything else to send.

Indigo picked up the envelope and shook it again. The small solid thing moved around.

The envelope was already damaged. If the thing inside it just happened to fall out, Keely couldn't be too mad. Indigo slid her little finger in the gap where the flap was unstuck and turned the envelope upside down. The thing fell against her finger. A corner, smooth, maybe wooden. She wiggled her finger. The gap got a tiny bit bigger. And a tiny bit more. That was it. Suddenly, the thing fell into her palm.

Indigo stared at it. It was a kid's toy, a small wooden crocodile. Its body was painted cartoon-green and the white on its teeth had peeled, but Indigo knew that already. She closed her hand and squeezed. The chipped bit at the tip of its tail dug into her skin. She knew that was going to happen too. And she knew how heavy it should feel, even though her hand was much smaller the last time she held it.

Oh, God!

Indigo made it back into her room and slid down the door on to the floor. She unplugged the smoking straighteners and shoved them aside. It was too late. The envelope couldn't be stuck down again. The crocodile couldn't be shoved away into the dark.

Breathe.

14

She lay the crocodile on her rug, ripped the flap off the envelope and emptied the rest of the stuff on to the floor. She poked at a wodge of tissue. The toy must have been wrapped in it. It looked like it had bitten its way free. Then two sheets of paper, one A4, with the social services' address. The other one was smaller, old-fashioned notepaper, folded over.

Indigo scanned the first letter. *Dear Keely . . . Olive Bankes . . . Mahalia's mother . . . long-term dementia . . .* Yeah, Indigo knew that, but that came on ages ago. More writing. Social services were supposed to send this to Keely sooner. *We want to apologise for the unfortunate delay.* No surprises there. Keely was supposed to use her judgement . . . and call if she would like further support. Indigo almost laughed. Keely said that whenever she tried to call them, by the time she got through, Indigo's social worker had changed twice.

And who the hell decided that Indigo needed Keely's judgement? She'd had enough lectures about growing up and taking responsibility for herself. So that was exactly what she was going to do. Take responsibility. She unfolded the creamy notepaper and spread the letter flat against her knee. The writing was on just one side of paper, but the sentences were spaced out, in different colour pens. Sometimes the letters were neat and tight. By the end, they seemed to struggle across the paper.

15

My beautiful Indigo,

Time is short. This morning I woke up in a strange room, but they said I have lived here for many months now. It won't be long before it's all gone. Even when the words are taken from me, I know you will still be in my heart.

I have asked the care home to post this to you after I pass.

I have written out the address on the envelope first, in case I forget!

I'm not sure how long this letter will be, because writing is hurting.

I post this letter every night.

I want my spirit to rest in peace.

Forgive your father. Find him. Forgive him.

Mahalia told me. Not H. Just me.

Love love love,

Your nanna

Mahalia told me. What the hell could Mahalia say? She was dead! Because that bastard . . .

Indigo's temples felt like she'd pushed the straighteners against her skin.

Breathe! Breathe hard.

This must be a joke from some crappy social worker she'd wound up ages ago and forgotten about. Maybe it was the care worker who'd yelled at her about the apples and the tree. She'd got the sack for that. *She'd* want revenge.

Forgive your father. That was the biggest piss-take ever.

It felt like that giant spider from earlier had got into her head and was running around her brain.

Another breath, letting the air sink through her body. That was better. Start again. Read it slowly. Hold every word before moving on to the next one.

My beautiful Indigo . . . still be in my heart . . . after I pass.

Indigo's key worker had made a special visit to tell her that her grandma had died. They'd probably told Keely to keep an eye on her too, just in case she couldn't keep it all in, but Indigo had got that one right, watching the key worker talk, but fading out her words to silence. Indigo couldn't even remember what her grandmother looked like, even with the photos they'd sent.

And now this. A weird letter from a mad old woman who kept forgetting where she lived. Proper mad. She must have been. She wanted Indigo to forgive Toby Scott *and* find him!

Find him? Indigo bloody well knew where he was – at the bottom of a cheap council grave with three other deadbeats buried on top of him. He didn't even deserve a headstone to tell people who he was. There was no way she was going up north to stand by that flat square of earth with her head bowed. Toby Scott. Gone forever. And good bloody riddance.

Except he wasn't totally gone, was he? He'd left her with the thing, banging round inside her, filling out her emptiness. The thing that was waiting to spring out at the people she was supposed to—

love love love

Thanks to him, she couldn't love them. Not ever. They wouldn't be safe.

She hooked her arms round her knees. She kicked out, flicking the crocodile away. The letter was stuck between her fingers; she couldn't let it go. She closed her eyes. She could feel it moving inside her again, stretching out, its heat catching at the back of her throat.

BREATHE, BREATHE, BREATHE!

Oh, God.

3

Bailey should have kept his mouth shut, then his head wouldn't be rammed up with Austin's opinions.

Bailey, man, what's going on with the Indigo thing?

You wanna see desperation? Hold up your phone, bruv, and snap yourself.

Man, no! Just no!

Bailey washed his hands and glanced in the mirror. He'd made it casual but Austin still noticed.

'Hair's looking good.' Austin shielded his eyes. 'Got a full ginger glow on.'

Bailey teased a flat curl from behind his ear. 'It's you, man. Blinding me with your jokes.'

He levered out a paper towel and tried to wipe his hands. This school stuff was as absorbent as a brick. He scrunched it up and threw it at the overflowing bin, but it bounced off and rolled across the floor.

Austin sighed. 'Even the garbage don't want you!'

Bailey pulled the door to the corridor open. ''Cause I don't belong with no rubbish.'

Austin raised his hands. 'You calling me rubbish? You wonder why you ain't got more friends?'

Bailey laughed. 'I got friends. I just feel sorry for you and let you tag along.'

They joined the flow heading down the science corridor. There she was! Indigo. In the middle of the crowd. Austin hadn't spotted her yet. Good.

'It's you who needs sympathy.' Austin swerved past a huddle of Year Ten girls. 'Sitting there all lesson with your big, sad love-eyes beaming 'cross the back of Indigo's head.'

'It's a nice head.'

'But the back ain't the bit that does the talking. Or anything else, bruv.'

'No, mate! Just don't!'

'Just don't, what? You're the one with the dirty mind! I'm talking smiling.' He elbowed Bailey. 'Like now. You fixed up your hair. Go flash your smile at her.'

Did the boy have X-ray eyes or something? Mum said men couldn't do more than one thing at once, but Austin managed to run off his mouth *and* mind other people's business at the same time. Bailey should have brought that paper towel out of the toilet. He could have shoved it in Austin's mouth. It would dry solid and close him down for a bit. And then Bailey would sweep through the stream of Year Twelves and draw level with her. And maybe, just maybe, this time when he tried to talk to her, he wouldn't feel like he'd bitten off a chunk of iceberg.

'Go on!' Austin urged. 'Ain't no one in your way.'

Most of the other kids had filtered into their classrooms. There she was. Bailey took a deep breath. To hell with Austin. He was going to do it. He was going to say something, even if it was some pathetic crap about the poem they'd had to review for homework. He quickened his pace.

Austin grabbed his shoulder. 'Serious, bruv?'

'Gentlemen!' Mr Godalming brushed past them. 'If I'm late, you're even later.'

The teacher hurried down the corridor, sweeping Indigo along with him. Bailey watched them turn left into the humanities corridor. It was probably for the best. Austin was the worst wingman in the world.

They went into the English room

Austin was grinning. 'Girl's waiting. Better check your 'fro.'

Indigo was at her table, right up front. She was crossed. Arms, legs, even the pens on her desk, one over the other, like she was warding away vampires. Bailey hoped she'd got her eyes crossed too, because she was looking straight at the slimy man-mollusc Levy, who was giving her his smiley side-eye. Bailey felt sorry for her. It must be tough enough starting half a term after everyone else, without being stuck with Levy and a constant view of Godalming's crotch.

'Settle down!' Godalming held up the worksheet. '"Praise

Song for My Mother". I'm going to be deeply optimistic and assume that you've all read it and thought about it.'

Indigo sank into her seat.

'Come on, you lot!' Godalming's spotlight stare swung around the classroom. 'Can you try and *pretend* to be interested?' He looked over Bailey to the table behind him. 'Mona? What do you think the poet is trying to tell us?'

Mona groaned. 'It's too hot, sir.'

She was right. Bailey could almost see the heat wavering off the walls. One day someone was going to sort out Pitt Academy's mad heating. Indigo leaned forward and shrugged off her jacket, hanging it over the back of her chair.

'You're doing it again.' An Austin whisper was as quiet as everyone else's bus chat.

'What?'

'Laser eye. On the back of her head.'

'I told you. I like her head.'

'I don't get the stripy hair thing. The girl looks like—' Austin's hand clapped to his mouth. 'I get it, man! She's got the zebra crossing. You got the orange beacon. Together forever in road safety harmony.'

Godalming's glare circled round again and landed on Austin. 'Yes?'

'Yes, what, sir?'

'Yes, share your observations about the poem.'

'We were talking about the fried plantain smell, you

know, how plantain is universal. Everyone loves plantain.'

Godalming nodded. 'Thank you, Austin. I'm sure your discussion on the cultural ubiquity of plantain is deeply relevant.' He turned towards the whiteboard. 'Meanwhile, other thoughts, please?'

Austin leaned in. 'I got a new name for her.'

'I don't care.'

'It's Big Bang.'

'I don't care.'

'Wanna know why?'

'I'm telling you, man, I don't—'

'Soraya's cousin told her Indigo got chucked out of her last school because she right-hooked some kid called Stivo.'

'I know that.'

'Yeah, but it wasn't like she just punched him.'

Levy was giving Indigo the proper eye now. Bailey was surprised she didn't have to wipe the slime off her face.

'I heard about Stivo. He likes to touch up girls even when they don't want it.'

'Soraya's cousin said she went proper mental, though. Shouting, swearing, everything. Big explosion, like she was making a new universe. One of the teachers got hit too.'

'What are you trying to say?'

'She could turn on you, man.'

'I don't grab up girls.'

'Maybe she hates all men. Even good boys like you.'

And idiots like Levy. So far, it looked like she wasn't into him, neither.

'Austin, you need a filter, man. You know how people like to talk crap when anyone new starts. You said that Isabella girl was Adele's cousin.'

'I thought she was.'

'Thought wasted, bruv. It was total crap.'

Godalming was highlighting the first verse of the poem on the whiteboard. 'Water. *Deep and bold and fathoming.* What do you think that means? Saskia?'

'Maybe her mum tried to drown her when she was a baby, sir.'

A big laugh went up.

Godalming wasn't giving in. 'Are you saying that motherhood can be nurturing *and* dangerous?'

'Yeah, sir.' Saskia's voice was slow and sly. 'Some mothers are dead good, you know what I mean? Some of the other ones are dead bad.'

Indigo twisted round and hit Saskia with a look that should have killed her. Levy whistled.

Austin sucked his teeth. 'Oh, gee. And you know the boy Stivo was Saskia's cousin, right?'

'Serious?'

Indigo was blasting out *proper* laser-eye. Bailey could almost see the pin-thin beam of light burning a hole in Saskia's forehead.

'Um. An interesting take, Saskia.' Godalming glanced around the class. 'Anyone else?'

Indigo's hand shot up. Godalming took his time noticing her.

'Here, sir.' Levy looked proud that he'd managed to get out two words in a row.

'Thank you, Levy. Indigo, what would you like to say?'

'I'd like to say that Saskia's an arsehead.'

Levy whistled again. It was probably easier for him than talking.

Godalming dropped his voice like it was just him and Indigo in the room. Bailey strained harder to listen, just like everyone else must have been.

'Let's just focus on the poem.'

'Sir!' Saskia had stood up. 'You're gonna deal with that, right?'

'Later, Saskia.'

'If that was me, I'd be sent out.'

'Sit *down*, Saskia!'

Indigo was staring at her desk. It was just as well. Saskia had her screwface on. She scraped her chair back hard and sat down.

Austin raised his eyebrows at Bailey. 'See? Godalming would rather wind up Saskia than be the dude who destroys the universe as we know it.'

Indigo slipped deeper into her chair, her legs stretched

out under the table. Her mouth was moving, like she was praying. She didn't look the religious type, though maybe mini skirts and stripy hair had got big for Christians.

'Sir?' Carly was waving her hand. 'It's like the poet's back inside her mum. Really deep.'

Godalming grinned. 'Now we're getting there. Right, young men and women. You have thirty minutes. I want you to write an appreciation of "Praise Song". Think form, think theme, think literary devices. What is the poet trying to tell us?'

Indigo was still silent praying. Or maybe she was trying out a string of curses to lay on Saskia later. Levy leaned forward and waved his hand in front of her eyes. Indigo gave him the finger. Levy mouthed something. He got two fingers that time. Good. Ever since primary school, girls seemed to feel they were lucky if Levy threw them a second glance.

'Appreciation!' Godalming said. 'Now!'

Indigo's head bobbed down as she rummaged in her bag. Big streaks of blonde hair, big streaks of black. Of course! Austin must be dragging him into the Land of Stupid, because Bailey should have got it straight away. Whose hair was like that? Debbie Harry! Blondie, cover of *Parallel Lines*, 1978.

So Indigo was into Blondie? She must be. Now they really had something to talk about.

The bell made Bailey jump. He jammed his notebook into his bag and dropped his pens on top of it.

Austin said, 'She's escaping.'

'She looked stressed. I'm gonna give her some time.'

'Always the stalker. Never the talker.'

'Profound. I'm surprised you haven't sold that one to Kanye.'

'Saskia!' Godalming had pulled himself up to boss-teacher height. 'A word, please.'

'Sir, it's lunchtime.'

'Then let's be quick.'

Saskia hooked her bag over her shoulder and strolled towards the front. She paused by Bailey, smirking. Here it came. Again.

'Modelling for McDonalds yet, Ronald?'

Bailey met her sharp little eyes. 'You not got anything else?'

'It's still good.'

'Nah. It's stale. They don't even use the clown any more.'

She made a face at him. 'I know a clown when I see one.' She sauntered up to Godalming.

Austin shook his head. 'That girl's got cheek! At least your hair's real, man. There's a village in Brazil full of bald women because of her.'

Bailey laughed. 'You saying that to her face?'

'I just did. Her face is too far away to hear me. You

27

coming to Rooster C's? I promised Soraya I'd meet her at lunchtime.'

'I'll leave you two to it.'

'Bailey?' Godalming was holding out a plastic folder full of worksheets. 'I forgot to give this to Indigo. If you see her, can you pass it on? If you don't, just drop it at my office.'

'Yes, sir.'

Bailey pushed the folder into his bag. Behind him, Saskia was mouthing off at Godalming. He closed the classroom door and followed Austin into the corridor.

'Wow!' Austin said. 'I'd better get Roosters to serve my wings up raw.'

'What?'

'I told you. Indigo's a walking explosion and you've just been nominated to pass her six weeks' supply of Shakespeare's best. If Big Bang goes off, it'll be barbecue for miles around. Good luck, my friend.'

He patted Bailey on the shoulder and doubled back past the English rooms towards the quad.

The whole school was on the move, heading down to the canteen or out for chicken and milkshakes. Where would Indigo go? Bailey had clocked her at Rooster C's just the one time and even then, she'd come in, checked the queue and walked out again. But she did make it to the common room sometimes. On Monday, she'd been curled in a chair with her headphones clamped on. He'd walked past her twice. She hadn't looked up.

'What's your name?' A teacher had stopped in front of Bailey. She flicked her plasma screen-sized glasses on to the top of her head.

'Sorry, miss?'

'Your name.'

'Bailey, miss.'

'What's your first name?'

'Bailey is my first name, miss. Bailey Mason-Lyte.'

'Right. Yes. But I shouldn't have to ask you that, should I?'

She pointed to his chest.

'Miss? Oh.' He tugged the lanyard and his ID card popped out from under his shirt.

'You know the rules. It must be visible at all times. If I catch you again, I'll report you to your tutor.'

He nodded. He wasn't going to miss this crap when he left. Was Mum as hardcore in her school? Best not to ask.

The teacher strode on past him to terrorise some Year Sevens. Bailey had ended up outside the canteen. He might as well check for Indigo, even though Pitt Academy still didn't believe that no sixth former was spending out on a cheese roll and a bag of crisps when hot wings and chips were the same price just down the road.

But Indigo *was* there. By herself, with her headphones on, eating a yoghurt and checking her phone. A few tables away, Mona and a couple of her mates were rolling a Coke can across the table to each other, their eyes on Indigo.

And Indigo was carrying on like she didn't know they were there, when any second now, Saskia would be roaring down the corridor looking for revenge.

Bailey pulled the folder out of his bag. It was slippery in his hands. He watched as Indigo tucked back a strand of black hair that was flopping over her phone, still not looking up at anyone. All he had to do was go over, give her the folder and . . . they could go to the common room and get a coffee or something. Quick, though, before Saskia got back from bashing Mr Godalming.

He needed one word. Just one. 'Hi'. His tongue was on lockdown, though.

'Yo! Ronald!' Mona, doing her best Saskia impression.

Bailey ignored her, but Mona's voice must have bust through Indigo's music. She looked up, caught Bailey's eye, then down at her phone again.

Just 'hi'. It had to be now. He went across to her.

'Hi.' It sounded like he'd coughed the word out.

Nothing. She must have turned her music right up. Mona muttered something and her mates sniggered. Bailey fought against the blush that was rising on his cheeks. The last thing he needed was his face matching his hair. He pulled out a chair and sat down opposite Indigo. She flipped back her headphones and looked at him. It wasn't just the hair – she'd gone for the proper Debbie Harry look, lipstick, eye shadow, everything. Though Indigo's eyes were gold brown, not green, and there was a big silver stud punched through the top of her ear. He hadn't noticed that before.

Now he must seem all intense, staring at her. He kept his eyes on her ear.

'Do you want something?'

'Sorry.' His mouth was slowly loosening. 'Godalming asked me to give you this.'

He laid the folder on the table. It sat there between them.

'Right. Thanks.'

Bailey's chair jerked forward. He looked round. It was Levy, giving Indigo a big wink. *Well done, Levy. You managed to kick a stationery object.* Levy swaggered off and sat next to Mona, who grabbed his hand like it was about to fall off his wrist.

'Jesus,' Indigo said. 'Even my finger can't be bothered with him no more.'

Bailey said, 'He's always been an idiot.'

'Yeah?'

'I've known him since nursery. Most of us went to the same primary school.'

'Lucky you.'

He deserved that. What was worse than an English lesson caught in Godalming's groin-line? Being reminded that everyone else has known each other since they were five.

But she hadn't got up and gone. She'd even kept her headphones off. This was his chance.

Coffee. Common room. Now.

He said, 'Indigo? Do you want . . .'

Indigo frowned. 'Serious?'

He hadn't even asked her yet! Was that good or bad 'serious'? 'Well, I was thinking . . .'

Now he could hear it. Mona was singing. Her voice wasn't bad, neither. She was giving it out to 'Mama Used to Say', the old Junior Giscombe song.

'Yeeessss!' Saskia made her entrance, waving her hands and wiggling her hips through the canteen. 'Tuuuunnne! Sing it, sister!'

Indigo looked like she'd been zapped by a stun gun. She was rigid, eyes wide.

Bailey said, 'They just like attention.'

Indigo didn't move. Mona and her mates had started on 'Mamma Mia'. Other kids were turning to stare at them, teachers too, as if Saskia was leading a cheesy pop flash mob.

Indigo's chair shot back, she stood and raced off. A cheer went up from Mona's table.

Mona gave Bailey a sweet smile. 'Are you into nutcases now?'

'No,' Bailey said. 'You were the last one.'

'Hey! Look what I found!' Saskia's long gold nails were unhooking a jacket from the back of Indigo's chair.

Mona whooped. 'Nice!'

'Yeah. Nice.' Bailey held out his hand. 'I'll give it to her.'

Saskia readjusted her chewing gum. A lump bulged in her cheek. 'Don't think I can trust you, bruv.'

'Oh, come on, Saskia! You know how much grief she's going to get if she's stopped.'

'Yeah. That's why we have to keep it safe for her.'

Saskia threw the jacket towards Mona. It fell short and flopped on to the dirty floor. Mona picked it up between her fingers and thumb. A big, greasy stain oozed across the lining.

'Damn! We can't give it to her like this!' Saskia caught it as Mona chucked it back. 'We're gonna have to clean it.'

Bailey went to grab it, but Saskia threw it low. The jacket skidded across the floor, into the puddle of leftovers by the waste recycle bin.

Saskia rubbed her hands together. 'You say a word, Red Boy, and we're gonna make sure wherever your little honey goes in this school, we're there too. You understand?'

Mona strutted over to the waste bins and stood there, arms folded.

Saskia said, 'You didn't answer me? Do you understand?'

Mona stepped back, grinding Indigo's jacket sleeve into the slops.

Saskia said, 'Yeah. You understand.'

Indigo stopped running. A kid close behind her cussed hard. Indigo could cuss him back, but not now. If she opened her mouth, if she let out the words, she wouldn't stop there. The thing was ready, making her bones vibrate against her skin. Pushing, pushing.

Please. Not here.

Those bitch girls. It was deliberate. They were poking at her. They wanted to set it off. If she could find the Reflection Room she might be all right. She'd sit down with silence around her, fill her head full of good things. Make the thing go back.

Left? Right? Across the quad? It was all the bloody same. Why was every new school designed to catch her out? She'd try left. Good, a noticeboard. That would help. No! It was just more crap about Pitt Academy transforming lives.

A load of Year Eights were pouring down the staircase next to her. She closed her eyes and leaned against the wall.

Breathe. Her stomach jumped, like it was laughing at her. She had to try harder. She needed the right pictures in her head. She had to see them properly, her counsellor had said.

MrsWeasleyLinGiselle. Breathe.

Not working.

MrsWeasleyLinGiselle. Breathe.

The hook and pull inside her.

MrsWeasleyLinGiselle. Breathe.

She touched her stomach.

Having breakfast with Mrs Weasley and her kids in their magic house. Lin from *Spirited Away*, giving her a bun in the bathhouse dormitory. Getting a piggyback off Giselle from *Enchanted* while they ran through their New York apartment. It was only pretend, but anything was better than what was trying to escape from her.

She opened her eyes. The Year Eights were gone, their shrieking voices fading away. And she knew where she was. She should have gone across the quad. She dashed out of the door, straight across the grass square and in the other side of the building. Yeah! There! The Reflection Room.

Indigo opened the door. It was empty. Good. It was hers, they'd said, to use when things were getting too much, but it was hard to chill if some stressed-out kid was shouting at their support worker. She went over to the water cooler, pushed the button and held a plastic cup underneath. She knocked back the water and shivered as it arrowed down into her belly. She filled her cup again and sank into one of the soft chairs.

She was done for the day. Maths catch-up would have to wait. She was getting out of this dump and going home. And maybe she'd slip the letter out of her pillowcase. Maybe she'd read it again. And she'd definitely send a picture of it to Primrose. She'd know what it was about.

The door clicked open. It was a chunky Year Seven girl with a furious face. She glared at Indigo. What? This little girl was going to start something?

Yes, she was! Her chin jutted forward. 'What are you staring at?'

Indigo pulled out her headphones and shoved them on. 'Room's all yours.' She scrolled through her playlist. 'Atomic'. Dead right. She rammed the volume up, and opened the door and stuck out her head. Not too manic. She stepped into the corridor.

'You!'

A teacher. She was wearing enormous glasses that made her look like a Powerpuff Girl. She gestured for Indigo to take off her headphones. Indigo paused Blondie and pushed them down round her neck.

The teacher frowned. 'What's your name?'

'Indigo. What's yours, miss?'

'I'm Miss Devrille.' A smile played across the teacher's face. She stepped closer to Indigo, looking her up and down. 'Where's your jacket?'

'What?'

'The dress code, Indigo. You and your parents signed up to it. Your skirt's too short as well.'

Her jacket. Jesus. Keely had forked out something big for that, way more than her allowance from social services.

Indigo had promised – *sworn* – that she'd take care of it.

'Those aren't black tights, Indigo.'

Indigo had run out of the English room as quick as she could. Maybe her jacket was there.

'Your shoes—'

Her jacket. She needed her jacket. And, oh, God . . . scrabbling, scraping, pushing.

MrsWeasleyLinGiselle. Breathe.

MrsWeasleyLinGiselle. BREATHE.

It wasn't working!

'Indigo? Did you hear me? I'll be phoning your parents.'

The hole, edges squeezing against each other, pushing it up.

'I get it, miss! I don't care about your crappy uniform, but I need to—'

The teacher's eyes widened. They filled her whole glasses frame. 'Who's your Head of Learning?'

'My jacket!'

The bloody cow shook her miserable head. *Breathe. Breathe.*

The teacher touched Indigo's arm. 'You can pick it up later. I think we need to see your Head of—'

'NO!' It came out like a howl.

The teacher said something, but it was hard to hear beneath the sound of Indigo's own breath, the throbbing beneath her skin, her whole body feeling like it had been

37

dropped in a cauldron of boiling water.

'Time to call your mum or dad.'

'My mum's dead, you idiot! And my dad killed her!'

And now Indigo was splitting apart. Her knuckles snapped in pain as they hit a wall. And she was crying because it hurt inside and out and maybe if she didn't stop, all of her would melt into tears.

4

Bailey knew there was no point running for the bus. Even if he got there, it would already be jammed with St Ecclestia girls. Things would be extra-hyper and Bailey wasn't in the mood.

'Yo!'

Austin was jogging towards him.

Bailey raised his eyebrows. 'Yo?'

'You stopped, didn't you? You gonna wait for the next one?' Austin checked his phone. 'Six minutes.'

Bailey shook his head. 'Not in any hurry. I was going to check out the record place.'

'Flash Tracks or Final Vinyl?'

'Got time for both.'

Austin fell into stride beside him. 'Soraya told me Big Bang went off today!'

'I was there.'

'Seriously, man? You actually witnessed her in action?' Austin was going to need an operation to prop his jaw back.

'Saskia's crew took her jacket. I was looking for Indigo to tell her.'

'Her jacket got took? And that was enough for her to go off?'

'Suppose so.'

'I heard she clonked that teacher, big time.'

'That's crap.'

'So what happened?'

'It was just . . . Forget it.'

'Oh, come on, Bailey! Give us the goods!'

'Next time I'll film it, right, mate?'

'Don't come over so holy. You were the one in the audience. You. Not me.'

No answer to that one. Dad once told him about the only time he remembered Bailey having a tantrum. He was two and they were by a pond in Victoria Park. Bailey had wanted to wade in, the same way he did with the paddling pool, and nothing Dad had said would convince him it was a bad idea. In the end, Bailey's valve had blown and he'd thrown himself on the ground, screaming. Dad just lay down next to him and waited for him to finish, while people walked round them, staring.

Indigo's valve had blown, but no one lay down next to her. All anybody did was stare. Including Bailey. And it was Bailey's fault. He should have snatched the jacket from under Mona's heels. He'd let it go way too easily.

He said, 'Did you know?'

'I told you, man! Big Bang!'

'No,' Bailey said. 'That her mum's dead.'

Austin made a face. 'Yeah. Everyone does.'

'I didn't.'

'That's 'cause you don't talk to no one.'

'I talk to you.'

'I thought you knew.'

'And her dad? You know about that too?'

Austin looked embarrassed.

'Jesus, Austin. You looked her up.'

'Just like you're going to do when you get home.'

'No . . . well, maybe. Do you know what happened?'

'It was when she was a kid. Her parents were on drugs and they think her dad just got a bit mad and killed her mum. He pleaded guilty straight away.'

Bailey blew out his cheeks. 'Dad's worked with kids who've gone through stuff like that. But I didn't expect . . .'

'What?'

One of them to be in my English class.

Austin gave him a snidey smile like he knew what Bailey was thinking.

'Saskia and Mona and that, they were in the canteen, singing songs about mums. And that poem from English.'

You were moon's eye to me . . . God.

'Yeah,' Austin said. 'I suppose it's a bit rough.'

'A bit rough? She starts a new school and everyone's

taking the piss out of her dead mum. No wonder she went mad.'

'You could have comforted her.'

'Austin, man. I'm being serious.'

'Me too. Girl was upset and you were standing there with the tourists.'

'It wasn't like that.'

It was even worse than that. Bailey had simply walked away, hoping she didn't see him.

Austin nudged him. 'Man, I'm trying to work out who's doing the stalking here. Her or you.'

'What do you mean?'

'She's over there. By Old Hat.'

Yes. She was. Outside the junk shop looking at the window display.

'She's probably just waiting for a cab.'

'Then the girl's richer than me and you. If you take her out, she buys the food.'

'I'm going to talk to her.'

'Sure she's not going to punch you?'

'Joke's over, Austin. You're right. I was just a tourist. I need to make it up to her. And you're not coming.'

Austin shrugged. 'Bailey, bruv. I want to keep these bones in one piece.'

He skulked away down the street, breaking into a run to catch a bus. Bailey crossed the road towards Indigo.

Suddenly, she turned around. She must have caught his reflection in the window. Bailey's hand auto-cruised to his hair, but he turned it into a neck scratch.

The neck scratch evolved into a little wave. 'Hi.'

A much better 'hi' this time. He didn't sound like a cat forcing out fur balls.

Indigo cocked her head sideways. Since he'd last seen her, she'd drawn her eyeliner on thick and pulled her hair into a high ponytail. *Since he'd last seen her.* Crying and crumpled against that stupid teacher.

She said, 'Are you following me?'

'Um. No. I sometimes go to the record shops.'

She glanced sideways to Final Vinyl at the end of the parade, then back at him.

'I thought . . . I just wanted to say I'm sorry about your jacket.'

Her jacket. Yeah, and for watching her freak out by Mr Grinley's science room.

Indigo's eyes narrowed. 'What do you mean?'

'I saw Mona take it. I tried to find you and . . .'

She stared down at her shoes. 'And?'

'Sorry. Are you all right?'

She kept her eyes on the pavement. 'It was . . . I didn't mean . . . sometimes things just go off. Did lots of people see?'

'It was after lessons started. No one was really about.'

Though classroom doors had opened and faces peered out.

She looked up, straight at him. 'But you saw, right?'

He had to meet her eyes. 'Yes.'

She blinked but didn't look away.

His mouth was moving. 'Do you fancy a coffee?'

Her lips twitched, then her face set serious again.

'I need to get my foster mum a present.' She turned and walked into Old Hat, stopping in the doorway. 'You in school tomorrow?'

'Yeah.'

'Maybe I'll see you then.'

'Yes!'

A real smile and she disappeared.

The junk shop was jammed with furniture, bed stuff, plates, everything. Indigo waited by the window, watching him walk away. He looked back and she ducked behind a stack of suitcases. She'd smiled at him. She had to hold it in next time.

She moved away from the window, holding her school bag close. Her day had been crap enough without knocking a load of china things off the shelves. The owner seemed cool, though, kind of a young Snape with ear stretchers. He gave her a nod and a little grin before sticking his nose back in his magazine. She bent over a collection of tiny glass animals. A zebra, a buffalo, a giant cockerel, a polar bear. No crocodile. She picked up a little yellow elephant; it was cute, but the end of its trunk was chipped. She replaced it on the shelf. At least she'd stopped shaking now. She wouldn't have dared come in here an hour ago.

She'd gone off at school again. God. She'd told the bloody counsellor that Pitt Academy wasn't going to be any different. It was just one more place for her to get chucked out of. Her face was heating up just thinking about it. Her eyes were prickling too. If she ended up crying, her tear ducts would squirt out steam. She'd said stuff, she knew that. And her knuckles hurt. She must have bruised them. She'd knocked that stupid teacher's glasses off, but she didn't feel sorry about it. Nothing was torn, nothing was broken. And when she'd talked it through with her tutor and the counsellor, it was obvious she'd been provoked. They'd found her jacket, but it was full of mank from where those bitches had thrown it behind the waste bins. Keely was getting some compensation for that. And there'd be 'a period of grace' until she bought another one. That meant never, because Indigo wasn't going to stay. Pitt Academy *was* the school that transformed lives, just into something even crappier.

Her phone buzzed. She was supposed to get back to her mentor. And her therapist. And the emo girl standing in while her keyworker was having a baby. If Indigo made all their meetings, she wouldn't have time for any bloody lessons. *And* she had a missed message from Felix. How the hell did he know? Keely must have called him after she was dragged off the shop floor to talk to the school. At least Indigo had persuaded Keely she didn't need to come in person.

But this text wasn't from any of them.

Hi sis! Gonna be at Euston tomoro. Getting train at 6. Meet 5.30?

Primrose! Indigo tapped back.

Yes!! Where?

Starbucks by the loos.

Can you meet earlier?

Sorry. Lots of jobs to do. See you tomorrow. Xx

OK, sis. Xxx

Primrose was going to be in London! For a proper meeting, face to face, second time ever. And this time, it would be just them, no social worker pretending not to earwig their conversation.

The shop owner was too busy reading to see her grinning to herself. Now she could buy something for Primrose too.

Something tickled the side of Indigo's face. It was a silvery-grey shawl hanging over a lampshade. It was beautiful, decorated with tiny glass beads and a delicate lacy fringe. Indigo checked the price tag. Sixty quid. No chance. She'd only got twenty and now she needed two presents. Keely wouldn't mind something cheap; she never

46

expected anything, anyway. Primrose, she was different. She was a proper sister, both of them made from little bits of Mum. Primrose deserved something important, something to match the first gift she'd given Indigo – the small, metal badge shaped like a rainbow. One colour for each of them, Primrose had said. A place where sisters and brother could be together. It was tucked away in Indigo's jewellery box. Maybe she'd put the wooden crocodile in there, next to it.

What would Primrose like, though? She said they'd already chucked loads of stuff. There was no point shipping out tatty old things when they could buy new in Australia. And what about the kids? She was Aunty Indigo, even if she'd never met them. Should she get them something too? No, she'd wait until they were settled in their new place.

Indigo manoeuvred between a chest of drawers and a rocking chair. She crouched to examine a china hand, with lockets dangling from the fingers.

'Excuse me?'

The owner looked up, smiling again.

'How much are these?'

'Between ten and fifteen pounds.'

Indigo unhooked a small silver locket and clicked open the casing. It would be too cheesy to put a picture of herself in it, but Primrose might ask her for one anyway.

5

Indigo slipped the key in the lock.

'Honey?'

Her breath caught. Keely. Shit! She was supposed to be at work. She'd promised Indigo she wouldn't leave early. Maybe it was something else. Social services had called! She'd be sitting there with the emo girl waiting to ask about the letter that came this morning.

Nuh. Indigo knew how it worked. *Call me if you would like further support.* That meant it was down to Keely to make the move. Still, though, Indigo could slam the door shut again. She could run back down the stairs and away, just like she used to. But this was Keely.

Indigo closed the door and manoeuvred around Felix's stacked-up boxes in the hallway. She poked her head into the lounge. Keely was alone, sitting on the sofa, hunched over her laptop.

She blew Keely a kiss. 'You looking at porn again, Kee?'

'Very funny. Though internet dating's probably not much different. It's a complete scam and sodding addictive.'

'Why can't you just meet someone? You're in a shop all day.'

'Indigo, any man who thinks my uniform's sexy is the man I don't want to meet'. Keely pushed the computer aside. Even she did the head-tilting thing.

For a minute the words were on Indigo's lips. *The stupid postman couldn't be arsed to wait until I opened the door and he pushed through an envelope and it ripped and . . .*

'I'll happily go up to the school and whoop those girls' backsides.' Keely smiled. 'But your tutor suggested it might not be a good idea.'

Indigo swallowed back the words and returned the smile.

'Yeah. Though she's wrong.'

Keely came over, put her arm round Indigo and drew her towards the sofa. 'Was it a bad one?'

Indigo shook her head. There'd been worse. Though she could have done without the audience. She carefully laid the shop bag on a cushion. 'I bought you something.'

Keely kissed Indigo's forehead. 'You didn't have to.' She opened the bag and lifted out the teapot. 'Oh, thank you, hun! Felix wants to take our big red one. Did you know that?'

'He's got a sugar daddy! Can't he get his own?'

Keely rolled her eyes. 'Come on, Indigo! Wade's only five years older and they've been together more than a year now. That's marriage compared to my last two relationships.' She flicked the spout. 'Hear that? That's the sound of a pot begging for tea. But I don't need a present, you know that.' She peered into the bottom of the bag. 'What's this?'

Indigo picked up the small jewellery box that young Snape had packed the locket in.

'It's for Primrose.'

Something flickered in Keely's eyes. 'That's a nice thing for you to do.'

Indigo opened it to show her.

'A locket,' Keely said. 'What a lovely idea. Are you going to send it to her?'

'She's coming to London tomorrow. I'm going to meet her at Euston before she goes back to Birmingham.'

'She's coming to London? That's the first I've heard of this.'

Indigo felt herself shift away slightly. 'I only just found out.'

'Do you want me to come with you?'

'You met her before. You know she's all right.' And there were new things to talk about now.

Keely looked like she wanted to smile but her face didn't agree. 'It's just that I know she's going away and sometimes it can be a bit tough saying goodbye.'

Like Indigo didn't know that! She was the biggest expert in goodbyes.

'It's not going to make much difference, Kee. We'll just

text and Skype like we usually do.'

This time, the smile and face agreed. 'Of course. I forgot. I'm a technology immigrant, remember? Not a native, like you lot.'

'You've seemed to work out the dating thing all right.'

'Except for which button I'm supposed to push to find the right man. And, by the way, that stupid teacher who had a go at you? She's seriously not going to bother you again.'

Indigo stood up slowly, like there was no reason to hurry. 'Cool. Thanks, Kee.'

'You're going in tomorrow, right?'

'Yeah. Suppose so.'

'Good.'

Indigo backed out of the lounge and straight into a stack of cardboard boxes.

'Careful!' Keely called.

'They're blocking my door!'

'I know! I've told him. It won't be long now.'

Indigo shoved the boxes aside and slid through the gap into her bedroom. And it was *her* bedroom, not *the* bedroom. Keely was cool about the Blu-Tack stains when Indigo moved her postcards around. She'd replaced the curtains Indigo didn't like with a blind, even though the curtains had looked new. Keely didn't nag too much about tidying, neither. Not *too* much. And she'd never come into Indigo's room without Indigo's permission, let alone snoop around in places that had nothing to do with her.

Indigo sat on the bed and pushed her fingers under the pillow until they touched the envelope. She had to sort herself out first. She was still coated in college. She kicked off her platforms and peeled off her socks, stripped off her shirt and her skirt. She retrieved the can of Sure from her bed and sprayed it round her room until the Pitt Academy stink was gone. Toe warmers on and . . . the lacy leggings? Yeah. They were under the bed. The Placebo sweatshirt still smelled of that curry Felix spilt on it. She should never have lent it to him in the first place. But it could get one more wear before another wash.

Indigo slid the frayed envelope from underneath her pillow and emptied the crocodile into her hand. She sank on to the floor, leaning back against her bed. Outside, a burst of car alarm was making the dogs bark and the Irish bloke in the flat above had started yelling over the balcony at invisible people.

'Hun?' Keely must have knocked, but Indigo hadn't heard her.

She made a fist around the crocodile and stared at Keely's feet. She was wearing the tiger-paw slippers Felix got her last Christmas.

'Fancy one?' Keely was offering a bottle of iced tea.

'Cheers.' Indigo held out her free hand.

Keely moved across the room. Luckily, the envelope was face down on the bed. Even if Keely saw it, she wouldn't see her own name on it. She sat down next to Indigo. It must have been hard, as Keely's shape didn't make it easy for her to get to the floor. They sat there side by side for a while. Keely's arm slipped round her shoulder. Could people smell of shop? Keely did.

'You're going back to school,' Keely said. 'I'm so proud.'

'Thanks, Kee.'

'And I know I've said it a million times, but if you want to talk, I'm always here for you.'

Indigo was squeezing the crocodile so tight, the wooden tail was going to stab through her hand and out the other side. 'I know, Kee. I'm all right for now. Thanks.'

'You sure?'

Indigo rested her head on Keely's shoulder. 'It was only two girls. And they're idiots.'

'Being an idiot is no excuse.'

Keely's neck was warm against Indigo's cheek. If Indigo opened her hand, if she reached back to the bed and gave Keely the envelope, Keely would understand why she'd opened it. She'd keep Indigo in a hug, she'd say the right things.

Forgive your father. For what he did to her mum? For making Indigo what she was? The same apple, from the same tree, with the same thing inside her?

Indigo shuffled away from the hug. 'They gave me loads of catch-up stuff. I'd better get started.'

Keely heaved herself to her feet. 'Of course, honey. I'll leave you to it.'

As the door closed, Indigo opened her hand. When she stuck the crocodile back in the envelope, its shape was marked in her skin.

The front door slammed before Bailey could catch it. Dad must be down in the kitchen with the back door propped open.

'That you, Bailey?'

'Yeah.'

Dad was staring at some packets of meat. 'Duck legs. Your mum loves duck.'

'Why don't you do something veggie for her?'

'She does veggie for me, so I should try and cook meat for her.'

'She doesn't mind veggie, Dad.'

'I know. But it's nice to treat her.'

Most nights you could serve Mum plectrums on a plate and she wouldn't notice. She usually had her fork in one hand and a pen scribbling on a big pile of papers in the other.

Dad stabbed the plastic with a knife. As the air whooshed

out, he wrinkled his nose. 'Is it supposed to smell like that?'

Bailey sniffed. 'I can't smell anything. What are you doing with it?'

'Roasting it in red wine.'

'And what are you going to have?'

'Veggie sausages, probably.'

Dad wrapped kitchen towel around his fingers and fished out a duck's leg from the packaging. He dropped it on to a chopping board.

'Dad?'

'Mm?'

'Have you ever lost it?'

'Lost what?'

The second leg plopped on to a plate. Dad unwrapped his fingers and squirted washing-up liquid on to his hands. He started scrubbing at his nails with a wire pad.

Bailey said, 'Your temper. You know, really lost it so you couldn't stop.'

Dad shrugged. 'Maybe a couple of times. Your Uncle Len was a horrible little sod. He'd have provoked Gandhi to violence.' He jammed a corner of the pad under his thumbnail. 'It's probably best not to blow a gasket in my line of work. Why do you ask?'

'Just wondered.'

Dad rinsed his hands and wiped them on the tea towel. He looked at the duck. 'The recipe says I need blackcurrant jelly. I've only got strawberry. Do you reckon that's okay?'

'Don't know. Maybe you should ask Mum.'

Dad shook his head. 'No. I want it to be a nice surprise.'

Mum was very surprised. She sniffed the plate, then picked at the meat in silence. Dad sat opposite, chewing his veggie sausages. The duck was okay, but even Bailey couldn't eat the puddle of hot, globby strawberry goo it was sitting in.

Dad said, 'Sorry, Viv. I think I got something wrong.'

Mum gave him a little smile. 'I really appreciate it. You tried. And it's sort of funny.'

Dad pronged a sausage and held it out to her. 'Have this.'

'It's okay. Our Head of English left today, remember? I'm full of cream cake. Do you mind if I go up?'

'No. Go ahead.'

Mum pushed her chair out, touching Dad's shoulder as she left. There was a pause at the front door. She was probably lifting her big bag to take upstairs with her.

Dad sat back. 'Who knew? There are two types of blackcurrant jelly.'

'And none of them are strawberry, Dad.'

'Rub it in, Bailey.' Dad shoved Mum's plate on top of his, the strawberry wine sauce slopping on to the leftover mash. 'You do your music practice. I'll clean up. Reckon Shuu fancies sweet and sweeter duck, tonight?'

'Don't try it, Dad. Cats like strawberry jam even less than Mum does.'

Bailey was in the right mood for his guitars. On the first landing, the door to Mum's tiny office was closed, but Bailey could make out her shape behind the bevelled glass panel. Mum had been angry at dinner; Bailey had seen it. It was like a little ripple that went through her when Dad served the meal. But she'd swallowed it and even managed to say something nice. Anger was weird. Mum held it in, pretended she was happy. But with Indigo, it had been like a whirlwind was building inside her, until her anger burst out.

He stood outside the music room. Dad used to pretend the guitars were getting up to mad adventures when no one was there, like in *Toy Story*. Even now, Bailey imagined them rushing back to their places when they heard him coming. He opened the door. Yes, his Gibson Melodymaker was slightly askew on its stand. He unhooked it and plugged it into the amp.

A few hours ago, Indigo had smiled at him. She was standing so close he could smell her hairspray. God. Concentrate. What was he going to play? *See you tomorrow.* She'd meant that for real, right?

He could transcribe some Muse. Or go heavy with Led Zep.

Maybe Indigo was just being polite. Or stringing him along. And even if she wasn't, she could do it again, freak out and start yelling. Did he seriously want that stress?

Bailey ran his palm across the Gibson's strings – A, B, G, D, E, A. He'd got it. He strummed a D chord. 'One Way or Another'.

Blondie.

6

Bailey scanned the sixth-form common room. As usual, it wasn't worth the energy. The principal had made all that fuss about a new student-friendly design, so how had they ended up with somewhere no one wanted to be? The architect had clearly decided that windows were an expensive luxury sixth-formers didn't need. The only action was over by the vending machine. Someone must be telling big jokes because Mona and her mates were laughing like they were being choked.

Austin said, 'She's not here.'

'Who?'

'Big Bang Girl.'

'Who said I was looking for her? And her name's Indigo, remember?'

'You never come in here. I left you two getting all cosy yesterday and now you look like you're looking. She promise to meet you here?'

'Like I'd tell you.'

'Did you check out the stuff about her?'

Of course he had. The dad and mum in the bedroom. Indigo, just a tiny kid, on the other side of the door. Jesus!

Mona spotted him and whispered something to Saskia. Saskia made a kissy face and slowly ran her fingers through her hair like she was teasing up an afro. Bailey turned his back on them. If he could zap one part of his memory, it would be the bit that held the info that he once went out with Mona.

Austin kicked the back of his ankle. Bailey almost went down. 'What the hell, Austin?'

'Your girl. Due south.'

'Why don't you just stick an aerial on your head and broadcast, mate?'

Indigo must have sneaked in ninja-style. She was leaning against the trophy cabinets, like she was summoning up the energy to be bothered. Her bored look slid over Mona and her mates, the scattering of prefects, Bailey and Austin, the crisp packets on the floor.

Austin's eyebrows bounced up and down. 'You got a six-foot ginger afro and she wants to pretend you're invisible?'

But there had been a little something, Bailey was sure. A twitch that was supposed to branch into a smile, like outside Old Hat yesterday. Indigo slumped on a chair in an empty corner, fished around in her bag and pulled out her headphones and a yoghurt. She jammed on the headphones, peeled the top off the yoghurt, dipped in a finger and scooped it into her mouth.

'Oh, man.' Austin screwed up his face. 'Get the girl a spoon.'

'You ever seen yourself eat wings?'

'Very funny. You going over, then?'

'Yep.'

'Man, I have to witness this.'

'Thought you knew it all already, bruv.'

Indigo was scrolling through her phone. Did she choose that seat especially? Bailey couldn't even go and sit near her because the only chair close by had her bag on it. He'd have to stand awkwardly and bend over to talk to her.

Austin gave him a little shove. 'You wanna do it while you still *got* hair?'

'Yeah, Austin. Jokes.'

He glanced towards the vending machine. Mona and her mates had gathered into a pack, whispering together. Mona's crew specialised in volume. The sudden quiet wasn't good.

And then it started. 'Mamma Mia'. Four of them, moving closer to Indigo with poodle-faced Saskia running the solo. This was *Groundhog Day: the Remake*. Bailey, stuck in this scuzzy common room, reliving the moment until he did the thing that was right. Whatever that thing was.

Austin said, 'You gonna be her hero?'

If Bailey gave them mouth, they'd give it back double. He shot a sideways look at Austin. That boy could keep up the chat until he won. Bailey needed to get lessons. So, what, then? Maybe Bailey should plant himself between Indigo and Mona. Yeah, one Bailey against the four of them. That was going to work. If he was in an American feel-good high school show he'd go one better than them, brandishing his Gibson and knocking out the best riff ever. Something by Blondie.

Indigo didn't look like she needed a hero. She was slowly sliding her finger around the inside of her yoghurt pot, headphones still on, like she was oblivious. Why didn't she look up? Give him a clue? Done with the yoghurt, she threw the pot over a chair into a bin. Perfect shot! Saskia's voice wavered, then carried on, even louder.

Indigo stood up. Suddenly, Saskia found herself singing a solo as the other three stepped away. Indigo flicked back her headphones and one by one, she looked Mona, Saskia, Betti and Kay in the eye. Then she gave them the finger, slow motion. Headphones on again, she sauntered off towards the science wing.

Hell.

That was . . .

She was . . .

Bailey ran after her. 'Indigo?'

She kept walking. Those bloody headphones. He tapped her on her shoulder and she spun round. Bailey had to stop himself jumping back. Bloody Austin and that Big

Bang stuff. She was biting her lip, frowning. Maybe Bailey should try Dad's social-worker smile. Friendly and calming, Dad said.

Indigo's expression didn't change. Silence.

He stopped smiling. 'Those girls are idiots.'

'Same as yesterday, then.'

'Yeah.'

Her eyes looked darker today, more copper. The murky light in the common room didn't do most people favours. It was working okay for her, though.

He said, 'I just thought, you know, you dealt with them really well.'

'What was I supposed to do? Join in?'

'We could have had a sing-off.'

Yes! A faint smile. 'I'm not singing Abba.'

'I had a song ready in my head. Do you know Blondie?'

She touched her headphones. A proper smile now, not big, but there. 'Might do.'

'There's a song called 'Rip Her To Shreds'. It was the first track they released here, but no one bought it. It was about the crap stuff newspapers say.'

'I'll look out for it.'

Over Indigo's shoulder, further along the corridor, Austin emerged from the toilets, flailing his hands in the air, miming an explosion.

Bailey tried to block him out and took a deep breath.

'Do you fancy a coffee or something?'

'Now?'

'Er . . . I've got politics.' But he could miss it, couldn't he? He'd never bunked yet, not even from music, when he had to sit through the stuff he already knew. 'If you're not busy now, there's a new place opened by the creperie.'

She shook her head, but kept that smile. 'It's all right.'

'What about later? Around four?'

'I've got family stuff at four.'

He clamped his mouth shut. He almost said it back. *Family?* Like he was surprised. Of course she was going to have other family. The stuff he'd read last night said that her mum had loads of kids. Indigo probably had masses of niece and nephews.

She couldn't have noticed his mouth fail because she was still here. He smiled again. His own smile. Not Dad's.

'When's best for you?'

Indigo let her bag flop to the floor. 'If you reckon you can skive politics, we can . . .'

Suddenly, Austin was by Bailey's side. He gave Indigo a big grin. 'Hi! Love the zebra hair!'

Indigo swore, grabbed her bag, swung round and strode off down the corridor.

Bailey glared at him. 'Austin! You stupid, or what?'

Austin looked incredulous. 'I was saving you, man. Even from a distance, I could see that wasn't going well.'

'You're talking crap!'

'You ever seen an exploded person?'

'Yeah. In the same place you did. On your Xbox.'

'Laughs, mate.' Austin gave him a sideways look. 'I don't want to encourage you, but if you really can't help yourself, you could always invite her over to your house.'

'Like when my parents are in Paris?'

'Your parents are cool, Bay, but you wouldn't want them around. Not if, you know, the world starts spinning backwards and she really gets into you. And maybe, you could invite some of us over too, so it doesn't look like you're taking advantage of the girl.'

They started walking towards the Lilian Bader block.

'No, Austin. I'm not having a party.'

'Come on! Your folks will never know.'

'My neighbours will. Mrs Skinner will probably livestream it from her bedroom window.'

'Your parents will be too loved up in Paris to notice. And what's the worst thing they're going to do if they do find out? Talk to you?'

'You been round my house lately? My folks barely talk to each other!'

'Mine, neither.'

'Yours live in different continents, Austin.'

They stopped on Lilian Bader East Corridor. Bailey waited for Austin to head towards his class.

Austin said, 'I'm serious about Indigo. I know you can't help it. Your parents are full of this goody-goody, save-the-bad-kids stuff. You must have absorbed it in your cot. But that girl's got problems. Big ones. Can you handle it?'

'Thanks for your concern, but you're too late. We're going for coffee.' *Maybe.*

Austin stretched out a sigh until it looked like his body was ready to cave in. 'My Aunty Essie's a nurse at the fracture clinic in Guy's. She says they fix bones really good in there.'

Bailey grinned. 'The only thing that's getting broken is your heart when you see how wrong you are!'

Indigo deserved a damn medal. There must be a form somewhere that you had to fill in to get one. She'd ask Keely to find it for her. She'd faced down those stupid cows in the common room, impressed Bailey – not on purpose, though – *and* managed to give a couple of right answers in maths catch-up this afternoon. Yeah, a proper heavy gold medal with her name carved into it.

Then to top it all, she was heading for a proper face to face with her sister. It was going to be hard. They'd only found each other a few months ago and now Primrose was moving to the other side of the world. But blood was strong. If you needled out drops from both their arms and tested them, you'd see they were family. The first time they'd met, she'd kissed Indigo, a little one on each cheek. It was stupid, but Indigo hoped that maybe this time Primrose would hold her hand.

And there *was* new stuff to talk about. She had a phone pic of their grandma's letter. The wooden crocodile was tucked in the front pocket of her rucksack. It was next to the box with the locket and the rainbow badge. It was like she was making a nest of good things.

Indigo checked out the common room. It was quicker to zip through than go all of the way round, but she didn't need any of them idiots singing at her right now. She'd judged it right. It was dead. She'd get to the station good and early, settled and ready for when Primrose got there. Should she give her the locket at the start or the end? It was all wrapped up and Keely had even given her a little gold bow to decorate it.

Indigo ran through the common room, popped out of the sports-block exit and sped down the back entrance to the main road. And stopped.

Mona and Saskia were at the bus stop, looking at something on Mona's phone. They were in with a mix of younger kids from another school. And Bailey was there! But he'd got his stupid mate with him. Bailey gave her a little smile, though there was no way she was giving anything back with that bigmouth, Austin, next to him. She peered along the road. A bus was on its way and it'd better not be full. Indigo needed to be on it.

The driver must have been stuck in first gear, but at last the bus pulled up. And, yeah, there was room. Mona and Saskia pushed their way to the front. That was fine by Indigo. She needed full calm. She touched her stomach. All right, so far.

Indigo tagged on behind the group of younger kids. As the hem of Saskia's arse-skimmer headed upstairs, Indigo slid into a seat at the front next to an old woman and checked the time on her phone. She was still fine. She tapped out a text so Primrose would know she was on her way. They'd sent loads of texts to each other when they'd first linked up, though Primrose took a bit longer to reply now. It was hard, she said, with three young kids and a full-on move to deal with.

The driver slammed on his brakes. Indigo lurched forward, almost dropping her phone in the old woman's lap.

The old woman shook her head. 'Stupid fool wants to meet his maker.'

'Who?'

'The vagrant.'

Indigo had to crane round an extra-tall kid standing in the aisle to see out of the front window. A trampy-looking bloke was in the middle of the road staring down the driver. Suddenly, he dodged the traffic to the other side and went gunning along the pavement to the next bus stop.

The old woman touched Indigo's knee. 'Don't move, darling. Or he's going to end up sitting next to me.'

The driver shouted something and the bus started again. That was good. Indigo didn't need any bus crap today. She finished her text and pressed 'Send'. The road was pretty clear as they pulled away from the stop. She'd still be on time. Someone poked her shoulder. She looked up, and straight into Saskia's eyes. Mona was right behind, smiling like her teeth were trying to push their way out of her mouth. Indigo flipped her headphones on and stared at the ground. Tomato sauce was spilled on the aisle floor and Saskia's boot was bang in it.

Typical. Indigo's battery was down to eleven per cent. She had to save the rest in case Primrose called. She couldn't turn her music on, but they weren't going to know that.

'Hey, Indigo!' Everybody must have bowed their heads to make way for Saskia's voice, doing that looking and not looking thing.

Indigo pretended to nudge up the volume. What was that song Bailey told her about? 'Rip Her To Shreds'. She should have checked it out.

'D'you get your jacket back?' Even music full blast wouldn't have wiped out Saskia's loud mouth. 'I heard you got a bit mad about it.'

Deep breath.

If Indigo didn't look at Saskia, nothing could happen.

Saskia lived near here, didn't she? The bus stopped and the doors opened. Indigo could get off if Saskia didn't. She could wait for another bus or use the taxi account that Keely had set up for emergencies, because if she wasn't careful, this was going to be an emergency. Suddenly, she wanted to dip her hand into her rucksack pocket and grab the crocodile, but not with Saskia's eyes hot on her.

The bus doors slid shut. Shit! Indigo should have moved herself instead of sitting here, just bloody thinking about it.

And they were singing again. For God's sake, couldn't they leave it?

'You not joining in? That's a diss, man.'

Indigo made herself look up at Saskia's bundle of hair, the nose ring, the jaws grinding on a piece of gum.

A shiver and a flicker inside her. She swallowed hard. *Please. Not now.*

Indigo knew she had to get the next move right. Headphones off, slow and casual. Eyes steady, face blanked out.

'Not dissing you, Saskia, but only dogs make noises like that.'

The crappy song stopped. Saskia laughed. It sounded like she was rolling gunk in her throat. 'You calling me a bitch? That what you saying?'

Yes! Breath coming so deep it must be pulled out of Indigo's toes. Her chest felt jammed with barbed wire,

70

as if all the words she was still holding down were covered in spikes.

'Big diss, nut-head. You should be honoured.' Saskia was rolling her wet chewing gum between her fingers. 'You're getting special attention. We don't sing for everyone.'

MrsWeasleyLinGiselle.

MrsWeasleyLinGiselle.

It hadn't worked last time. Why should it now?

'Crawl away, Saskia.' Indigo's voice sounded like it had been run over.

Saskia turned back to Mona. 'She don't appreciate us, man.'

Little claws. Dig, dig, dig. Needles of heat.

Saskia stretched the wet, warm gum between her fingers and thumb. It looked like sick skin. 'You ready with the tune, Mona?'

Of course Mona was. 'Mamma Mia . . .'

'Why don't you two just leave it?'

What? Who the hell was that? All eyes turned to the back of the bus.

'It's always the same old boring crap.'

Indigo knew that voice. Oh, God. It was him, Bailey, pushing his way towards Saskia. Doing a big Rescue-Indigo-in-Public thing. Hadn't he seen? She'd managed all right in the common room.

But not yesterday. Not in the corridor outside the science rooms.

71

Saskia jerked her head forward and sucked her teeth at him. Then her hand moved, quick. Indigo caught the blur and moved her head, feeling Saskia's fingers catch her hair. What?

Saskia was screwing out Bailey. 'Red Boy! I told you to mind your own business. Indigo Mental Case is ours.'

'You stupid little cow! Didn't you hear? The boy said "leave it"!'

Bailey had clapped his hand to his mouth like his voice had jumped out and carried on without him. The earbudders across the aisle from her were looking around to find the source of the diss. Indigo followed where they were looking. It was the homeless guy, the one who'd run to catch the bus. He was standing in the wheelchair space, pulling his beanie hat with both hands. He'd stretched it so far it almost met beneath his chin. His face looked proper tramp-red, like he rubbed it against a doormat every morning.

'You!' He let the hat go and pointed at Bailey. 'You're the only decent one on this bus!'

Bailey gave him a small nod, like his voice was still hiding.

'Better than these stupid little bully-bitches!' Spit shot out of the tramp's lips that time. 'All of you ganging up on one kid. Big and clever, ain't you? Go on! Do it some more!'

72

Saskia's eyelashes twitched. The cow was definitely thinking about it.

The bus bell rang, one, two, three times. Of course, everyone wanted to get off now. Saskia was opening her mouth again, but before any more crap came out, the driver swung hard towards the next stop. Saskia staggered and Indigo slipped past her and out of the opening doors.

Breathe.

Yeah. She could. Just.

She turned her back to the road as the bus passed her by. She didn't need to see Saskia's sneering face through the window. And she still had loads of time to get to Euston. She was near the crossroads and most of the buses were heading that way. She took another deep breath, hunched up her shoulders and let them relax. That was too easy. Something was missing. Her bag. Her bloody bag! Primrose's locket. Her badge and her crocodile. Everything All on the floor by that old woman's feet, speeding through the amber traffic lights on the way to Angel. It wouldn't stay unnoticed for long, neither. Even now, the Queen Crapheads must be tearing through her bag and chucking around her stuff. Her crocodile, hitting a window . . .

Breath couldn't come. The heaviness was pressing too hard against her lungs. She leaned against a traffic light post, closed her eyes.

'You okay?'

What? She let her eyes open to a squint.

Bailey was standing there. 'I thought you might need this.'

Her bag? God. All of her squashed breaths were trying to jump out at the same time. She tried to take it but her arms were all flop.

He said, 'It's all right. I'll hold it until you're ready.'

Her lungs hurt and her heart and her stomach. And she was ready to cry.

He sort of half-looked away and at her at the same time. Good. She didn't need an audience right now. Especially as she wanted to cry even more.

He said, 'The homeless guy noticed you'd left it. I think Saskia was going to fight him for it. Not sure who would have won that one.'

Just behind Indigo, the traffic lights were beeping. It sounded like the alarm on Keely's cooker clock. Indigo had to say something, do something, move. She took her bag and pressed her hand against the front pocket. The box, the wooden animal, pressed her back.

'Thanks.'

'No problem.'

She peeled herself away from the post and made it to the island in the middle of the road. The lights turned green and buses and vans flashed in front of her.

'Do you know Ms Fraser? She's Head of Year.' Bailey was

still beside her. 'Maybe you can tell her about Saskia.'

Indigo nodded. What was he going to do? Escort her to Euston?

She said, 'Thanks, Bailey. I'm all right now.'

'I . . . I live this way.'

God, now she was blushing. He must think she was even more weird. Okay. Though maybe he wasn't following her, but he was definitely hanging back. His legs were longer than hers. Usually he must walk much quicker. She let herself look at him. He wasn't bad-looking, just a bit different. She'd seen loads of mixed-race kids with afros, but none of them that gingery brown. It was big too. His eyebrows were darker, though, and his eyes, seriously dark.

He said, 'Was that yours?'

'What?'

'It sounded like a text.'

'Yeah.' Her phone was in her bloody hand too. She checked it.

Sorry, sis. Problem with childcare. Had to jump on an earlier train. Skype this pm.

'Shit.' A pull across her chest. Short breaths. But at least she could breathe. She bit her lip. She was not going to cry. She was going to keep going, one foot, then the other, then the other.

He said, 'Bad news?'

'I was supposed to meet my sister.' She could get

the words out and they didn't sound too different. 'She just cancelled.'

'Sorry.'

'Yeah.'

'Will she be okay to meet you another time?'

Indigo shrugged. Even if she tried to explain, he wouldn't get it. All the butterflies before the first meeting, then seeing Primrose for the first time and feeling they were joined. Then all the sneaky Skype calls because Primrose's husband didn't like it.

One foot after another after another after another. Four feet. Her platforms. His trainers.

'Um . . .' Bailey was staring at the side of her head. 'Saskia got your hair, didn't she?'

Indigo touched behind her ear. Her finger poked a big clump of stickiness. 'Jesus! The bitch!' She tugged at the gum, but it ground in deeper. Indigo wiped her fingers on the traffic-light post, but the gunk seemed to like her better.

Was Bailey smiling? If he was, he killed it quick.

She glared at him. 'Do you think it's funny?'

He shook his head so hard his hair waved. 'I was just thinking about Saskia's face when the tramp started up. I don't think anyone's called her a bully-bitch out loud before.'

Indigo would have. And more. But then things would have got too serious. 'Why's she like that?'

'I don't know – she's being going on like that since infants.'

Silence, then beeps. They crossed over. Though where the hell was she going now that Primrose had blown her out? She glanced at Bailey.

'She called you Red Boy. That's about your hair, right?'

'Sort of. And because I'm mixed race.'

'I don't get it.'

'It's one of those old time things. If you've got light skin.'

'That means my mum would have been red.'

Her mum? How the hell had she let that slip out? Time for that awkward silence.

He said, 'Do you look like her?'

She frowned. Was he taking the piss? No, his face was serious, open.

'A little bit.' She could tell him more too. Her mum had dark hair with a purple fringe and a big, gold stud through her nose. Or she did in the photo from when she was pregnant with Indigo. 'Funny, no one asks that.'

He looked upset. 'Sorry.'

'No,' she said. 'I don't mind.' Not if it was about her mum.

They walked along. She still had no idea where she was heading, but it was better than going straight home and having to explain about Primrose.

She said, 'Do you get lots of grief about your hair?'

'I did when I was little. Not so much now.'

'Why didn't you cut it?'

'That's telling people like Saskia they're right.'

She let herself smile. He smiled too. If his resting face was cute, his smiling face was cuter. They manoeuvred past a drunk woman outside Costcutters.

He said, 'I got good at getting gum out.'

Indigo's hand zipped up to her hair. She remembered Saskia's jaws mashing and grinding and stopped before she actually touched it.

'I'm gonna cut it out.' Secretly. In her room. She didn't need to give Keely more stress.

'You don't have to.' He probably didn't realise he was stroking his own hair. 'There are other ways. My mum's a teacher, so she's a gum removal expert.'

Yeah. Somehow Indigo could have guessed his mum was a teacher.

'She's been in some tough schools, pupil referral units, all sorts.' Now, he was fiddling with a curl above his temple. 'She's had to get it out of other kids' hair. And her own.'

'What does your dad do?'

'He's a social worker.'

'A social worker?'

He nodded. She could tell him everything she knew about social workers, but let the words hang.

He said, 'I'm sorry about your parents.'

'What?' If there had been an awkward silence, she'd missed it.

'Your parents. I'm . . . I'm really sorry.'

'Yeah. Me too.'

No, she hadn't missed it. Here it came, shouldering its way into the space between them. Bailey's face was wrinkling like he didn't know what look to put on for her. At least he was trying. Maybe she'd been too harsh.

'You've got a teacher and a social worker, I could say the same thing about you.'

His mouth opened. Right. She'd got that wrong. Now he looked even more confused.

She sighed, 'Everyone knows, don't they?'

'I didn't. Not until . . . well, I couldn't work out why Saskia and Mona kept singing those songs.'

'How did you find out?'

'I . . . someone told me.'

It would have been that mate of his. You'd need a stapler to keep his mouth shut.

'Did you Google me?'

'I . . . er. Sorry.'

He stared at his trainers. They weren't Pitt-Academy-approved, neither. Not bad for a teacher's kid.

She stopped to turn and face him. 'So aren't you going to ask?'

Confused face again. 'What?'

'Do I remember it? Or where's my dad now? And the younger kids always want to know if I'd seen my mum's body.'

'No! I wasn't going to ask any of that!'

'You know all about me, then?'

If the traffic was quieter, she could probably have heard the cogs whirring in his head trying to click on the right answer.

'No . . . it's just . . . I wasn't going to ask because . . . well, I sort of wanted to.'

'What stopped you?'

A little smile. 'My dad's a social worker, remember? He's been asking me questions all my life. I reckoned it must be way worse for you.'

She nodded.

He carried on. 'It must be weird everyone thinking they know stuff about you. Even when you start somewhere new.'

Too bloody right, it was.

He stroked the side of his face like he was trying to get the cogs to slow down. 'I suppose I didn't want to pretend that I didn't know, even though I didn't for ages. And then when I did, I thought maybe you were sick of people going on about it too.'

His trainers must be talking to him because he was staring at them hard.

'Bailey?'

He looked at her, like she'd just given him permission. He was blushing and it made her want to smile.

'The thing is, I don't really remember it anyway. Sometimes I think I do, but maybe that's because of all the stuff I read. I used to Google it too.'

He raised his eyebrows.

'I thought I'd better know what other people were reading about me. But it used to make me   it wasn't a good idea. I haven't done it since I've been with Keely.'

He said, 'Do you like where you are now?'

'Yeah! Keely's all right. My foster brother's an arse, but he's leaving soon. Anyway, I'd better get back and sort out my hair before Keely gets home.'

He was fiddling with the curly bit behind his ear again. 'I live near here. The invitation's still open. I can show you how to take the chewing gum out.'

'Go back to your house?'

He'd stopped looking at her. He was staring across the road, behind them.

'Bailey? Are you asking me back to your house?'

'Yeah. Sorry. I just thought I saw that homeless guy. The one from the bus.'

Indigo stared the way they'd come. Kids from another school, a woman on an electric scooter.

'He went into the betting shop,' Bailey said.

'You sure it was him?'

Bailey shrugged. 'Maybe not. But if you'd like to come back, it's this way. And I can make you that coffee.'

It *was* the same guy, Bailey was sure. On the bus, he'd been just in front of Bailey. When the bus stopped, Bailey had watched him grab the door rail, stepping off the bus like he'd used his day's worth of energy running to catch it. Then Bailey had to squeeze his way past him, before Saskia made another grab for Indigo's bag.

Indigo said, 'Maybe you should invite him for a coffee too.'

'Yeah.'

'Do you think he's following us?'

Was he seriously going to say 'yes'? He'd already asked stupid questions about her mum. *Do you look like her?* Jesus! Maybe he could have styled that one off if things were normal. But in Indigo's situation – God. She'd been all right, but Austin must never hear about it. Ever. It would be number one, with a golden star, on his list of 'You said *what*?'s. And now Indigo must think he was Mr Paranoid. She had every right to turn round and run in the opposite direction. The homeless guy had probably been heading to the betting shop anyway.

'Of course he was following us.' Bailey flicked his hand through his 'fro. 'It happens all the time since I was called up as the new Bourne. I don't like to boast, but I could have laid out that whole bus in twenty seconds. I just didn't want to give myself away.'

Indigo laughed out loud. Yes! If Bailey strained hard, he'd hear an actual big bang as Austin's heart shattered to atoms.

Bailey said, 'I live down here.'

She followed him, a couple of steps behind. 'Nice!'

His place wasn't much different from everybody else's: a slim, terraced house with the kitchen in the basement, and a couple of rooms on each floor. Bailey opened the little gate and waited for Indigo to go ahead, squeezing her way between the dustbin and the garden waste recycler jammed in the concrete space between the hedge and the house. Last year, Mum had painted the front door bright blue and planted pots full of bulbs to make it look more cheerful when she came home from work. Now there was just a row of limp plants that no one got round to watering.

Bailey fished for the key in his jacket pocket. The mortice was unlocked, so Dad must be back. He'd better stay out of their way. The last thing Bailey needed was Dad's social-work radar going into meltdown when Indigo walked in.

He pushed open the front door. 'The kitchen's at the bottom of the stairs.'

'Cool.'

Indigo picked her way over the random collection of boots and trainers in the hallway without a second look and headed downstairs. Mona had always been a bit sniffy about his messy house. Her mum wouldn't even let family in unless there'd been a full-on house clean first.

'Oh, hello!' Dad's voice, from the kitchen. 'I'm Ed.'

'Indigo.'

From the top of the stairs, Bailey saw they were shaking hands. *Nice one, Dad. Who shakes hands with teenage girls, for God's sake?* Social workers or creeps. Just as well Indigo knew which one Dad was.

Dad smiled up at him. 'You all right, Bailey?'

'Yeah, thanks, Dad.'

Behind Dad, the kettle clicked off. Hopefully, he'd make his tea and go. Nope. No such luck. Dad leaned against the work surface, settling in.

Bailey followed Indigo down. 'Dad, your water's boiled.'

'So it has.' Dad looked from one to the other. 'So what are you two up to?'

Indigo twisted her head to show him. 'Some bitch stuck chewing gum in my hair.'

'Blimey,' Dad said. 'That's miserable.' He ran a hand over his super-short cut. 'I've had a bit of that in my time. That's why I keep it like this now. Or that's what I tell people. Sadly, my follicles aren't what they once were.'

Bailey said, 'Do you want me to make your tea for you?'

Dad was shaking his head. 'Chewing gum's a real pain. Bailey's hair used to collect it. Do you know how to get it out? You can—'

'It's okay, Dad.' Bailey eased past Indigo into the kitchen. 'We've got it sorted.'

Dad held up his hands. 'All right! All right!' He shifted himself from the counter and finally topped up his mug with hot water. He wiggled his tea bag in it and dropped it in the bin. 'But I strongly recommend peanut butter.'

Dad took his tea and thumped upstairs.

'Yeah,' Indigo said. 'He's definitely a social worker.'

'Telling me. But if I hadn't told you about him, would you have known?'

'Yeah, of course.' She pulled at the gummed up hair. 'Some blokes would have a heart attack when someone like me walked into their kitchen.'

'Like you?'

She gave him a little smile and touched the hem of her skirt. 'It's like they're trying not to look at you, so you can't see what's in their head. But your dad, it didn't bother him at all. He shook my hand!'

Bailey laughed. 'He's always done that with my friends, even when I was little. Mum used to organise birthday parties for me, with games and treasure hunts and all sorts of stuff. Half the kids just wanted to hang out here with Dad because they thought he was so cool.'

85

'Do you think he's cool?'

The kitchen faced west and the afternoon sun fell across the counter and a patch of floor. It was reflected in Indigo's eyes, making the hazel almost gold, darker around the pupils. She blinked and he quickly looked away.

'Do you?' she said.

Did he what?

'Do you reckon your dad's cool?'

'Er, he's all right. Though Mum won't think so. He's supposed to wash up.'

The sink was full of breakfast stuff and even the box of cornflakes was still on the table, all four flaps open, like a shout. Bailey went over to make it quiet.

Indigo said, 'What's the thing about peanut butter?'

'It gets chewing gum out of your hair. So does oil. And WD40.'

She screwed up her face. 'Crunchy or smooth?'

'WD40?'

'No,' she laughed. 'Peanut butter.'

'Smooth,' he said. 'Or I suppose the peanuts would get stuck too.'

'You've got some, then?'

He opened the cupboard over the sink and showed her the big jar. 'Probably left over from when Dad had hair.'

She moved a stack of recipe books from a chair on to the table and sat down. 'Let's do it.'

Yes, let's.

He was going to massage peanut butter into her head. His forehead was heating up like the sun was catching him too. Mona had hated Bailey touching her hair. She said it cost too much to let anyone start raking up the frizz. And to be honest, he didn't like people's hands in his, neither. Too many memory scars from when he was ten, sitting in the bath while Mum yanked the comb through his tangles, keeping his legs crossed so she couldn't see any further down. God, now his face was proper infrared. At least Indigo couldn't see.

Can I rub your head with Sunblest Smooth? Another one for Austin's list. He unscrewed the jar and spooned a blob on to his palm. He held it under her nose.

'Sure about this?'

'I've got gum and Saskia-slobber in my hair. Anything's better than that.'

'Okay.' He started working it through. He remembered Mum saying that you had to keep at it until the oil sank in. Was it just him who could hear the slushy squeaky sound? He should put the radio on or plug his phone into the dock, but his fingers were all greasy.

This wasn't the way he'd pictured their first – whatever this was. Not when he'd sat behind her in English, etching her hair, her neck, the shape of her ears into his memory. Or that time he'd seen her sitting by herself in the common room, gone in to talk to her, but carried on walking past. Or when he'd followed her to the library and sat there pretending to read *The Audacity of Hope* while she worked her way through a big book of film photographs. He'd watched her pause on the pages, running her fingers over the women's faces.

Imagine if his thoughts could travel down his fingers through her hair and into her brain.

He stopped rubbing. 'Would you rather do it yourself?'

'No, it's okay. You can see better. Has your dad been a social worker long?'

'Yeah. Since leaving uni.'

'Where's he working now?'

'He does agency work, so he can be anywhere. For the last few weeks he's been in Barnet. Why?'

'Just being nosy. There's always been social workers round my family, so sometimes you think you're going to bump into one who knows you.'

That would kill things. Imagine if she'd met Dad before and hated him. 'Do you recognise him?'

Indigo shook her head. The greasy hair slid between Bailey's fingers. 'But it's always a bit weird thinking I could be sitting in McDonalds and someone's there who knows more about me than I do.'

'Yes,' Bailey said. 'It must be really weird.'

'Yeah.' She twisted round to face him, making the hair

he was holding pull taut. She didn't seem to notice. 'Like everyone in Pitt Academy digging up stuff about me online. What one did you read?'

God. What was he supposed to say? *The full page write-up in the South London Gazette. Drug-crazed man smothers helpless wife in front of baby.* Though now he knew. She wasn't a baby. She was four.

He said, 'A local paper thing.'

'Do they mention my name?'

'No.'

'Good. They're not supposed to. But everyone still finds it and knows.'

'Sorry. I shouldn't have looked.'

'Everybody does. It's what happens afterwards that's crap. You know, like bully-bitches singing to you on the bus. Thanks for trying to make them shut up.'

'It didn't work though, did it?'

'I'll get my foster mum, Keely, on to them. She's been dying to for ages. That should stop them.' She touched her hair, brushing his finger. 'Can it come out yet?'

'I think so.' He wrapped kitchen roll round the gum and gave a little tug. The gum slid off easily.

'Here.' He showed her the gooey mess.

She wrinkled her nose. 'Thanks.'

He threw it in the bin and washed his hands. 'Would you like a drink? There's Coke, tea, juice. Even coffee.'

'Tea's all right.'

'There's normal, Earl Grey, or Mum likes the herbal stuff.'

Indigo rolled her eyes and was about to say something but bloody Dad thumped back downstairs. Indigo must be a tractor beam, pulling him in.

He grinned at them. 'Mission accomplished?'

Indigo touched her hair. 'Yep!'

'Excellent! If you're bunging the kettle on, Bailey, can you do me another one?'

Bailey tried to meet Indigo's eyes, but she was looking at Dad. What sort of look was that? Mona used to go on about Dad being quite hot, though that was only to wind Bailey up. No, Indigo wasn't Dad-struck; her expression was more thoughtful. Bailey pulled the kettle off its stand and turned on the tap. He filled it up halfway – just enough for him and Indigo.

Dad rolled up his sleeves. 'I'd better sort this washing up before Viv gets home.' He wet a tea towel and handed it to Indigo. 'Here, you might need this, to get the rest of the peanut butter out of your hair.'

'Thanks.' Indigo settled down on a stool by the breakfast bar, next to the sink. She was rubbing her hair, still looking at Dad. Bailey turned on the kettle and sat down at the table. The magazine on top was open on a page of recipes. Dad had circled one for lentil shepherd's pie.

Indigo said, 'You're a social worker, then?'

'Yes. But don't hold it against me.'

'Some of you lot are all right.'

'Thank you.'

Dad upended the washing-up liquid bottle and squirted it under the running water. Mum always complained that he used way too much.

Indigo said, 'You know the files and stuff, where you keep all the reports about us?'

Dad turned off the tap and swished the water with his hand. 'I know them well.'

'Is everything true in them?'

'Professionals don't lie.' Dad turned back to the sink and started the Brillo pad along the inside of a frying pan.

Indigo scowled at him. 'I didn't say that.'

'Dad?'

Dad straightened up. 'Sorry, that came out a bit harsh. Us social workers have a habit of getting a bit defensive. What I meant was that we can only go on the information that we're given. If it's a really complex case and social services have been involved for a long time, well, you can imagine.'

She doesn't need to imagine, Dad.

'Everyone has their say. Health workers, nursery workers, mental health team, teachers, all of them. Maybe police reports.'

Dad pulled the plug and turned on the cold tap. He

rinsed the plates and bowls, stacking them in a wobbly heap on the dryer. Indigo was looking at him the way Shuu did when she realised her food bowl was empty.

Suddenly, Bailey felt a flash of anger. He might as well be eight again, with kids only coming to his party so they could chill with Dad. Dad had never seemed to notice what was happening then. He must do now. This was different. Why didn't he go back upstairs until Indigo was gone?

Indigo said, 'Do you reckon they make mistakes?'

Dad turned round, leaning against the sink. His hands dripped water on to the floor. 'No one's infallible. So, yes, sometimes, people make mistakes.'

Indigo was crumpling the tea towel into a ball. The silence was so heavy it could almost block the sunlight. This was when Shuu should earn her right to live here and slink in and rub herself round Dad's ankle or sit by the cat food cupboard and whinge a distraction. But the cat always did have crap timing.

Indigo hopped off the stool. 'I just get the bus from the top of the road, right?'

'Yeah.' Bailey glared at Dad. 'I'll walk with you.'

Upstairs, the front door opened and closed. Dad was wiping his hands on his jeans as Mum came down. She gave Bailey a tired smile as her eyes swept over the stack of crockery, the cereal on the table and Indigo. They stopped on Indigo. Both Mum and Indigo were standing there, looking at each other.

Dad said, 'Hi, Viv. You're back early.' He looked from Mum to Indigo. 'Um . . . Do you know each other?'

Indigo bobbed past Bailey, past Mum, up the stairs. Bailey dashed after her. He caught her at the door.

'Is everything okay?'

'Yeah.' Her cheeks looked like she'd caught his infrared and whacked the power up. 'Are you sure? You and Mum . . .'

'I'm all right. I just want to make sure I'm home when my sister calls.'

'I'll come with—'

'I'm all right.'

'Yeah. Okay. But Indigo, I was wondering if—'

And he'd missed it, the moment he could have asked for her number. She was already running towards the main road.

Back downstairs, Mum had dropped her heavy bags on to the kitchen floor. 'I know that girl.'

'Her name's Indigo,' Bailey said.

Mum flipped the kettle on. It turned off almost instantly, still hot from the forgotten tea.

That red face must be potent, because it was spreading across Mum's face too.

'God . . . yes. Indigo.'

7

Viv! Bailey's mum was Viv! And her face! She looked like she was going to have a heart attack. She probably would have had a full-on body fail if she'd come in when her son was rubbing peanut butter into Indigo's hair. It would have served Viv right. Now Indigo got why that counsellor kept going on about keeping a daily journal. Imagine writing down what just happened. The bus, the hair, Viv . . . and the day wasn't finished yet.

At least she'd made it home in record time, like the buses had driven out of her head and along the road towards her. She was calling Primrose in thirty minutes, so she'd better get thinking straight. She had to forget Viv. Forget Saskia. Forget Bailey's fingers stroking the skin beneath her hair. Indigo bit back a smile. Even with the squelch and grease, she'd just wanted to close her eyes and lean into him. When she'd turned round to talk to him, the back of his hand had brushed her neck. Just thinking about it now made the little blood vessels in her scalp prickle.

God. She was pathetic. She had to push him to the corner of her brain. Even there, his hair would make the shadows glow . . .

For God's sake! It was twenty-four minutes and counting to the Skype. They needed to sort out another meet-up so she could give Primrose the locket. And she wouldn't have the locket at all if Bailey hadn't got her bag back.

FORGET BAILEY!

Indigo readjusted her laptop on her knees and turned up the volume on *Heir Hunters*. Two blokes in suits were having a chat about some money left in a will. It was funny how she used to be hungry for this stuff. Really, it was just private detectives for dead people, with lots of scrolling down computer screens and blokes in cars knocking on doors. It was best when they found a distant relative and told them they'd got a thousand pounds coming their way.

Who Do You Think You Are? was even better. Famous people ended up crying. It was good to know that other people had complicated families.

Yeah, even Bailey's wasn't as simple as he thought. Weird that he didn't know it.

'Indigo?'

Her bedroom door opened. She nudged down the laptop cover.

Felix clocked the laptop and shook his head. 'You can't fool me. Or Keely. You have to learn to clear your browser history.' He came in and pushed the door shut with his bum. 'All fosterers have to take an exam in internet safety, you know. Their desks are suspended over a shark tank and if they get even one question wrong, the rope's sliced. Unless, of course, this is all totally innocent and you're being wrongly accused . . .'

Indigo flipped up the lid so Felix could see the screen.

He rolled his eyes. 'Oh, God. You're not back on the tears at tea-time stuff, are you? It's even worse than I imagined.'

'I bet when you move out you'll watch every single *Heir Hunters*, just to remind yourself of me.'

'I bet I won't.'

She threw a sock at him. He caught it in his fingers, screwed up his face and tossed it away. 'Pungent and toxic.'

'There's toe jam in there too. What do you want?'

'Just to see you.'

'I'm not helping you move any more bloody boxes.'

'I wasn't going to ask.' He stepped over her college clothes. They were sprawled on the floor like she'd collapsed and leaked out of them. His big foot just missed the locket box and crocodile on the rug. She had to stop herself leaning forward to grab them.

Felix sat down on her desk chair. 'How are things going?'

'Why?'

'Just asking.'

'Why are you just asking?'

The seat creaked as he twisted side to side. 'It's been you, me and Keely for a few years. And it's all changing.'

'So what? Things are always changing. It was never going

to be forever, was it?'

He gave her a searching look. 'Didn't you ever want that, though? A forever family.'

'How many kids have you known who got adopted?'

'A few.'

'And they all stayed adopted, right? None of them got dumped back into care. I don't know about you, but I met a few it didn't work out for.'

'Weren't you going to be adopted?'

She glared at him. Like he didn't know how much this crap hurt. 'I think my mum's parents were thinking about doing it. That really worked out, didn't it?'

'You were young and cute. You must have looked just like the kids they have in those bus-stop adverts for adoption. Why didn't social services keep on trying?'

'You seriously came in here to talk about this stuff? I've been with Keely the longest out of anywhere. But it was never going to be *forever*. Not for you or me.'

Felix sighed. 'Look, Indigo, believe me. You can come round to see me and Wade any time. If you want to.'

'You keep saying.'

'We mean it.'

'Yeah, thanks.' And she would go round, maybe for the first month or two. Then they'd meet up less and less, with even less and less to say to each other. The council would find her somewhere to live that was even further away.

That's the way it usually worked. His SIM must be like hers – full of contacts he hadn't used for years.

The bloke in the flat above was humping his vacuum cleaner up and down. It sounded like he was blowing a trombone into the floor. Indigo jacked the volume up on *Heir Hunters*. The car on the screen was so loud it could be driving through her room.

Felix pushed himself to his feet. 'We've been family for three years, Indi. My door's always going to be open for you, wherever you are.'

Then he was gone.

Indigo paused the programme. She'd been feeling all right, but now everything was churning again. She ran into the bathroom, turned on the tap and splashed cold water on her face. She held out the strand of hair where the gum had been. It was still a bit clammy and she could smell peanuts. She'd give it a proper wash in the morning. Fifteen minutes and counting. She had to get ready.

She went back to her room. 'Pull Up To The Bumper' was blasting through Felix's wall. Wade had bloody better like Grace Jones. Indigo settled her laptop on her chair and fast-forwarded *Heir Hunters* to where they found the dead bloke's cousin. He lived in a small house in Newcastle and didn't look particularly happy.

Four minutes and counting. Indigo called up Skype.

Primrose picked up straight away. She'd pulled her hair into a high bun and that made her face look more like Indigo's. Anyone seeing them together would know they were sisters.

Indigo blew a kiss. Primrose batted back a little smile. Last time, Primrose had blown a kiss too. Indigo let her hand drop down, resting on the locket box.

'Sorry about earlier,' Primrose said. She blurred for a moment, as she readjusted her laptop camera. 'Kieron's got a bit of a chest infection and his childminder told me to come and get him early. Pete couldn't leave work.'

'That's okay.' Primrose did look really sorry. 'It's not like you're going next week. You can come down again.'

'We're sort of busy sorting things out. I'm not sure if I can.'

Not sure? 'But you don't leave for ages! I can come up to Birmingham. I don't mind.'

'There's lots to do.'

Okay. Calm down, Indigo. Keep it sweet. 'Yeah. I suppose there must be loads of packing.'

'Indigo?' Primrose was chewing at her thumbnail. 'I wanted to see you for a reason.'

'I know. We're doing it for Mum. Like you said, social services broke our family up. We can put it back together again.'

'I was wrong.' Primrose was shaking her head. 'I can't. We can't.'

'We can't what? I don't get it! What do you mean, Primrose?'

'It's a dream, Indigo. We're . . . we're ruined. Nothing good can happen.'

What? Who's ruined?

'Indigo, I wanted to see you today so we could say goodbye properly.'

Goodbye? Primrose didn't have to use that word. Not when she was tearing another scrap of Indigo's heart away.

'It's not goodbye, Primrose. Things don't have to be any different. They have Skype in Australia, don't they?'

Primrose looked behind her. 'Just a minute.' She disappeared and Indigo heard a door bang shut. In the corner of the screen, Indigo watched her own face. She wiped her eyes on her sleeve and took a deep breath. This wasn't what Primrose wanted. It couldn't be. Primrose had come looking for Indigo. Real family bonds were too strong. And now there was even more for them to find out together. Indigo reached over and picked up the crocodile, let it lie flat in the middle of her palm.

Primrose settled herself back down. 'It's damn impossible getting privacy in this house.'

'Yeah,' Indigo said. 'I know what you mean. Listen. Something weird happened. I got this letter and—'

'Please don't, Indigo!'

'It was from our gran, Primrose. She said I had to find my dad and—'

'For God's sake! Stop!'

'But . . .'

'Indi, hun. You have to understand. I've had to deal with this for so much longer than you have. I can't do it any more.' Even in low res, Indigo could see that Primrose was crying.

'Do what? What do you have to do?'

'I can't hang on to it. To you.'

'I don't know what you're talking about.'

This was the wrong Primrose, not the same one who'd been waiting, all nervous, in the social worker's office, who'd jumped up to kiss Indigo the first time she saw her. Who took five, six, pictures of them with their cheeks squashed together. Pete must have got to her! That's why she was doing this!

Primrose rubbed her temples. Her thumb slipped back to her mouth and she started on the nail again. 'Me and Pete have been talking about it.'

Yeah. Pete, the jealous git! Always trying to pull Primrose and Indigo apart.

'One of the reasons he took the new job was to help me. He said I needed to be somewhere completely different, with no reminders. There had to be a proper reason to shift all five of us to the other side of the planet and that was it. It wasn't for him. It was for me.'

'But it doesn't matter where you go.' Indigo knew her

voice was getting louder. She took a deep breath in and tried again. 'It doesn't matter, because we're still sisters. We're doing this for Mum, remember?'

'How can I forget? Not now I'm a mother too. It's hard, Indigo, bloody hard, to get things right with your kids. I went through crap when I was little, but I'm doing my best. Just me and Pete, working at it. I've seen the files. I know how much help our mum got. She still mucked it up. Every time.'

'But she tried! You told me that!'

'Yeah, Indigo. She did try. And maybe one day she would have got it right. But she didn't have a chance to get there, did she?'

Indigo bent closer to the camera. 'Primrose?'

Primrose's teeth, up and down her thumb, like she wanted to work her way through to the bone. 'Our mum never got the chance because your dad killed her.'

Primrose's face filled the screen as she leaned forward. She must have grabbed a tissue, because as she moved back, she was wiping her nose.

Indigo wanted to say something, put her side across, make the argument, but her brain was full of empty speech bubbles.

Primrose dropped her tissue out of sight and started fiddling with her bun. 'This is what happens to me every time I think of this stuff. Something inside me makes me want to explode. I can't keep taking it out on Pete and the kids. They had nothing to do with this shitty mess. It's not fair on them.'

'I . . .'

I . . . what? The empty bubbles in Indigo's brain got bigger until all that was left was dead space.

'I love you, Indigo. Sorry.'

The connection broke. Indigo tried the number again. It rang. No answer. And again. And again. *Ring. Ring.* Nothing.

Indigo shoved the chair, hard. It slammed against the desk. The laptop jerked forward, almost toppling off the seat. Indigo pushed herself back across the floor, the cheap rug scraping her skin. Right now, that felt good. Her foot kicked something. It was the box with the locket inside. Indigo flipped the lid and held the locket up. The light caught a tiny scratch across the case. Primrose would never have bloody worn it in the first place! Indigo yanked the case off the chain and threw it across the room. It clipped the window and dropped behind the shelves. The chain trickled through her fingers on to the floor.

Why didn't it come when she needed it? The shuffling, the pulling, the burst of heat taking over? That's what she wanted now. Not the nothing. Not the emptiness.

She crawled over to her bed and dropped face down on to her duvet. It was starting, the slow pull into herself, as the gap inside her got too hungry.

Bailey unplugged the amp and rested the Gibson on its stand. His concentration was shot, so what was the point? If he'd been any good at song writing, he'd have had a whole album's worth now. 'The Girl All Alone'. 'High Heels and Hazel Eyes'. And there'd be a bonus track, 'Stressed Out Viv', for the proper fans who knew where to look for it.

He opened the music-room door. Voices drifted upstairs. Mum and Dad in the kitchen.

Mum's voice. 'Indigo—'

Bailey held his breath, but the rest of Mum's sentence soaked into the walls. He needed to be a couple of steps lower. He moved quietly and sat in the shadow of the stairs that led from the hallway to the first landing. He could just about see through the spindles into the back of the kitchen. Dad was in yellow rubber gloves, kneeling on spread-out newspapers, scrubbing the oven. The stink of cleaner was wire sharp, even from up here. Mum, or at least her hand, was holding a glass of wine.

Mum said, 'What did she say to you?'

Bailey leaned forward.

'I've already told you.' Dad carried on scraping.

Glass up, pause, back down again. The wine level was definitely sinking.

'It was a big family,' Mum said. 'The same mum, different dads.'

Silence. The scraping stopped. Dad looked up, towards Mum. Bailey moved back. 'Rod Stewart's got eight children with five different mothers.'

'Don't get all self-righteous with me, Ed! This isn't about knocking up blonde models. This is about children born into chaos. It's not fair.'

Bailey couldn't peek round. Any movement might catch Dad's eye.

Mum was carrying on. 'This is the stuff you know inside and out, Ed. When the poor woman keeps pushing out the babies, even though they all get taken away.'

'People can change, Viv.'

'Really, Ed? I suppose I must bow to your judgement on that one.' Wine glass up. Wine glass down. Nearly empty. 'Indigo was the sixth. It's hard to forget them because of the names, a whole bloody rainbow of them. Scarlet and Coral were twins. Then there was Primrose and a boy called Teal. Another girl, Bluebell and one after Indigo. You don't have to guess what she was called. '

'Our son's named after the Central Criminal Court.'

The wine glass clinked on to the work surface. 'I'm not sneering, Ed. I'm just trying to remember. She was called Mahalia, the mother. She had the usual problems – booze, on and off heroin, and all the mental health crap that comes with it. You know the way it is. Women like that are a magnet for every exploitative little bastard for miles.'

Maybe Dad nodded then.

'She had the twins when she was fifteen, I think. Her parents tried to help her, but as soon as she was seventeen, she took the kids and ran off to live with the dad's family. Bristol or somewhere. It was one of those families . . .'

The fridge door opened and a cork squeaked out of a bottle.

'Do you want anything, Ed?'

'When I'm done.'

'Those poor children were there for three long years until the dad's brother was locked up for sex with an under-aged girl. It was normal in that household. Even his sister had older men staying over. She was fifteen.'

Dad's voice was quiet. 'And the twins?'

'Nothing that anyone could tell. But Mahalia wouldn't leave their dad, not at first. So Scarlet and Coral went into care.'

Jesus! Indigo's family's life as told by Mum. And Bailey was sitting here listening in. This was private stuff. He should go back to the music room and close the door.

Bailey shuffled down another step.

Mum was still going. 'I think Primrose was taken on by her dad's family, and Teal, his dad was French and took him back to France.'

'I wonder if he ever saw his mum's family again.'

'What do you think?'

'No. Probably not. If things were as chaotic as you say, I

can't imagine his dad would make the trek over. What about the next child?'

'Bluebell was adopted from birth. I only ever met Indigo. She was seven or eight. She shouldn't really have been in a pupil referral unit. She was very bright, but when she lost it, she really lost it.'

'You can understand why,' Dad said.

'I'd like to hear you say that when a screaming kid's wrenching a chunk of hair out of your head.'

Dad said, 'It happened. When I had hair.'

Bailey didn't hear Mum laugh, but the bin opened and closed, then the fridge door went again and a can ring pull was opened.

Mum said, 'Use a glass, please, Ed. And she didn't say anything else to you?'

'Who?'

'Indigo, Ed! Who do you think?'

'Like what?'

'I don't know! Anything!'

A patter of footsteps on the stairs above Bailey. Shuu launched herself off the step above and landed by Bailey's feet with a moany meow. Bailey tried to nudge her away with his toe.

Mum was talking again. 'So what do you think's going on between her and Bailey?'

Seriously, Mum! She and Indigo had been staring each

other out like a referee was going to ding Round One. And now Mum wanted to make it about him? As if!

'For God's sake, Viv! I don't know! It's not really our business anyway.'

Thank you, Dad.

Shuu sank a claw into Bailey's thigh. Bailey bit back a swear word and pushed her off. The stupid cat hurtled downstairs, yowling.

Dad called, 'Shuu?'

Bailey stood up. 'Sorry, Dad. I stood on her tail.'

'Really, Bailey? She's not exactly hard to see!'

He carried on into the kitchen, making it look like that was always the plan. Shuu raced to her empty food bowl, looking back at him with an expression of sheer hate. Mum slugged the last of her wine and glared at Dad, who had his back to her again, wiping the hob.

Mum said, 'You should ask him, Ed.'

Bailey said, 'Ask me what?'

Dad gathered the scraps of crusty food into his cloth. 'It doesn't matter.'

Mum shot Dad a look. 'Yes, it does.'

'No, it doesn't.' Dad scrunched up the newspaper from by the oven door. 'It really doesn't.'

Bailey looked from one to the other. 'Mixed messages.'

Mum glared at him. 'This is not a joke.'

Bailey said, 'What is it, then?'

'Nothing.' Dad dropped the dirty newspaper in the bin and peeled off his gloves.

'You're not helping,' Mum hissed.

'Because I'm not bloody psychic.' Dad picked up his glass of Guinness and brushed past Bailey, out of the room. Mum made a point of ignoring Dad's disappearance.

Bailey said, 'Well, Mum?'

She tried a smile. 'I was just asking Dad about Indigo.'

'Why?'

'She's doing her A Levels, isn't she? I don't think many people who knew her before would have seen that coming.'

'Jesus, Mum! Are you snobbing on her?'

'God. Sorry. That sounded all wrong.' Mum ran her hand along the work surface, like she was checking for crumbs. 'She had a tough start. Have you . . . do you know about her parents?'

'Yes, I do. Thanks, Mum. How do you know her?'

'From a special education unit in Medway, of all places. She was in Year Four.'

'Did you teach her?'

'Not really. We did some art therapy stuff. I was only there six months or so, though I always wondered what happened to her. She was very clever, but a bit of a whirlwind. When she got angry, you really knew about it. I wonder if she sorted that out.'

Work-in-progress, Mum.

Bailey opened the fridge. They were obviously due a shopping delivery, because the only thing in there was a bowl of green pasta stuff that Dad had cooked two days ago, and some rotting celery.

Shuu wound herself round Mum's ankles, meowing. Mum checked the cat-food cupboard.

'Sorry, Shuu, you'll have to wait. Or go and harass Ed. He's the one who forgot to top you up.'

Shuu did her squeaky pathetic noise and gazed at Mum. 'Oh, for goodness sake, cat! Bailey, can you pop out and get her something?'

'Now?'

'Yes. Now. I don't often ask. And don't get any fish flavours. It makes her sick.'

It had started to rain. Bailey could see it dribbling down the glass panel in the back door.

'Um, Bailey?' Mum's eyes seemed to dart around him. 'You and Indigo, are you . . .'

'Are we what?'

'Is she your girlfriend?'

Yes. He should say it just to wind Mum up. 'She's my friend. What's the problem?'

'There's no problem, Bailey. I'm just glad it's that way.'

'What do you mean?'

'I don't mean anything, Bailey. My rucksack's by the shoe rack. A tenner should be enough.'

8

Bailey was happy to be out. Right now, he could carry on walking along the main road, down to the crossroads and on and on. All the umbrellas had disappeared at home, but the rain wasn't as bad as it looked. Dad was watching football in the sitting room when Bailey left, door shut. Bailey had seen the flicker of the game through the window as he walked away. Mum had gone back to her office. Shuu was sulking in the kitchen. If a giant alien sliced his house in half, it would look like a computer game with two little figures and the bloody cat, all on different levels, doing their own thing, in their own rooms.

Mum had never come out with this crap before. Mona's older brother had done time inside but Mum hadn't had anything to say about that – although she hadn't looked particularly sad when Bailey told her he'd ended it with Mona.

Mum had absorbed too much teacher. The mum bit was shrinking away. Home wasn't school, she had to understand that. She had to stop trying to control him and Dad.

'Oi!' The voice cut through the rush of traffic. Bailey nearly looked up, but stopped himself. He wasn't in the mood for the guys who hung around BetQuick, asking for money.

'You! Indigo's pal!'

That voice. Bailey knew it.

'Yeah! You!'

A homeless guy was standing by the bus shelter. Not a homeless guy. It was the one from earlier.

'You coming over here, or do you want me to come to you?'

Bailey's head was yelling, 'Keep walking! Quick!' The guy must have followed Bailey here, keeping his distance on Essex Road. He *could* just be here by coincidence. There were enough betting shops to keep *Ocean's Eleven*, *Twelve* and *Thirteen* happy. But he knew Indigo's name. How the hell did he know that?

Bailey crossed over to the bus stop. The drizzle was working its way into his hair. Rain did him no favours and it hadn't done the homeless guy any, either. He'd pulled the beanie right down to his eyebrows and his damp face was grey in the shadow of the shelter. He was holding a bulging plastic bag that clunked when he moved.

He said, 'You got money for coffee?'

Bailey held out two coins. 'That's all I can give you.'

He knocked Bailey's hand away. The money fell into a puddle. 'I'm not a bloody beggar!'

Bailey felt his face redden. He bent down to retrieve the coins. 'So what do you want, then?'

'You're Indigo's friend.'

'I don't know what you mean.'

The guy's eyes blazed. 'I look like this, but it doesn't make me stupid, right?'

He needed a mirror! He needed to understand how he did look!

The man sank back on to the bench in the bus shelter, clutching the bag of cans tight on his lap. 'I need to make things right for Indigo.'

'You did. You got her bag back for her. I gave it to her.'

'Tell me the truth. I need to know. Are you her friend?'

Say no, and he could carry on to Nisa Foods, pick up Shuu's dinner and go home. Though he'd have to go round the long way in case he passed the bus shelter again. But . . . the homeless guy was looking at him, waiting. The rain had soaked his trousers like he'd been standing outside the shelter, watching for a while. And Bailey was Indigo's friend, wasn't he? He'd taken chewing gum out of her hair, for God's sake.

Bailey said, 'Yes. I am.'

'Good. We need to help her.' The cans knocked together as the homeless guy stood up. 'Let's get out of this soddin' rain.'

'I don't think so.'

'You're not really her friend, then.'

'Yes, I am.'

113

'If that's true, you'll come with me.'

Right. Bailey had gone out to get cat food and now he was following a tramp up the street to a takeaway.

The food joint was warm and not too busy. The guys behind the counter gave them a quick look over, but didn't say anything. They must be used to all sorts picking up their cardboard boxes of wings. Bailey aimed for one of the three tables set aside for punters wanting to eat in. It was a little way back from the window, but the place was so brightly lit that no matter where they sat, anyone could peer in and see them. The rain was getting worse. Hopefully no one walking by was taking time to window-shop fried chicken, though, knowing Bailey's luck, Saskia and Mona might be taking a rainy stroll right now.

Bailey said, 'Do you want anything to eat?'

'Pizza. Cheese and tomato.'

Bailey would have to break into Shuu's tenner. He went to the counter and ordered. Just a Coke for himself. It wasn't like he was going to be here long. He glanced back at the table. Under the harsh light, the stains on the homeless guy's jeans looked like they'd been there for years. So did the dirt under his nails. He had the start of a street drunk's swollen nose and his chin bristled with black and grey stubble. No, this was definitely going to be quick. It was a bloody stupid idea to come here in the first place. If he hadn't mentioned Indigo's name, Bailey wouldn't be here at all. It was probably just a fluke.

Bailey took the food to the table and sat down. The pizza smell was mixed with something heavier, like damp, old carpet and sweat. The homeless guy tore off a chunk of pizza crust and dropped it on to the side of the box. He tapped his cheek.

'Choppers. Not in good nick.'

Bailey said, 'Does Indigo know you?'

The tramp took a bite of pizza. The skin on his neck wrinkled and relaxed. "Course she doesn't.'

'So how do you know her name?'

'That would be telling.'

'That's why I'm here. So you can tell me. You were following us, right? If you're stalking her, I could tell the police.'

'Go ahead. Pentonville's shit, though it's better than some of them hostels.'

'You've been in prison?'

'Not proud of it.' More crust was ripped off and discarded. 'Last time, I took some stuff from a garden centre. Don't know why. How much does a bag of slug pellets go for these days?'

'You went to prison for that?'

'On recall. A slap on the wrist for being naughty again.' He wiped his hands on the side of the box. His fingers were shiny with grease and dirt. 'Where are my manners? You just bought me supper. The least I can do is introduce myself.' He held out his hand. 'I'm JJ.'

Bailey braced himself and shook it as lightly as he could. 'I'm Bailey.'

JJ nodded. 'Good job you came along when you did. I wasn't sure how much longer I could wait. That rain gets into you.'

'You've been waiting since I got home?'

'Yes.'

'Did you see Indigo when she left my house?'

'Yes.'

A police car screamed by. JJ's eyes followed the lights until they disappeared.

Bailey said, 'She doesn't know you, but you want to help her, right?'

'She met me when she was a kid. She won't remember. I—'

He started coughing, bent over, fist against his chest. He pushed the pizza away from him. He'd torn it into strips, but it looked like you could put the whole thing back together again. He'd probably only managed a couple of bites. The coughing was going on and on.

JJ wheezed, 'Water, please!'

Bailey went back to the counter and bought a bottle.

The manager pointed to their table. 'You make sure he stays good.'

116

'Yeah,' Bailey said. 'I will.'

Bailey opened the water and put it on the table. JJ took a slug. He was right. His teeth definitely weren't in good nick.

'Cheers.' The words came out as a gasp.

The coughing eased, though JJ was still hunched over, like he was expecting a second episode.

Bailey said, 'When did you meet her?'

'I knew her parents.' He glugged back more water. 'Do you know what happened to them?'

'Yes.'

JJ looked ready to start coughing again, but managed to hold it in. 'No one had no excuse for that. You hear about these things . . .' He shook his head. 'The crowd changes. You take that for granted. Sometimes they get clean. Sometimes they even stay clean. And there's the ones who cane it, and the new'uns who don't know their measures. They're the ones the ambulances come out for. But Toby and Mahalia . . . no. It shouldn't have happened.'

He killed her! Of course it shouldn't have happened!

Bailey said, 'Did you know them well?'

'Too well.'

'From before Indigo?'

He nodded. 'We went back a long way.'

'I heard about the stuff in Bristol, with Indigo's twin sisters. Do you go back that far?'

JJ's fist crunched down on the pizza box lid. 'I am not a fucking nonce!'

'I didn't say—'

'I know about Bristol! Mahalia told me! And I knew her. Nothing like that would ever happen to her kids and it didn't, you understand me? It didn't even happen in Bristol! She protected them. But they still got taken away. She had her faults, but that . . .' He punched the lid again. 'No!'

'You!' One of the takeaway guys was out from behind the counter. 'You don't make trouble here.'

'No.' Bailey frowned at JJ. 'We're all right. Sorry.' He lowered his voice. 'You have to keep it quiet or we're going to be out in the rain.'

'I'm not a nonce.'

'No. Sorry. But you still haven't told me who you are. Or why you want to help Indigo.'

JJ leaned in closer. Bailey was hit by a blast of the sweaty-carpet smell. He had to stop himself moving away. 'Like I said. I'm a friend of her parents. I did something . . .' His eyes narrowed. 'Not what your nasty mind's thinking, right?'

'All right. Sorry.'

'Get me that coffee and I'll tell you what this is about.'

At this rate, Shuu would be eating air. Bailey went to the counter to place yet another order. Behind him, he heard the clang of tin cans. *God, please don't break into the Special*

Brew in here.

JJ hadn't. As Bailey took the drink back, he saw an A4 envelope on the table. JJ split three sachets of sugar into the coffee and stirred it hard. It slopped over the table, just missing the envelope.

JJ said, 'I've come to you because you didn't just sit there and let it happen. You're like me. You opened your mouth against those bitches. Then you made sure Indigo was all right.'

Yeah, he had. He'd had his own reasons.

JJ looked round, like he was checking no one was close. He dropped his voice, bending over his coffee, stirring and blowing it. Bailey had to move closer again.

'I knew her mum on and off. She was all right, May. Her proper name was Mahalia, but not many could remember that. She'd had her problems before. She'd had five kids taken away and for a while it was like she'd given up. Hers was the place you went back to when you wanted to carry on with the drink. There was other goods there too, for those of us who wanted it.'

Bailey nodded. Indigo's life. Second instalment.

'Then May got pregnant. Toby, the guy she was with, didn't touch the heavy stuff. She was sure she was going to keep this one. The place got tidy. All the other stuff was knocked on the head, along with all the hangers-on that came with it. Baby was born. It was all good. For a couple

119

of years they were all right. Kid doing fine. May too. Toby looked like he was a good influence, but then Toby got caught for supply. It was money, May said. They were struggling. He had a decent amount on him and was banged up for nearly a month. And all the sleazy gits came creeping back to May's.'

'How do you know?'

JJ took a sip of coffee. 'I was one of them. But it wasn't just me. There were others. May was back on the gear too. It wasn't good for a kid, especially one toddling round the place.'

Bailey's phone buzzed. Mum's number. He turned it face down. 'So Indigo got taken away as well.'

'Yeah. But she was lucky. Her grandparents had her. They loved her too.'

'So what happened?' That came out wrong, like Bailey was hurrying JJ to get to the bit where Indigo's dad . . . when her dad did it.

'I went away. I thought if I got out of the area, things would change for me. But you take things with you, don't you? I ended up in the clink, over Suffolk way. When that was done I came back to London. May was on-off with Toby – she'd had another baby while I was away. Violet. She was taken for adoption straight from the hospital. But May was trying, I could see it. She'd even cut down on the drinking. Toby, though. It seemed like something happened when he was prison.'

'What do you mean?'

'He went in good and healthy. Came out different. Some do. May's mum wouldn't bring Indigo round the flat with Toby there. And when May went round her parents', she said she just got grief.'

'You said you did something.'

He sighed. 'Yeah. I did. I'd seen how close May used to be with Indigo. I'd seen how she tried. I thought maybe if she got to see her daughter properly, things would change for her.'

'You went to Indigo's grandparents?'

More sirens. An ambulance and a couple more police cars. JJ was stirring his coffee again, half turns, like he was drawing a smile.

'I knew where her nan took her to play. I went a few times, just to be sure. One day, Indigo was playing with her little toys in the sand pit and a kid fell off the swings and was making loads of noise. Indigo's nan went over to see and I picked up Indigo and took her to her mum.'

'You kidnapped her?'

'No!' JJ wiped his face. 'She was always going to go back!'

'But her grandma! She must have been . . . God!'

JJ pushed the envelope towards Bailey. 'Her nan was ill then but didn't know it. Maybe I made it worse . . . it's a bad world, isn't it? People like me can do all this rubbish to our bodies and we're still here. Indigo's nan, she wasn't old, but her marbles were already rolling away. After it happened, Indigo's granddad said he couldn't look after his wife *and* his granddaughter. And that was that.'

One of the takeaway staff came over for the pizza box. He looked at the heap of shredded pizza in the middle. 'You all good here?'

JJ ignored him. Bailey nodded.

'Yeah,' JJ said again. 'That was that.'

'You left Indigo there . . . in that flat . . .' Bailey said, 'while her dad . . . Jesus! Why?'

'I'm not proud of it.'

'Why?'

'A guy I know called. He had something for me. I wasn't going to be long.'

'You went to score?'

'I told you. I'm not proud of myself. They were all right when I left. They were playing with her. But I should have known. Toby could turn on a sixpence. Prison did that to him. He wasn't like that before.'

'Jesus!' It was filling Bailey's head. The squalid flat, the crying child. The struggle on the other side of the bedroom door. 'What do you want? You can't dump all this on her! She's got enough on her plate.'

'I know what she's going through. I know how the system works. I was a care kid too.' JJ tapped the envelope.

His greasy fingerprint gleamed in the middle and the corners were wrinkled from bashing against the cans in the bag. 'It was my fault she got split up from her family. I want to make amends.'

'Like how? Isn't it too late for that?'

'No. It's never too late. There's a picture in here. I want you to take it to Indigo's granddad. He's all she's got left. She needs him. And he needs her. Indigo's nan died a few months ago.'

God, that was tough. Her mum, her dad, her grandma. 'Do you think she knows?'

'Social services would have told her. That's why she needs to find her granddad. It's just them now.'

Bailey shook his head. 'I don't know who he is. And even if I did, I couldn't just turn up out of the blue.'

'His name's Horatio. He runs a garage in Deptford. I've written it down for you. It's in the envelope.' They looked at each other.

'I can't.'

'Why not?'

'I can't turn up at a stranger's door telling him to get in touch with his granddaughter. What if he already had a chance to and didn't want to?'

'That's why you need the picture. To show it's for real.' JJ had nudged the envelope closer to Bailey. 'Take it.'

Like it was easy to carry home a big envelope like that.

Dad's social worker radar would be pinging left, right and centre. And JJ may not be paedo, but he had definitely been following them. So that did make him a stalker.

What if Indigo really did want to get to know her granddad, though? He'd looked after her. It wasn't his fault that Indigo couldn't live with him.

He said, 'How did you find Indigo?'

'She wasn't hidden. I bumped into one of the boys I was locked up with and he took me to the free computers in the library. Some idiot had put up a picture of her, taking the piss because she got thrown out of school.' He frowned at Bailey. 'It shouldn't be allowed. No one keeps their mouth shut these days.'

Bailey stood up. 'Thank you for asking, but I can't do it.'

JJ closed his eyes slowly, opened them again, like it took a big effort. 'Why can't you?'

'Because it's . . . because it's her life. It seems like everybody's prying into her business and I don't want to. It's not fair.'

'Of course it's not fair! That's exactly why you should do it! Kids like you, you've got everything. You're planning to go to university, right?'

'That's nothing to do with—'

'And if things don't work out, you're going to live with Mum and Dad. Save some money. Go off travelling. You think Indigo's got those chances?'

'My dad's a social worker. There are funding schemes. He says—'

'Schemes? Bollocks to schemes! When you get passed from stranger to stranger, you don't want schemes. You just want family.'

'Yes, but . . .'

But what? It was just an envelope. He didn't have to do anything with it. He could take it now if it would make JJ stop.

JJ said, 'You're her friend.'

'Yes.'

'You going to help her, then?'

Bailey picked up the envelope and slid it beneath his jacket. 'I can't promise.'

JJ folded his arms. 'I don't believe in promises. It's what people do that matters.'

Bailey waited for a bus to speed through a puddle before opening the door. He turned back to JJ. He was tearing open another sachet of sugar. He stirred it into the dregs of his coffee. The takeaway staff looked ready to pounce on him any minute.

Bailey said, 'Where are you staying?'

JJ gave him a tired look. 'Why? You giving me a lift home?'

9

Felix skidded a piece of toast over the table. 'You over your huff, then?'

Indigo knocked the toast back to him. 'Bugger off.'

Felix took another swipe. The toast shot into Indigo's lap. 'Gooooalllll!'

'You stupid or what?' Indigo slammed it butter-side-down next to his plate. Grease oozed from underneath.

Keely pulled a tray of bacon out from under the grill. 'God, I'm going to miss these tender moments.'

Indigo said, 'It's your fault. You make us do this stupid breakfast thing.'

'I know, I know. I just thought it might be nice. Once a month, that's all. Some crispy bacon and some friendly conversation.'

Felix picked up the toast and wiped the table with kitchen roll. 'Reckon the two of you will carry on this rich tradition without me? Or are you getting someone else?'

'Like anyone could fill your shoes.' Keely plonked the plate of bacon on to the table. 'Help yourselves. Or are you vegetarian this week, Felix?'

'Not this week.' He picked up a rasher and dropped it

on to his plate. 'What about you, Indi?'

'Like you care!'

Indigo felt Keely glance over. She kept her eyes on her plate and stabbed a couple of rashers. She ate them straight off her fork.

Felix said, 'You didn't answer, Keely. Are you getting someone else?'

Indigo's stomach was hurting. She shouldn't eat so fast.

Keely slid into her seat. 'I don't know. You're a hard act to follow, Felix. Indigo too.'

Indigo prodded another rasher. 'I haven't gone yet.' It was meant to come out light, but there was a short, hot silence.

Keely stroked her arm. 'Of course you haven't.'

But they were all getting ready for that, weren't they? Keely had upped the cooking lessons and there were extra meetings with social workers where they sat around a table and talked about Indigo's future. She'd been allocated a personal adviser called Rohita who kept going on about learning to budget. She'd told Indigo about a new block of one-bedroom flats in Edmonton, not far from Silver Street Station. They'd be freshly decorated, Rohita said, and Indigo should be able to get some cash to help with a fridge and a cooker.

A couple of days later, Indigo had gone to look at the flats. As the bus stopped at the lights by Seven Sisters, she'd seen a young blond bloke pull down his trousers and start peeing against a tree. Right there, in the middle of the day, with all the people walking past pretending to ignore his naked arse. He was probably just a few years older than Indigo, but it looked like he didn't care about anything at all. She'd got off at the next stop and taken the bus back, staying on it all the way through Dalston, past Liverpool Street Station until it crossed London Bridge. Then at London Bridge, she'd waited and got the very same bus right to the end of Keely's road. *Her* road.

Felix burped. Indigo wrinkled her nose.

'Jesus, Felix! That stinks!'

'Yeah. Well, now I've got your attention, I want to remind you that it's your turn to load the dishwasher. Me and Wade want to hit Ikea before the masses.'

Indigo made a kissy face. 'Need candles for your love nest?'

'Enough,' Keely said. 'When you come back, Felix, please move those boxes. I've got no toes left to stub.'

'Yeah, sure.'

Felix pushed out his chair, stood up and stretched. His fingers could almost touch opposite kitchen walls. At least there'd be more room without him.

'See y'all later.'

Keely buttered a triangle of toast. Indigo got up and started pulling the plates towards her. Bloody Felix never ate his crusts. And he peeled off all the bacon rind. She scraped the leftovers into the food bin and stacked the plates in the dishwasher.

Keely said, 'Indigo?'

There was still some toast in the rack. 'You going to eat this, Kee?'

'Indigo? Please, sit down and tell me what's stressing you out.'

Indigo opened the fridge and found the carton of smoothie. Felix always shoved it in the back, hoping she wouldn't find it. Hands were on her shoulders. Keely, guiding her out of the kitchen, round Felix's boxes and into the lounge. She nudged Indigo on to the sofa, sat next to her and put her arm round her.

'Is it school?'

'It's shit.'

'Maybe so. But your social worker's right. This is last-chance saloon. You just need to hold it together for long enough to get what you need out of school. But that's not it. I know you, Indigo. What happened with your sister?'

'What do you mean?'

Keely was leaning forward, like she was getting ready to catch anything Indigo was going to throw at her. 'You were supposed to meet her yesterday and you were going to give her the locket. But you haven't mentioned anything about it. Usually you're bouncing around after you've been talking to Primrose.'

'She cancelled.'

'She cancelled?'

'Yeah.' A tiny tug, that pulled thread, just behind her belly button. 'Her kid was ill.'

Keely took Indigo's hand. 'I'm sorry. And the Australia plan's still on, I suppose?'

Indigo nodded.

'I thought you didn't mind that? You were still going to text and Skype and whatever.'

Indigo shook her head. The bacon she'd eaten felt like it was spinning round, squashing flat against her insides.

'What, then, Indigo? I don't understand.'

'She wants to make a new start.' The words came out in gulps. 'Without me.'

'Without you?'

'Because . . . because of what happened. Because of what happened to our mum. '

Keely breathed out sharply. 'She had no right to hoist that crap on you. That was *nothing* to do with you. You understand me?'

Indigo tried to nod, but her head wouldn't work. She knew Primrose was right. It was *her* dad that had killed their mum, not Primrose's dad.

'Primrose has made her choice. I have to say, I don't

130

agree with it and I'm angry on your behalf. But that doesn't help you, does it? I'm here for you, Indigo. I always will be. Even when they drag you away from me, I'm never going to abandon you. Do you believe me?'

Indigo had to keep looking at her knees, at the moth hole in her leggings, at the spot of bare skin. Keep staring. No blinking. 'It's just . . .' *There's a letter. It should have come to you. I opened it and—*

'I'm not real family.'

'No. But . . .'

'But I'm all right, though.'

Indigo managed to hook out a smile. 'Not bad.'

'That'll do me. Let's finish in the kitchen and go out for a bit of shopping. I'll stand you thirty quid to spend in H&M.'

'What about Camden Market?'

Keely made a face. 'Oh, God. Okay.'

For a few seconds, Bailey was confused. Then he got it. He lay in bed, completely still. There were no Dad sounds. The house didn't give that slight shake as Dad ran up and down the stairs trying to remember things, or the bang as he pulled the front door shut a bit too hard. No second or so of silence before Dad's feet went pounding along the road.

Of course. It was Saturday. Dad didn't leave for another

hour. He was probably having a coffee in the sitting room, surrounded by gear for the youth football team. Mum would be in the small room already working. Dad always used to take her up coffee too. He'd sit on the bed talking to her while she grumbled about the kids' spelling. That hadn't happened in a while, though Dad was convinced their weekend in Paris would change that. Coffee and bed, he'd said. Then he'd grinned at Bailey's embarrassment.

Bailey turned on to his side. When he'd returned home last night, the kitchen was empty. He'd fed Shuu, crept past Mum's office, taken the envelope up to his room and tipped the contents on to the bed. He'd had a look, but it had been too much to get his head around. He'd shoved it all back in the envelope and left it on his bedside table.

His phone went. He reached over to answer it. Damn. It was Austin.

Bailey said, 'Yo.'

'Don't "yo" me. You haven't, have you?'

'Haven't what?'

'The tickets, man!'

'What—' Oh, God. 'Sorry, Austin!'

'Sorry? I've been stalking that gig for months! Fall Out Boy in our town hall, Bailey. You ever think that's going to happen again?'

'I could try now.'

'The tickets went in forty-five seconds.'

'So I probably wouldn't have got any anyway.'

'You don't know because you didn't try. If I had a bank card, I would have done it myself. But you offered, man! You offered! You're going to have to make it up to me.'

'Two lunches.'

'Five measly pounds in Rooster C's? That's an insult.'

'Three lunches.'

'Man, you're proper awake, right? Because it sounds like you're dreaming. I'm talking real compensation.'

'Like what?'

'Wake up!'

'I am not having a party, if that's what you mean.'

'You owe me.'

Austin rang off. It *was* crap about the tickets, though it was Bailey who should be making the noise. He was the proper fan. Austin only had time for the new stuff.

Bailey rolled out of bed and opened the curtains. The weather had cleared overnight. Downstairs, the front door opened and Bailey watched Dad striding away, the sports bag full of shin pads and footballs swinging by his side. Bailey picked the envelope off his bedside table and emptied it out again. Last night, he'd gone to buy Whiskas and come back with a mission from a tramp. God.

Then another thought wriggled in. No matter how much he tried to clear it, it wouldn't go. If this was a computer game, he'd been handed a power-up, a power-up in the shape of a photo.

It was an A4 black-and-white glossy print, a mother with a newborn baby. The mother looked Turkish or mixed race, her fringe flopping over her face into her eyes as she bent to kiss the bridge of her baby's nose. The baby looked – well, like a baby. It had a fat round face, no eyebrows, and was squinting up at its mother. A date was written on the bottom. December, the year before Bailey was born. It would be right for Indigo, but no matter what way Bailey looked at the picture, he couldn't see her in there.

He turned it over. Wobbly pencil words were scrawled across the middle.

Indigo's granddad is Horatio Bankes, a mechanic in New Cross.

But that wasn't all. Bailey had almost missed the scrap of paper that fell from the envelope when he took out the picture the first time. It was a faded Tesco's receipt and JJ had written over the top of it.

Ivygables House is at 11 Swift Avenue in Camden

Bailey had Googled it. It was a hostel for homeless men. What else could it have been? He'd Googled Horatio Bankes too. He was still the proprietor of Nelson's Motor Repairs. The picture online showed closed garage doors with a small tow truck outside.

And now he'd agreed to go and knock on those doors and introduce himself to Indigo's granddad, all behind her back. Why the hell hadn't he got her number yesterday? Well, he would have if Dad hadn't refused to disappear. And Mum hadn't come bursting in and surprised everybody. But even if he had, would he really do it? Call her and tell her that the homeless guy actually was following them and had sent Bailey on a mission? How the hell would that conversation go?

Hi, Indigo! You're being stalked by a homeless guy called JJ and he snatched you from the park when you were four.

It was all too mucked up. Maybe he should take the envelope to the police.

There's this sort-of-homeless guy who looks like he drinks Superbrew for breakfast. I bought him a pizza and he told me he kidnapped a kid.

Except the kid was seventeen and Bailey couldn't stop looking at her in English class. It would be worse if the police believed him too. They'd probably take the photo as evidence.

It would be like resetting the game just when you were reaching top level.

Bailey slung on his trackie bottoms and headed

downstairs. Mum wasn't around after all. That was good – no questions about how he was spending his weekend. In the kitchen, he opened a cupboard and pushed aside the granola. Why did Dad always try and hide the Nutella? He dropped some bread in the toaster and sliced up a banana.

He could go to New Cross, just to see. And, if the situation seemed right, he could introduce himself to Horatio Bankes. But only if. They'd find a little quiet spot and Bailey would do his best to explain. Dad always said that kids could tell when adults were lying to them; you had to be honest and appropriate. And that's how Bailey would play it. He had the journey down to think of the words he was going to use. If the situation seemed right.

The train south was virtually empty. The scattering of passengers along the carriages were plugged in, like Bailey. A blast of Led Zeppelin mix and his whole head dissolved into hard chords. Indigo must do that too, jack the music up so hard there wasn't any room for anything else.

The outside world zipped by. Graffitied backs of buildings running parallel to Shoreditch High Street, then slipping through the tunnel underground to Shadwell. Canary Wharf. Surrey Quays. Until finally stopping at New Cross. He muted Jimmy Page, pushed the door button and stepped on to the platform.

Outside the station, Bailey checked his GPS and

headed towards the main road. According to his map, he should cross over to the one-way system, then hang a left into a cul-de-sac. An eight-minute walk. Or he could do the reverse thirty-second walk back into the station and on to a train. The traffic lights turned red. Bailey crossed over. Forward.

For once, the GPS was bang on. Eight minutes exactly. Bailey turned a corner and Nelson's Motor Repairs was straight in front of him. It was a tiny place between a Methodist Church and a nail bar, in a short street blocked off to cars at one end. The garage sign looked newer than the rest of it, bright yellow with the current London phone code. A tow-truck, probably the same one from the picture, just about fitted on the small forecourt. Two men in mechanics' overalls were outside. One was older, mixed race, in his sixties, tall and big with close-cropped hair like Dad's. The other one was eighteen or nineteen, Somali-looking, though his accent was pure London. He seemed to be getting grief about some part he hadn't ordered. The old guy was seriously unhappy.

Suddenly, both of them noticed Bailey and turned to face him. The young one looked like he wanted to knock Bailey out with a spanner. Bailey felt for him. Who wants to be told about yourself in front of an audience? The older guy was scowling, but then his shoulders lifted like he was taking a big breath.

Indigo's granddad?

He said, 'Rif, just get back inside and make a start on the Volvo.'

Rif skulked off through the double doors behind the tow truck.

The old guy could have been a boxer in the past. His bigness didn't look like fat, more strength squeezed into an oily overall.

He said, 'Do you want something?'

Yeah! A clue about what's honest and appropriate right now.

'Well? I've got work to get on with!' The guy turned away.

Bailey forced his legs into action and crossed the road. The back of his throat pulsed as if it was fighting against speaking. *If the situation was right.* Was it? The words shot out. 'Is Horatio Bankes here?'

He looked Bailey up and down. 'Why?'

'I . . . I was told to meet him.'

'Who by?' Suddenly, the guy smiled. 'Lots of our customers recommend us. That's how we get our business. Word of mouth. You got something that needs fixing?'

Yes. But not a car.

'Sorry. It wasn't a customer.'

The smile flicked off. 'Who, then?'

'It . . . it was a man I met. He said I needed to see Horatio Bankes.'

'What's this man's name?'

'JJ.'

'JJ what?'

'I . . . I don't know.'

'Jesus!' The mechanic turned away. 'Come back when you've found your brain.'

'He . . . he wanted me to tell Horatio about Indigo. Are you . . . are you Horatio Bankes?'

The guy stopped, turned round and moved towards Bailey. The overall was probably blue once, but now it was grey with oily smears, getting closer and closer. Oil had worked its way into the creases of the man's fingers and the back of his hands. He stopped, centimetres away. Bailey could smell him, the oil and something mixed with it, fresh and spicy, maybe aftershave. He frowned down at Bailey. His eyes were light brown and flecked with dark. If the sun caught them, Bailey imagined them turning gold. Indigo's eyes.

'Yes. I am. Who the hell are you?'

'My name's Bailey. I'm Indigo's friend.'

Horatio moved closer. 'Who?'

Keep still. Hold your space. Honest and appropriate. 'She's . . . she's your granddaughter.'

'I don't know what you're talking about.' His voice was quiet, like he was telling it to himself.

Bailey fumbled the envelope from his bag and slid out

139

the picture. 'JJ asked me to give you this.'

Horatio snatched the picture and studied it. For a second, he seemed to shrink into his overalls. 'Where the hell did you get it? Jesus Christ. This had better not be some sick prank.'

'It's not. Please. I need to talk to you.'

The baby and its mother flapped in Horatio's hand. 'Come inside. But I'm busy, you understand?'

Bailey nodded. Though he didn't. How could the man be too busy to hear about his granddaughter?

The garage could have passed as a storage place instead of a business fixing cars. A Volvo was jacked up in the middle of the cluttered space, Rif's legs sticking out from underneath it. A couple of motorbikes seemed to be abandoned in a corner. Plastic storage containers were stacked against the walls along with piles of tyres and old car parts. An old-fashioned sewing machine sat on a work-table next to a length of tartan. The radio was tuned to Capital, playing the old Peter Gabriel song that Mum always sang along to.

'This way.' Horatio led the way to a makeshift office at the back, a plywood cubicle with an empty window frame set in it. A desk was pushed against the brick wall. Horatio dropped the picture on the desk and leaned against it. 'Behind you.'

A fold-up chair was propped against the plywood.

Bailey tugged it open and sat down.

Horatio was studying him. 'So, you're called Bailey.'

'Yes.'

'And you have a picture of my daughter.'

'Your daughter?'

'The woman with the baby. My daughter, Mahalia.'

Of course it was. Bailey had been too busy looking for signs of Indigo in the baby to think too much about the woman. He felt a blush rising. 'Sorry. I think so. I wanted to ask you—'

A phone blasted out. Horatio reached into a pocket. 'Need to get this.' He squeezed past Bailey's knees into the workshop.

Bailey sat back on the chair and breathed out. If his heart beat any harder, blood would spurt from his ears. But he had come to the right place. This *was* Indigo's granddad.

Horatio's voice was rising outside in the workshop, a dispute about paying an invoice. Without Horatio's bulk, it was easier to look around the office. The desk was piled with papers, receipts, invoices and flyers from suppliers. A Man United calendar hung from a nail on the brick wall behind it. Framed photos were propped on a metal filing cabinet to the right of the door. Bailey leaned forward. In the closest one, Horatio was just recognisable in a smart suit, his arm around a white woman in a fancy hat. Their faces were close together, smiling. The photo next to it was mounted in a silver frame. Bailey squinted hard at it. He picked up the picture from the desk. Yes, it was a smaller version of the photo in his hand.

Horatio was standing by the door. 'You've clocked it, then.'

Bailey nodded. 'Is the baby Indigo?'

Horatio didn't move. 'You take a picture from a stranger and you don't ask who the people are in it? You didn't check with him where he got it? If it's his to give?'

'He said . . .'

'Well, one bit of advice, Bailey.' Horatio moved so close they were almost foot to foot, bending right over him so Bailey couldn't see anything else. This room had stopped being an office. It was a shoebox full of heavy air with Horatio's solid body blocking the only exit. 'This is nothing to do with you.' Horatio straightened and opened the door wider. 'Go.'

Honest and appropriate. And it *was* to do with Bailey. He'd been standing in the science corridor watching when the world closed in on Indigo. He'd walked away when she cried.

He said, 'She's . . . she's my friend. JJ said you're her only family. He said you'd want to see her.'

Horatio thumped the filing cabinet. The office wobbled. 'Who is this man who thinks he can tell me what to do?'

'He . . .' *Appropriate.* 'He said he was a friend of Indigo's parents.'

'A friend? He was just one of the junkies and liars that leeched off her?' *Bang!* Horatio's fist hit the metal again. Both pictures toppled over. 'Why is he crawling out of the woodwork? I bet he wants money. That's all they ever want.'

'No, he just wants . . . he said if you and Indigo meet again . . . he said your wife died.'

A heartbeat. 'Cockroaches, all of them.' Horatio flung the door right back. It hit the plywood walls and the office wobbled again. 'One of them stole Indigo from the park, did you know that, Bailey? From right under my wife's nose. They took her to that place and left her alone while that monster killed my daughter. And you come here because *a friend* of Indigo's parents told you?'

'I'm sorry.'

'Olive never forgave herself. Maybe it was better she forgot everything in the end. I had to remember for both of us.' Horatio's phone was going again. He glared at the screen and threw it on to the pile of invoices. 'The social workers said Indigo didn't see anything.' He tapped his head. 'I see it every day. My daughter on the bed. My little granddaughter on the floor. Can you ever understand how much it hurt us to give Indigo up? But I had to make the choice. Care for Indigo or care for my wife. And in the end, I had to give up my wife, too.'

143

Bailey slipped the picture into the envelope. It seemed to take a very long time. He half-expected Horatio to reach out and grab it, but Horatio didn't seem to be looking at anything. He moved aside so Bailey could get out and the door shut behind him. Rif had slid from under the Volvo and disappeared. Bailey glanced back. Horatio's wide shoulders were framed by the office window as he sat at his desk, still.

The walk to the station was much quicker. The train was waiting, but it wasn't leaving for a while. Bailey sat right at the front, four seats to himself. As soon as he got home he was going straight up to the music room. He'd unhook the Gibson electric, plug in the headphones and amp and close his eyes as the electricity thrummed through the wires. He leaned back against the train seat. Right now he needed The White Stripes, loud.

Indigo should have listened to Keely. She wished she was a kung-fu expert so she could high kick and chop her way through Camden Market. Who would she slice down first? The packs of twelve-year-old girls in eyeliner and fishnets who kept stopping in front of her? The grumpy stall holders who sold the same stupid things for the same stupid price? Or the ancient blokes with red mohicans who moaned when tourists took photos of them? Maybe she'd start in this shop, with its rack of rancid plastic mini skirts and electronic burp sounds blasting through the speakers.

Indigo went back outside. Keely was still waiting by the wall, checking her phone.

Indigo said, 'Can we go?'

Keely tucked her phone away. 'The magic words, hun.'

They jumped on a bus to Holloway Road where Keely knew a really good second-hand shop. Indigo bought a white dress like the one Debbie Harry wore on the cover of *Parallel Lines*. And even better, she found some white shoes to match. Keely forked out on a long, gold knitted cardigan for her date with a bloke off the internet.

When they finally made it home, Felix had been and gone. He'd taken more of his boxes and left a pack of tealights on the kitchen table.

'At last,' Keely said. 'My toes are praising the Lord.'

'And I can get into my room.'

'Yes,' Keely smiled. 'As a foster carer, I definitely fail on the health and safety front. Do you have any plans for later?'

Indigo shrugged. 'Don't really know.'

'I thought you'd want to show off your new clothes.'

Yeah. There was a thought. Indigo had looked damn good in that dress and if she left her hair loose she'd be seriously Debbie Harry. 'I might meet up with a friend.'

'Any friend I know?'

'No.'

Kelly raised an eyebrow. 'A girl that's a friend or a boy that's a friend?'

'A boy.'

Keely had her worried face on. 'A boy from where?'

'Don't worry, Kee. He's in my English class.'

'Ah-huh?'

'And he's got mad hair. A big ginger afro.'

Keely laughed. 'My cousin's girl's growing one of those. Though it's just one big ball of tangles at the moment. Where does his live?'

'In one of the posh houses past the junction. The kitchen's downstairs from the hall. I wasn't sure about that.'

Keely's laugh was killed quick. 'You've been to his house, Indigo? I've told you! You have to be careful!'

'Serious, Kee, I'm not stupid.' Far from it. Indigo and her mates had compared enough notes on this stuff. 'And Bailey's nothing like that idiot Stivo. His mum's a social worker and his dad's a teacher.'

'It doesn't matter what his parents do. It's no guarantee.'

Indigo picked up the bag with her dress and shoes. 'Don't you trust me?'

'This isn't about trust. It's about bloody worrying.'

'I bet you'd be worrying even more if I'd met him on the internet.'

'Very funny. But it's my job to worry about you. And I intend to do my job well.'

Indigo backed into her room, dropped her shopping bag on the floor and flopped on to her bed. Jesus! Sometimes Keely took this stuff way too seriously! *Is this what it's like in real families?* She closed her eyes. As she moved her head, the letter slid about beneath her pillow. She reached under and let her fingertips rest on the paper. She knew the words by heart. Her grandmother's writing must have wriggled off the page and crept through the pillowcase, into her head.

Just before breakfast, she'd had a nose online. It was still dark and she was never going to get back to sleep anyway. She'd found a little article about her grandmother's death. She'd had dementia for ages before she died, but there were only a few words about that. All the rest was about what happened before, with the old picture of the door to her parents' flat. Her imagination had pushed the door open and she'd seen a hallway, a sitting room, a bedroom. She'd smelled burnt toast, dirty mugs. And then the door had slammed shut.

Indigo sat up. She was all breath and emptiness. It was Saturday night. She was not going to lie here, waiting for the hole to open up inside her. Felix was with Wade. Keely was going out with her internet date. Even Primrose was probably watching a film about Australia with Pathetic Pete.

She'd just got all that grief from Keely. She might as well make it worth it.

Indigo retrieved her new white shoes from the bag and balanced them on her toes. Keely had noticed they were a little bit scuffed at the sides, but they'd driven the saleswoman down to a fiver. She flipped one shoe then the other on to the floor, she rolled off the bed next to them and spread the dress on the rug. She searched out a picture of the cover to *Parallel Lines* and laid her phone next to the dress. Perfect.

10

Bailey had to admit it. The tabs to 'Stockholm Syndrome' were tough. It was like Muse were setting their fans a deliberate challenge. Loads of people had given it a go, transcribing their arrangements and filming themselves playing them. Bailey wanted to play it the way *he* heard it, not some pumped up version by an intense thirty-year-old in Kyoto. He took a sip of Coke. This time round he'd focus on the timing. Next time, he'd review his chords. Then . . .

Then nothing. It wasn't working. Drowning his brain in music wasn't pushing out his other thoughts. Instead, they'd become a sped-up slide show with a Muse soundtrack. Indigo. Horatio. JJ. The photograph of a woman and her baby. All of them, one after another, skidding on a loop behind his eyes.

He played back the song's intro and scribbled some notes.

'Bailey?'

His parents were standing by the door. Both of them together – that wasn't a good sign. Last time they did the joint announcement thing, their old cat had died. But when Bailey saw Shuu earlier, she'd been very much alive. Dad was looking down at a toe poking through a hole in his sock. Mum's hair was still wet from the bath, stuck flat to her head but curling up at the edges. Even in that small space, there was a gap between them.

Bailey flipped back his headphones and swivelled his chair round to face them. He looked from one to the other. 'What's happened?'

Dad wiggled his toe. Mum sighed.

Suddenly, it hit Bailey. 'You're splitting up.'

Dad shook his head so hard he almost butted the doorframe. 'No! What the hell gave you that idea? We're going to Paris, for God's sake!'

Mum glanced at Dad and away again. The parents who'd always made a big deal about talking things through were doing a crap job of it right now. Mum came right into his room. Dad followed. For a second, Bailey imagined them trying to come through his door side by side and getting stuck, like in an old slapstick film.

God! Bailey did know what this was about! One of their friends had spotted him in south London. He could style that off, though, say he'd been to check out a second-hand guitar he'd found on Gumtree. But what if he'd been spied with JJ in the takeaway? That was going to be harder to explain. He rested his pencil on his notebook.

Mum said, 'I just want to clear up something from last night.'

Shit. It *was* JJ. Bailey had to keep his face blank. 'Last night?'

'It's about your friend, Indigo,' Dad said.

Did they put a bug in Bailey's trainer or something?

Dad continued. 'We've always trusted you with girlfriends. You know that.'

Girlfriends? There'd only been two! Dad's toe was drumming a solo.

Bailey said, 'What's this about?'

'Go on, Ed.'

Dad darted her his annoyed look. Then his attention returned to Bailey. 'Indigo had a particularly difficult start in life.'

'You could say that, Dad.'

Dad looked like he wanted to be teleported to Mars. 'Even before the awful tragedy. She was removed from her parents when she was little.'

Removed. Like verrucas. 'Why are you telling me this?'

Dad sighed. 'Your mum thinks it's important.'

A killer glare from Mum. 'So do you, Ed.'

'Yes. I do.' Dad's hand was on Bailey's shoulder. 'This isn't about Indigo. This is about you. We're your parents and we care about you.'

'What do you mean it isn't about Indigo? All you've done is talk about her.'

Dad's hand felt heavy, like it was keeping Bailey in place.

'There's something called attachment theory. It means that some children from unstable family backgrounds have trouble forming healthy relationships.'

Bailey glanced down at his desk. Those notes he'd sketched looked nothing like the Muse song. If he kept staring hard enough, maybe he'd catch the music in his head, Chris Wolstenholme's bassline hammering over his parents' voices.

Mum said, 'Are you listening, Bailey?'

'Yeah. I just heard Dad reading out of the Social-Workers' Handbook.'

'That's not helpful,' Mum said.

Dad finally released Bailey's shoulder. 'We're not saying you can't be friends.'

'Not at all,' Mum agreed.

Bailey looked from one to the other. 'I know exactly what you are saying.'

Dad was opening his mouth, but Bailey didn't need to hear it. He lifted his headphones on again and pressed 'Play' on the video. As Matt Bellamy's fingers skidded up and down the fret, Bailey felt his parents move away from him.

Six o'clock. Bailey pushed back his headphones. He'd been fiddling with the song for hours. Now he'd broken it apart, he could never just enjoy it again. Shuu had crept in and set up camp on a newspaper on Bailey's bed. Downstairs,

Dad was blasting out his dub collection; Mum must be off somewhere. Bailey's phone buzzed. He checked his messages. Austin was getting tickets for the new Marvel film. Apparently the nine o'clock screening should be free of popcorn-chucking ten-year-olds.

Bailey shot back a reply. Yeah, he was up for the film, but Austin'd better not bring Soraya. When they'd gone to the Foals gig together, Bailey spent most of the time watching it by himself, while those two swallowed each other's tongues.

Bailey's phone buzzed straight away. Austtin was offended at the suggestion. Anyway, Soraya was out with her mates. And double anyway, who didn't get the Fall Out Boy tickets? And triple anyway, who should be paying compensation to who?

Bailey pulled his laptop towards himself and reinstated his headphones.

Half seven. Shuu was curled into a ball, flat out. Dad's music still thumped through the floor. He was probably in the kitchen, creating some culinary wonder for Mum. Bailey went downstairs and slipped on his trainers and his zip-up.

'I'm off!'

'Where to?' Dad called.

'Cinema, with Austin.'

'Have a good time. Do you want me to leave you something to eat?'

'Thanks, but we'll probably grab some food later.'

'Okay.' Dad's voice faded back into the kitchen.

Bailey clicked the front door shut and walked towards the main road. As he hit the corner, his phone vibrated. Austin needed to calm down. Bailey wasn't even late yet. Or, more likely, Soraya was going to be there after all.

What r u doing now? A number he didn't recognise.

New message. **Meet me by dalston junction.**

Who had his number? Mona had deleted him for sure, the same way he'd done with her. Celene? He hadn't heard from her since she moved to Plumstead.

Maybe . . .

Nah, Indigo didn't have his number yet. Austin had probably borrowed Soraya's phone and was having his version of a joke.

Who's this?

Three, four, five seconds. New message. **Who do u think?**

Pause. A picture. The cover of *Parallel Lines*.

Yes! Bailey looked up. No one was around to see him grinning. He saved the number and replied.

What time?

Nine, ten, eleven seconds. **About 9.**

Bailey had reached the end of the street by the bus stop. One way took him to the cinema, the other to Indigo. He scrolled back to the last message from Austin.

Reply. **Sorry, mate. Have to change plans. Got a date.**

'Hurry up, Indigo! I can't go out with my breath stinking of garlic bread!'

Indigo rubbed a cotton-wool bud under her eye, easing away the smudged eyeliner. That was better.

'Nearly done.'

'You said that half an hour ago.'

'Yeah, well, I am now.'

The red lipstick made her look all mouth, even though the tutorial said it should balance out her eyes. She wiped it off and slicked on her usual colour. That was better. Mascara or falsies?

'Indigo!'

'Yeah, all right, Kee! If he wants to see you, he's gonna wait!' God knows where her eyelash glue was. It would have to be mascara. 'And you know what they say about keeping them keen.'

'Not up for taking the chance, Indigo.'

Indigo opened the door. Keely stepped back.

'Blimey, girl! You look gorgeous. He'd better appreciate you. Where are you going?'

'Not sure yet.'

Keely frowned. It was the only time she ever looked old. 'Not to his house, Indigo.'

Indigo flashed her most reassuring smile. 'Of course not.'

'Okay. I'll try and stop worrying. A bit. Do me a favour, though. Write down his number for me.'

'What for?'

Keely smiled. 'In case you go on a robbing spree and deport yourselves to Spain. It's just in case of emergencies, Indigo, and I can't get hold of you.'

Indigo rolled her eyes. 'Okay.' Bailey's number. The last contact. She forwarded it to Keely.

'Happy now?'

'Perfect. Leave your phone on, though. And I'll text you and Felix the address where I'm meeting this guy, Larry, just in case I don't come back.'

Indigo said, 'Does he look like a serial killer?'

'You judge.' Keely scrolled through her phone and showed Indigo the screen. 'What do you think?'

'Could go either way, Kee.'

'That's what I thought. But you know. Books and covers.'

Indigo kissed her on the cheek. Her lipstick left a faint mark. 'Have a good time.'

Kelly sniffed. 'Is that my Gaultier, Indigo?'

Indigo gave a little spin. Yeah, she could walk all right in these sandals. She landed by her bedroom door. 'You're going to be late, Keely. You said you didn't want to keep Larry waiting.'

'Thanks, Indigo. But lay off my Gaultier, please. It's the only expensive one I've got.'

The bathroom door shut and the key turned. Indigo waited. The shower turned on. Good. That gave her more time. She crept into the kitchen and opened the cupboard door. Keely didn't drink, so why did her brother keep bringing her back booze? Maybe it was revenge for something she'd done to him when they were kids. Indigo paused. The shower was going full blast in the bathroom. She shifted the bottles aside. Limoncello. Miduri. Retsina. She hadn't heard of half this stuff, but . . . she pulled out a bottle and smiled. Tequila. She'd definitely heard of that. It was a quarter-bottle, just the right size for her sparkly shoulder bag. They'd need something to drink it from. She checked the cupboard over the sink. Yep. Got it.

Bailey was twenty minutes early and he hadn't even been walking that fast. Dad said when he and Mum first came to Dalston, it was rough, with drug couriers on bikes outside the betting shop and prostitutes in the abandoned houses. Now there were fountains in the square by the library and they'd even done up the kebab shop with red leather banquettes. The bar opposite the station was jammed, with more people outside, smoking. Bailey could hear live music, something folky.

The workmen's barriers by the station made the

pavement too narrow and everyone walking past was jostling him. He moved just inside the entrance, where he could still see both bus stops.

38, 242, 277. Bus after bus pulled up. People poured into the bars and around Bailey, into the station. He checked the time. It was just past nine. Maybe it *was* a joke. He couldn't be sure it was Indigo who messaged him. Austin was probably crouched down in the kebab shop filming Bailey's stress. Another bus, a 56, stopped across the road. Bailey moved out of the station. Was that Indigo, standing in the aisle? It was hard to see. The bus pulled away and he waited for the mass of people to clear. God, it was Indigo. It was like his heart gulped. She looked amazing. She was wearing a white dress with matching high-heeled sandals and a black leather jacket. Her hair was backcombed and rolled up, with a few strands hanging down her neck.

She spotted him and waved. He weaved his way through the queuing traffic, towards her.

He said, 'You look good.'

She smiled. Her eye shadow made her eyes more copper, like in the common room that time. Eyes just like her granddad's. Bailey had to shove that – JJ, his parents, all of it – to the back of his thoughts. Just for the minute. Just until he worked it all out.

He said, 'What do you fancy doing?'

'I have a plan.'

'Cool.' Because he didn't. Even if there'd been one, it would have collapsed into a muddle as soon as he saw her.

She opened a sparkly shoulder bag. 'I brought something.'

He looked inside. 'Tequila?'

A small bottle of it, complete with a bright yellow label decorated with a cartoon donkey in a sombrero.

She said, 'Do you like it?'

'I've never had it. Last year, there was a party and Saskia had so many shots she ended up in hospital for the night. It put me off.'

'Yeah, anything to do with Saskia would put me off too.'

He laughed. 'Where did you get it?'

'The first shop that didn't ask for ID.'

'How many shops did you go to?'

'Just one.'

Their eyes met and she laughed. 'Next time I might buy the banana cream rum or the melon liqueur.' She shifted closer to him to let a woman with a trolley pass. Bailey smelled perfume, something sweet and heavy.

She said, 'You ever played London Bingo?'

'No. What happens?'

'Not quite sure, but I was on a coach once, coming back from a camping trip. Some kid called Zac had a bag full of those miniature bottles, brandy and stuff. We all had a list of different things, cow, tractor, whatever. If you saw one, you had to have a drink.'

'Didn't the staff notice?'

Indigo laughed. 'They were too knackered after a week with us lot! They only woke up when Zac's twin brother vommed. So you up for it?'

'Do you have a list of London stuff?'

'I'm gonna trust you to tell me. I haven't lived in London much.'

'And it's a shot every time we see somewhere famous?'

Indigo rummaged in her bag and brought out two egg cups. One was shaped like Humpty Dumpty, the other one was plain white. 'My foster mum doesn't drink. It was the best I could do. Classy, right?'

He laughed. 'Completely.'

Indigo hooked her arm through his. 'I reckon we should take the first bus and change after each shot.'

'Why?'

'Just to make it more interesting.'

Indigo's leather jacket was brushing against his arm and for a second, her hip bumped his. *Sorry, Austin. Even the Black Widow in her skin-tight leggings couldn't be better than this.*

A 56 came first, heading towards St Bart's Hospital.

'Come on,' Indigo said. 'Upstairs. That's the best view.'

The seats at the very front were taken. Indigo clicked

towards the back and sat in the corner by a window. She patted the seat next to her. 'Hurry up! We might miss something.'

Her dress sprawled across the gap between the seats, bright white against the blue checks. She pulled it over her lap to give him more room. When she leaned forward, he could see their reflections in the window, faces cheek to cheek.

The bus headed across the traffic lights at the junction and down towards Essex Road.

Bailey said, 'See that?'

'The big church?'

'I went to nursery there.'

Indigo handed Bailey the Humpty Dumpty egg cup. She fiddled around in her bag and brought out the tequila. 'New rule. If it's a landmark to you, it counts.'

She poured a shot and grinned at him. He smiled back. His throat had to be like a letterbox – click open, click shut. Down in one. He breathed in. His nostrils smouldered and – *whoosh* – it hit his belly.

Indigo gave him an approving look. 'Excellent work.'

Had she done this before? Not just with kids on a coach, but with other guys? Maybe Bailey had to pass some kind of test. A couple of African women came and sat bang in front of them. It was like he and Indigo were cut off from the rest of the bus.

'Look!' Indigo tapped the window. 'This one's mine!'

They were passing the old bingo hall. A sign said that it now belonged to a church. 'You? In there with all the old grannies?'

'No! One of my foster mums was a proper bingo addict, though. She kept coming home with toasters.'

'When was that?'

'Can't remember. It's a bit of a blur, sometimes.' She poured herself a shot and knocked it back quickly. She blinked. 'That's rough, man.'

'No wonder the guy in the shop was happy to get rid of it.'

She wiped her lips. 'Yeah. Best off without it.' She rang the bell. 'Come on.'

'Where?'

'We're supposed to change buses. We should have got off at the church.'

Bailey was still holding his egg cup. He shoved it in his jacket pocket and followed Indigo downstairs and off the bus. A 38 pulled up straight away. That would take them past Sadler's Wells. And Finsbury Town Hall. Four landmarks in and he wouldn't be able to speak.

'Hurry up!' She took his hand and led him up the stairs, her dress swishing round her hips and legs. She'd played it all casual, but Bailey could feel his heartbeat thud as their palms touched.

The top deck was busy. They had to sit separately across the aisle from each other until they reached Angel tube station. Then virtually everyone got off and they moved to the front. Indigo took off her jacket and leaned forward against the rail. The dress was sleeveless, with thin shoulder straps and cut in a V at the front, gaping as she moved. He looked away.

They passed Sadler's Wells. Bailey kept quiet. Finsbury Town Hall. They passed that one safely too.

Indigo shifted in the seat so her thigh rubbed against his. He nearly pressed back. Not yet, though.

'Bailey?'

'Yeah.'

'There's something I have to ask you.'

You knew about Horatio all along. You sent JJ to test me. I did plan to tell you. He turned towards her.

She said, 'Did your mum say anything about me?'

He nearly blew out his cheeks, right in front of her. 'She said she recognised you.'

'What did she say?'

'She remembered doing art stuff with you at a PRU in Medway.'

'Is that it?'

She told me your life history. She warned me away. 'More or less.'

'I was in a special unit. I got put there because . . . because

I used to fly off the handle.' Indigo was staring out at the road. He had to lean in close to hear her. 'They said it was like I'd go a bit mad.'

He said, 'Is that what happened at school?'

Her cheeks were starting to redden. Should he put his arm round her? Or would she think he was just feeling sorry for her? The bus was passing a long stretch of high wall with a garden behind it.

He said, 'That's Gray's Inn, famous barristers' chambers.'

He took Humpty out of his pocket and offered it to her. She unwrapped the bottle and sloshed in more alcohol. It slid down his throat like greasy bleach.

Indigo replaced the bottle. 'I might have yelled at your mum. I was a bit hyper, then.'

'She's used to people yelling at her.'

'Like who?'

'Kids at school. Parents. Even a couple of teachers, when she's had to tell them about something they've done wrong.'

'Have you ever yelled at her?'

'Not that I can remember. Maybe when I was little.'

She was staring out of the window again. No landmarks, just buses and taxis and the hi-vis cyclists. Suddenly, she twisted around to face him. 'It's from him.'

'What is?'

'The thing inside me, the thing that makes me blow my top. You know like when kids have a tantrum?'

'Yeah.'

'It's like that. The counsellors reckon it's taken longer for me to deal with the anger. But it's not that. My dad had it. A thing. He passed it on to me. It waits until there's a trigger and then it goes mental and I'm not there any more, it's just the thing.'

He reached across for her hand. She let him take it. He should tell her that he knew there was more to her. There was the Indigo who'd laughed in his kitchen. The Indigo whose face lit up when he said he liked Blondie too. It was all these things about her that made him want to be here now. But his mouth was a mush of words. A few of them could be the right ones, but how would he know? He could keep holding her hand, though, tight in his.

He said, 'Do you remember the first time it happened?'

'Sort of. I think I was about four or five. I was doing a painting at the kitchen table and I had it in my head that I was going to send it to my mum, even though I knew I couldn't.' She frowned. 'There was a really fat, grey cat and it jumped up and knocked water all over my picture. And then . . . it felt like there was a snake inside my stomach. Something big, like a python. The stupid cat had woken it up and I could feel it untwisting itself and stretching. And the weird thing is, it was horrible and nice at the same time. It was like, before that, I was just empty and I didn't know. The thing sort of made me feel full. And then it burst out.

After that it's a bit blank. I'd torn up my painting. And I'd thrown the jar of water against a wall. There was glass and painty water everywhere. I wasn't very popular.'

Bailey said, 'I can imagine you weren't.'

She gave him a little smile, then turned to the window. Shit. He had said the wrong thing. He'd known it as soon as he heard himself. She'd poured all that out to him and that's what he gave back. *I can imagine you weren't.* A bit jokey, a bit too light. Something one of his old aunties would say. No wonder she turned away from him.

He said, 'I'm sorry. It must have been pretty scary when you realised what happened.'

'Yeah.' He'd got that right, at least, because she shifted back towards him. 'It was. I was sent to a counsellor but I didn't want to talk about it in case it happened again. I got moved on too. But I think that's because I painted the cat's ears red.'

She slid her hand out of his and rested it on his knee. 'Where are we?'

'Coming up to Shaftesbury Avenue. If we get off now, we can walk to Covent Garden.'

'That's famous,' she said. 'Very famous.'

Indigo hooked her arm back through Bailey's as soon as they were off the bus. He liked that, she could tell, and she could feel his body move with every step.

166

Had she really just spouted all that stuff about the thing to him? At least she had managed to shut up in time. She could have splurged all the other stuff, like the time she was sitting in Joanna's office trying to explain about the emptiness. She'd sketched out a picture – a giant, swirling black circle with something jagged and twisted inside. Though all she'd wanted to do was draw Toby Scott's face. She'd told Joanna how much she hated it when the thing clawed its way out and went wild, how everybody thought that was the problem. But it was worse when it was quiet. That's when the emptiness was bigger and deeper.

Joanna had said, *It isn't unusual for people like you to feel like this, Indigo. You've experienced some very big losses. Your parents, of course, but every time you move too.* How many times had it been by then? Nine? Ten? Indigo had looked at the photo of Joanna with her kids and husband that was always on the bookcase. Four grinning faces plunging down a flume in an adventure park. Suddenly, Indigo hadn't been able to say anything else. Joanna could never understand. Most people couldn't. Though maybe . . . She tightened the loop of her arm, bringing Bailey a little closer. He'd said something stupid, but he was trying.

He said, 'Are you okay?'

'Yeah. Thanks. You sure you know where you're going?'

'Of course! Though if I'd had any more of that tequila, we'd be walking in circles by now. We go left here on to

Drury Lane and carry on to Covent Garden.'

'Is it far?'

'Not too bad.'

'Good. These shoes are killing me.'

'We'll find somewhere to sit down when we get there.'

The streets were narrow and full of people – tourists and foreign students, phones up, clicking selfies. There was a theatre, but the show must have started because the doors were closed. On the left was a big, pale building flanked with columns.

She said, 'What's that?'

'It's the Freemasons' Hall.'

'Famous?'

'If you're a freemason.'

'That'll do.' They stopped on the corner. She fished out the tequila and her egg cup.

He said, 'Shall I pour?'

'Yeah. Thanks.'

A splash in hers and then she held Humpty while he topped it up. They clinked the cups together and knocked it back. He winced.

She said, 'Are you feeling it?'

'Every time.'

'I mean, has it gone to your head?'

He touched his hair. The streetlights made it glow. 'I've got protection. What about you?'

His hand reached towards her head, then he pulled away, looking embarrassed.

'It's okay.' She took his fingers and guided them to the strand of hair dangling by her cheek. 'It's not the first time you've been in my hair, is it?'

He laughed. 'No. Though it's the first time without peanut butter.'

A tremble of something. Not the usual shuffling and scratching. She blinked hard and touched her stomach.

He let his hand fall. 'Are you sure you're all right?'

'Yeah. Fine.'

'You looked like you were feeling a bit sick.'

'No, nothing like that.' She slipped her hand into his. His fingers instantly curled round to claim hers.

It was quiet now, but there'd definitely been something. It wasn't just the hot, oily tequila, though she could feel that, all right. It was like pulling the laces tight on her DMs, feeling the boot close in round her ankle. When Bailey touched her hair, the space inside her shrank. Just a tiny bit. When his fingers curled round hers, it shrank a little bit more.

She glanced up at him. He must have caught her movement, because she was looking straight into his eyes.

He said, 'You sure you're okay?'

'Yeah.'

'It's just down there, by the tube.'

169

'What is?'

'Covent Garden.'

'Oh, yeah.' And she knew where she was now. 'When I was in Kent, the social workers brought us to see the big Christmas tree.'

'Did you like it?'

'I loved it.' They skirted round the crowds outside the tube station, past the shops, down towards the market.

She squeezed his hand. 'What about you, London Boy? Do you come here at Christmas?'

'We used to. We'd go skating at Somerset House, then come here for a pizza.'

'You and your mates?'

'Sometimes.' Pause. 'Or just me and Mum and Dad.'

That pause.

'It's okay,' she said. 'I've got used to it. Some people have a mum and dad.'

His face worked like he was trying to find the right reply.

She said, 'I suppose I've had loads of different mums and dads instead.'

He smiled. 'I suppose so.'

A girl in a tiny skater skirt and stacked platforms went striding past them. She gave Bailey a quick, secret glance. Indigo couldn't see if he returned it. She wiggled her fingers until they locked between his and his palm was warm against hers.

She said, 'Did you go round London a lot as a kid?'

'Yeah, I suppose so.'

'Did you go to London Zoo?'

'Yeah. I loved the giraffes. And we'd go to the Aquarium too.'

'Did it have killer whales?'

'No. But there's a stuffed blue whale hanging from the ceiling in the Natural History Museum.'

She gave a dramatic shiver. 'I hate stuffed things. If something's dead, why'd you want to fill it full of sawdust and hang it from a ceiling?'

'I suppose they thought—' His arm tensed. 'Yeah. You're right.'

She was. Who'd want to keep looking at dead things?

She said, 'Nearly there, right?'

'Yes. Nearly there.'

That must be why the streets outside the pubs were so crowded. Still loads of tourists, but also lots of blokes holding pints and women with wine glasses.

She said, 'Have you ever been to Buckingham Palace?'

'God, no. My parents wouldn't even sign the letter for me when there was a school trip. They're serious republicans.'

'What do you mean?'

'They don't agree with the royal family.'

Indigo laughed. 'I didn't know you had to agree with

them. They're just there, aren't they? I used to draw Buckingham Palace when I was a kid. I thought it must be a really special place. Like Hogwarts for the Queen.' She nudged his shoulder with hers. 'Covent Garden's a landmark, isn't it?'

'Completely and totally.'

There wasn't much tequila left and it was starting to fire bullets through her brain. They sank their shots and she poured again, emptying the bottle. 'What can this one be for?'

He spun round slowly. 'I reckon we should toast The Lion King.'

'Is it near here? I've always wanted to see it!'

'It's just down the road.'

'Yeah,' she said. 'I'll drink to that!'

They banged their egg cups together.

Bailey examined Humpty. 'Is this yours?'

'No. I just found it in the cupboard. It could be Felix's.'

'He lives with you and Keely, right?'

'I suppose I live with them. He's been with Keely for longer than me, since he was about ten. He's moving out this week.'

'Where's he going?'

'He's got a Sugar Daddy.'

'A what?'

'He's got an older boyfriend. Wade. He's a bus driver.'

'How old is he?'

'Felix? He's eighteen. That's why he's moving out.'

'No. I mean his boyfriend.'

'Wade's twenty-three.'

'That's not so old.'

'You reckon? Maybe I should do that. Find a bloke in his twenties to look after me when I have to move.'

Bailey's face clouded over. Damn. That was tequila moving her mouth. Why had it seemed such a bloody good idea at the time? The stuff was proper foul.

She said, 'Can we sit down?'

He guided her to a bench. She was starting to feel a bit saggy. The seat was cold and damp and they sat on the edge, facing each other, their knees touching. She leaned towards him. He had freckles, but you had to be right up close to see them. His eyelashes were long and much darker than his hair. It was weird how people turned out.

She said, 'I like your eyelashes.'

He was supposed to laugh then. But he looked dead serious. Shit. The tequila was really mashing her up, getting her to say wrong random things. It was like the donkey on the label had come alive and kicked her in the brain.

He said, 'Indigo, there's something—'

She kissed him. Lightly. Just the tip of her tongue against his lips. She sat back. 'Yeah?'

'I . . . It doesn't matter.'

She stood up, reaching her hand out to him. 'Come on. Let's go to the market.'

Past the shops into the real market and just like Camden, this one was bloody rammed with tourists. Holding Bailey's hand made it different, though. Indigo was more than just a visitor. She was with someone who belonged. They wandered past the stalls – jewellery, candles, bags. Bailey let go of her hand and picked up a green trilby from a stall. He held it just above his afro, eyebrows raised.

'Nah,' she said. 'Not you.'

Bailey shrugged at the stall holder and replaced the hat on the pile.

The music from the shops was having a battle with an opera singer blasting out from the lower floor. She nudged Bailey. The cosmetics shop next to them was playing 'One Way or Another'.

She said, 'Boys don't normally like Blondie.'

He grinned. 'Umm. They do.'

'No, not just Debbie Harry. I mean the songs.'

'Of course we like the songs! Though, it was my mum who liked them first. I learned how to play "Sunday Girl" on guitar for her birthday. I was about seven. Then I really started listening to them. Their drummer's one of the best in the world. He's amazing!'

'You like him more than Debbie Harry?'

His eyebrows shot up. 'Are you trying to tell me I'm a music nerd?'

'Yes!'

He shrugged. 'I need time to come up with an argument against that. How did you get into them?'

'I don't know. I've just always liked them.' There must have been a first time she heard them. But it was like learning to read – someone must have taught her. What she could remember, though, was the moment when it all made sense. It was when she found out that Debbie Harry didn't grow up with her birth family neither.

The song finished.

Bailey said, 'Shall we go and see who's making the racket downstairs?'

They peered over the railings. The singer was a skinny guy in a tight purple suit. He looked nothing like his voice. The crowd around him were clapping like it was the best thing in the world.

'Excuse me.' It was a girl in her twenties, probably Japanese.

She held up her camera.

'Sure.' Bailey reached to take it from her.

'No,' the girl said. 'You. Together.'

Bailey's eyes sparkled. 'Happy with that?'

'Yeah!' Indigo struck a pose, jacket pushed down to show a shoulder, hand on hip, like in the magazines. Bailey lounged against the railings. The girl took the picture and showed it to them, then ran back to her friends who were waiting by the ice-cream place.

'Wow! London Boy!' Was it cool for Indigo to smile this much? 'You're going to be famous in Japan!'

'Wow! London Girl! You'll be standing right next to me.' He stroked a fold of fabric by her hip. 'Or maybe she's a Blondie fan too.'

'You got it!'

'Your outfit and the *Parallel Lines* cover? Yeah! Of course!'

She tried to make her voice jokey. 'You didn't say anything.'

'You distracted me with tequila.'

She sighed. 'Yeah. S'pose so.'

He slipped his arm round her waist. 'Fancy going round the courtyard to see the performers?'

Her mouth said, 'Yeah,' but her heart was too loud in her ears to hear it. He'd scooped her in and she'd let herself be scooped. His fingers were resting at the top of her bum, by the thin waistband of her knickers. Was that on purpose? If it was Stivo, he'd already be butt-palming her. But this wasn't Stivo. Definitely not.

They were moving out from the main market, past the jewellery and gift stalls. She'd have to hook up with some of her old mates and bring them here. They'd love it. Amber would be into those hats and that cat cushion – Rubi would kill for that. And the silver dangly earrings, perfect for Mischa. Indigo should buy them now to take up to Mischa's next month and maybe find something for Mischa's kid. But that meant pulling away from Bailey. She'd come another time.

A troop of jugglers had set up outside the church. One was a drag queen Beyoncé, another could be Lady Gaga and the other one . . . was that supposed to be the Queen?

'Bailey?'

His hand had slid under her leather jacket, cosy against her spine. He looked down at her and smiled. Her stomach felt like it had yawned then closed tight.

She said, 'Most of the time, I feel like a weirdo. But I don't now.' Not with you.

'It's hard to be weird in London.'

'When your dad kills your mum, you're weird anywhere.' He'd stopped smiling. She'd gone too far again. Bloody tequila. She turned towards him. His hand slipped off her spine. 'It's just . . . I feel a bit normal.'

He nodded. 'If there are things . . . you know, stuff that stresses you, you can talk to me. I don't mind. I might even be able to help.'

She took his hand. 'I've talked to hundreds of people. I like it because I don't have to talk about it to you.'

That sounded wrong too. How could she get him to understand? Right here, holding his hand, she was like all the other people standing in the crowd, watching the show. Clubs whirled in the air, pink, green, orange, higher and higher. Suddenly, Beyoncé threw a club really high and cartwheeled away, her oversized gold heels clonking on to the cobblestones. The Queen twirled into place, catching it. Half a second later and the trick would have failed. The clubs would have clattered to the ground.

Indigo took Bailey's hands and slid them back under her jacket. She felt them pressing through her dress. The material was so thin she imagined him leaving fingerprints on her skin.

He bent down so his mouth was by her ear. His hair tickled her cheek. 'Okay. But if you ever want to talk . . .'

She tilted her head so her lips slid across his cheek. 'Okay.'

Beyoncé and Lady Gaga were hurling flaming torches at each other. Cameras flashed and kids cheered. Indigo kissed him again, a proper kiss, spit and tequila, holding him tight.

11

Austin snapped the chocolate biscuit in two. Loud. Brutal. Deliberate.

He said, 'Do you know how bad it got?'

So bad that he had to come round first thing and tell Bailey in person.

'I almost shoved popcorn up his nose.'

Bailey closed his eyes and rubbed his nose bridge. 'Almost?'

'Bailey, man, you've never heard my brother snore! Get it in your brain! If I stuck popcorn up there and it came out full force – *bang!* We're Muslim! We can't do that crap.'

Crap. Like inside Bailey's head. Tequila wasn't alcohol. It was chemical warfare. Austin filled the kettle, tap full on, kettle held far below. The sound was making Bailey's stomach shiver.

'There's this James Bond film.' Austin slammed the kettle on to its stand. 'An assassin tries to kill Bond with poison. Do you know how he does it?'

'Dripping it down a cord and he kills the girl instead. *You Only Live Twice.*'

'I thought your mum didn't do Bond films.'

'Dad does. When she's not here. Anyway, what's your point?'

Austin opened the fridge door so hard all the jars inside rattled. 'My point is, there's lots of clever ways to kill a man.'

Was there a standard rate of brain cells destroyed per millilitre of tequila? It must be a serious bundle because Austin was not making sense. 'You think Indigo's Velcroed to my bedroom ceiling with a bottle of poison and some dental floss?'

'I dunno, Bailey. You could be into that stuff. But maybe she spiked your drink last night. How much did you have?'

'Not much. It was a tiny bottle to start with.'

'Anything to eat?'

'A slice of pizza from one of those stalls on Charing Cross Road.'

'Oh, God.' Austin was staring at him. 'That was your big mistake. Though I can't say I'm sorry for you.'

'I never had a go at you about Soraya. Even though you blew me out loads of times.'

'Because, my good friend, there was foreplay. I built up to it slowly. I didn't let you down until at least . . .' He poked the half-biscuit in his mouth, chewing it with his mouth open. 'Not until at least the third date.'

The front door opened and closed upstairs. Dad's voice filtered down, having a one-way conversation with the cat.

Austin unhooked a third cup from the mug stand. 'Look who's home.'

'You promised, remember?'

'Are you asking me to lie to your parents?'

'Yes. Because you promised me.'

'I didn't promise nothing. You made a request and I said I'd give it consideration.'

Dad's footsteps on the stairs, coming down. Why the hell couldn't Bailey just say it as it was? It was already trying to burst out. He and Indigo had taken two buses to get home last night, just to make the trip longer. She refused point blank to let Bailey walk her to her door, but she'd messaged him when she was in. A picture of her in her room with a wall of postcards at the back.

Dad shook his head slowly. 'There's a good reason why I'm a vegetarian. It all stemmed from an unfortunate moment with a hot dog from a vendor in Trafalgar Square.'

'He just doesn't listen, does he?' Austin gave Dad his wise smile. 'I said he should have pizza, but no, he insisted on that kebab. When he sees something he likes, it's hard to change his mind.'

'Yes.' Dad laughed. 'That's how he ended up with his first guitar. You brewing fresh? Pour me one, will you?'

Austin topped up the teapot with boiling water and poured milk into the three mugs. 'I'm already ahead of you.'

Indigo had said she was busy today. Maybe she'd have

to change her plans if her head felt anything like his, whomped by a spiked mallet. She'd seemed all right last night, though. More than seemed. When he woke up this morning, he could still smell her perfume on his sweatshirt. And there were messages. Last night. This morning. There must be even more by now. But he wasn't going to check until Austin left. And that didn't look likely any time soon.

Dad was stirring sugar into his tea. 'So how was the film, then?'

'Could have been better.' Austin looked expectantly at Bailey. 'What do you reckon?'

'I bow to your opinion.'

Come on, Austin, man! You've made your point! Like he didn't know that Bailey just wanted to heave himself off the stool, shuffle upstairs and slide back into bed. Even if every time the duvet moved, it sounded like the New Year's Eve fireworks on the Thames.

Austin had swapped to his angelic face. Oh, God. Here it came.

'Bailey says you're going to Paris.'

Dad paused with a slice of jammy toast halfway to his mouth.

'Yes. Why?'

Austin offered up his sweetest smile. 'I just wondered what it's like. I thought maybe me and Soraya could go there.'

'Aha!' Dad managed quarter of the slice with one bite,

pink crumbs sticking to the side of his mouth. Bailey blinked hard and swallowed. 'So you've outed yourself as an art lover, Austin. Or is it the grand sweep of Haussmann's architectural vision that captures your imagination?'

Austin's smile didn't falter. 'Yeah. That too.'

'Good to hear,' Dad said. 'My assumptions about you have been challenged.'

Bailey couldn't resist it. 'What assumptions, Dad?'

Dad was obviously glad he'd been asked. 'Just the usual gossip that zaps up and down the parent hotline. Something to do with a rave at Maisie's house when her mum was away on a hen weekend. Know anything about that, Austin?'

Austin made a good job of looking confused. 'I can't remember . . . oh, yes. I think I stuck my head in. There was no one I knew so I went again.'

'I heard the police came,' Bailey said.

'Yeah,' Austin hissed. 'I heard that too.'

'And what about when your aunty went off to Nigeria for Christmas?' Dad sipped his tea. 'There just happened to be a party on Boxing Day. Quite a big party, according to the hotline.'

Austin's face drooped in remorse. 'That was my cousin. A couple of us promised Aunty we'd check her house was okay. My cousin found out we had the key and there was no stopping her.'

183

'I'm sure there wasn't,' Dad said. 'Didn't some of your aunty's neighbours try? Your cousin was less than cooperative.'

'Yeah. She's proper feisty. Drives my uncle mad.'

'So just to recap.' Dad dropped another slice of bread into the toaster. 'I appreciate your interest in our possible forthcoming trip to Paris. And I am pleasantly surprised that your interest lies in the city's treasury of art and history and not, apparently, in the rich opportunities of a parent-free house.'

Austin shook his head hard. Any second now, it would fly off and slam against the fridge.

'Well, thanks for your hospitality, Ed.' Austin gulped the last of his tea. 'I told Mum I wouldn't be long. I just came to check that my boy was good.'

'Yeah,' Bailey said. 'Thanks. I appreciate your kind concern.'

'Treasure it,' Austin said. 'You never know when you're going to need my concern in the future.'

As soon as the door banged shut after Austin, Dad turned to Bailey.

'I can never work out if he's really a bad influence or just pretending to be.'

'He's right about the parties,' Bailey said. 'None of them were his fault.'

'He just happened to be there.'

184

'Yes. Something like that.'

'That doesn't fill me with much hope.' Dad was filling the kettle again. Maybe one of the interview tests for social workers was how many buckets of tea they could drink in a minute. 'At the moment, your mum's not sure if she can fit in a trip away, but I'm trying to persuade her otherwise. I don't want extra stress worrying about whether the place is being ripped apart.'

'It won't be, Dad. Seriously.'

'I have to trust you, Bailey.'

'You can. Honest.'

'Good.' Dad unhooked a frying pan. 'Fancy some scrambled eggs?'

'No, thanks.'

By late afternoon, Bailey's body was feeling normal. Austin had sent him a link to a Swedish kid who played rock versions of Disney love songs. It was probably meant to make Bailey feel more nauseous, but the boy had got it so wrong. Last night he and Indigo had gone into the Disney Shop in Covent Garden. She'd held up a toy lion cub and whistled 'The Circle of Life'. She was good at whistling. The Swedish kid played a decent thrash version of it. Bailey flipped the link over to her. Maybe that would prompt her to reply to his last message.

There were probably so many things about her that he

didn't know. Then there were the things he did know about her and hadn't told her. He'd meant to tell her, just after he'd put his arm around her. But then he'd felt the slide of her leather jacket against his zip-up and tried not to stare as the dress moved against her legs. And suddenly his head had been crowded with all the reasons why he had to keep quiet.

Reason one. JJ looked like he drank a bottle of whisky a day. What if he'd just read about Indigo in a newspaper and was hallucinating it all? That sometimes happened to bad alcoholics.

Reason two. Bailey had gone to New Cross, hadn't he? Horatio had made it clear. He didn't want to know.

Reason three. What did Indigo say? She didn't want to remember that stuff.

So in the end, it was good that he'd kept his mouth shut.

Still no reply to his message. That was two she hadn't answered. What if Indigo really hated Disney and he'd got the wrong end of the stick? Why wasn't there an app where you could call back messages you sent to someone else's phone? He ran a finger across his lips. Tequila removed skin cells too.

He needed music. His head could handle it now. He flicked through his vinyl. Muse, Muse, Blondie? Maybe. Led Zep. Arctic Monkeys. Yeah, Arctic Monkeys. 'Mad Sounds' was about right. He set it up on the record player

186

and maxed the volume. Yes. Better.

He pulled open the drawer and lifted off the old notebooks covering JJ's envelope. There was no chance of his parents happening to find it in there. He tipped out the picture. Now he'd seen Indigo up close, he still couldn't say that the baby was her. But it must be because Horatio had the picture too. And that was definitely Indigo's mum. He'd seen that same look on Aunty Maria's face when she'd had her first kid. Both of them looked like they'd never let their babies go.

Keely was dancing with the Hoover. Indigo didn't think she meant to, but that's the way it looked. Keely's arms went in and out. Her bum wobbled. And there were a few fancy steps in there too, as she swung the Hoover around the coffee table in the sitting room. Indigo should have stayed in her bedroom, but since last night, it felt a bit small. Or there was too much of her to fit in there.

She curled her legs up into the armchair to let Keely clean underneath.

'You could stop watching and help,' Keely yelled over the motor.

'I'm doing the polishing,' Indigo yelled back.

'With a pencil and bit of paper.'

'I can't polish properly until you're finished. Else everything's going to get dusty again.'

Indigo looked down at her notebook. She wouldn't write his name, just in case Keely noticed and asked more questions. There wasn't even that much to tell her. But what there was, Indigo was going to hold close. She needed two columns – YES and NO. In the first one, she wrote just one word – cute, in small, light letters. And Bailey *was* cute. But so was Stivo. He'd said his granddad was Greek, and Indigo used to imagine Stivo in a little white tunic, spearing monsters. Though in real life, Stivo was a monster moron. So, cute was good, but it wasn't enough. Bailey could turn, the same way Stivo did.

Next, for YES – Viv. Indigo turned her smile away from Keely. If only she'd had a secret camera when she'd seen Viv, she'd have kept the picture forever.

Keely was banging the Hoover against the skirting board. Indigo was surprised that next door hadn't come knocking to complain about their sleeping baby.

Under Viv in bigger letters – normal.

It was still with her now. Even when she held the wooden crocodile in the dark last night. Even when she lifted the corner of the letter and ended up reading it through again. All that was part of her, but when she was with him, she'd felt the emptiness shrinking back. That's how other people felt. Normal.

Her phone pinged up another message. Letting him hang on, that was normal too. She'd just have to see how long she could hang on for.

Keely turned off the Hoover. 'I don't know why I bother. Nobody cares if this place is clean.'

Indigo closed her notebook and tucked the pencil down the side of the seat.

'You might meet someone really gorgeous on a date. You can't bring them back to a tip.'

'I wish.' Keely flopped on to the sofa.

'Was last night another crap one?'

'He was ten minutes late, so I was sitting in the bar by myself like an idiot. Then when he finally got there, he went and bought a big, expensive bottle of wine without asking me first.'

'Did you have any?'

''Course not. I would have thrown up on the spot. Though that would have ended the torture quickly. How was your night?'

'Cool. We hung out in Covent Garden.'

'Hung out?'

'Yeah.'

'So it wasn't a – what do you young people call it? – a hook-up.'

'Jesus, Kee!' Her face must be the colour of Bailey's hair.

Keely laughed. 'Sorry, hun. I didn't mean to embarrass you. I'm glad it went well. Much better than mine.'

'Did your bloke get narky because you don't drink?'

'Not at all. He just drank the lot himself.'

So had Indigo and Bailey. Tequila that smelled like nail-varnish remover. Every drop of it. She managed to squeeze back a giggle. 'What did you talk about?'

'Me? Nothing. Him? Himself. For two hours flat. I got in one question. I asked him if he liked to cook and do you know what he said?'

'What's your favourite pizza?'

'If only. What he actually said was, "I used to have a wife who did all the cooking. Why have a dog and bark yourself?"'

'A dog? He called his wife a dog?'

Indigo nearly laughed, but then she spotted Keely's face. She was close to tears. Indigo uncurled from the armchair and slid on to the sofa next to her.

'Did you punch him, Kee?'

'No, I sat through another twenty minutes of his crap, then made a run for it when he went off to the loo.'

'Good. Did you hear from him again?'

Keely shook her head. 'No. I sent him a text to say that my mum fell down the stairs and I had to go off to her.'

'In Jamaica?'

This time Keely laughed. 'Yeah, but he didn't know that. The thing is, this guy was a complete and utter git, and somehow I still ended up lying to save his sad little ego.'

Indigo laid her head on Keely's shoulder. 'You'll find someone.'

'I'm starting to wonder if I want someone. Sometimes, I don't know . . . working in a stupid supermarket, smiling at complete idiots. And that's just the managers. Maybe I should go and spend time with Mum. Six months. A year, maybe. Or go somewhere completely different. Somewhere special.'

'You'd have to take me with you.'

Keely stroked Indigo's hair. 'It wouldn't be the same without you.'

That wasn't a yes.

Keely left just after two and she wasn't due back until half eleven. She'd taken Indigo's advice, though, and put on some make-up. She'd squirted on some Gaultier too. Who knew who was coming into the shop today?

Indigo plugged her speakers into her laptop and clicked on her playlist. The Creatures, 'Right Now'. Bailey must have been staring at his phone waiting for her, because as soon as she messaged him, he replied straight away. Was that normal? Who cared? She was crap at hanging on.

Indigo retrieved her make-up box and mirror from the bedroom. She propped the mirror on the coffee table and scraped back her hair with a band. She dug out a cover stick. That spot had to go.

When she was Skyping Primrose, she used to look from Primrose to her own little square of screen to see how much they looked like each other. They both had small ears and the same shocked-looking eyebrows, but Primrose was darker, because her dad was from Antigua. Whether you liked it or not, you always took something from your dad.

She poked the cover stick back into the make-up box. 'Right Now' finished. It was a pity it was short. Next song, 'Union City Blues'.

Funny how she hadn't flicked through her life-story book since she'd been with Keely. A social worker must have spent ages arranging those pictures, writing little notes so she knew who everybody was. When she was living with the Corrigans, it was always open – the blurry photo of Teal's fourth birthday party, Scarlet and Coral in matching sleepsuits on a tartan blanket and Violet, just a tiny scrap in an incubator, six weeks early. She'd stare at them for ages, looking for the thing that made them family. And that thing, of course, was Mahalia, their mum. It was easy to forget the dads. Well, easy to forget the ones that weren't Indigo's. She'd only got one picture of him. He was about ten, with some other boys in a football team. She always skipped that page.

Her stomach twitched. She imagined the thing opening one eye and then another, slowly stretching until its nails tapped Indigo's insides. She breathed out slowly and shifted back up into the armchair. She picked up her notebook, dug out the pencil from under the cushion and skimmed through to Bailey's page.

Yes
Cute
Viv
Normal.

Below that, she wrote: I can tell him things. He didn't laugh or take the piss. He just drew her closer.

She wrote it again: Normal. Pushing the pencil hard into the paper so it pressed through every page. Normal. Normal. Normal.

Last night, with the colours whirling around them and the tequila thick on her tongue, it was easy to pretend the other stuff didn't matter. But she was here now, with her grandma's letter under her pillow and her life story in a plastic crate at the bottom of her wardrobe. A few minutes online and anyone could know her past life, with photos too. Pictures of her parents' flat popping up on screens in countries she'd probably never heard of.

She wasn't normal, was she? She'd never be normal. But she could tell him things. And he made her *feel* normal.

The NO column was still empty. There were always *NOs*. In the past, she'd made herself ignore them.

She ran her finger down the blank space. Bailey's dad

was a social worker. Like she needed any more of them in her life. And there was that complete idiot friend of his. She didn't need moron sidekicks, neither. But that was the small stuff.

It was *NO* because . . .

She'd had to let Felix go.

She would have to let Keely go.

She couldn't let Bailey get anywhere close. Then she would never have to let him go.

She dropped the notebook on the floor and caught a glimpse of her face in the mirror. That cover stick had made the spot worse.

She turned the mirror face down. Why bother anyway if this was going to be it? Sitting in the middle of Keely's flat by herself. And next year, she'd be sitting in some poky room in Edmonton, also by herself. Indigo, just a big hole of emptiness with the rest of her body stretched round it. She was like one of those donuts from the cheap shelves in supermarkets. Everything seemed all right until you bit into the middle and then there was just nothing.

Though when she was with Bailey last night, it was like there'd been something else inside her, something sweet and good. Not filling the space all the way up, but enough. You think there's nothing there and then the first splodge of jam hits your tongue. You just want to smile.

She picked up her phone. Another Bailey message. *Sure you don't want to meet up?*

Bailey opened the fridge and fished out a Dr Pepper. Mum was hungry. Dad wasn't. It was a really big deal to them.

'If you can wait an hour,' Dad was saying, 'the fish will be fully defrosted.'

'It would be fully defrosted if you'd taken it out earlier.' Mum reached round Bailey and pulled out a wedge of Brie. 'You can't do everything on the hoof.'

'Since when do we have a big lunch?'

'Since I told you I'd be going round to see Marla tonight. Her mum's back in hospital and she's feeling a bit desperate.'

'Right,' Dad said.

'Right what?'

'Just right.'

Bailey flipped the tab on his can. Mum turned to him. 'I can do pasta for us now or your dad can cook you fish later.'

'It's okay.' Bailey kept his face calm and indifferent. 'I'm going out.'

'Oh,' Mum said. 'Where?'

Deep silent breath. 'Just to Austin's.'

Dad shook his head. 'You two'd better not be plotting.'

Mum spun round to him. 'Plotting about what?'

Dad tried a little laugh that didn't work. 'Nothing. I was just joking.'

'Of course you were.'

They glared at each other. The fish could have defrosted just from Mum's look.

Lies worked by being close to the truth. And being simple. 'Austin's having a FIFA day. There's a few of us invited.'

That bit was true. Bailey *had* been invited. And he'd definitely been planning to go, until the message from Indigo. He held his phone tighter, as if Mum could see deep into the SIM and read it for herself.

She said, 'Who's going?'

Bailey shrugged. 'Austin's usual crowd.'

'Is Indigo going?'

'For God's sake,' Dad said. 'Leave it.'

Yes, please, Mum. Leave it.

Mum slammed the cheeseboard on the counter. 'Is she?'

His phone never usually felt so slippery. 'Maybe. Soraya's been invited. And her mate, Jade.' He owed Jade, for passing on his number to Indigo. 'They probably won't come, though. FIFA doesn't do it for most girls.'

Mum looked ready to argue with him about that. Then her shoulders dropped and she started peeling away the packaging from the Brie. 'Any idea what time you'll be home?'

'I don't know. If Austin's losing, it'll go on forever.'

'Just make sure your homework's up to date.'

Dad opened the freezer and shoved the half-frozen plastic tray of salmon in. 'I might be on the sofa when you come back. Try not to sit on me.'

'There's a spare room,' Mum said acidly. 'No one needs to suffer.'

Bailey left them to it. It was like standing in the spot where they crossed the streams in *Ghostbusters*. Mum hadn't been this stressed since the last Ofsted inspection.

Back in his room, Bailey called Austin. He answered straight away.

'You blowing me out again?'

If they were doing video, Austin would be sitting on the floor of his bedroom surrounded by stacks of games. Leaning against the wall behind him would be the special whiteboard he'd bought for his FIFA marathons along with the gold, plastic champion's trophy with a list of names written in black Sharpie.

Bailey said, 'What makes you think I'm blowing you out?'

'So you just called to say you love me?'

'I'm being polite in advance. Because I *might* not make it.'

Austin sucked his teeth. 'The girl's making you stupid.'

'She's not. I want to see her.' And feel her warmth. And kiss her again.

'You've known her five minutes and suddenly she's taken over.'

'That's crap, Austin.'

'Yeah? Twice in twenty-four hours, man!'

Bailey should have sent a text. A quick apology and nothing else.

'You're heavy with my favours,' Austin was saying. 'I can't spare you no more. You have to balance things up.'

Bailey rubbed his face. There were still a few cells of brain that couldn't deal with Austin right now. 'Okay. Yeah.'

'Yeah, what?'

'If my parents go to Paris, I'll have people round.' *One big 'if'. Right now, they don't even want to be in London together.*

'Oh.' Now Bailey wished he could see Austin's face. 'Yeah.'

Austin hung up. Bailey checked the last message from Indigo.

OK. You choose the place. Let's meet.

No pressure, then. What was going to beat last night? Maybe they could do proper landmarks without scrambling their brain cells with tequila. Tower of London? St Paul's? She'd mentioned Buckingham Palace, hadn't she? Though did she really want to hang out in the Queen's yard with a million tourists? And she could go to any of those other places any time she wanted. It sounded like her foster mum would do anything for her.

He opened his music-book drawer and pulled out JJ's envelope. Indigo had said she didn't want to talk about it. That was one of the reasons she liked him – for once, she could forget it all. He opened his bottom drawer, the one with the t-shirts too mashed up to wear again. He slid the envelope under the clothes and shoved the drawer shut.

So, where was he going to take her? It had to be somewhere special, somewhere she wouldn't normally go . . . Yes. He had an idea.

The day was brighter than he'd expected, though that could be the last knockings of the tequila. Mum had retreated to the garden. Dad was vacuuming the stairs. New people were moving into the flat opposite; they seemed to have too much furniture to fit in a basement. The main road beyond Bailey's street was clogged as cars tried to pull out of the Seventh-Day Adventist Church car park. The tables outside the new organic café were filling up. The usual guys were begging outside BetQuick's.

A 38 bus was due in eight minutes. Walking to the junction would be quicker.

'Oi!'

Oh, God, no.

JJ was standing by the bus stop. Bailey glanced around; there was no one around he knew.

JJ was wearing the same grey beanie hat; maybe it never came off. Tufts of dark hair poked out from underneath. He'd swapped his jeans for tracksuit bottoms with a padded waistcoat over his hoodie even though the day promised sunshine. Dad had a hoodie he wore when he went running, but nothing like that. Funny, they were probably about the same age.

Bailey said, 'Were you waiting for me again?'

JJ laughed. It caught in his throat and he seemed to struggle for breath. He was looking paler than before, puffed up and swollen with a rough-looking cut above his left eyebrow. 'If you give me your phone number, you'll save me the bother.'

Yeah. Very funny.

Bailey said, 'How do you know I'd be coming this way?'

JJ pointed. 'Because you live down there.'

'You know where I live?'

'Yeah.'

Great. So at any moment, he could knock on their door and introduce himself to Mum and Dad. Bailey would get in from college and see the three of them sitting around the dining room table, their faces turning towards him as he came through the door.

He said, 'Sorry, I haven't had a chance to talk to Indigo yet.'

JJ nodded. 'Did you go to Indigo's granddad?'

'Yes.'

'Thank you.'

'But . . .' Bailey hadn't even managed to test this conversation on himself yet. 'Horatio doesn't want to see her.'

'What do you mean?'

'He says it's too late now.'

'It's never too late. You have to try again!'

The bus was coming. Bailey's travelcard was in the palm of his hand. 'He was really clear about it. He didn't want to be involved.'

'You have to go back.'

'Sorry.'

The bus doors slid open and Bailey jumped on. He skimmed his card across the scanner and ran upstairs, sinking into the last free double seat. He peered out of the window on to the street. JJ was nowhere to be seen. He was lucky that Bailey had bothered to listen to him at all. Bailey didn't know anyone else who'd let a homeless guy get a word in. He pushed in his ear buds. Vintage Kinks, Dave Davies hammering the guitar like he hated it.

The bus shifted a few metres and stopped, caught at traffic lights. A stream of cyclists jumped the red and shot towards central Hackney. There was a movement beside Bailey and a flutter of shadow on the window, the smell of old alcohol and stale skin. Grey tracksuit bottoms. Stained trainers.

No! This must be a joke!

JJ sat next to him, so close their thighs were almost touching. Everyone must be sneaking little looks at them, counting down in their head until Bailey moved.

In two stops' time, they'd be outside the station. What if Indigo was already waiting there? JJ would get off the bus right behind him.

The bus swerved to miss a grocery van; Bailey and JJ knocked shoulders. Bailey popped out his ear buds and looked at him. JJ was sitting with his hands on his knees, staring ahead. A woman across the aisle caught Bailey's eye and smiled in sympathy. Did JJ notice? Bailey didn't smile back.

Bailey said, 'I tried.'

'You have to keep trying.'

Bailey kept his voice low. 'Her granddad doesn't want to see her.'

'That idiot!' A jab of energy that wasn't there before. JJ wiped his forehead with his sleeve. The sun was angling through the window straight on to them. 'Then tell her. Tell her about her granddad. Take her there.'

The whole bus must be straining to hear what they were saying. 'I can't.'

JJ leaned towards him. 'Yes, you can. Just open your mouth and start talking.'

'It's not that easy. Indigo said she doesn't want to go over that stuff. It's not fair to make her.'

The bell was going off, again and again. A dust van was crawling ahead of them, the bin men taking their time collecting their bags of rubbish and throwing them in the back. A girl in a bright red kilt and white t-shirt was dodging round the empty boxes and bin bags. Her sparkly shoulder bag swung to and fro. Bailey's belly flipped. Indigo.

The bus stopped and she was lost in the crowd of passengers that were getting off.

JJ said, 'Tell her.'

'What?'

JJ was tugging at the bus seat. His knuckles were cut up and shiny, like they hadn't finished bleeding. 'You promised.'

Just past Bailey's shoulder, Indigo emerged from the crowd and was walking up the street. Bailey shifted round, trying to block the view. He glanced at his phone. He couldn't even send her a message with JJ sitting right there, looking at him.

'It's not that simple,' Bailey said. 'What am I supposed to say? The guy who kidnapped you from the park followed me home and gave me your baby picture. He's the same guy who left you alone when your parents— Jesus!'

Someone rang the bell for the station stop. There was always a delay here while a load of passengers got on. So even if Bailey managed to squeeze out to the aisle, JJ would still have enough time to follow him. The clock on the bus said Bailey was dead on time. If he got off at the next stop, he could sprint back and not be too late. A long pause.

The dust cart moved a few metres and stopped again.

Cars in both directions hooted. It seemed to make the bin men even slower. He heard the doors open downstairs, even though they were still some way from the stop. More passengers were pouring out.

'Look,' Bailey said. 'I'll talk to her.'

'When's that?'

'I don't know! Soon!'

'When?'

Shit! He was going to miss the next stop too! The driver was going to go straight past! It was hard to keep the anger out of his voice. 'Just leave me alone!'

Silence in the bus.

'Excuse me,' Bailey said. 'I need to get off.'

JJ didn't move.

'Please?'

JJ shifted his knees sideways so Bailey could slip through. He felt the burn of the other passengers' eyes on him as he turned the corner on the stairs.

There were steps behind him. No, no, no!

Bailey had seen people flip before. Once, Austin's older brother started yelling abuse at a bloke he thought jumped the queue in Burger King. It had made Bailey cringe. Now, he understood. He could feel himself filling up with heat and words. Maybe this was how it felt for Indigo, especially the first time, with the python uncurling slowly, squeezing the part of him that kept him calm.

He wasn't going to look round. He wasn't going to see the dirty joggers and trainers and the puffy face and the scar. Just for a second he'd pretend it was someone else standing so close to him; it was the woman who'd felt sorry for him, or the old bloke in the Chelsea shirt who'd been sitting in front of them.

It was anyone apart from this bloody tramp.

Bailey stepped off the bus. Glancing up, he saw faces pressed against the window, gazing down at them.

Indigo would be at the station now. Maybe she was checking her messages, not too worried yet.

Bailey walked down a side road. God knows where it went, but JJ was following him like a tired, shabby shadow. Bailey stopped and faced him. 'What do you want?'

'You have to tell her! You have to make it right!' A gob of spit flicked out.

'I tried!' Bailey's voice was rising. 'Why can't you just leave it alone?'

'Because *she* will be alone, you stupid kid! Soon, there'll be no one left for her.'

JJ leaned against the wall, his face in his hands. If Bailey sprinted hard, he wouldn't be too late. JJ was in no state to follow him. He fired a quick message to Indigo.

Bus stuck. A bit late.

JJ was murmuring something.

Bailey moved closer to her. 'I'm sorry, JJ. I have to go.'

205

JJ was even paler now, the cut starker on his forehead, one hand pressed on his stomach.

Turn around. Walk back to the main road. You can call an ambulance from there.

'Bailey?'

Bailey moved closer.

Wrong way! The bus stop's down there!

JJ was staring at the ground. When he lifted his head, his eyes had trouble finding Bailey. 'Toby was the good one. Not me.'

He lurched forward, crumpling on to his knees.

Oh, God. JJ was going to die. Right there on the street.

'You'll be okay, JJ. Just hold on. I'm calling an ambulance.'

JJ's mouth moved. A breath of voice. 'My brother, Toby. He was the good one.'

Bailey looked around. There was no one around to help them.

JJ swayed back against the wall, banging his head. Bailey felt the thud in his own head. He crouched beside him.

'Did you say your brother . . . ? JJ?'

JJ's head slumped sideways and he vomited. Flecks of it caught Bailey's shirt. Oh, Jesus! Oh, God. Bailey held his breath and turned away.

'Hang on, JJ.' Bailey went straight through to the emergency line. Where exactly were they? It was just an alleyway off Essex Road! Why the hell didn't the council put up street signs? And no! He didn't know the postcode. What were the symptoms? Was the man conscious? Bailey didn't know. No, Bailey wasn't related. No, he didn't know anything else about the sick man.

He's an alcoholic. He's homeless. He took a toddler from the park and he's been sorry ever since.

'They're coming in five minutes.'

It was like life was flopping out of JJ, his head, his shoulders, slipping sideways. Bailey sat down next to him, bracing himself to take JJ's weight.

Five minutes. If he left now, he'd be about fifteen minutes late. But the stink of vomit was all over him. And if he moved away, JJ would fall.

'JJ?' Nothing. He touched his arm. 'It's Bailey.'

Still nothing.

Sirens were screaming towards them, but this was London. There were always sirens. *Please let these be the right ones.*

12

Indigo's phone buzzed. It was over the other side of the room, from when it'd bounced off her waste bin and landed next to her white shoes. *Bastardy stupid idiot.* He couldn't even give her a proper reason! Some crap about someone getting ill on the bus. He could have walked it from his house to the station, she knew that. Did he think she was stupid? Even she'd walked more than she usually did to get there on time.

Big bastardy stupid idiot.

Indigo had stood outside that station for twenty minutes. Twenty sodding minutes! And who should come slinking by? Mona and that creep, Levy. When she'd looked up from her phone, there they were. There was no way Indigo could avoid them. She just had to stare them out while they took their time walking past her. They must have clocked straight away what she was doing. Waiting. Waiting for someone who wasn't going to turn up. As soon as they were out of sight – and that bitch, Mona, kept looking back – Indigo virtually ran to the bus stop. It was just as well that no one was home, because the last thing Indigo needed was Keely to see her like this.

Indigo grabbed her pillow and squeezed it into her chest. *Breathe deep.* Covent Garden had been fun, but that was it. Lipsin' with a cute boy who didn't lunge in for a quick grope. She'd thought she needed more from him. That was crap. No, Bailey hadn't turned the same way Stivo had. This was worse. Bailey had almost made her believe something different about herself.

She squeezed the pillow tighter, pushing in her nose so deep she could hardly breathe. It reeked of hairspray and Gaultier. If she squeezed hard enough, the whole thing would disappear into her, all the sweet stuff pushed out by a heavy lump of nothing.

Her phone buzzed again. She launched the pillow across the room. It skimmed across her desk, sending her nail varnishes flying.

A knock on her door. Her stomach leaped. Bailey had found out where she lived. He'd somehow got in.

'Indigo?'

No! Not bloody Felix!

'Bugger off!'

'Don't be so rude.' The door opened a sliver. 'Especially as I came all this way to see you.'

'The 253 from Holloway. Big deal.'

'It was actually. I'm not into the bus thing like you are.'

Felix eased himself into her room and stood with his back against the door. He nodded towards the pillow and scattered varnish bottles. 'I don't like you when you're angry.'

'You don't live here any more. So you don't have to like me at all.'

He sighed. 'No. I don't have to like you, but I do.'

She sat up, catching sight of herself in the mirror. It looked like someone had tried to fingerpaint her face with mascara.

He said, 'What happened?'

It was a fight to keep her expression blank. 'Nothing.'

'You put your make-up on with your eyes closed, do you?' He held his hand to his ear. 'And is that a phone I hear?'

He moved over and sat on her bed. Not that he was invited.

He said, 'Who is he?'

'Who's who?'

Buzz. Another bloody message.

'He really wants to talk to you,' Felix said.

'How do you know it's a "he"?'

'I would have worked out if you were a lesbian.' Felix swept his arm round the room. 'His fault?'

'I got stood up.' If she'd written that in her notebook, the words would have been tiny.

NO.

He makes you want him then lets you down.

Felix nodded. 'And he's sorry, right?'

'Yeah.'

'Have you answered?'

'No.'

'Do you like him?'

She squeezed her lips together.

'Ah ha.' Felix smiled. 'Are you likely to bump into him?'

'He's at college.'

'Excellent. You can play him good and proper. He has to earn you. He has to know what you're worth. Do you know what I mean?'

'I know, but . . .'

'You're pregnant.'

'No! It's just . . . he . . .'

Felix slid over and slung his arm round her. He let her cry, even though she knew her mascara must be splodging his t-shirt. He kissed her cheek. 'You and him, you'll sort it out. As long as you remember you're valuable, Indigo.'

How did you work it out? What should she count?

She sniffed back a sob. 'You're lucky. You've got Wade.'

'Wade's okay.'

Eh? This wasn't the way Felix sold it to Keely. 'Just okay? I thought it was a big love job.'

Felix looked embarrassed. 'I didn't mean it like that.'

'What did you mean?'

'I mean, me and Wade went to look at this crappy studio I'd been offered and we decided that we'd give it a proper go together. I suppose I had to make a decision. Do I keep looking out for someone better or do I try . . . I don't know. Just try. Wade's been really patient with me. I decided to try.'

She sniffed again. Were there really more tears left? 'I haven't got a Wade.'

'You've got me and Keely.' She just managed to stop herself shifting away. He stroked her hair. 'I know you're trying to get rid of us, Indigo, but we're going to stick with you.'

'You can't.'

'Yes, we can. What your dad did, it's nothing to do with you. He was a different person. You're you.' He stood up. 'If you keep pushing everyone away, you'll never have a Wade. Or anyone else. You have to make yourself believe it!' Felix scooped up her pillow and whacked her with it. 'Or you'll cost Keely a fortune in pillows.'

Felix left her door open. She could hear him pulling out drawers in his bedroom – his old bedroom. There was still loads of his stuff here. Keely kept moaning about it.

He was calling her. 'You haven't seen my blue headphones, have you?'

The ones under her bed? 'No!'

Another message hit her phone. Indigo rolled off her bed and went to retrieve it. Bailey. She turned the screen to face the rug.

13

Bailey wanted to talk to her. No, he didn't *want* to. He *had* to. Though she was doing everything she could to avoid him. He'd sent three days' worth of sorries and she still wasn't replying. He could write a proper message, an email, something that tried to explain it all. He'd snapped a shot of her baby picture and it was sitting in his gallery waiting for him to attach and press 'Send'. But now there seemed too much to say, things that were too hard to write down. It was his fault. He shouldn't have bottled it at Covent Garden. No, go back. He shouldn't have followed JJ to the takeaway. He should have left the two pound coins in the puddle and walked off.

So what would he say to her? *Please, Indigo, hear me out. The homeless guy who is stalking me is the same guy who kidnapped you. Oh, and he says he's your uncle, but he was about to fall unconscious when he said it, right before he puked on me. (He's all right now; well, he's out of hospital at least. I checked.) I don't know if it's true. I don't know his real name so I can't find anything about him. He said that Toby Scott, your dad, was the good one. I can't find anything about that, either. Sorry.*

In fact, wherever Bailey looked, the only thing Toby Scott got mentioned for was killing his girlfriend, Mahalia. Or sometimes it was his wife. The newspapers didn't seem bothered about finding out if they were married. He appeared in different places, not just newspapers. There he was, in a blog about male violence. And again in a defunct forum for social workers. There was even a stupid, sick death tour walk around Deptford. Bailey was tempted to leave a comment on that site, but it looked like it hadn't been updated for years.

Reading it all had made Bailey start to feel a bit sick. The facts were more or less the same in most reports. Indigo's parents had been drinking and doing other stuff, probably crack. Mahalia had a convulsion and fell unconscious. Toby thought she was winding him up. The pillow started as a joke and then he got angry and didn't stop.

And it all happened with Indigo on the other side of the door.

How the hell could JJ say Toby was the good one?

Bailey wiped his search history. All the different goes at 'Toby Scott's brother' and 'Scott baby kidnapper' looked weird. Nothing useful came up anyway.

'Bailey!' Mum, calling up the stairs. 'You're going to be late!'

He flicked his computer on to standby and went down. Mum was in the sitting room on the sofa, a mug of coffee in

214

one hand and her phone in the other. She looked up.

'You don't look even close to ready.'

'It's Wednesday. First lesson's at eleven.'

'Oh. Sorry. I forgot.'

Mum sipped her coffee and thumbed the screen at the same time.

'What about you?' Bailey said. 'You've usually left by now.'

'It's that conference, remember? Over in bloody Wandsworth. It's a pain in the arse to get to but it's easier than a day in school.' She checked her phone. 'TFL says there are no major disruptions, but you never know. I'd better get going.'

Bailey sat on the arm of the sofa. Mum laid her phone on the cushion between them.

She said, 'Is something up?'

'Not really.'

'I don't doubt you love me, Bailey, but you rarely come and sit next to me by choice these days.' She glanced across at the clock on the bookshelf. 'Does your account need topping up? You'd best ask your dad.'

'It's to do with Indigo.'

Mum put her coffee cup down on the floorboards. 'Right. I'm not sure I've got time to discuss this now.'

'I was wondering about her dad.'

Mum's eyes widened. 'Her dad? Why?'

Good, he'd taken her by surprise. But he'd have to tread carefully. Mum was always good at seeing right through him.

'You know when you and Dad were talking in the kitchen the other night?'

A quick, guilty look then a frown. 'You mean when you were sneaking about eavesdropping?'

Good knockback, Mum. He smiled. 'I could hear you both from upstairs.'

She smiled. 'Touché.'

'I was wondering what happened to her dad.'

Mum's smile transformed to her teacher stare. She slipped her phone in her bag. 'You just wondered, Bailey? Well, for whatever reason you're "just wondering", there's not much I can tell you. He went to prison for manslaughter and I heard on the grapevine that he died there.'

'Did he have any family?'

'Good God! Who knows?' Mum sighed. 'Bailey, he suffocated his girlfriend with a pillow. If he had family, I'm sure they'd keep very quiet about it.' Mum stood up. 'I'd better get going. Though I still want to know why you're so interested.'

'Interested in what?'

Dad was in the doorway, tea in hand, like he was waiting for his turn to use the room.

'Nothing, Ed.'

Dad drew back as Mum slid past him. He nudged the door shut as he came in.

'I was just asking about Indigo's dad,' Bailey said.

Dad sat down in the sofa dent left by Mum.

'You and Mum were talking about Indigo's mum. It seems like her dad doesn't get mentioned.'

'You can understand why.'

'I know. But I was thinking about the stuff you talk about sometimes. You know, how everyone goes on about the times when things go wrong. Social workers get all the blame.'

'Yes . . .'

'But usually social workers have done the best they can. All the right things have happened but something bad still happens.'

'True. What's that got to do with Indigo?'

'I was wondering if that's what happened with Indigo.'

'Indigo? She was one of the lucky ones.'

'Lucky? You serious, Dad?'

'Sorry. That was a bit crass.' Dad stretched out his legs. He was sporting socks with holes again. 'What I meant was, she wasn't harmed. I know it sounds tough, but her mum obviously wasn't able to care for her and she was placed somewhere safe.'

'Until she got taken from the park.'

'I don't know the details, Bailey, and I'm also curious to

know why you're so interested.'

'It just seems a bit rough for Indigo. Not having any family about.'

'Learning to appreciate us as you get older, are you?'

'I've always appreciated you, Dad.'

'Of course you have.' Now it was time for Bailey to get the social worker look. 'But I really don't think you should be snooping around Indigo's past.'

'I'm not. I was just interested.'

'Some things are buried deep in the archives and, frankly, I think they should stay there.'

'Maybe, if I was Indigo, I'd want to know more.'

'She can read her file when she's eighteen.'

'And that will have everything she needs to know, will it?'

'You're going to be late, Bailey.' Dad clicked the remote control. A woman in a blue suit was interviewing the Home Secretary. Dad turned up the volume.

'So what horror is being foisted on us today?'

Bailey stood up. 'Do you reckon it's as bad as your dad killing your mum?'

As Dad opened his mouth to answer, Bailey closed the door quietly behind him.

The door of the English room opened. Bailey watched them come in. Neema first, then Rudy. Indigo was trailing behind them. She flipped her blue headphones down on to her neck. She was pushing the dress code to the max, in a black mini, bare legs and clumpy black shoes. Her shirt was tight against her black bra strap.

Austin nudged Bailey. 'Man, keep your eyes on stalks.'

'Yeah, Austin. A bit louder.'

If Indigo heard him, she didn't show any sign of it. She slouched at the table in front of him, leaning into her bag and pulling out her pencil case. Her nails were orange with white tips. She was so close Bailey could have touched her shoulder.

'Okay!' Mr Godalming held up his book. 'Lady Macbeth. Transgressing femininity or plain old psychopath?'

Austin's hand shot up. 'Psychopath, sir.'

'Really, Austin? Let's hear your theory.'

Austin made a great show of consulting the post-it notes on his pages. Indigo didn't turn around. Her fingers were moving back and forward across the table like they were part of a conversation. They *were* part of a conversation. She was mouthing something to Levy. Levy grinned and gave her a little thumbs-up.

Levy Osborne? What the hell? He was like a jellyfish dressed up as a dolphin. On the surface, he was everybody's mate, but underneath all the friendly stuff, there was a sting and way too many arms. And now Indigo was smiling at him, twiddling a strand of her hair. It was the same place where Saskia had stuck the chewing gum.

Bailey glanced behind him. Mona was glaring daggers. Well, if Indigo wanted to dig at Mona, then she'd just have to deal with the crap.

Indigo bent sideways to adjust her ankle sock. Did she flash him a look just then?

'So, sir, a psychopath.' Austin flipped his notebook shut.

'Fascinating treatise, Austin.' Godalming gazed round the class. 'Anyone want to argue against him?'

'Yeah!' Everyone turned to Mona. 'Some women are just bitches.'

Godalming managed to carry on looking enthusiastic. 'Care to build a case for that statement?'

Mona sat back, arms folded. 'No, sir.'

Her eyes were on Indigo and Levy. They were busy whispering to each other. Bailey picked up his pen, scribbled some notes, highlighted the relevant passage on his worksheet. He could just see past the potted plants out of the window. If he really wanted to, he could count the plane contrails stretching across the sky. Anything but look at that idiot Levy.

Austin whispered in his ear. 'She knows she's winding you up, bruv. Just make like you don't care.'

'I don't.'

'Then what's with the laser-eye? Aimed at Levy. Set to annihilate.'

Indigo was out of the door as soon as the lesson was over. Austin sniffed and scraped the floor with his shoe.

'Girl moved so quick, there should be a scorch mark.'

Bailey shrugged. 'And what?'

They headed out of the humanities corridor and on to the quadrangle. Indigo was nowhere to be seen. She and Levy must have sloped off together.

Austin shot Bailey a side-eye. 'Soraya says Levy never keeps one girl. He's nasty. If he left his body to medical science, they'd probably cure every dick-mould known to man.'

'I don't care, Austin.'

The crowd was thinning out by the exit gates. Austin gave a royal wave to a sullen Year Eight who'd been stopped by a prefect trying to creep out for lunch.

They walked up to the row of chicken shops near the roundabout.

Austin said, 'You do care. I wish you didn't, but you do.' They crossed over to the central traffic island. 'Thing is, Mona reckons that Levy's hers, right? You know Mona, man. The girl's got fists like Tyson and teeth like Suarez. Anything happens to Indigo and you'll be wading right in there, dragging me with you. My mum's running three jobs now. I can't be spending time in hospital and stressing her out.'

'So what are you saying?'

'When you throw your party . . .'

'Austin!'

'Man, you promised. But look, it's not just for me. Like I said before, invite Indigo over. Tell her there's other people coming. Then engineer it so you spend some "Bailey and Indigo" time.'

Bailey sighed. 'It's not that simple.'

Austin stopped so suddenly, a woman behind bumped into him. 'Man, you got me telling lies to your parents! You think that's simple?'

'For you, yes. Anyway, I've had your back before.'

'Yeah, you let me copy a bit of homework. When we were nine. Look, even last week, you blew me out and then turned up at my place covered in tramp puke. I lent you my shirt *and* I let you join in with us.'

'You were losing. You needed me. And, just in case you're interested, the tramp's been discharged from hospital.'

'They told you? I thought you had to be like family, or something.'

'They couldn't tell me much, but they said he wasn't there any more.'

'Maybe he's dead.'

'He's alive.'

'That's good,' Austin said. 'Maybe you can get some money off him for a new shirt.'

'Man!'

'Seriously, bruv. You're better than me. I see those drunk guys lying there and I just step round them.'

They'd landed at Rooster C's. It was jammed up with Lea Dale college kids.

Austin made a face. 'Wings 'n' Tings?'

They walked round through the alleyway to the chicken place opposite the park. It seemed no one could be bothered to go the little extra because it was empty.

'Look, man, I appreciate everything you've done,' Bailey said. 'But I'm not even sure if Mum and Dad are going to Paris. They're not even sleeping in the same room together.'

Austin slapped his coins on the counter. 'Mine sleep in different continents. It works for them.'

But not for mine.

They took their chips and sat on a bench by the children's playground in the park. A woman and a toddler were chasing each other through the swings. A couple of girls from St Ecclestia's were skiving off and playing on the see-saw. The street drinkers were in their usual clump under the trees.

Austin threw a chip to a pigeon. 'Seriously, man. You're special, helping out a wino.'

'He's not just a wino.'

'Who is he, then?' The pigeon's mates were flying over. They looked expectant. Austin flung out a few more chips. 'Well?'

If I tell you, you'll open your big mouth to Soraya. Then Soraya will have to tell Jade. Then Jade will set up a special group chat to discuss it.

'I mean, you shouldn't call him a wino.'

'Jesus, Bailey. Your parents really went overboard with you, didn't they?' He gave Bailey a sideways look. 'But that means they'll be okay about a gathering. Just a few mates. We'll get in Creed or GFA. Maybe some beer.'

'You don't drink, Austin.'

'No, but I'm not selfish that way. So we're game on!' Austin reached a greasy hand across to Bailey to shake it.

'No, man,' Bailey said. 'Take my word as it is.'

'Hey!' Austin pointed to the park entrance. 'You want words? There's a whole load of cusses coming this way.'

Mona was standing there, by herself, for a change. She clocked Austin and Bailey and came marching towards them, scattering the foraging pigeons. She jabbed a finger at Bailey.

'You gonna rein that bitch in?'

Austin whistled.

Mona said, 'You hearing me, Red Boy?'

'Yeah,' Bailey said. 'I'm hearing you, I'm just not understanding you.'

'That bitch, Indigo. She needs to look whose man she's taking.'

Bailey kept his voice calm. 'Why you telling me?'

224

Mona had a nasty little grin on her face. 'Everyone's seen you loving up to her.' She made a big kissing noise. 'On the bus, a couple of weeks ago. My sis said it looked like you two were planning to make babies, right there and then.'

Bailey felt his face going red.

Austin cleared his throat. 'Bailey, man! My mum takes that bus!'

Mona looked like she was going to hit Austin. 'Did I ask for your contribution?' She was back, jabbing at Bailey. 'Your little nutcase took my ticket for Dubsweepers on Friday. Me and my sisters, we're going anyway. If we see her anywhere near him, man, she's going to hospital, you hear me?'

Austin stretched his hands behind his head. 'You mean she's training to be a nurse?'

Mona ignored him. Her eyes were on Bailey. He wasn't going to nod, not to her. But she must have seen something in his face, because she smiled. 'Yeah. You hear me.'

She turned round and stomped away.

Bailey looked at Austin.

Austin said, 'No.'

Bailey said, 'I didn't ask you anything.'

Austin dumped his chip wrapper in the bin. 'Yes, you did. You asked me to abandon my superior musical taste to come to Dubsweepers with you on Friday.'

'No, I didn't.'

'That's good, because I'm taking my little cousin to prayers.'

Bailey checked his phone. 'The six o'clock prayers, right?'

'I'm not telling you nothing.'

14

'Indigo!'

'What?'

'Turn it down! I'm not up for another argument with next door.'

'I thought you liked Grace Jones.'

'Not when she's louder than a jet plane.'

Indigo stared at her bare face in the mirror. She should win prizes for her 'up yours, Bailey' look. The wind must have changed this week, because this seemed the only one she could do now. It was the right look for tonight, especially as Soraya reckoned Bailey was going to be there.

The main band was supposed to be dub rap kids. She'd checked them out on YouTube, but the wobbly camera and crap sound made it impossible to see what they were about. The band was the least of her problems, though. Levy was going to try and stick his tongue in her mouth and the thought made her want to throw up. If they ended up on a bus, his hands would be burrowing away at her. If she was stupid enough to rest her head on *his* shoulder, he'd be groping at her boob. God.

Indigo held the mirror away from herself. She should

turn up like this, in her old t-shirt and PJ bottoms. No make-up, nothing. They were only going to some ratty pub in Camden. She didn't need to put herself out. She smoothed a sticky-out hair on her eyebrow. Except – she needed war paint. Proper stuff. She skimmed through pictures on her phone. Siouxie Soux? Yeah. Good look. Indigo could go a bit easier on the eyebrows, but those lips. Perfect. Indigo rubbed a spot of concealer into the dark patch under her eyes. And clothes? The tartan mini, that would do, along with the black sleeveless polo neck. She had a rubber-studded necklace somewhere. She laid the top and skirt out on the carpet, her lace-up platforms next to it. Sorted.

Levy was waiting for Indigo as she came out of the station. He was in gym-boy uniform, jeans and a tight t-shirt that showed off his muscles. His trainers looked like they'd never been worn before. He slowly looked her up and down. Mainly down.

He said, 'Nice skirt.'

'Thanks.'

He grabbed her hand. 'I got used to Mona in her heels and stuff. I like something different.'

Something? Indigo glanced downwards. All she could see was Levy's fist, her fingers lost somewhere inside. She pulled her hand out.

He frowned. 'What's up?'

'You're still technically with Mona, right?'

'Why's that matter now?'

He managed to catch Indigo's hand again, and this time he held it tighter.

Camden at night was worse than Camden by day. More foreign students, more goths, whole families of tourists and a bunch of junkies by the station trying not to look too obvious. Levy tugged her along like she was a naughty kid. Maybe he'd give her sweets at the end.

They turned into a side street with a few shops and an old pub.

'That's it,' Levy said.

He kept her hand until he pushed open the door for her. Then he stepped back, probably having a good old look at her bum as she went in ahead of him. Yes, there it was, a tiny little pat as his hand flopped down.

The pub was old-style, with a swirly red carpet and wooden tables and chairs and a few old blokes drinking pints by themselves. Levy's mates were hard to miss. Most of them had shaved heads and were crowding round a corner table, laughing and talking over each other.

One of them raised his hand. 'Hail, Levy!'

They were looking at her now. One of them gave Levy a little wink.

She looked around. 'Where are the loos?'

'Other side of the bar.' Levy pointed to some double doors. 'That's where the gig is. I'll meet you up there.'

Indigo could feel their eyes still on her as she walked to the Ladies. She dived into a cubicle and locked it. She sat down on the closed seat. Someone had scrawled 'Friday I'm In Love' in black felt-tip on the door. Good luck to them. They'd never met Levy.

Indigo should have listened to herself. She should have messaged Levy saying she had her period, or something else that he wouldn't bother to answer, because she had to admit it. This was a crap idea. It wasn't that she even wanted Levy! Him and Mona were made for each other.

But she was here now. She had to go through with it. Like Felix said, if Bailey wanted her he had to work for it. He had to see how much she was worth.

Indigo unlocked the cubicle and checked herself in the mirror. Yeah, she was still looking good. She opened the door back to the bar. Thank God, Levy and his mates had gone ahead. She pushed open the double doors and walked upstairs.

The gig room was poky and pretty empty. Levy had shown her a promo picture of the place with a crowd of people moshing at the front. It must have been a different pub or a really clever angle, because this place could never look like that. Levy was up on the small stage mucking around with some microphones. He jumped down and came towards her.

He smiled. Okay, that was one of his good points. When he smiled you felt like you were the only person in the room. Then his hand brushed her arse again, like it was a total accident.

She shifted away from him.

He said, 'My mates are over there. '

Yeah, Levy, they're the only other people here.

He moved closer and didn't even bother disguising the arse pat this time. And his hand stayed right there, on her left bum cheek.

He said, 'They're happy to guard you for the night.'

'Guard me?'

'Yeah! All my girls get treated like queens.'

He managed to snag her hand again and lead her over. She recognised a couple of them from college, but they all looked the same in their tight t-shirts, jeans, box-fresh trainers. There must be a dress code to be Levy's friend. They all looked her up and down, Levy-style.

A short one with a man bun said, 'Nice hair.'

'Thanks.'

'You're welcome. My name's Jez.' He smiled, and his eyes flicked between her face and her boobs. Great, she was going to be stuck with a peeper.

'We've grabbed a table,' Jez said. 'It can get a bit full on when the band come on. Fancy sitting down?'

'Yeah,' she said. It was near the fire exit, handy to slip out when nobody was noticing.

Austin was going to combust.

Why the hell had he let Bailey drag him out to Emo Zombieland?

Do you know what he really loved doing on Friday nights? Playing Tattooed Hipster Dodge, that's what!

He should have put his foot down!

And on and on and on. Not even Camden's noise could block him out. They pulled to a halt as a middle-aged couple in front of them stopped to take a selfie by a giant boot.

Austin sucked his teeth. 'These people never seen a big shoe before?'

Bailey swerved round them. 'Come on!'

'Do you know what, man? We're going to get there and they won't let me in.'

'Why?'

'Because you ain't nobody without some ear stretchers.'

'There's a place over there if you're desperate.' And a bus stop. Bailey didn't need Austin. It had been a reflex to ask him, but there were times when his mouth was a liability. Tonight looked like one of those times. But here he was, trying to keep pace with Bailey, fighting through the tourist jam.

Bailey checked his phone. 'This way.'

They peered down a side street. A group of white guys with shaved heads were smoking outside a rundown pub on the corner.

Austin chuckled. 'You seriously want me to go in there?'

'You don't have to. I'll be all right.'

Austin shook his head. 'You dragged me here, bruv. I want to see things through.'

A black guy in a suit and trilby came out of the pub and started talking to the smokers. They flicked their cigarette butts on to the ground and followed him inside.

Bailey bit back his smile. 'Old-school ska, skinhead-style. My dad's era.'

'Pity. If I had a choice between knucklehead racists and Mona on the rampage, I'd probably take the racists. Better chance of survival.'

Bailey looked up to the second-floor windows. What was he expecting? Indigo sitting on a windowsill, letting her hair down for him?

Austin pushed the door open. 'You coming?'

They walked through the empty saloon bar. As they pushed open the double doors at the end, the dub beat banged down the stairs towards them. Bailey bought tickets from the girl at the table outside and they went in.

The room was hot and loud. A small stage was set up for the band at the end, a drum kit, a keyboard, an army of mics. It was going to be a tight fit up there.

Austin wrinkled his nose. 'Do they wash the walls with Stella, or something?'

'I can't see if Indigo's here,' Bailey said. 'Let's get to the front.'

'That's wall-to-wall people. I'm not breaking my way through that.'

'Suit yourself.'

The DJ flicked 'Mute' on the dub and a small cheer went up. The girls in front must have sewn their shoulders together. Bailey stood on tiptoes. He could just see the black guy's trilby.

Austin said, 'If you can't see Indigo, Mona can't, neither.'

'You think that's going to stop Mona?' Austin should know better. Mona would steam through the crowd with her sisters, knocking heads together like bowling pins.

'So what's your plan? You taking on muscle-boy Levy?'

'Indigo isn't like Mona. She doesn't want men fighting over her.'

'The last few days, it looks like she doesn't want you at all. Ever going to tell me what happened?'

'Nothing to tell, bruv.'

'That's why we're stuck in this dump on a Friday night. Because there's nothing to tell.'

More people were squeezing into the small room. Bailey's t-shirt was damp from heat; at least this black

Ramones one hid the sweat. The girls in front suddenly shifted apart so Bailey could see the stage. The black guy was obviously still talking, but his words were drowned out by the noise bouncing off the walls.

'They have to sort that mic,' Austin said.

'They are. And look who's doing it.'

Levy was at the edge of the stage, adjusting a guitar lead. He moved to the back and tweaked a drum mic. He should just let loose his tentacles and sort all the instruments at the same time.

Bailey said, 'If he's there, Indigo's by herself.'

'If she's here at all. I reckon she's tucked up in bed laughing herself sick because you and Levy are idiots.'

'I'm going to have a look.'

'And then what?'

'Get her out of here. Try and talk to her.'

'When you're done, come and get me. I'll be outside getting fresh air. Even my spit's tasting of Camden Brew.'

Bailey watched Austin push himself backwards through the crowd. Maybe he'd carry on down the road and go home.

The wall of bodies had fixed itself solid ahead. Indigo was on the other side of it. He knew she was. And if Mona got here first, things were going to get way too complicated. A cheer went up. Overhead lights gleamed off the shaved heads that were coming on to stage. A trombone solo –

Bailey could just about see the shine off the brass. The beat kicked in. So did the dancing. Bailey took a deep breath and began weaving through the crowd. A dark ponytail swished against his face. Indigo? He dodged round two old blokes and looked back. How the hell did he think one of those old boys could be her? He pushed his way forward and she was there. There! Standing right up close to the stage. A smile started in Bailey's chest and worked its way towards his face.

Indigo turned away from the stage and scanned the crowd. Just for a second, her eyes locked on to Bailey's. They widened and she quickly looked away again. But she stayed where she was.

A hand clamped down on Bailey's shoulder. Austin looked like he'd just run round the block.

'They're here!'

'Who?'

'Who the hell do you think? Mona! She's got Renée with her and some other girl I don't want to be starting a fight with. It's like Charlie's Angels went rogue.'

Bailey tried to peer over Austin's shoulders, but all he could see was bouncing dancers.

'Where are they?'

'There's a back way, a fire exit.'

'Shit.'

On stage, the band was still blasting, but some of the crowd seemed to have lost interest. Something better was obviously happening at the side of the stage. Bailey took a deep breath and shouldered his way through, Austin following.

A tall guy in front wouldn't give way, but Bailey could see Mona, screwface, chin jutting forward, hands on hip. Bailey elbowed past, ignoring the tall guy sucking his teeth and muttering. There was Indigo. Dead still, screwfacing it right back. He opened his mouth to call her, but held it in. If she looked away, Mona would go for her.

Austin nudged Bailey. 'Look, man, see? There's three of them. Charlie's Demons.'

'Shut up!'

Austin was right, though. Mona had back-up. The tall one in the glitter boots, that was her sister, Renée. The other girl in the red stretchy dress? She looked like she could be a sister too. They were standing right behind Mona, like they were going to break into a dance routine. Except, their faces were mean, as if the only reason they'd come was to punch people.

Indigo hadn't moved. Is that how it happened at school? Just before? No, when she'd flipped it had been quick. That's what had made his heart beat. But maybe that thing didn't always burst out. Maybe it uncoiled slowly, waiting before it attacked. And if it did, all the idiots here would have their phones in the air filming her. There'd be strangers round the world sniggering and sharing stupid comments.

That slimeball, Levy, jumped off the side of the stage, and gave his mates a thumbs-up.

Bailey moved forwards. Indigo moved even quicker, a hard push that sent Mona flying backwards. Austin gasped and Bailey felt his own breath stick. Mona's pin heels skidded on a patch of wet floor and she lurched into the girl in the stretchy dress. Stretchy-dress girl was knocked off balance and both of them slammed into an old white guy in a pork pie hat. Austin whistled and clapped.

Renée spun round towards him. 'This funny too?'

Her arm swung back ready to clout Austin. He dodged away in good time. With a mouth like his, he'd had plenty of practice.

'Calm yourself!' A bouncer planted himself between Renée and Austin.

'It was her!' Austin was pointing. 'Didn't you see?'

'Grass!' Renée pushed past the bouncer. 'You need big man to fight for you?'

The bouncer was smiling, shaking his head. 'That's enough, love.'

'Enough?' Renée let loose a string of cuss at the bouncer. The band had stopped playing and was watching from the stage, the trombonist holding his instrument like he was about to add musical accompaniment. Levy appeared next to Mona, smiling and suckering her towards him. She was yelling, pulling away, but not too hard.

Indigo? A fire exit door at the right of the stage was edging shut. The sound system kicked in again, blasting bass-heavy dub. Maybe the organisers thought the beats would weigh everyone down. The girl in the stretchy dress was yelling at Austin, but Austin was giving it back good. The bouncer looked like he was trying to work out what to do with them. Mona's mouth had slowed, but now her and Levy were both hard-eyeing Bailey. He backed out of the fire exit, ran down the stairs and banged out of the door on to the street.

He was in an alleyway, home to every wheelie bin in Camden. The dub from upstairs was still loud, but other noises were mixing in – the honk of a lorry horn, bus engines, a traffic light beeping. He wasn't far from the main road. Austin was still up there. The dub cut off and a cheer went up as the band started back up. Everything had calmed down. Austin would survive. He always did. Right now, Bailey needed to find Indigo.

The alleyway opened on to a small car park on a council estate. Bailey walked through, eyes on his phone. Indigo wasn't replying. Did she even come this way? He tried again. **Where are you?** He turned on to a one-way system with a bus stop a few metres away. It was empty. Left took him towards Camden Market and the canal, right and it was the main bus route back to Hackney. Knowing his luck, whichever way he went, Indigo would have gone the opposite.

His phone flashed up an image. Camden Lock. Indigo's number.

There was a caption. **5 mins, right?**

Yes. If he was beamed up and teleported.

He hurtled across the road to catch the bus towards Camden centre.

Indigo pressed her back against the wall. If she pressed any harder she'd crash right through it. If she was dropped off the roof of that clothes shop, she'd hit the pavement and bounce right up again, powering all the way to the moon. She must be glowing, full of the stuff that turned skinny boys into superheroes.

Indigo had won. She'd won! There she was, face to Mona's mutt-face and the thing was full-on scrabbling inside her, hooking its way up, fast, like there was a rocket underneath. Then she'd seen Bailey and it was like it lost its grip. Yeah, Indigo had pushed that bitch, Mona. Yeah, Indigo had been mad. But it was all her own mad. It came from her head, not from the heat and dark inside her.

The thing usually wiped her brain. It was like its way of forcing her to do it again and again and again. But Indigo could remember every detail of what just happened and it was making her glow more. Levy's pervy smirk. Mona's bright-blue nail tips grabbing at the air. Her girl-gang mate bouncing back against the poor old bloke behind her.

Bailey, his mouth open like he was calling her.

A tall, slim black girl was clicking along the street opposite – short tartan skirt, black top, heels, almost the same stuff as Indigo. She was taking quick, long steps, head held high. She knew she looked good. But yeah, Indigo looked good too.

Indigo checked the time. Was he seriously going to make it in five? It had taken her over twenty minutes to get here. She'd walked round that bloody council estate twice by mistake. Two minutes left. *Please, Bailey. While I'm still glowing.*

Indigo moved over to the low wall on the bridge over the canal. A couple of girls were making out by the lock gates. They hadn't even bothered to take off their big rucksacks. They just had to kiss each other right then, right there, no matter what people thought. Indigo knew that feeling. Even with tequila burning her tongue and three dudes dressed like women chucking clubs at each other and homeless guys guilt-tripping tourists for money, even with all that, she'd *had* to kiss Bailey in Covent Garden.

'Oi, bruv! Down there!' A short boy who could have been a reject from Levy's tight t-shirt posse was hanging over the wall. He turned and grinned at Indigo like she was part of the joke. 'A couple of lesbos! Look!'

His mate shook his head. He was about twenty with a harsh undercut and a flop of dark hair on top. 'I'm sorry about him. He doesn't get out much.' He really did look a bit embarrassed.

The girls had separated. One of them, the tallest one, flicked two Vs. Some of the drinkers outside the waterside bar cheered her. Reject stuck up his finger and twisted. Indigo turned away. Reject was close enough for people to think she was with him.

His mate said, 'We're heading to Red Dog. If I get him under control, fancy joining us?'

Indigo shook her head. 'I'm waiting for someone.'

He smiled. 'Don't blame you.'

He nudged Reject and they wandered away. This time last year, she'd have given it proper thought. She'd have convinced herself it could be fun even while 'No' flashed up in her head like the red traffic-light man. But she was learning to listen to 'Stop'. Maybe she was changing. She didn't have to flip and freak out. She didn't have to smile at idiot boys just because they talked to her. Green man. Walk on.

Reject and his mate disappeared behind a crowd of early clubbers. Indigo turned back to the canal. The water was too far away to see her smile in it.

Down by the lock gate, another couple were swallowing each other's tongues. Some YouTube kid must be filming a lipsin' marathon there. It was a boy and a girl, this time, dressed like they'd just left an office. Suddenly, the girl swung away, bent over and threw up in the canal. Her boyfriend jumped back and stared at her. When she'd finished, he put an arm round her and led her away down the towpath. Respect to him.

'Indigo?'

Her heart flicked against her rib cage.

Bailey was crossing the road towards her. Her mouth was taking charge before her brain kicked in, grinning at him. She was still glowing, though, and grinning *was* normal. She pushed herself away from the wall. He stopped in front of her. His face was shiny with sweat.

She placed her palm on his cheek. 'Better?'

He nodded.

He leaned forward and kissed her forehead. If he had X-ray eyes, he'd see heart dents inside her ribs. Her arms ached to stretch round him.

But he took her hand. That would do for now.

He said, 'I think we need to talk.'

'Yeah.' And even though he sounded like a social worker, she smiled.

They headed down the steps towards the market. Most of the stalls and shops were still open and along the canal, an army of food trucks wafted smells around them. A bloke in a bright green waistcoat had set up an old-school ghetto blaster on a bench. The music was tinny, almost lost under everything else.

They crossed the bridge and stopped halfway, shoulder to shoulder, staring out at Camden.

She looked down at his reflection. 'Levy's a bit of a meathead.'

'Yeah. Him and Mona deserve each other.'

She nudged his shoulder. 'Did you and her deserve each other?'

'Ummmm.' He laughed. 'Probably. I think she went out with me for a dare, but we got on all right. Then she fell in with Saskia and got a bit stupid.'

'How long were you together?'

'A few months. Not long.' Bailey's hand slid closer to Indigo's on the railing. 'Why?'

'Just trying to work out why she's on at me.'

'She thought you stole her meathead.'

She frowned at the watery Bailey. His little finger stretched out to stroke her thumb. 'It's just if . . . you and me . . .' If they what? 'I don't want to have to deal with her crap.'

'She'll get bored.'

'Bloody hope so. It's like she's deliberately winding me up, like she wants to make me . . . you know. Go mad.' The words fell out of her before she could stop them. 'Did you and her ever . . . did you?'

'Did we what? Oh. We were at a party once and ended up in a spare room. We got pretty close, I think.'

She raised her eyebrows. 'You think? You don't know for sure?'

'There was never really the right time. Or the right place. And my parents gave me this lecture about how important it was that sex was dignified.'

Laughter exploded out of her. 'Dignified?'

'Yes. They gave me rules. Girls had to be over sixteen, as much over as possible, and we had to use condoms.'

'Did you ever bring anyone home?'

'With Mum doing spelling corrections in the room below? No chance.'

She turned sideways so his arm slid away. 'Keely does late shifts sometimes.'

'Does she?'

For God's sake! How long did he need to work it out?

She walked the rest of the way across the bridge.

'Indigo!' He ran to catch up with her. 'Sorry! I just didn't think . . . I didn't think we'd got that far yet.'

Her felt her face flush. 'Aren't I worth it?'

Splashes of orange spun in the air. The busker by the Lock market was juggling fire.

'Indigo, you are worth it.' He turned her face towards him. In this light, his eyes were as dark as the canal. 'The first time you came into our class, I couldn't stop looking at you.'

'I know.'

'You noticed?'

'It was hard not to. Especially with your big-mouthed mate spreading the word.'

Now Bailey smiled. 'Austin's all right.'

'If you say so.'

'I just didn't think things were that serious between us yet. I thought they were and then you blanked me and went off with Levy.'

'I'm sorry.' She stepped towards him and linked her hands around his back, resting her head on his chest. He was damp. He must have run most of the way to get to her quick.

'Don't be. Indigo, there are things I have to tell you.'

His thighs rubbed against hers. His cheek was resting on her hair. She had to hold this moment, somewhere safe, but where she could pull it out when she needed it. She could feel his words on her skin.

She said, 'Sorry?'

He pulled away. 'Indigo! Didn't you hear anything I said?'

'Photo something? Sorry. Oh, Jesus!'

'What?'

Of course, his back was to it.

A tramp was peeing into a bush. His trousers were piled around his ankles, bare arse on show. It was just like that kid in Edmonton. An older version.

'That's disgusting,' Indigo said.

Bailey was biting his lip. It made his face lopsided. 'Maybe he can't help it.'

'Yes, he can! I was put in this home once, one of the temporary ones. There was this kid who had all sorts of head-crap going on. Every time a new kid came, he'd break into their room and pee over their stuff. I had these new pyjamas and a load of make-up in my bag. Nobody warned me because he'd peed on all their stuff too. I opened my bag and everything was all swishing around.'

'Shit!'

'Nah. But maybe I was just lucky.'

He frowned. 'Oh, my God!'

And he was laughing again. She wanted it to go on and on.

'Come on.' She nudged him. 'We don't want to watch him finish.'

The tramp was standing back, like he was admiring his work. He yanked up his trousers and stumbled off.

Bailey said, 'It sounds like you went through some really rough stuff.'

She shrugged. 'It's all in the past. I can't change any of it, can I?'

'But it seems . . . I don't know. Really big. You found your sister . . . there might be other people in your family. What if they want to get in touch?'

My beautiful Indigo,

Time is short. This morning I woke up in a strange room, but they said I have lived here for many months now.

She let her fingers slide down his palm. 'I'm starving. Fancy getting me a hot dog?'

He sighed. 'You might have to have it with chipotle chutney.'

She screwed up her face. 'Better go down the kebab shop, then.'

15

'Bailey!'

One day, Dad would realise that he didn't have to knock so hard.

The bedroom door opened a slit and Dad's face peered through. 'You haven't forgotten, have you?'

'No, Dad.'

'Get up, then!'

Bailey's phone said 10.30 a.m. The alarm should have gone off an hour ago. Bailey examined the settings. Nice one. It was set for 9.30 p.m.

Dad rapped on the door again. 'Come on!'

'Coming!'

Dad'd better be bloody quick. Indigo said 11 o'clock. Dead on. Bailey rolled out of bed and glanced at the mirror opposite. He looked like he was planning a session of serial killing. He seriously needed to sort those afro clumps before he dialled up Indigo. He wiped sleepy dust out of his eye and tried to tease out his hair. The back was squashed, but that could wait. It wasn't like she was going to see that bit on Skype. He opened his door and plodded upstairs.

Dad had already carried the desk chair from the music room to the top floor and positioned it under the loft hatch.

Dad said, 'Hold it, can you?'

Bailey gripped the chair back. As Dad climbed on, the seat kept trying to swivel away. Bailey held it tighter. Right now, Indigo was getting ready. She'd promised something a bit special today. It was like she felt she had to make it up to him. Just when things were getting good between them, she had to go and spend half term with her mate. It was good that she was going. Bailey got it. Indigo and Mischa had been tight at their last home and Mischa was having a crap time with men. She was lonely and had no one else. And yes, he was a bit sad wanting her here with him. But he did want her. If he wasn't careful, when he called her up, he'd be gawping at her in the same way Shuu stared at Dad when he tipped out the Cat Treats.

'You got it, Bailey?'

'Yeah.'

Dad eased the cover to the loft hatch aside, grabbed the edges of the loft and heaved himself up and in. A click and the loft light was on.

'Blimey,' Dad said. 'We need a serious clear out in here.'

He'd said that the last time. And the time before that. But the boxes of stuff never moved, though once he'd come down with a gig programme signed by Joe Strummer from The Clash. It was a present from Mum. Another time, Dad had found an old photo album from their early days together. They'd seemed to spend half their time on protest marches.

'Okay,' Dad called down. 'I can see them.'

Good. Bailey needed to be in front of his laptop very soon and without the mad hair. Indigo reckoned that time was tight, just until Mischa came back from taking her kid to the doctor's.

'Ready, Bailey?'

A small red suitcase dangled from the hatch. Bailey grabbed it and propped it by the airing cupboard. Dad poked his head out. A few threads of cobweb dangled from his eyebrow.

'Your old highchair's up here!'

'I know. You told me last time.'

Dad sighed. 'We really need to pass it on.'

His head disappeared again. *Hurry up!* Bailey should have just got a train and gone up to Lincoln to see her. But when he'd suggested it, she'd been really annoyed. This was her time to spend with her mate. Then she'd come up with the Skype dates. Pity Mischa was never out at the same time his parents were. Thanks to Dad, today's chat was going to be really quick. It was probably just as well. Yesterday, he'd almost tipped the photo out of the envelope and showed her.

'Here!' Dad's grey case was hanging down now. Its corners

were worn and frayed and one of the wheels looked wonky.

'You sure about this, Dad?'

'It's good for one more go.'

Bailey took the case and rested it next to Mum's. Dad manoeuvred himself from the loft on to the chair, closed the hatch and jumped to the floor. He flicked the cobwebs from his head.

'I'm glad you're going,' Bailey said.

Dad gave him a suspicious look. 'Why's that, Bailey?'

'Mum didn't seem into it, but you managed to talk her around. What's stressing her?'

'She's got a lot of work on.' He hoisted up the chair. 'Can you get the door for me?'

Bailey went ahead, opening up the music room. Dad skirted round the guitars and plonked the chair with its back against the desk.

'We done, Dad?'

Dad sat down. *No!* He had his social-worker face on too. Why the hell had Bailey left his laptop here, sitting on the desk behind Dad? His phone was all right for Skype, but Indigo said the bigger screen was better.

Bailey said, 'Is this the take-care-of-the-house lecture?'

'You're not my worry, Bailey. It's Austin.'

'It's all right, Dad.'

Dad wiggled the seat to and fro, making it squeak. 'The problem is, I was once a teenage boy too and your

252

look of innocence is making me very worried indeed.'

10.59 a.m. Indigo was opening her laptop, calling up the connection. Dad didn't look like he wanted to move. He had to be given something. Something honest and appropriate.

'Well, there is one thing, Dad.'

'Uh-huh?'

'I've told Austin he can come round on Friday. It's just to play some games, same way we do at his house. And you know no one would dare mess up Austin's.'

'Games?'

Yesterday, Indigo had laid out everything on the bed so Bailey could see. Skinny leg jeans, Banshees t-shirt, bright red bra, tiny knickers. She'd been sitting there in a little shirt and shorts. Then that ruddy toddler burst in and jumped on her back.

'I said *what kind of games*, Bailey.'

Dad was sipping at the info. He needed a bigger gulp.

'Um . . .' Bailey lowered his voice. 'Some of the ones Mum doesn't like. Maybe GTA 5. Or Bloodborne.'

'Ah.'

Squeak, squeak. To and fro.

'And that's all?'

'Yes, Dad.' And it must be eleven now. Maybe just past. And, yes! Dad was standing up!

'Don't let me down, Bailey.'

Dad was fully vertical. He was patting Bailey's shoulder. Dad was out of the door!

Bailey grabbed the laptop and sat down, back against the closed door. He logged on and plugged in the headphones. The Skype icon was already flashing.

'Hey!' Indigo blew him a kiss. Her hair looked soaking wet, hanging loose and heavy and clinging to her bare shoulders. A trickle of water was running down the centre of her chest. His minimised face on the screen looked like a cartoon, wide eyes and open mouth.

She'd said it was going to be something special.

'Indigo?' He just managed to keep a stage whisper.

She moved her phone down and up, so he could see the towel wrapped round her. He could make out tiles behind her; she was sitting on the edge of a bath.

She said, 'I thought you'd blown me out.'

'Sorry. I had to do something for Dad.'

'We haven't got long.' She held the phone further away; the wire to her earbuds pulled taut. Grey tiles, a blue wall, a soap dish stuck on to a wall. She hooked her fingers into the edge of towel, where it was tucked under to keep it together. 'Are you ready?'

'Yeah.' Little screen-Bailey licked his lips. Jesus, he looked like one of those dodgy blokes in a crime reconstruction. He wiped his mouth. That was even worse.

Indigo tugged the towel apart. She was wearing a

strapless bra underneath. It was pulled tight across her breasts, damp from her skin. She gave him a little shimmy. She spun round, looking behind her. Bailey heard hammering on the door at her end.

'Shit!' She pulled the towel back around her. 'The little sod's back already.'

She blew him another kiss and killed the connection.

Bailey closed the laptop and sat back. His heart was running double-time and his head must be burning a hole through the door. Out on the landing, Dad was on the phone. It sounded like he was talking to the agency, organising work for when he came back from Paris. And in four days' time, he and Mum would be gone.

Indigo stuck her hair up in a band and wrapped it in the towel. Nial was supposed to have chicken pox but if this was what he was like when he was ill – God, no wonder Mischa was washed out. Indigo rubbed in her body lotion and slipped on her jeans and t-shirt. They were a bit wet from the shower, but it was easier to dress in here than in the kid's room. Even though he was supposed to be in with Mischa, he wasn't giving up his room easily.

She opened the bathroom door.

'So what's his name?' Mischa was waiting outside. There was a slight smile on her lips.

'Huh?'

'You've started talking to yourself, then.'

'Of course not.'

'Jesus, Indi! You weren't flashing your bits in there, were you?'

'No!'

Mischa was giving out the hard look. Nial shuffled over and pushed his hand against Indigo's, wanting her to hold it. His fingers were covered in something sticky.

'It's all right, baby.' It was funny how Mischa's voice had got all soft since she'd had Nial. 'Me and Aunty Indigo are just talking. Nothing bad.'

Nial squeezed Indigo's hand tighter. Indigo unstuck herself, picked him up and kissed the bit of cheek that wasn't covered in goo. He wriggled round until he was balanced on her hip and put his arms round her neck.

'It's okay, Nial.'

They stared at each other. There was a dribble of honey by the side of his mouth. She wiped it away with a corner of towel.

She said, 'Do you want to go and play now?'

He nodded.

Indigo lowered him to the ground and he ran towards the sitting room. He dived straight into the fort they'd built out of sofa cushions.

'He's going to miss you,' Mischa said.

'He's lucky. He's got you.'

'Yeah,' Mischa laughed. 'He is bloody lucky, right?'

They moved into the kitchen. It must have started off as a cupboard, before the council found out they could fit a tiny fridge in it.

Indigo pulled out the stool from under the breakfast bar. Nial's cornflakes were still splashed across the counter.

'You're really good with him, Misch.'

Mischa grinned. 'I know! Better than expected, right? Want a drink?'

'Yeah. Thanks.'

Mischa opened the baby fridge and took out two cans of lemonade. There wasn't much else in there with them. Indigo must do a little shop for her tomorrow. Mischa leaned against the door frame so she could see into the sitting room.

'Who is he, then?'

'Who?'

'If you weren't talking to yourself, there must have been someone on the other end.'

'His name's Bailey.'

'How old?'

'Same as me.'

'Another bad boy?'

Indigo laughed. 'His dad's a social worker.'

'Are you serious?'

Indigo pulled the tab on her lemonade. It was the

own-brand stuff where they designed the can to look cheap. 'You make it sound like he's a nonce or something.'

'No . . . it's just . . . I dunno. I never thought you'd get into goody-goodies. Or . . .' Mischa gave her an evil wink. 'Has he gone the other way? You know, like the girl in *Footloose*.'

Indigo took a sip. It had that weird taste from when they took out the sugar and put chemicals in instead.

'He's a bit good.'

So good, his eyeballs nearly hit the camera when he saw her bra. If that was Stivo or Levy, they'd be yelling for her to take it off.

'A bit good. Right.'

The TV blasted on in the sitting room. Indigo almost fell off her stool.

'Is that Nial?'

'Yeah. I've tried hiding the remote, but he just screams. And anyway, I don't worry if he watches a bit of telly. We do other stuff too. He's a real star at his nursery.' Mischa slugged back some lemonade and made a face. 'I forgot how rank this is. But don't change the subject. You and Bailey. How far you got?'

'Mischa!' Sodding blushing made it look all wrong. 'It's just really started.'

'Aw, bless. Enjoy it while you can.'

'Mummy?'

Nial was so small next to Mischa. How could anything that tiny keep its balance?

Mischa hoisted him on to her hip. 'Okay, hun. We're going to the park soon.'

He pointed at Indigo.

'Yes, Aunty Indigo's coming too. And we're going to pack your bag for Dad's, right?'

Nial nodded.

'It's good Geoff's still about,' Indigo said. 'Most guys would have scarpered.'

Mischa lifted the can to Nial's mouth. Lemonade dripped down his chin.

'It's always been a big love job. Soon as he saw Nial. No questions asked.'

Indigo took the tiniest sip and put the can down. '"No questions"? What was he supposed to ask?'

'Geoff might be a bit dumb, but he can count.'

'But you and him got together in Worcester House, right?'

'Yeah.'

'Not bad, since boys and girls were supposed to be on different landings.'

Mischa shook her head. 'That's where we met. Everything else came a bit later. And yeah, those care workers had invisible tripwires and Superman ears. Nothing got past them.'

Nial kicked his legs against Mischa's side. She plonked him on the floor and he ran back to the telly.

'Nine months back from Nial, Geoff was in prison.'

'Serious?'

'Yeah. Just coming up for trial. He pounded some corner shop guy who wouldn't give him credit on cigs. He went down for eight months and served five.'

'Jesus, Misch! He never did that stuff to you, did he?'

'No! We weren't really together then, though he'd still come round sometimes. He was taking stuff that was making him a bit psycho. I really didn't need the aggro.'

'And Geoff was all right about Nial?'

'I was the only one going to see him when he was inside. When I started showing, he wasn't going to tell the lads it wasn't his, was he? He got out just after Nial was born. He said he always wanted a son.'

'And he seriously didn't mind that you'd gone with someone else?'

''Course he did! I was every kind of slag going, but in his head, Nial was separate.'

Indigo nodded towards the sitting room. 'You ever going to tell him?'

Mischa shrugged. 'If him and Geoff stay good, why bother?'

'And if they don't stay good?'

'I dunno. What am I going to say? I met your real dad at

260

Flamingo's and had a one off?'

'No, Misch. You don't have to say it like that.'

'Right, Indi. What about "the bloke you think is your dad couldn't be because he was in prison for beating up an old Asian guy who didn't want to give him free stuff"?' Mischa lifted the can to her lips then suddenly emptied the drink into the sink. 'It's shit, Indi. I'm just doing the same bollocks my mum did.'

The can slammed into the bin. The TV must have turned off because everything was silent.

Indigo slid off her stool and put her arm round Mischa. 'You're doing all right, Mischa. Really all right. Nial's lovely.'

Mischa wiped her eyes on her sleeve. 'Yeah. I know. I think I'm just a bit jealous of you. I'm glad you've found a good one. Even if you're giving him a flash-up in my bathroom.'

'I. Am. Not.'

Mischa laughed. 'So stop blushing, then.'

The bus was jolting like it wanted to bump Indigo out of Bailey's head. That wasn't happening. There wasn't just one Indigo in there, there were billions of them, printed on every cell in his brain, and all of them were Indigo in the bra that was like a white skin, with the trickle of water running down her chest.

The bus stopped and he crossed over to Austin's block.

He pressed the buzzer. And again. He tapped up another message, but they must be stacked in Austin's storage like Lego bricks. He buzzed again.

'What?' London accent. Female. Must be Binrin.

'It's Bailey. Is Austin there?'

Pause. 'You might as well come up.'

The door clicked and Bailey pushed it open. He walked the stairs up to the third floor. Austin must live in the sweetest smelling block of flats in London, though knowing Austin's mum, she was never going to let the cleaners skimp on bleach and freshener. Bailey knocked on the door. It was funny how the planters bolted beneath the windows seemed to have found their own sun-spot. One year, Austin's mum had grown chillies there and he and Austin had dared each other to eat a whole one. Bailey had thought it would impress Binrin.

Binrin was holding the door open, looking as unimpressed now as she was then.

She said, 'You need to get them back together, before all the food goes sour.'

'Who?'

She made her face. 'You're a crap friend, aren't you? Didn't you hear? My little bruv got dumped.'

'Soraya dumped him?'

'Yeah.'

'Damn!'

'Exactly.' Binrin moved aside to let him in. 'How come you don't know?'

'He's been playing hard to get.'

'After you left him to get beaten up in the pub?'

'You've only heard his side.' Though she wasn't far off. 'Is he in his room?'

Binrin nodded. 'What's in your bag?'

Bailey held it up. 'Biscuits.'

'Good ones?'

'Oreos, double chocolate.'

'Good call.'

Austin's door opened down the hallway. He glared at Bailey. 'I thought I was having a nightmare. Then it turned out to be true.'

Binrin rolled her eyes. 'Drama King.'

'Freezer Queen.'

'Yeah. Whatever.'

Austin shut his bedroom door and nodded towards the kitchen. *Jeremy Kyle* suddenly blasted out from the sitting room.

As usual, Austin's kitchen looked like the 'after' scene from an advert for anti-germ cleaner. Bailey sat down at the only wooden table he'd ever seen that had no rings on it. Austin turned his back to fill the kettle.

Bailey said, 'What happened?'

'When?' Austin snatched teabags out of the canister and

threw them in mugs. 'When you left me to get killed by the Camden hillbillies? Or when Soraya made me feel like Levy's dick?'

'What?'

Austin held his thumb and finger close together. 'This big.'

'I take your word for that.'

'I don't know for sure. I'm only estimating. Coasters, please.'

Bailey spread a couple on the table and Austin banged down the tea. Bailey held out the bag of biscuits.

Austin looked inside. 'Seriously? No ginger nuts?'

'You know I don't like them.'

'So even biscuits are about you.'

Austin skimmed another coaster on to the table, followed by a plate. He emptied the Oreos on to it.

Bailey took a sip of tea. Why did Austin's brew always taste like it had passed through a cat first? 'At least you're not in lock-up.'

Austin's face hardened. 'You still think this is funny? You blew me out. You let me down. Then you abandoned me to a bunch of demon witches and a bruiser from Jamaica on a mission to kill all Nigerians.'

'You mean the bouncer? He really said that?'

'Action speaks louder than words.'

'Did you run your mouth off at him?'

264

Austin slurped his tea. 'Yeah. Right. Blame the victim.'

'I'm sorry, man. Really.' He examined Austin's face. 'You don't look damaged.'

'When that girl in the red dress kicked him, he lost interest in me. Anyway, it's been so long, damage would have healed by now.' He gave Bailey a side-eye. 'Was it worth it? You know, abandoning your lifelong best friend?'

Indigo, in the bathroom with her towel open. 'What can I say?'

'Nothing. Your face says it already.' Austin dunked his biscuit. When he lifted it out, the bottom half crumbled back into the mug. 'Jesus.' He pushed the tea away.

'What happened with Soraya?' Bailey said. 'I thought you and her were . . .' He hooked his fingers together. 'Like that.'

'That's the problem.' Austin hooked his own fingers together. 'None of that at all.'

'But she told you from the start that wasn't going to happen.'

'She changed her mind.'

'She did?'

Austin took his mug over to the sink and emptied out the biscuit mush. He swilled it with water and refilled the kettle.

'She said it's been a while now. That things were proper between us. She thought we should move it along.'

265

'So why aren't you celebrating?'

Austin gave a dignified sniff. 'Shows how little you know me.' He made a new mug of tea and sat down again.

'You're saving yourself, then?'

'Yeah,' Austin said. 'From instant death. You seen her dad?'

'He's the one with the mobile phone stall, right?'

'The man makes his own eclipse. You want to talk to him? You need a climbing rope to get close enough to his ears.'

'Has he had a word with you?'

Austin shook his head. 'He doesn't know I exist.'

'Even now? Man, that's impressive! How d'you manage that?'

'Soraya's got five brothers and sisters. All of them look out for each other.'

Bailey tried another mouthful of tea. 'So why does she want to risk it?'

'She thinks I'm getting it somewhere else.'

'Are you?'

Half a biscuit shot across the table and bounced off Bailey's nose. 'I'm telling you this stuff and all you can do is take the piss.' Austin stood up. 'That's why I didn't bother messaging you.'

He stalked off back to his bedroom, slamming the door. Binrin stuck her head out of the sitting room.

'He's proper cut up, you know. Sort it out, Bailey!' She noticed the biscuit on the kitchen floor. 'And you'd better sort that out too.'

Bailey retrieved the Oreo and stuck it in the bin. In the sitting room, a couple were yelling at each other about DNA results.

Bailey knocked on Austin's door. 'Come on, mate!'

'Go away!'

Bailey opened the door. Austin was lying on his bed, the boot-up screen for *Assassin's Creed* flickering on his big monitor.

'Sorry, Austin.' Bailey stepped over a heap of trainers and sat on the armchair. The FIFA whiteboard was propped next to it, still declaring him and Austin as winners of the last tournament.

He said, 'D'you remember that homeless bloke on the bus?'

Austin didn't answer.

'Remember? He called out Saskia for giving Indigo crap and grabbed Indigo's bag for me.'

Nothing.

'It was him who collapsed the other day. I was with him when it happened.'

'So he's your new lifelong best friend then?'

'No. He kidnapped Indigo when she was a baby.'

Austin rolled on to his side and stared at him. 'He. Did. What?'

'It's all a bit weird. Indigo lived with her grandparents when she was little. The homeless guy's called JJ and I think he's Indigo's uncle.'

'Her uncle's a hobo? And he kidnapped her?'

'Jesus, Austin! He's not a hobo.'

'Sorry, Bailey. My dad isn't a social worker. In our house, we call them hobos. And that's the thing you're stressing about? Because I said "hobo"? Priorities, man. What does he want?'

'He says he wants to get Indigo back in touch with her granddad. Her grandma died earlier this year and JJ thinks . . . I don't know. He wants them to be a family.'

'So why doesn't he do it himself?'

'He said Indigo's gran was already a bit ill and he made her worse when he kidnapped Indigo from under her nose.'

'So you're his foot soldier?'

'Very funny.'

Austin sat up. 'I mean it. Your dad knows about all this stuff, you talked to him?'

'I'm talking to you, mate.'

'Only because I'm pissed at you.' Austin turned back to face the wall. 'Some hobo turns up out of the blue. He's got you running round doing his business and you don't have no clue who he is. Good luck with that.'

Bailey stood up. 'Thanks for the advice.'

'Any day. And don't even think of cancelling the

gathering. I'm going to tell Soraya about it now. Just in case. Indigo coming?'

'Yeah.' Straight from the station, to be with him.

'And she'll be hanging out the whole weekend, right?'

'Maybe.'

'That's a yes, then.'

16

Why did Dad always dump the Hoover in the right place to catch Bailey's toe? Just a little to the left and Bailey would skim past it. But here, just here, it always got him. Dad must run a special computer programme that calculated the best position and angle of hose placement to bash Bailey's foot.

Dad must be hinting, though. Reminding Bailey to give the place a good clear up before he and Mum got back.

His phone buzzed. It was from Dad, a picture of Mum outside their hotel. She still didn't look like she was in the holiday mood.

Bailey checked the time. He had to get a move on. Jeans on, t-shirt, hoodie, notepad, pencils. Trainers, door key, done. Shuu would have to wait for breakfast until he came back. She was hardly in danger of starving.

He jogged towards JJ's bus stop. Weird how Bailey almost expected to see the trackies and beanie as he got closer. Not today, though. There was just an old Turkish-looking woman with a trolley. He was only going two stops, but any time saved was good.

When he passed this bus stop on the way back, would it

still belong to 'JJ'? Or would he have another name?

Another phone message. It was Indigo. She'd been out shopping with Mischa and had just made it to Lincoln station. She was going to drop her bags home before coming round to Bailey's.

Brilliant. It gave Bailey more time.

And she was coming. He wanted that so much, but it was like he was Harvey Dent from *Batman*. What if he found out something today that burned him badly? He'd be the Hackney Two-Face, tossing a coin, trying to work out what to tell her.

The library was busy. There was a little kids' story time on the ground floor and some kind of adult computer class in a room off the side. The archives, though, were right at the top. He retrieved his notepad and pencil and stuck his bag in the locker.

The room was about double the size of the common room at school. A few people were sitting at tables, heads bent over books. An older bloke was peering into what looked like an old school reel-to-reel microfilm machine.

The woman sitting at the information desk was trying to meet Bailey's eye. She smiled. 'Can I help you?'

Excuse me, I need to find out about the brother of a murderer.

He smiled back. 'I need some information about someone, but I'm not sure where to start.'

271

Anywhere else and that would sound dodgy, but the woman seemed to expect it.

She said, 'Family?'

'Yes.' Just not his.

'Do you know their name?'

'Not their proper one.'

'Ah. That could make things more difficult. Do you have any details?'

'His brother's name.'

'Okay. That's good. Were they from this area?'

'I'm not sure.'

If she wanted to roll her eyes, she hid it well.

'Most of the information we have is local, but you could start over there.' She pointed to a row of computers. 'We subscribe to a few family history sites and it's a good place to start playing detective. The best advice is to start with what you know and take it from there.'

Bailey sat down at the last free computer at the end of the row and opened his notebook. He'd made more notes for this than the whole of this term's politics course so far. He glanced back at the information desk. The woman was busy at her own computer. If she looked over right now, she'd see he wasn't as clueless as he seemed. But he'd follow her advice. He'd start with what he knew.

None of the newspapers had mentioned Toby Scott's brother. A few claimed that a friend of the family had taken

Indigo from the park to the flat, but they were all more interested in going into details of how Indigo's mother died. The articles always gave Indigo's parents' ages, so Bailey could work out when they were born. If he'd needed to, he could have used that to find out where Toby Scott was from, but he'd have to splash out on a copy of the birth certificate. He'd gone back to the violence against women blog. The writer had compiled an inventory of perpetrators, complete with biographies. Toby Scott's wasn't that long. He was born in Margate and been in care for most of his life. He'd had a couple of convictions for shoplifting and one for supply, but no history of violence. He'd been a casual labourer on building sites, but in the months before, he'd been off work ill. The blog didn't say with what.

There was more about Indigo's mum, Mahalia. The article mentioned the children, but not in much detail. Did Indigo ever read this stuff? It was nothing she didn't know, but it must be odd that everyone else could know it too. It had been bad enough for him, sitting on the stairs listening to his parents.

Right. He needed to hurry up. What did he know? Toby Scott, day, month, year of birth. He tapped the details into the family history site. Ah – birth registration. Not much detail, though it must be him, born in Margate. And that must be him again. A death certificate, aged thirty-seven, in Liverpool. No more details available unless Bailey sent off for a copy. He scrolled though the Toby Scotts. He stopped and clicked. He and Mahalia did get married, but not for a year or so after Indigo was born. Maybe things were going well then.

Bailey rubbed his head. He hadn't really got anywhere. He still had no idea if JJ was really Indigo's uncle. Austin was right. He could be anyone. Bailey had jumped right in without thinking this through.

'Found what you need?'

The information woman was standing behind him.

'Not really.'

She said, 'What have you got so far?'

'Nothing about the person I'm looking for. But I've got his brother's info. Birth, death, marriage.'

'You could check their mother's info, though I've found the women's information doesn't always come up in a search. But one idea. If you want to shell out, you can get a copy of the marriage certificate.'

'Why?'

'My brother was one of my witnesses. They sign the registry too. It's surprising what you find in the small print!'

'So anyone can just get a copy?'

'If you've got the right info. Yes.'

The bus back was one of the slow ones, where the driver decided that the empty bus lane was just decoration.

Another message from Austin. **Just get off and walk.**

Doors are closed. What do you expect me to do? Climb through the windows?

Yh

When Bailey turned the corner into his street, Austin was waiting on the doorstep. He was carrying a massive sports bag.

Bailey poked the bag. 'You got Soraya in there, or something?'

Austin screwed up his face. 'Man, I should have thought of that.'

He bumped past Bailey down into the kitchen and thumped the bag on to the table. 'Just think of me as your dark-brown Mary Poppins.'

'Too weird, Austin. What's in there?'

Austin unzipped his bag. He carefully lifted out his Xbox. Controllers and games were underneath. 'Essential equipment. You got snacks?'

Bailey opened the junk food cupboard.

Austin whistled. 'Man, your folk like their crisps.'

'Dad buys them. Me and Mum eat them.'

Austin extracted a family-sized bag of chilli tortillas. 'I'm happy to help out. Booze?'

'Beer and some bottles of cider in the fridge. And you said you asked Jade to get wine.'

'Her sister's going to pick some up for her. What does

Indigo like? Apart from tequila.'

'I don't know.' Though if she'd drunk that tequila, she'd probably drink anything. Mum had some fizzy wine in the fridge. They could have that when everyone was gone and Bailey would go out tomorrow to replace it.

Austin opened the pack of tortillas, shoved a handful in his mouth and crunched down. 'Call these chilli? Your dad needs to get his money back.'

'Austin! You changed your mind quick, man!' Bailey fished out the pack of condoms stashed between *World of War* and *Let's Dance*. 'My parents' room is out of bounds, right?'

Austin gave him a pained look. 'I told you. Even if one little rumour gets back to Soraya's dad, me and her would have to go and live on an island in the middle of the sea. And not a nice, warm island, neither. We're talking somewhere with snow. And ice. It's that, or . . .' He made a slicing motion near his crotch. 'These little baby blockers are for you, Bay. Your other ones must be well past their use-by-date now.'

'Nice touch. But unnecessary.' Bailey shoved the condoms into his back pocket. He'd stash them in his bedroom drawer later. Just in case.

Someone was knocking on the front door.

'That'll be my honey,' Austin said.

'Soraya?'

'She had to leave before her dad came back from work.'

'But I thought . . .'

Austin grinned. 'She's prepared to rethink.'

'You'd better let her in, then. Before she rethinks herself back to the bus stop.'

Austin raced upstairs. Bailey picked up the console and followed. Soraya and Austin were chatting in the hallway, head to head, intense. Bailey left them to it and took the console into the sitting room. Mum still moaned about the big new TV, even though it made Dad so happy. Bailey started to plug in the cables. Outside, the voices stopped. Through the crack in the door, Bailey could see them, arms round each other, full-on kissing.

Indigo had snapped a picture of the last two things going in her rucksack – the red bra and little knickers. He should have told her that he didn't need all that. All he wanted was her.

Indigo turned the key in the lock and dumped her rucksack in the doorway. Jesus! Did trains always do crap like that? She could have walked it quicker, in the bloody white shoes she'd bought on Holloway Road. It was good to be home, though. Keely's place wasn't posh, but it was a palace compared to Mischa's tiny flat. Though, they'd had a good time last night, dancing like mad witches and bad-eyeing any blokes that came anywhere near them.

The flat was quiet. Keely wouldn't be home for a couple of hours, so Indigo could blast her music loud. Blondie or Grace? Grace was the opposite of Debbie Harry, all black and edges. Yeah, tonight was for *Nightclubbing*.

Bailey had called it a 'gathering'. What the hell was that? She'd been to parties, but never a bloody gathering. She'd just wanted him, the two of them, no one else. That's what they'd been working up to. But Bailey wouldn't back down on his big promise to his stupid friend. If they were going to stay together, at some point they were going to have to talk loyalties. He'd made her a promise, though. None of his mates were sleeping over. That meant one thing. All the time she was up at Mischa's, she'd tried to stop thinking about it, but couldn't.

Indigo made a face in the mirror propped against the wardrobe. She squeezed a blob of concealer on to a pad and dabbed it under an eye. Tonight's look – Debbie's tough punk flow mixed with Grace's 'don't give a shit'. Indigo bet there weren't any tutorials for *that*. She should start her own channel.

'Polishing up your bumper, Indi?'

Indigo almost poked herself in the eye. Felix was standing in her doorway.

She hurled a box of tissues at him. He ducked. 'Bloody knock, right?'

'I did. You were blasting Gracie too loud to hear. You

278

nearly ready?'

'What?'

'It was Keely's birthday yesterday.'

'I know. I texted her and she said one of her new blokes took her out.'

'And tonight *we're* taking her out.'

Indigo shook her head. 'No, we're not.'

'I told you.'

'No, you didn't.' She massaged the concealer in with her fingertips. If she didn't do it properly, she'd look like she had burn scars.

'Yes, I did.' He held up his phone. 'I can show you all the sent messages.'

'Then I must have forgot to put it in my calendar. I'm busy tonight.'

Felix came right in and pushed the door shut.

Indigo dropped her pad on the floor. 'Felix! You don't live here any more. You've got no right to be in my room!'

Felix frowned. 'Stop shouting! Wade's out there!'

'I didn't invite him!'

'It's his treat, so please try and be polite, Indigo.'

'I can't be polite because I'm not going.'

'What's more important than Keely?'

'I'm going to a gath— a party.'

She could see Felix watching her in the mirror. 'Whose?'

'Not that it's any of your business, but I'm going to tell

you so you'll leave me alone. Right?'

He gave her one of his slapable smiles. 'It's that boy, isn't it? The one whose mum's a social worker.'

'It's his dad. But yes. So can you bugger off now? You've left your man all alone.'

She tested her grey eyeliner on the back of her hand. Where the hell was her sharpener? She'd tear off her eyelid if she used that.

She caught Felix's eye. 'You still here?'

Felix took something out of his pocket. 'Look.'

There were four tickets fanned out in his hand. '*The Lion King*. Good seats.'

She threw the eyeliner back on the bed. 'I'm busy, right? I'm not going.'

'Wade bought them.'

'He didn't ask me.'

'Indigo?' He turned her music down. He bloody turned her music down!

She stood up, hands on hips. 'I'm trying to get ready!'

'No, Indigo. Just listen!' He dropped the tickets on to her desk. 'You like Keely, right?'

'Yeah. She's all right.'

Felix gave a proper smile at that one. 'Yeah,' he said. 'All right. We both know she's much better than that. Yesterday was her birthday and it's probably the last one you're going to spend with her. The least you can do is show her that you appreciate her.'

'I could be here longer. The law's changed.'

Felix shook his head. 'Anyone mentioned it? I reckon Keely's still got her big plan. After you're gone, she's going to give up the shop job and go off to Jamaica.'

'That wasn't definite.'

'She's had to deal with a lot of crap from both of us,' Felix carried on. 'I thought it would be nice to spoil her a bit. Don't you agree?'

Yes! But why should she always feel grateful to her foster carers just for being bloody nice to her?!

Felix sat down on the edge of her bed, stirring her cosmetics round with his fingers. 'So this boy . . .'

'He's called Bailey.'

'You and Bailey . . . has shagging been involved?'

Her face must be glowing through her concealer. 'You turning pervy, or what?'

'Ahh,' Felix smirked. 'I get it. That's what tonight's about.'

Indigo searched around for something else to throw at him. She picked up the *Nightclubbing* CD cover. She gave it a good flick of her wrist, but still missed him by miles. Felix watched it land on her pile of dirty clothes.

'I take it I'm right, then.' He opened her lip balm and sniffed it. 'But seriously, what's the worst thing that can happen if you don't see him tonight?'

That wasn't the point! She *wanted* to see him tonight. So badly.

'D'you reckon he's going to get off with someone else?'

'No.' She tested it in her head. Soraya was gorgeous, but for some stupid reason, she was completely hooked on Austin. Indigo hadn't seen anyone else in college giving Bailey a second look. But that girl in the mini skirt, when they were in Covent Garden – she'd definitely given him the eye. So maybe there were others.

'If he's having a load of people round, then how's he going to pay you any attention? Don't go, Indi.'

'I want to go.'

Felix slicked lip balm across his mouth. 'If he doesn't see you tonight, he's going to want you so much more tomorrow.'

'Yeah, but . . .'

'And he stood you up, remember? And you gave him another chance.'

'He said there was a reason.'

Felix dropped the lip balm; it bounced off an eye shadow palette. 'You're playing *his* game, Indi. You go around tonight, you jump under his duvet and then what? Are you sure he's still going to want you tomorrow?'

'Yes!'

'Ever been wrong on that one?'

Nice one, Indigo. Felix was never going to hold on to your secrets.

There was a knock on the bedroom door. 'Felix?'

'Sorry, Wade. I'll just be a minute.' Felix stood up. 'Your decision.'

He picked up the tickets from her desk and left her. She could hear voices murmuring behind the door. Time for Grace, back on, loud. She finished her make-up – matte eye shadow, thickening mascara and dark red lipstick.

A message. From Bailey. **What time are you coming?**

Reply. **Let you know.**

She slipped on her tight jeans, vest and the black jacket from the charity shop in Lincoln. She pulled her hair into a ponytail and twisted it into a loose bun, studying her back view in the mirror. Yeah, she looked good.

A knock on her door. It was Felix again. 'Keely's home!'

Indigo unhooked her sparkly bag from the drawer knob and opened the door.

A small crowd was squeezed into Bailey's sitting room and none of them was Indigo. None of them were Austin or Soraya, neither, but the door to Mum's office was closed. When Bailey stood on the landing to try and call Indigo again, he'd heard laughter coming from inside.

Where the hell was she? He'd heard nothing from her for hours. He'd checked to see if there'd been any bus crashes in Hackney that would stop her getting to him. Nothing. No police incidents, neither.

Jade was having a giggling fit on the sofa. Zombies were swarming across the screen, but she didn't even know how to shoot the gun. Clifton was snuggling next to her, doling out his wisdom. Russell emptied the rest of the cider into Lena's paper cup and dropped the empty plastic bottle on to the floor. A few drops of cider dribbled on to the wooden boards.

'Bailey!' Jade was waving to him. 'You coming in or what?'

'Yeah! In a minute!'

Music blasted from the kitchen, Run DMC. That must be Valentine; he was the only one into that stuff. He called it his spliff-building vibes. Jesus, Bailey didn't need Mum finding weed dregs in the sink. He peered down the stairs. Shit! Valentine had his papers out.

The door. Three loud knocks. Yes! Indigo! It was past eleven, but that was all right. They had the rest of the weekend. He threw open the front door, grinning. It was pushed so hard the hinges creaked. Bailey staggered backwards.

The guy on the doorstep must have been wearing four puffa jackets, one on top of the other, because no one could be that huge.

He said, 'Where is she?'

Bailey tried to push the door shut. 'You've got the wrong house.'

The visitor shoved past Bailey. 'Soraya!'

Oh, God! Bailey hadn't recognised him in the darkness, but he should have. Who else was that massive? He filled the whole hallway. How the hell did he know where to come?

He scowled down at Bailey. 'Don't even think about talking crap to me. Where is my daughter?'

'Soraya? She's . . . she's in the garden. Downstairs. You have to go through the kitchen.' Bailey made the words loud, over the splat of exploding zombies.

Soraya's dad stomped downstairs. The sitting room door opened and Jade skidded out and up the stairs.

Soraya's dad yelled from the kitchen. 'You taking the piss?'

Bailey ran to join him. 'Sorry. I thought she'd gone to get some fresh air.'

Her dad looked around at the wine and cider bottles and Valentine's abandoned papers.

'Where are your parents?'

'Out for the night. They're going to be back soon.'

The giant shook his head slowly. 'They know this is going on, then?'

'Yeah. They said I could have some friends round to play computer games.'

Soraya! Austin! You need to be out of that room NOW!

'Computer games.' Another glance at the cigarette

papers. 'Your dad does the youth football, yeah?'

Bailey nodded.

'I'm going to have to have a word with him.' He stomped back upstairs. 'Soraya!'

Austin, pull your pants up now, man!

'Dad?' Soraya and Jade were standing by the front door, coats on. 'We were just leaving. You got the car?'

Soraya's dad was looking at her like he was checking every detail. 'You were just leaving, were you?' His voice dripped disbelief.

Soraya opened the door. 'Yeah!' She gave him a bright smile. 'Let's go!'

Jade managed a little wave back as the door slammed shut behind the three of them.

Bailey ran upstairs to Mum's office. Austin was lying on the sofa bed, fully clothed, thank God. Mum's work had been dumped in sloping piles on the floor.

Austin gave him a weak smile. 'That was close.'

'Yeah,' Bailey said. 'Because I saved your arse.'

Austin hoiked himself to sitting. 'Who's left downstairs?'

'Everyone else.'

'Indigo?'

Bailey shook his head. 'She's not answering, neither.'

'Sorry, mate.' Austin looked genuinely sympathetic. 'Let's go down and smash the hell out of Mario. She might come later.'

'Yeah.'

'Unless Mona's taken out a hit on her and she's lying in a gutter somewhere.'

'Thanks for that, Austin.'

He followed Austin into the sitting room. The volume was rammed up high and tortillas had spilled over the sofa.

Austin handed him the controls. 'Come on, man. Let's play.'

17

Indigo took a big glug of her coffee. She'd emptied two of those little tubes of sugar in it. She should have chucked in another two. The closer she got to Bailey's house, the more her body was slowing down. She wanted a full-on sugar rush, the sort that made her feel her head was going to burst. She wanted to blank out all the things that could go wrong. Felix had better be damn right. What if waiting a bit longer didn't work? What if Bailey had given up and got off with someone at the party? She could knock on his door and he'd slam it in her face.

Last night was all right, though. Keely had always wanted to see *The Lion King* and burst into tears when Felix presented her with the tickets. And Wade was more than 'okay'. He really did seem to care for Felix and he even had a few words with that miserable woman in front who glared at Keely for singing along to 'Circle of Life'. But even then, Indigo couldn't stop thinking about what would be happening if she was with Bailey. It shone in her head. Stroking his fingertips, the back of his hands, his arms, underneath his t-shirt, feeling the shape of his ribs. She imagined shifting his t-shirt up and away, over his shoulders.

In the interval, she'd taken out her phone. Ten missed calls and twenty-two messages. Felix nudged her and mouthed, 'No.' She'd dropped her phone back into her bag. *Turn up and take the boy by surprise. He'll be even more grateful.* But what if it was her that was surprised? If she knocked on the door and Mona opened it, wrapped in a towel? There were lots of ways to get revenge.

Another mouthful of coffee. Indigo's heart was making more noise than the audience at the end of last night's show. Two more stops and she had to get off. Why was she putting herself through this? She'd blanked out that question when she'd had her shower, when she'd shaved her legs, when she'd raided out her underwear drawer for the nice black Topshop knickers. She was taking relationship advice from a guy who didn't do girls, for God's sake.

Her stop. *Bailey's stop.* She rang the bell and got off the bus.

Bailey's street was as quiet as usual. She touched her lips. Good, they weren't too spitty, but her breath must stink of coffee. She walked along the path, took a deep breath and knocked on the door.

He opened it almost straight away. He looked at her and broke into a smile. Her mouth grinned right back.

He held up a bin bag. 'I was just putting this out.'

'Yeah.'

'It's from last night.'

'Yeah,' she said. 'Sorry. It was Keely's birthday. Felix got her surprise tickets for *The Lion King*.'

His face was serious. 'I tried to call you. And I messaged you.'

Felix said she should offer no explanations, though all that sugar was making her thoughts skid round her brain, looking for a way out. 'I wanted to come. I really did. But I couldn't.'

He frowned. 'Nothing weird happened, did it?'

She laughed. 'Yeah, there was a farting warthog. And some dancing hyenas.'

'Huh?' He smiled. 'Oh, yeah. The show.' He dropped the rubbish by the front door. 'Would you like to come in?'

Sugar. Caffeine. Heart. *Beat, beat, beat*.

'Yes, please.' Indigo nudged the door shut behind them. 'Who came last night?'

'Jade, Soraya, some others me and Austin have known since primary school.'

'What about Mona?'

He laughed. 'Mona? And Saskia with a baseball bat? Not the best idea.' He opened the door to the lounge. 'What do you reckon? Presentable?'

'Yeah. Good.' It was tidier than Keely's. And that TV was big as Indigo's bedroom window.

'Austin helped me with the tidy up. He owed me a favour.'

290

'What? For being his friend?'

'No, he's all right. Honest. Soraya's dad came looking for her. He's built like Hulk, if Hulk was on steroids. I made sure they didn't get caught.'

Indigo giggled. 'Did you get Black Widow to sing him a lullaby?'

'I keep her in the music room, just in case. Fancy meeting her?'

'Yeah.'

They looked at each other. He couldn't have been out of bed that long. He was wearing faded old jogging bottoms and his hair was all uneven. If she sniffed him, she'd smell sleep.

She said, 'When do your parents get back?'

God, would he think that was a big hint? And that was a sneaky look he gave her, up and down. Though not creepy, like Levy and his mates.

He said, 'Tomorrow afternoon.'

The cat strutted up and wrapped itself round Bailey's legs. He bent to stroke it.

Suddenly, he looked up at her, straight into her eyes. 'I missed you last night.'

'Yeah. Me too.'

'Are you hungry? I could do us some brunch.'

'I'm all right.'

The ruddy cat meowed. He ignored it. He stepped

forward and took her hands.

Sugar. Caffeine. Heart. *Beat, beat, beat.*

He said, 'Wanna meet the Black Widow, then?'

'What?'

'In the music room.'

'You seriously have a music room?'

His shoulder brushed hers. 'It's really just a spare room with some stuff in it.'

She said, 'Upstairs?'

'Yes.'

He walked up behind her. She imagined his hand soft on her waist, but he was keeping his distance.

There were three doors on the first landing. One, slightly open, was a toilet. She pointed to the door in the middle.

'This one?'

'Good guess.' He pushed it open.

He seriously was into the music thing. One, two, three sodding guitars. An electronic keyboard. Some percussion stuff.

'Your guitars have their own bedroom! Jesus!'

'Not really.'

'Yes! Really, Bailey!'

Now he looked a bit worried. He should! He was showing off! She moved past him into the room, pinging a string on a bright blue guitar resting against a wall.

He said, 'That was my first guitar.'

'Do you still play it?'

'It's a bit bust. Mum bought it from the school music department when they were making room for some new stuff.'

Indigo picked it up. She must be holding it wrong because it felt like she was trying to squash a giant fly. Bailey was watching her with a tiny smile on his face.

She said, 'No drum kit, then?'

'Mum's office is next door. It wouldn't have gone down well.'

'Yeah,' she said. 'I suppose not.'

She rested the guitar back against the wall and looked around. There was an old armchair loaded with music books. The bookcase was jammed too. How many books did he need?

She pulled one out. '*The Best of Blondie*?'

He nodded. 'Dad bought it for me after I learned "Sunday Girl" for Mum. He thought it would encourage me to keep practising.'

'Did it?'

He grinned. It made his ears move.

She said, 'I wish I could play something.'

'Do you want me to teach you?'

'Okay.'

She moved closer to him. He should be able to smell the Gaultier perfume. It had worked in Covent Garden.

She said, 'Which guitar shall we use?'

'Do you want to try the Yahama?' He pointed to a boring-looking light brown guitar on a stand. She'd have preferred the blue one.

'Why that one?'

He unhooked it. 'It's a good size for you.'

'Is it expensive?'

'Sort of mid-range.'

'More than a hundred quid?'

'Yeah.'

She grinned. 'Sure you trust me?'

'Yes, Indigo. I trust you.'

'Good.' She lifted the guitar over her head. Everything seemed to tangle round her.

'The strap's all twisted.' He unhooked it, straightened it and hooked it back on. The guitar dangled from her neck. 'Now your arm needs to go through.'

She stuck out her arm and looked at him. In Camden, he'd kissed her like he wanted to be part of her. In Covent Garden too. Now he was guiding her arm through the straps like she was anybody. But something was buzzing underneath, like the words hidden beneath noise when Keely tuned her crap old radio in the kitchen.

Indigo whacked the guitar strings. They screamed in pain as she strummed hard. For a second, his face creased up like it really was hurting him.

She flexed her hand. It'd bloody hurt her too.

He said, 'Ready to start?'

She turned round and moved backwards, so her shoulders rested against his chest. If he looked down, he could probably count every hair on her head.

She tapped the guitar. 'What's this bit called?'

'It's the neck.'

'How do I hold it?'

'You have to balance it and your hand needs to . . .' His chest shifted against her back. 'Relax and I'll move your fingers for you.' In a quick, soft movement, he shifted her thumb behind the neck. 'Then you stretch your fingers over the strings. Use your other hand to strum or pick or whatever you want, over the sound hole.'

She wished there was a mirror to see themselves in. Was that his heart she could feel? No, it was probably her own.

She said, 'Right. Now what?'

'I'll teach you a chord. What about a D?'

Like that meant something to her. She shrugged. The guitar pushed up against her chest.

He said, 'It's the first chord of "One Way or Another".'

Blondie.

'Okay.'

'Just place your first finger on the fourth string on the second fret.'

For God's sake! She spun round, almost clunking him

with the neck. 'I've no idea what you're on about! Just show me!'

He went to pick up another guitar.

'No! On this one.'

'Yeah. Sure.' He sounded dead casual. But he moved behind her again pretty quickly. He stretched his arms around her, one hand on the string running along the neck, the other helping her cradle the guitar.

He said. 'Does this feel okay?'

'Yeah.'

'Now, all you need . . .'

She could feel him breathing. If she held her own breath, she might feel the pulse running through him. He was burbling on about her middle finger and her ring finger and how she should push down as hard as she can. The word 'modulation' was warm air on the back of her neck.

'Let your fingers go loose.'

She had to press down and feel the strings against her skin. She turned slightly and breathed him in. He smelled of hot cotton and something slightly sweet. Was *that* his sleep smell? One little twist of his head and he could kiss her neck. Why didn't he? His head was so close her thoughts should just trickle into him.

'Go on,' he said. 'Strum.'

Or he could move his hand to her waist, round to her stomach and pull her into him. Under that t-shirt, his chest was a skinny boy's chest. She was happy with that, way better than a buffed-up steroid-sucker like Levy who thought his puffy pecs and guns meant he was God.

He said, 'Do you get it?'

Her heart was going mad. She couldn't let it jump into her voice. 'Get what?'

'Keep your fret fingers where they are and strum. Like you did before.'

She did. And, yeah, it sounded much better. But what was he going to do? Spend the next few hours teaching her the whole song, note by note? She should have just dived through the front door and grabbed him straight away.

She said, 'Enough for now!'

She wriggled out of the Yamaha and balanced it on the stand. She laid her hand on his chest. His ribs were sharp under the thin material. She could feel him taking slow breaths. Out, slowly in. She smiled up at him and slipped her hands under the edge of his t-shirt. He took a tiny step back, blocked by the old armchair, t-shirt pressing against the back of her hands.

He said, 'Are you sure?'

'Are you?'

'Of course I am. But I want to know about you. I care about you.'

Suddenly, she wanted to cry. With Stivo, she'd been scooped into things, hands on her before she had a chance to say a proper yes. But this time, she was sure.

He said, 'Indigo, maybe we should just talk.'

'No more talking.' She reached up to him and kissed him. He frowned, just for a second, then he was kissing her back, his arms around her, folding her in. Her fingers crept upwards and at last, they were twisting through soft curls on the base of his neck. She stepped away from him and scooped off her t-shirt, lifting it wide so it didn't get stuck on her ears.

'Indigo?'

For God's sake! She put her hands on her hips. 'You've got five seconds to decide, Bailey. Then I'll put my t-shirt back on and leave.'

He must have counted to two at the most, because they were mashed together again, just the thin layer of his t-shirt between his skin and hers. He kissed her neck. She closed her eyes and rested her cheek in his hair, turning her face so she could bury herself in it. She caught his scent again. It must be the stuff he used for his afro.

He said he cared about her, words she'd heard before, bouncing around inside her, leaving little bruises. But this time was different; she knew it. She scrunched his t-shirt into big wads, lifting it higher and higher until his arms dropped free and she tugged it over his head. He reached round to hold her again, kissing her, his fingers drawing lines up and down her back. It tickled and tingled at the same time.

She said, 'Are we staying here?'

'No.' He kissed her forehead. 'I don't want my guitars to get jealous.'

He linked his fingers in hers and she followed him to the top landing. In those few steps, Indigo felt herself tense. She imagined the thing jolting awake, trying to fight back as the emptiness got filled up with the good stuff.

Bailey's bedroom. Grey walls, silver study lamps, posters, a bed with the duvet in a heap at the bottom. He clicked on his laptop. A guitar squealed.

She said, 'God, Bailey. Is this your romantic music?'

'Sorry. It's Muse. I've been trying to teach myself a couple of their songs.' He scrolled down. 'Arctic Monkeys?'

Not exactly romantic, either, but better.

Bailey sat down on the bed. She sat next to him. Suddenly, she felt cold, more naked than she was. He looped his arms round her and she let herself be drawn towards him.

He stroked the goosebumps on her arms. 'Do you want a t-shirt?'

She nodded.

Before she went to Lincoln, she'd known how much she wanted this. Downstairs, she'd given him five seconds to decide. Now, she was shivering on a crumpled bed with a guitar yelling at her. What had she expected? All she'd thought about was being with him. And she was with him.

Bailey opened a drawer. He pulled out a t-shirt from the muddle of clothes. 'This okay?'

'Guns N' Roses?'

He smiled. 'Early phase. Before Axl went weird.'

She held up her arms and he slipped Guns N' Roses over, past her head, smoothed it down.

Sugar. Caffeine. Heart. *Beat, beat, beat.*

He said, 'Is that better?'

'Thanks. Yeah.' Kind of.

She lifted the duvet and they slid in together, arms, legs, chest to chest. He kissed her nose bridge, moving so they were eye to eye. They'd been this close before, but lying down, looking at each other now, was different. Bloody hell! She was blushing.

He took her hand and kissed her fingertips. 'We can stay here all day.'

She wriggled round, so she was lying on top of him. His arms were thrown back like he'd surrendered. She dragged the duvet up and over their heads. Bailey. Hair, skin, heat, heart. Her head nestling in the nook between his neck and shoulder.

She closed her eyes as his arms tightened around her.

'Bailey!'

A woman's voice, a voice he knew from outside of his dream. He reached for Indigo. She wasn't there. He opened his eyes. Indigo was sitting bolt upright, staring at the door.

Jesus Christ!

'Mum?' She was there, solid and real in his doorway.

Mum turned back and called down the stairs. 'Ed!'

Mum? And now Dad, in the hallway. What the hell? He and Indigo couldn't have slept for twenty-four hours. Mum was glaring at Indigo. Dad turned away.

'Come on, Viv. We'll let them sort themselves out.'

Dad shut the door as if he was trying not to wake someone. Bailey put his arm round Indigo. He could feel her tension beneath the t-shirt.

She said, 'I thought they weren't coming back until tomorrow.'

'They weren't. Well, that's what they said.'

She pulled free of him. 'I need my clothes, Bailey.'

He put a hand on her thigh. He remembered her skirt, his joggers, shucked off just before they fell asleep. 'We weren't doing anything. Just sleeping.'

'In your bed.'

'We're old enough, Indigo. If they don't like it, it doesn't matter.'

'Your mum definitely doesn't like it. Didn't you see her face?'

'Sometimes she can be a bit judgmental, but—'

'*She's* got no right to judge!' Indigo threw off the duvet.

'I'll go down and talk to them.'

Talk? That was going to be hard. His parents were loud. He was used to the sharp whispers, voices that rose but quickly fell again. This was different, full-on shouting. He glanced at Indigo. Her face was pinched.

'I'm sorry,' Bailey said. 'They're not normally like this.'

Indigo's eyes flashed. 'Your mum hates me. That's why.'

'She doesn't . . . she just . . .' But Bailey had seen it in Mum's eyes too. She hadn't been keen on Mona, but she was always polite, even if sometimes Bailey was sure that he could hear Mum's teeth grinding.

Indigo fished her skirt off the floor and wriggled into it. Bailey's joggers were there too, on full display for his parents when they made their entrance. She passed them to him and he pulled them on. Had Mum been there long before she called his name? Bailey hadn't bothered shutting the door when he and Indigo went in. It hadn't been his top priority. No one else but Shuu was at home. What if Dad had come in first? Maybe he'd have just shut the bedroom door and stuck a note underneath.

'We could go down together,' Bailey said.

Indigo shook her head. 'Shit! My t-shirt's downstairs. In the *music* room.'

He stroked her back. 'Hold on to Axl, for now. I'll pick up your other one.' He kissed the top of her ear. 'Maybe I can sleep with it under my pillow.'

She caught his smile and let herself slump into his arms.

302

There was a knock on the door. 'Bailey?' Mum's voice.

Indigo grabbed her shoes and jumped up. 'See? She can't wait for me to get out!'

Indigo swung the door wide. For a second, Bailey saw Mum's startled face, before Indigo rushed past her.

Bailey jumped up. Mum was in the way. He dodged round her.

'Bailey!'

'Later, Mum.'

He jumped down the last of the stairs and ran out into the street, barefoot. He was every cliché from every soap opera he'd ever seen. He padded to the end of the road and looked up and down. She wasn't there.

He walked back along the path into the house.

'We agreed!' Mum's teacher voice, for when the class wouldn't settle down. A different voice. A different Mum. 'Those kids must run rings round you, Ed. You're an easy touch.'

'No, I just try and be reasonable.'

'Says the world's biggest bloody hypocrite!'

Bailey let the front door click shut. The voices stopped.

His parents came into the hallway.

Dad said, 'Did you catch up with her?'

'No.'

'I'm sure she'll be all right.'

'How do you work that out?'

'We trusted you,' Mum said. 'And you lied to us.'

The door was open to the sitting room. Their cases were dumped in the middle of the floor. Dad's had keeled over.

Bailey looked at Dad. 'Is that what you think too?'

Dad didn't meet his eye. 'Viv's right. We trusted you.'

'Is this why you came home early? To check on me?'

'Oh, Bailey.' Mum went into the sitting room, picked up her case and took it upstairs.

'Dad?'

Dad shook his head. 'The trip seemed like a good idea at the time.' He went to retrieve his own case and wheeled it to the bottom of the stairs. 'At the time.'

He hoisted his case up the stairs. His parents' bedroom door opened and closed and the voices started again. Bailey went into the music room and shut the door behind him. Indigo's t-shirt was sprawled on the armchair. He held it to his face; her perfume was still strong on it. The Yamaha was over there. If he looked closely, he'd probably see the marks from Indigo's fingers across its body. He closed his eyes and called up the moment, Indigo standing in her bra, daring him to ignore her. Upstairs in his bedroom, she'd stretched herself on top of him, skin to skin, pulse to pulse. His heart was beating like it wanted to kick off a tune.

Bailey closed the music room door and slipped upstairs to his own room. His parents were smashing words back and forward on the other side of the wall. Indigo's name.

Bailey's name. Then all the stuff Mum hated about Dad.

Bailey pressed 'Play' on the laptop and pushed up the volume. Arctic Monkeys again. 'Mad Sounds'.

His phone was under his bed. He picked it up and tapped. **Are you ok?**

Indigo's reply bounced right back. **On the bus**

Want to be with you

Me too

Do you want to meet up in a bit? I can creep out

Felix is bringing K birthday cake. Tomorrow?

Yh

Talk later?

Yh

Bailey lay on his bed. His t-shirt drawer was slightly open. If he sat up, he'd see the corner of the envelope poking out. He'd almost given it to her with 'Appetite for Destruction'. He'd had the envelope in one hand, the t-shirt in the other and his mouth ready to blab. *'S'pose Axl can't help being weird, though. He thought his stepdad was his real dad until he found out that his real dad was murdered.'*

Then he'd looked back and she was shrunk into herself, shivering. He'd just wanted to make her warm again. But even when they were lying here, with her body leaving its print on his, his mind kept wriggling away. It wasn't fair. He knew this stuff about her and it lay there like a third skin between them. He had to tell her soon. Or not at all.

305

A light knock on his door. 'Can I come in?'

'Yeah.' Bailey sat up.

Dad shut the door and leaned against it. 'Are you and Indigo . . . is it a serious thing?'

Bailey nodded.

'She's had a tough time and sometimes these things leave scars. This has to work for you, okay?'

'Yes, Dad.'

'Good.'

That was it?

No. More words looked like they were on their way, but Dad just sighed and opened the door.

'Dad?'

'Yes?'

'Why did you come back early?'

Dad was caught, half in the room, half out. 'I told you. The trip seemed like a good idea at the time.'

18

Indigo looked like she'd squirted lemon in her eyes. Too much night talking. Bailey'd better look as crap as her. Just as well Keely wasn't here to say anything, but she'd still gone mental with the sticky notes.

HANG IT OUT PLEASE. On the washing machine.

Two of the bloody things on the fridge door. *THERE ARE BURGERS* and underneath *BUT DON'T FORGET THE SALAD.*

On the tall cupboard. *NEW KETCHUP IN HERE BUT USE OLD FIRST.*

And even on the kettle – the kettle! – with gaffer tape for extra stick. *NO MILK. BUY SOME PLEASE. TAKE MONEY FROM COIN JAR.*

Sorry, Keely. Later.

Indigo grabbed the last cereal bar and went back into her room. It wasn't just her eyes that hurt, her head felt like she'd been necking tequila again. There was too much going on inside it. Bailey, of course, and Viv. Bloody, hypocrite, mean-faced Viv.

Indigo needed to be out of the door in the next ten minutes, but there was something she had to do first. It would definitely help clear her head. She opened her laptop and scrolled through the emails she'd sent to Primrose. Jesus, there were hundreds of them. She slammed 'Delete' on every single one. Over to her inbox. Contact name – Big Sis. Two whole pages of messages. Photos of Primrose's kids and everything.

Indigo opened a message halfway down. Subject heading – *Full of love*.

Dear Indigo,

It's been the best thing in the world to find you. It seems like there's just the two of us left. Now we've found each other, we should never let each other go . . .

Select all. Delete. Was she sure? Yes. Primrose was so full of love, so grateful to find Indigo, that she'd dumped her as soon as her husband stared whining. Then moved to bloody Australia, to boot.

Indigo flicked down the laptop cover. Bailey said he was taking her somewhere special. The sun was out. Time to bring out the denim shorts.

She spotted him from the bus. He was outside the café by the bus stop, holding hot drinks. He came towards her as she got off.

'Hi.' His head bobbed forward and he kissed the side of her mouth. 'You okay with latte?'

He handed her the drink and pulled a handful of sugar packets from his jeans pocket. He held her drink again while she tore open the sugar and stirred it in.

He said, 'Five?'

'Yeah. It hides the taste of the coffee. You look like you need ten.'

'Am I looking rough?'

'A bit tired.'

She took his hand; it was warm from holding the drinks.

He said, 'It was all a bit weird in my house. Mum and Dad went from shouting to saying nothing at all to each other. Mum slept in the bed in her office.'

'The one where Austin and Soraya . . .'

'Yeah. Though I thought it was best not to tell Mum that.' He squeezed her hand. 'But it was good talking to you. It made everything else better.'

She didn't need the coffee. Her face was getting hot without it. They crossed the road to the station, swiped their travelcards and walked down the steps to the platforms.

He said, 'Platform three or four.'

A train was already waiting. It was new and bright, one long carriage from end to end. There were probably less than ten people on the whole train. Bailey propped his bag in the seat next to him, yawned and kicked his legs out straight in front. His t-shirt rode up, showing a stripe of skin. Yesterday, she'd been stretched on top of him. He must have remembered that too because he glanced at her and gave her a little smile.

She nodded towards his bag. 'Have you brought a picnic?'

'No. There's a café there.'

'What's in there?'

'Something for later.'

'That's mysterious.'

He gave another little smile and looked out of the window. The doors closed and the train pulled away.

She said, 'Is it all right to tell me where we're going?'

'Sure. It's the Horniman.'

A laugh burst out. 'The what?'

'I know. A museum set up by Mr Horniman.'

'His real name?'

'Unfortunately, yes.' He put his arm round her. She rested her head on his shoulder, catching a hint of his hair stuff. It was the same smell on his Guns N' Roses t-shirt.

The train pulled out of the dark station and on to a high track. Parks and playgrounds, quick flashes through building windows, an office, a kitchen, bicycles on a balcony. A massive girl and a bulldog sprayed on a wall. Tagged up train carriages on a roof. Past shining office towers and the Gherkin that always made Keely giggle.

Then back underground. Indigo closed her eyes. The train wobbled and her ear shifted against his neck. She could hear his breathing just below his skin.

She said, 'Wake me up when we're there.'

He stroked her hair.

Bailey's lesson for today – thinking about butterflies didn't get rid of them. His nan used to go on about fighting fire with fire, but she had nothing to say about fighting butterflies with butterflies.

What were his top three butterfly moments? Number three must be walking on stage to play 'Jumping Jack Flash' on his first Gibson guitar at the Year Eight winter concert. Number two: going to school the day after Onyx class's outing to the Horniman Museum.

And number one? Now. Right now.

Indigo's head was heavy on his shoulder. Maybe she really was asleep. He could always say that he dozed off too and missed the stop. They'd come back another day.

Surrey Quays . . .

Indigo's hair was down today. He wrapped a curl around his finger. She breathed out, moving closer to him.

Or he could leave the bag on the seat when they got off. By accident.

The train glided out of the tunnels back into the real world. New Cross Gate . . .

He kissed the top of Indigo's head. 'Just a little bit longer.'

She yawned. 'Cool.'

The full lunchtime sun hit them as they came out of Forest Hill station on to the main road. Bailey shuffled his bag to his other shoulder and looked up and down the hill. Did it always look like this? It was definitely different from when Dad used to drive them here. They'd leave Mum with a pile of work and always bring something back for her, a pencil, a magnet or just a postcard she'd stick on the freezer. She must have a whole drawer full of Horniman merch somewhere.

Indigo was looking at him curiously. 'Are you lost?'

'I'm in south London. The sun's in the wrong place for me.'

She squinted up at the sky. 'Huh?'

'It's a north London/south London thing.'

'Oh, yeah. I forgot. I didn't live in south London long enough to hate you north lot.'

He laughed. 'Maybe it's just as well.'

She was standing taller than him, on the slope of the hill. They were nose to nose, eye to eye.

She said, 'I don't feel like I'm from London at all.'

'Where do you feel you're from?'

She made a face. 'God knows. Nowhere, I suppose.'

He waited. Maybe he should just give her the picture

now. Open his bag, hand it to her, tell her she *was* from somewhere and they'd loved her. He took a deep breath.

She shrugged. 'It doesn't matter, though, does it? I've got you, London Boy. You'll make it good for me.'

As he slung his bag over his shoulder, the envelope flipped from one side to the other. 'I'll do my best.'

She said, 'Have you worked out how to find Mr Horniman?'

Bailey let his breath out. He hadn't realised he was holding it in. He didn't remember the sharp slope downhill. In his memories, he was higher than London itself and Dad was naming the buildings on the skyline.

He said, 'That way.'

She eyed the hill. 'You're gonna have to push me up that.'

He took her hand. 'No problem.'

No way was Indigo going to try and talk as she walked up that mountain. Anybody living at the top must have their own oxygen tents. The backs of Indigo's knees were slimy with sweat. The denim cut-offs had seemed a great idea when the sun poured through her window this morning. Now she wished she'd gone for the skinny jeans. At least, with his stride, Bailey wasn't going to see her from behind.

She said, 'How much further?'

It sounded more like a whine than she meant it to be. But it was sodding hot. Soon her hair was going to melt into her head. Mr Horniman had better be dead special.

'There,' he said.

She spotted the clock tower first, rising from a big, stone-coloured building.

She shaded her eyes. 'What's that?'

'Mr Horniman's totem pole.'

She giggled. 'Why's he got one of those?'

'He collected all sorts of stuff. When I was little, I used to think there were secret Indians living in the bushes by the totem pole.'

'Like in *The Indian in the Cupboard*?'

He grinned. 'You've read it?'

'I had a foster mum who loved it. She read it to us.'

'I had to read it in the school library. If I took it home, Mum would have written "Native American" all over the cover.'

Indigo laughed. 'For real?'

'Yeah. Mum can be quite full on.'

He was laughing too, but her laugh was gone. She already knew how full on Viv could get. She let go of Bailey's hand and slid her fingers between the museum railings. The coolness against her wrist spread through her body. That was better.

Bailey moved away. 'This is where their secret buffalo came to drink.'

He was standing by a stone fountain. A big green stain

314

had spread across the inside like a kid had dunked their mint choc-chip ice cream in it. One of the outlets was broken, coughing out drops of water.

'The buffalo should have just gone to the café,' she said.

'Is that a big hint?'

'Got it.'

He led her round the back of the museum. There was a massive queue for the main café, but there was one of those little trucks that sold drinks. This place really was popular. Just behind Indigo, a load of tables were joined together for a group of old people. Most of them were drinking tea or soft drinks, but one of the old women was knocking back beer, straight from the bottle. It made Indigo want to smile again. There were posh-looking mums and older kids in hoodies and a young blonde girl with Down's Syndrome chasing a pigeon. This was a place where anyone belonged.

Bailey handed her a bottle of ice tea.

She said, 'Thanks.'

'You're welcome.'

'No, I mean, big thanks. For bringing me here. It's really cool.'

He unscrewed his bottle and glugged half of it back.

She said, 'Man! You were seriously thirsty!'

'Yeah. I was. Ready for the tour?'

'Sure.'

He took her into a big, cool room with a domed roof,

everything white and light. A staircase led off to the floor below. Bailey was looking around as if he was confused.

She said, 'Is the sun still in the wrong place?'

'Very funny. The museum's had a bit of a makeover since I last came.'

'Is that good?'

'Yeah. But you know when things don't match the way you remember them?' He shrugged. 'I hope they haven't done anything to Big Daddy.'

Big Daddy was a walrus, a sod-off giant stuffed thing with tusks like swords, and evil little eyes. It was plonked on a fake iceberg, staring them out as they came into the gallery. It wasn't really called Big Daddy; Bailey's dad gave it the name after a wrestler on telly in the seventies. Bailey showed Indigo a picture on his phone. The original Big Daddy was a fat, old white guy in a leotard. The walrus was better looking.

'I used to think it was just pretending to be dead,' Bailey said. 'When anyone made too much noise, I thought it would wake up and dive off there and squash me.'

Indigo could imagine it, a mini Bailey gripping his dad's hand, silently begging everyone to shut up. He must have had to do some serious begging. This place was full of kids, running up and down and screaming.

He said, 'Shall we have a quick look round the rest of the gallery?'

Did he sound a bit sad? Maybe she should have been more enthusiastic, but it was just a big stuffed walrus. Was that what made this place special?

They headed further into the gallery. That's when it hit her. It wasn't just the walrus; this was a great, big room full of dead things. An ostrich, an elephant skull, a sloth, peacocks, foxes. And was that— God! A cabinet full of stuffed dogs' heads. Why?

At some point she must have unlinked herself from him, because they were standing side by side, a good gap between them.

She said, 'Why did you bring me here?'

He said, 'It's . . . it's one of my favourite places and I wanted to share it with you.'

A favourite place? Dead things everywhere, bones and bodies made to look like they were still alive. Tiny birds on ledges, beaks open, like someone shot them when they were singing.

'Indigo, honestly, I don't remember any of this. Maybe Dad just took me to the walrus and then straight out again.'

Did they look up and see it coming? What about those dogs? Did someone they loved and trusted do that to them?

'Indigo! Come on, let's go somewhere else.'

People died with their eyes open. She'd always thought her mum saw that pillow dropping towards her face. But Mischa had said it wouldn't have been like that. They'd reckoned Indigo's mum had a drug seizure. She wouldn't have known. But her dad knew. They'd found him crying on the floor by the bed. She'd read that he was still holding the pillow. Was that true? In her head, it was floating in the middle of the room, puffed up and pale on a sea of carpet.

'Please, Indigo.' Pulling at her arm.

Her mum, dead eyes, mouth open like a song or a kiss.

Indigo and Bailey, reflected in the glass cabinet, dead birds singing behind them.

Indigo turned and ran. The dogs, the birds, the squirrels, the walrus, all of them looking at her as she clattered out of the gallery and up the stairs. Was he calling her? Or was that just another kid screaming. There were hundreds of them, in carriers, on scooters, posh mums aiming buggies at Indigo's feet. Her breath was coming out of her in whistles.

Toilets? There! Except it was a locker room full of buggies folded in rows, ready to spring open and fire babies at her. She leaned against the wall, dropping her chin on to her chest. Her face was cold and sticky, sweat drying.

'What did the fox say?'

A burst of song coming from behind Indigo's shoulder. Not a quiet mumble song. The woman sounded like she was singing to a friend in another town.

'The ducks say quack!'

Indigo turned round. The singer was young, dressed in

318

black, with a cardboard duck's beak on string hanging around her neck. She clapped her hand to her mouth.

'Oops! Sorry. I've been with children all day. Sometimes it just slips out!'

A toilet came free. 'It's okay,' Indigo said. 'You go.'

'Cheers, hun.'

Indigo splashed water on her face. The heat was gone, her face nearly back to normal. The woman was singing again, in the toilet. Jesus, she was so happy she had to sing while she was having a pee.

Indigo could feel a smile fluttering inside. It wasn't ready to break the surface yet. She closed her eyes. The dogs' heads, the walrus, the birds all looked back at her, but their colour was fading. A deep breath. Another splash of cold.

Bailey was close by. She could feel the pull of him even from here.

The singing woman came out of the cubicle and washed her hands in the sink next to Indigo.

She said, 'Are you okay? It wasn't my singing, was it?'

Indigo shook her head. 'No. That was great! I'm just a bit tired. Thanks.'

The woman smiled. 'I highly recommend visiting the petting farm. One of the alpacas has had a baby. It makes everyone happy.'

'Yeah. Thanks.'

The woman headed out, then back in straight away. 'Are you Indigo?'

They looked at each other.

'If you are, there's a boy called Bailey waiting outside for you. I can tell him you're not here.'

'No,' Indigo said. 'It's all right. I'll be out in a minute.'

'Okay, honey.'

Something special. A room full of dead things. *Nice move, Bailey*. But he'd looked almost as stressed as her. Maybe he didn't know. Idiot! He should have checked! But he hadn't. And he was out there waiting and she was in here.

She opened her bag and took out her make-up. A quick fix of eyeliner and she'd be all right. She should have remembered. Even when you press 'Delete', all the crap sits around in a folder until you empty it for good.

Bailey wished he could fade into the wall. All the women coming out of the toilet were giving him the cold eye. Any minute now, a security guard was going to come over and ask some questions. But he couldn't move, in case Indigo came out and missed him.

Forget Austin's list of You Said *What*?s, this was going to lead the chart for worst dates ever. Austin's face floated in front of Bailey's eyes, jaw hanging low, eyes wide. *Bruv? You took her to a cut-off dog's head? Man!* Then Austin laughed so hard he evaporated.

Yeah. Bailey had done exactly that. On their second date, he'd taken Indigo to see a decapitated Alsatian's head stuck to a board. Indigo was probably racing back down the hill to the station. He checked his phone again. Nothing.

'Bailey?' Indigo's face was pale and water had dripped on to her top. Though her lipstick was bright and fresh.

He rushed towards her. 'Are you okay? Do you want to go home?'

She shook her head. 'It was a bit . . . I don't know. All those dead things.'

'Sorry.' If she looped her arm through his, he'd kiss her hair and he'd keep saying 'sorry' until she really believed him. Her arms hung loose by her side.

Her eyes focused on something just behind him and there was a twitch of a smile. 'Music room. Is that like yours?'

He said, 'Mine's way cooler.'

She gave him a little smile. 'Let's see.'

'Sure.'

He let her go first. Maybe she wouldn't want to stay for long. At home, he touched his guitars, even when he wasn't going to play them, pressing the hard skin on his fingertips against the strings. All he had to do was pick them up, plug them in and they'd burst into sound. Here were tubas and euphoniums and a carved lyre and an old wooden organ, every type of instrument, silent in their cabinets. Music caught in a cage.

Indigo was quiet, pressing her nose against the glass, moving on to the next cabinet.

His butterflies were swarming. His plans were all mangled. She was supposed to be relaxed. He'd been going to ease into it. But if he didn't do it now, it was never going to happen.

He touched her shoulder. 'There's another room, a really weird one. We used to go there on school trips.'

She looked at him. The low lighting in the room made her eyes plain brown. Her breath had left a smear on the glass. He didn't reach out his hand. Maybe he should have, but she was walking ahead too quickly, out into the light and noise of the atrium.

She said, 'Which way?'

'Here.' He opened the gallery door. It swished shut and the noise was gone.

Indigo looked around at the red walls and the collection of cabinets. 'Gosh. It must have been mental inside Mr Horniman's head.' She examined a cluster of bright blue butterflies pinned in a box. 'And bloody hell. Is that a torture chair?'

Bailey stood back while she studied it. The bag was getting heavier on his shoulder.

'Most of it's not real.' Indigo tapped the information panel. 'I mean, it's real. But only bits of it were used.'

'Yeah.'

Would she spot the mask or would he have to lead her there?

She wandered from case to case. 'He loved random stuff.'

A Buddha with some praying monks. A quick glance at the stuffed birds before she skimmed past.

She was by the wall now, the one with the masks. He could see her eyes sweeping across the display. She stopped. Looking at him, then back up again.

'Bailey?' She reached towards him, pulling the strap of his bag until he was beside her. 'Did you know this was here?'

'Yes.' He could probably draw the thing from memory. The jagged teeth, the cruel, sly eyes, the painted face. And bushed out on top, the mass of red hair. A warrior mask with a ginger afro. The back of her hand still rested against his chest.

Though now he'd brought her here, it felt stupid. After all her stuff it was a bit pathetic. But there was sympathy in her eyes.

He said, 'I think Dad avoided this room too, though that was probably because of the torture chair. I came here on a school trip, when I was about eight.'

'All the other kids noticed, right?'

He nodded.

'Yeah,' she said. 'Of course they would. What happened?'

'The teacher saw it and looked a bit embarrassed.'

'What did she say?'

'Oh, what a beautiful mask!'

A bubble of laughter popped out of her. 'Teachers really don't get it, do they?'

He shook his head, laughing too.

She said, 'Did they give you crap at school?'

It was so long ago, but he still felt that creeping sickness when he remembered it. 'All the usual stuff and extra. Someone drew a big picture of it with my name on it. It was bang in the middle of the wall in the PE corridor, in permanent marker, so they had to paint over it. Even that didn't work, so they had to move the PE lockers to cover it.'

'Did they know who did it?'

'Probably Saskia. But you reckon anyone was going to tell on her?'

Indigo turned to face him, resting her arms on his shoulders, her fingertips in her hair. 'But you didn't cut your hair?'

'No.'

She kissed his nose. 'Good.' Her face came back into focus as she moved back. 'It's that thing where everyone thinks it's big to take the piss and they just want to make you feel small and nothing.' Her eyes were back to how they should be, golden, with dark flecks. 'It works, even if you pretend it doesn't. You feel total shit and you think you should be someone different.'

He put his arms round her waist. 'I don't want you to be someone different.'

His lips brushed hers, but he made himself pull back. 'Indigo?'

'What?'

'I have to give you something.'

Her smile didn't quite touch her eyes. 'Is it my t-shirt?'

Damn! He should have brought that, instead. Or a copy of *Parallel Lines* signed by Debbie Harry and Chris Stein in 1978. Or JJ, to sort out the mess he'd started. Anything else.

But he was here now. He took the bag off his shoulder, laid it on the floor and unbuckled the straps. She watched him take out the envelope.

'What is it?'

'When you open it . . .'

She looked up. 'Are you sure you want me to?'

No.

Indigo tugged at the flap. Right now, he could be sitting on that torture chair, screwed in place, being slowly pulled apart.

She was easing out the picture. She gave a little laugh. 'This looks like my mum.'

Bailey tasted blood from where his teeth clamped down on his tongue.

'It is.'

'And is that . . . is that me?'

'Yes.'

She waved the picture at him. 'This is weird. Really weird. You've just given me a picture of my mum. And she's holding me. And I know this picture. I've seen it before. Where did you get it?'

He reached for her, but she jerked away.

Her voice was calm and cold. 'Tell me where you got it, Bailey.'

Maybe he could break the glass, sit on the chair and tighten the screws himself.

He said, 'There's something else in the envelope, a receipt.'

She banged the envelope on her hand. The receipt fluttered out. She mouthed the words. 'Ivygables?'

He said, 'It was the homeless guy on the bus. He followed me home and he asked me—'

'What homeless guy?'

'The one who yelled at Saskia.'

'The one in the hat?'

Bailey nodded.

'And he had a picture of me and my mum?'

Bailey nodded again. 'He said he knew you when you were a baby.'

Her eyes were wide, her mouth open, like she couldn't breathe. The picture crinkled as she held it tighter.

'What's going on, Bailey?'

'His name's JJ. He kept following me and asking me to help him.'

'Help him do what?'

'Please. Look on the back.'

She turned the picture over. 'Horatio. My granddad?'

'JJ blamed himself for splitting up your family. He wanted you and your granddad to get in touch.'

'My granddad? How the fuck does he know my granddad?'

Bailey closed his eyes. Life rewinding, back down the hill, back in the train, Dalston Junction station, past Mum's shocked face to yesterday morning. Indigo's cheek on his neck, her hand resting on his thigh.

'He said he knew your mum. He told me to check things out with your granddad first.'

Her mouth moved. *Check things out.* She looked at him, waiting.

'So I went to see . . . to see Horatio.'

'Horatio? It sounds like you're good friends now.'

'No! I just saw him once.'

She stepped back, leaning against the glass. 'You went sneaking round to my granddad's behind my back because some creepy tramp told you to. You really think that's right?'

He had. When he was sitting opposite JJ with the rain pouring down the windows outside, it had definitely been right. But now . . .

327

'So, what if I opened my bag and gave you pictures of your dad? Or I told you stuff you didn't know about your mum? You'd be all right with that, yeah?' She'd started off low, but she was getting louder, like the red walls were bouncing up the volume. 'Who is this mystery tramp who knows my mum and my granddad?'

'I . . . I . . .' He was in this deep. He had to continue. Be honest, yes. But what the hell was appropriate for now? 'I think he's your dad's brother.'

'He had a brother?'

Bailey opened his mouth. Maybe if he squeezed his belly, he could force air up to his lungs. Words were slipping out of his lips and moving, slow-mo, through the air to Indigo.

'He was the one who took you from the park.'

'The one who— Bastard!'

Her hands slammed into Bailey's chest and he staggered back, his head knocking against the cabinet with the masks. Not hard enough, though. If he looked up, it would still be there. Its sharp little teeth in its grinning mouth, staring at Bailey, the biggest joke of all.

The door opened. Children screaming. It closed again. Silence.

19

Running. The rush of it, through Indigo's arms, into her fingers. No stopping until she was in a different street, a different town, a different damn planet. And sounds, her feet on tiles, gravel, grass. Kids yelling in the playground, crows above the trees. Faces must have swung round, but she was carrying a photo, not a gun. A photo that felt like it could explode in her hand.

Indigo skidded to a stop, the photo flapping between her damp fingers. She was close to throwing up and her lungs were breathing knives. She sank to the ground, shuffling back to prop herself against a thick tree trunk. Eyes closed, her heart sounded like the drums from 'Atomic'. Bailey probably didn't even like Blondie! He must have been nosing behind her when she was scrolling through her music and struck gold.

She'd been so stupid. She'd trusted him. She'd told him about the thing for God's sake! All the time, he was collecting his own little secrets about her. And of course he really understood because kids took the piss out of his ginger hair! Jesus Christ! Indigo had fallen for it. And that made her the idiot, didn't it? He had a cat called something

Japanese and a room just for his guitars! God. It was always going to be wrong.

Her head drooping into the crook between his neck and his shoulder. Lying there as he stroked her hair . . .

Indigo opened her eyes. A deep breath in. She had to take hold of this. She'd seen pictures of her mum before; her life-story book was full of them. This was just another one. She straightened it out.

This picture was bigger than the ones she had already, on heavy paper, like someone wanted to make it special. She stared at the two faces. That baby could be anybody's. A clever Photoshop from a nappy advert or even just a friend's kid. Indigo held the picture at arms' length, slowly bringing it closer to her face. Yeah, babies all looked the same, just in different colours. But the woman, her mum . . . her eyelashes were so long they didn't look real. Indigo had noticed that in other pictures. And her mum's eyebrows, thick and flat with a tiny, smiley curve at the end, just like Indigo's. Did Scarlet and Coral and Teal have pictures like this? And what about Primrose? Did she have one too? Did she trace the shape of their mum's eyebrows on the photos, then over her own face? With a big picture like this, Indigo could see more than she ever had before. It wasn't just the shape of Mahalia's eyes, it was how she was looking down at the baby like she loved it.

Indigo let the picture touch her face, pushing it flat,

moulding it around her cheeks. Her skin was sticky with sweat. Maybe the picture would stay there until it became part of her.

'Are you all right, love?'

Indigo peeled her mum away. A quick, hard blink and she was back in the park. A woman with a small dog on a lead was standing a little way from her.

'Yes,' Indigo said. 'Thanks.'

The woman nodded and moved on. Nothing to see here except a teenage girl with a photo stuck to her face.

All those times Bailey had been kissing her, holding her, when they'd been walking through Covent Garden hand in hand, making their steps match . . . all the times she'd let him close enough to feel the gap inside her squeeze tight. All those times, there was this other secret stuff.

And it started with the tramp. The one who'd supposedly snatched her from her grandma and took her to that flat. The one who must have left her there while her dad picked up the pillow on the other side of the door.

He'd told Bailey he was her uncle, but that didn't change a thing. Her dad could have a hundred brothers and she wouldn't want anything to do with any of them. How dare he come back thinking he could just fix things? He'd already cracked open her life once. It was never going to happen again. Everyone thought they could make decisions about her, tell her how to run her life. And they'd got it wrong.

This tramp, this so-called uncle, was going to hear from her direct. Whatever crap he was brewing up with Bailey – he could shove it. She pushed back against the tree and made herself stand up. Loud and strong. From her direct.

The first bus came quick. The idiot sitting next to her – what was his problem, though? His legs were open so wide, she was squeezed into half of her seat. What was he going to do, land a plane in there or something?

She had two more buses to look forward to after this, if she wasn't going by train. And she couldn't risk that. Bailey had sent seven messages. He was still at the station, waiting. He could carry on waiting. He wanted to know she was all right. He could carry on wanting that too. His number was now blocked.

The bus stopped and Runway-Crotch moved to the free seat across the aisle. He gave Indigo a vicious side-eye as if it had been her hogging the space. She middle-fingered him back. He stuck on his earphones and stared out of the window. A pity. She was ready to take him on. That's why he looked away. He saw the shadow of something moving behind her eyes.

She rested her forehead against the bus window. Ivygables. The name made it sound like a country house with big gates and a butler to open the door for her. Even the picture on the website made it look posh. Then she'd read the words. '. . . *a residential care home with beds for thirty men . . . specialising in treating alcohol dependency (past and present) and drug dependency (past and present).*'

No surprise there. Except that he was still alive.

Next bus, Elephant and Castle, heading back north over the river. *Was the sun in the right place now?* She tapped her temples. Why was Bailey still clinging to the inside of her head? She needed that space to think.

What was she going to do when she got to Ivygables? Walk in and ask for JJ? What the hell did it stand for? Her dad was Toby Scott, but that didn't mean they weren't brothers. Half the people she knew changed their names when they came out of care. Mischa used to be called Lois.

King's Cross. Off this bus and on to the last one to take her to Camden. Her stomach felt like it was full of washing-up liquid. Every time the bus jerked, the bubbles bounced higher. Soap and air; she could taste it on her tongue. Everything inside her was squelch.

Camden. She rang the bell and got off the bus. Her phone map said all she had to do was cross over the main road and walk down a side road. There should be a park on her right and the hostel was at the end. She breached out. No froth came out of her nose. That was good.

Bailey had to go. He'd left it for five more minutes three times now, an hour and a half in all spent watching the trains heading to London Bridge and Dalston. He should have gone to the park instead. Maybe she'd felt that thing rising in her, maybe she thought she was going to explode and she'd run as far away as she could. Maybe she was still there, crouched among the trees, crying.

He checked his phone. Nothing.

When she'd lost it at school, her eyes had blanked out and it was like the outside Indigo had become someone different. In the museum, though, she looked like she was falling and he couldn't catch her.

A text. Mum asking if he was all right.

No, Mum. I'm not.

If Indigo had gone, there were two places she might head to. One was back to Keely's. The other . . . He clicked on the Ivygables site. The man who'd taken her. The man who'd arrived out of the blue and used Bailey to force himself into her life.

And Bailey had let himself be used.

A train heading north had pulled into the station. Bailey jumped on just before the automatic doors closed.

Another text. Dad, asking if he was all right.

No, Dad. I've made a big stinking mess of things and I think I need your help.

Dad was in the sitting room reading the newspaper.

Bailey said, 'Where's Mum?'

'Back garden. She thought it was time to attack the weeds.' Dad closed his newspaper. 'Is everything okay?'

Bailey closed the sitting room door and sat down. Out of the corner of his eye, he spotted a tortilla chip jammed between the floorboards by Dad's foot. Austin missed that one.

Bailey said, 'I didn't expect you back from Paris so early.'

A hint of a smile. 'Obviously.'

'Mum shouldn't have walked in like that.'

'You broke our trust, Bailey.'

'You don't get it.' Dad raised his eyebrows. 'I want to be with her.'

'It all seems to have happened very quickly, Bailey.'

Not for me. He felt himself blushing.

Dad said, 'Where's Indigo now?'

'I . . . I don't know.'

Dad's face clouded. 'What do you mean? I presumed you were with her this morning.'

'I was.'

'And?'

'Dad, I need to tell you something.'

Dad laid the newspaper on the floor. 'Go ahead.'

Bailey let it pour out of him – JJ on the bus challenging Saskia, trying to talk to Horatio, Indigo running out of the museum holding the photo of her mum.

For a moment Dad stared at the floor and said nothing.

When he looked at Bailey, his eyes were full of anger. 'What the hell were you thinking?'

'I thought . . . I thought I was helping.'

'By running around for the man who even by his own admission kidnapped her?'

'He was sorry. He wanted to change things for her.'

'What's his full name?'

'I don't know.'

'Jesus, Bailey.' Dad had never ever hit him. He'd almost got thumped himself a couple of times when he'd tried to stop people smacking their kids. But right now it looked like he was having difficulty holding himself back. 'You may well believe that you bloody well know everything, but you don't! You understand me? You don't.'

I know, Dad. That's why I'm sitting here now.

Bailey stared at the newspaper. Arsenal were underperforming and Wenger was under fire. They'd printed a photo of the manager frowning.

Dad said, 'He's at Ivygables?'

'Yes.'

'I know the place. It's for street drinkers. The ones who talk to themselves. The ones who'll never, in any sense of the word, be "rehabilitated". It's the place they end up, the end of the road, Bailey.'

'He didn't seem that bad when I met him.'

'I'll bow to your expertise.'

Bailey stood up. 'Forget it.'

Dad shook his head. 'What's your plan, Bailey? Sit down. We need to think this through.'

Bailey sat again. Dad's foot was on the newspaper, heel blocking out Wenger's face, leaving a frame of grey hair.

Dad said, 'Remember when Nan was in the care home? You'd do anything to get out of seeing her. Have you forgotten how scared you were?'

Nan, who used to grab Bailey's hand so tight it was like she wanted to twist it off at the wrist, suddenly singing the old lullaby Dad's granddad used to play on his guitar. And then she'd start crying and nothing Dad did could comfort her.

Dad said, 'Some of the men at Ivygables have alcohol-induced dementia. Psychosis. It's the tough stuff, Bailey. You really think she's going there?'

'Yes.'

'God. Poor soul. Who knows what she's going to find? And this JJ. Why now, Bailey? Why the hell would he reappear now?'

'I don't know, but there's one other thing, Dad.'

Dad's foot moved again, the sports page crinkling beneath him. 'Go ahead.'

'I think he's Indigo's uncle.'

'Mum's side or dad's?'

'Dad's.'

'So he's the brother of the man who killed her mum.' Dad stood up. 'Jesus, Bailey. Let's go.'

The sitting room door opened. Mum was still holding her muddy trowel. She looked from Dad to Bailey. 'I thought I heard you come back.'

'Yes.'

She frowned. 'And you're going out again.'

Dad retrieved his car keys from behind the mirror on the mantelpiece. 'Bailey's made a bit of a . . . shall we say, well-intentioned mistake. I'm going to see if we can sort it out.'

Mum crossed her arms. 'What's this about? Bailey?'

'Later, Viv. We need to go now.'

'Suit yourself.'

She closed the door behind her just a bit too hard.

Bailey said, 'Dad? Things between you and Mum?'

'Let's get going.' Dad's face was reflected in the mantelpiece mirror; he seemed to be doing the best he could not to look at himself. 'The traffic's going to be tough. There are nearly always roadworks round there.'

Indigo's phone was dead, but she didn't need the map any more. This was the park, a narrow stretch of grass and a playground with tyre swings and a couple of those duck things on springs that bounced backwards and forwards. A couple of kids were climbing the slide and a few people were dotted round the benches.

Ivygables was on the corner. Even getting close, it didn't look so bad; if she didn't know better, she'd have thought it was just a church. A group of men were hanging around the hostel door, smoking roll ups. One of them looked like he was checking out her legs in her shorts. She tried to stare him out, but what if it was him? What if he'd lifted her off the sand, away from the rest of her little wooden animals and taken her away? Or what if it was the grey-faced bloke who looked like he'd had a stroke? Or the dark-haired one in the baseball cap, muttering to himself? Did any of them look like the one on the bus? How could she remember when Saskia's stupid head had been in the way?

Breathe!

The pervy one jerked a finger towards the door. 'Rehanna's inside, if that's who you're after.'

Indigo walked past them, eyes straight ahead, through to the reception area. Just inside, on the right, an office had been partitioned off. Behind the clear plastic window, a woman with a blue headwrap was talking on the phone. She nodded a smile towards Indigo. The rest of the place was like a waiting room with chairs and tables and newspapers. An enormous window should have let in more light, but the light brown walls seemed to eat it all. The strip light was on but didn't make much difference.

'Can I help you?' The receptionist's smile was friendly and open.

'I . . . I'm looking for someone.' Since when did Indigo stutter?

'Are you one of the college volunteers?'

Indigo shook her head. 'No. I think . . . I think he's my uncle.'

'Oh!' The receptionist's smile widened. 'We don't get many family visitors here.' She started tapping the computer. 'What's his name?'

His name? Oh, God. 'He's . . . I just know him as JJ.'

'JJ? Are those his initials?'

'I . . . I think so.'

The receptionist squinted at the monitor. 'Can't find it.' She called into the office. 'Anyone know JJ?' She turned back. 'So sorry, love. There's often a bit of a difference between our clients' street names and the ones on their records. If you want to leave your details, I can ask around.'

'No. It's all right.' It felt like there were loops of elastic around her legs trying to tug her back down the street.

Outside, the smokers were still hunched together.

The grey-faced one caught her eye. 'Too much for you already, love? Us poor sods have got to live here.' He coughed out a laugh. None of the others joined in. Even the pervy one had lost interest in her.

'I'm looking for JJ,' Indigo said.

'JJ? He'll be in the park now, if he's not out back.' He

smiled at her puzzled face. 'The churchyard, love. It's our next stop from here.'

Indigo retraced her steps along the road to the park. Most of the people had gone, but a woman was pushing her kid on the swing. She kept looking over at a lone bloke sitting on the bench. A beanie hat was pulled down so tight it made his head look bulgy. After a couple of minutes, the woman let the swing slow to a stop and yanked her screaming kid away.

Indigo moved closer. Was it him? It was hard to see. The tramp on the bus was wearing a beanie, but loads of them did. He was also holding a can wrapped in a brown paper bag. Didn't he know? The paper bag made it worse. But he wasn't drinking, though. He was just sitting there like he was dead.

There was only breath in Indigo's mouth – no voice. She had to go closer, along the path, approach him side on. Old stained jeans. Trainers so run down his feet must flap out of the back of them when he walked. Could he run in them? With a child in his arms?

If she went closer, she might smell him. Thick, sweet beer. Unwashed clothes. Like a memory uncurling in her head.

Closer again. Just one step. And another one.

There should be someone else, arm round her shoulders, warm against her. The smell of soft hair, old t-shirts, sleepy skin.

One step.

The man called JJ stole her life once, but it would never happen again.

She took a deep breath. 'JJ?'

His head moved, like he'd heard something in the distance. His chin was patched with grey and white stubble that spread down his neck.

'Are you JJ?' She was louder. He must have heard. 'The guys in the hostel said you'd be here.'

He turned to her, squinting like it hurt to keep his eyes steady. 'You?'

'It's . . . it's . . .'

'You!' He stood up. The can slipped out of the paper bag and rolled on to a pile of twigs and litter. He grabbed the bench to steady himself.

Indigo jumped back. That dark, wet patch on his trousers, that was beer he'd spilt on himself. Beer. Just beer.

'You!' He dropped on to the bench again, pulled another can out of a bag beside him and snapped the tab. Beer frothed over his fingers. The stink of it made her stomach churn.

'Why did you do it?' She was yelling. The words had to hit him hard. 'You took me!'

He lifted his head. He had a proper tramp's face, just like the others.

'You let him kill her! And you left me there!'

'Indigo.' He gulped at the air and rubbed his arm across his face.

'You went and he killed her! You left me!'

Her words were too weak to reach him. His arm had sunk to his side, the slide of tears and snot wet on his sleeve. He was sobbing, a thick, heavy sound like it was too big for his body. He looked at her.

'Toby said you'd be all right.'

'He killed my mum!'

'Toby's the good one.' He turned away from her and tipped the can to his mouth. 'But there was a mad thing in him. I didn't know. A mad thing. That's what killed her. A mad thing.'

'A mad thing?'

Twisting and clawing and burning its way out of him. Blanking out his brain until it had done its worst.

A mad thing, shuffling deep inside her. Now the darkness was opening up. She was wobbling. She was falling. She was lost.

20

Dad had three dark spots on his earlobe. He'd once told Bailey that he'd got his ears pierced to impress a girl at school but the holes had gone all manky. Glancing at Dad now, it looked like someone had tried to stick a fork in his ear. It could've been Mum, with the mood she was in. Dad yanked the handbrake like he hoped it would open a trapdoor beneath Bailey's seat.

'Dad! A cyclist!'

Dad nodded and waited for the bike to pass then dodged round a stationary post van.

He said, 'I still don't get it, Bailey. Why didn't you tell me about this before?'

'Neither you nor Mum seemed open to questions.'

'Even more reason to ask.'

'Great logic, Dad.'

Dad pushed in a CD; it was old school dub, like they'd been blasting in the pub in Camden.

Dad said, 'I used to go to Ivygables now and again. Sometimes there'd be a dad or granddad or some other family member you'd want to consult about a child.' Dad shook his head. 'It was usually pointless. Even if they knew who you were talking about, they didn't want to stay in touch. They'd usually decided it wasn't worth it. There was nothing positive they could give.'

That's what Indigo's granddad, Horatio, had said. Except he'd held her as a baby, loved her like his child.

'They could help the child know its family,' Bailey said.

Dad managed a quick sideways look. 'Lots of those guys don't know their own history, or if they do, they don't want to remember it.'

They swung down a side street, passing a small park and pulled into the half-empty car park in front of a church building.

Dad opened the car door. 'Wait here.'

Bailey opened his side, slamming the door behind him. 'No, Dad.'

A few men were huddled by the stone wall on the edge of the car park. Bailey sneaked a look at them. In spite of Dad's horror tales, they didn't look particularly terrifying. For all Bailey knew, they could be badly-dressed teachers on their lunch break.

Dad pushed open the big wooden door, holding it for Bailey to follow. The lights were on already, even though it was only just starting to get dark.

'Hey, Rehanna!' Dad greeted the receptionist behind the plastic partition. 'Long time, no see!'

345

Rehanna gave a kind of squeal, the office door opened and Dad was covered in people. Mum used to joke about him being the world's most loveable social worker, though when she said it recently, she hadn't been smiling. As the wave of people carried Dad into the office, Bailey looked around him. If he was in a hotel, this would be the foyer. There were bookcases and armchairs and some charcoal sketches of Tower Bridge on the walls. A telly was fixed on a bracket high up, sound down, subtitles on. The place didn't smell bad, neither, a mixture of bleach and some incense stuff.

The front door was pushed open. A couple of the smokers came in, a smell of ash and mustiness carried in with them. The one in front stumbled, causing a chorus of swearing. The men headed to the stairs at the back of the foyer except for one, who dropped into a chair. He was wearing a grey beanie and broken-down trainers. A bag of cans thumped on to the floor, though it looked like he'd spilt most of his beer over himself.

JJ? Bailey realised he'd whispered the words.

More cans bulged in JJ's jacket pockets. He slumped sideways in the chair, eyes closed, as the plastic bag clumped on to the floor. The office door opened and Dad's laughter spilled out. A woman came and crouched by the chair and spoke to JJ. When he didn't respond, she gently removed the cans from his pockets, added them to the plastic bag and took them back into the office.

Dad appeared by Bailey's side. 'Do you recognise him?'

Bailey nodded. 'That's him. Was Indigo here?'

'It sounds like she came looking for him, but he'd already left. He has a spot in the park where he goes.'

'Did she find him?'

'I don't know. Let's hope not, Bailey.'

Bailey glanced over at JJ. He was bent over himself, chin nodding against his chest. 'We could ask him.'

'That's not a good idea. He's a heavy drinker. He might not remember meeting her even if we could wake him up. I told you. This is the place for men at the hard end.'

'He was okay when I saw him.'

'Was he? He's in a bad way. Hepatitis, liver disease and probably some early onset dementia.'

Dementia? JJ must be at least twenty years younger than Nan.

'He told me Indigo's gran had that too,' Bailey said. 'Maybe he wanted to say sorry to Indigo before he forgot.'

Dad sighed and put his arm round Bailey's shoulders. It felt like a long time since Dad had done that.

'I'm still angry with you, Bailey, but I can understand why you tried. Let's go.'

'Where?'

Dad released him. 'Home.'

'What about Indigo?'

'Rehanna said she'll call me if there's anything to tell.'

'Dad?'

'Yes?'

'Can you find out JJ's real name?'

Dad looked down at the drunk, still figure. 'Why?'

'It's just . . . I can check online, see if there's anything about him Indigo should know.'

'Bailey—'

'Please, Dad.'

Dad went back into the office. Even asleep, JJ didn't look at rest. His fingers twitched and his face moved like something was rippling beneath the skin.

At last, Dad's old mates let him go. Bailey breathed in the cool, outside air. His clothes and hair must stink of the incense smell.

Dad waved his key fob and unlocked the car door. They strapped on their seatbelts and Dad pulled out on to the main road.

'Did you get his name, Dad?'

'No.'

'Why not?'

'I didn't ask.'

'Dad—'

'You should never have involved yourself in this. I'm not going to help you make it worse.'

The Specials' 'Ghost Town', singing out from the

phone cradle on the dashboard.

'That's mine,' Dad said. 'Can you get it for me?'

Bailey answered.

'Ed?'

'It's me, Mum. Dad's driving.'

'Oh. Okay. I was phoning because . . . I wanted to tell you . . . It's about Indigo, Bailey. She came here and she was very upset.'

'Indigo came to find me?'

And he wasn't there! He was stuck in this bloody traffic jam with Dad!

'Mum! Has she gone?'

'Yes. Sorry, Bailey.'

Indigo had knocked on his door. She'd needed Bailey. She'd got Mum.

'Bailey, please let Dad know.'

'Dad?'

'Yes.'

'Why?'

Mum had disconnected.

Dad said, 'Well?'

'It was Mum.'

'Yes. I gathered that.'

'She said Indigo came around, really upset. But she's not there now.'

'Shit.' Dad's cheek twitched as if he was clenching his

jaws together. 'How was Mum?'

'Mum? Why's this about Mum?'

'Did she sound stressed out?'

'Indigo?'

'No. Mum.'

'Seriously, Dad? This isn't about Mum. You just gave me the whole lecture about what Indigo might find at Ivygables, but now, it's all about Mum.'

'You don't understand.'

'No. Because I'm not psychic.'

'Not helpful, Bailey.'

'Nor was Mum. For God's sake! Don't you care?'

Dad looked ahead, jaw set. Bailey slumped back in his seat. The north London traffic ground to a halt ahead of them.

Indigo closed her eyes, but it was like Viv's face was pinned to the inside of her eyelids. Viv. There were only two teachers who'd let the kids call them by their first name. Viv was one. The other was Dan, the speech therapist. Indigo hadn't meant to see them. She probably wouldn't have even cared. She was too busy being pissed off with herself for getting stressed out during a reading session. She'd stormed down the corridor and there they were, full mouth to mouth, eyes closed, everything. Viv must have heard something, because suddenly they pulled away from each other and were staring at Indigo. Dan whispered something in Viv's ear and hurried off. Viv looked like she was going to follow him, but then she spun round and strode right up to Indigo. She didn't say anything, she just stood there, looking down. Everything Viv was thinking was folded into that look.

When Viv opened her front door just now, Indigo had been hit by that look again.

Indigo had managed to force out some words.

'Is Bailey here?'

Viv shook her head, blocking the doorway like she thought Indigo was going to fight her way in.

'Do you know where he is?'

'No.'

And that look. The one that made Indigo feel small and nothing, that told her nobody would ever believe her. But things were different now. Indigo didn't have to tip up her face to see Viv. They were equal. She made sure Viv heard it loud and clear. Her dirty little secret wouldn't be secret any more.

Indigo got off the bus at the corner and walked towards the flat, the picture jiggling in her bag like it was laughing at her. She needed the thing now. She needed to feel it stretching, the claws tapping, the skin shifting on her bones. She needed it to fill up the hollow space and remind her what she was. Because she had to go through with this and she couldn't do it by herself.

351

She stuck the key in the door. The flat was silent. Keely's shop uniform was on a hanger hooked on the doorframe of the bathroom. Indigo sniffed. Was that Gaultier perfume she could smell? The door to Felix's old room was open, just a bed and carpet. Everything that was Felix was gone. After eight years, there wasn't even a fingerprint. Soon, that's how hers would look too, scrubbed clean of her. She had to make sure Keely wanted to get rid of every Indigo trace.

It was hot in here. The council must have muddled up the central boiler settings again. She turned on the tap in the kitchen and let the cold water run over her wrists.

Was *it* sleeping now, or waiting?

The herb plant on the windowsill was waterlogged and dying. The Chart was hanging lopsided on the fridge. Felix must have nicked the other magnet. Keely's Batgirl mug was drying on the rack, next to the Man United one. The handle had to be glued on after Indigo slammed it in the sink once. Indigo had broken other stuff too. But Keely had kept her.

Indigo swallowed. It hurt.

She'd hated Keely so much when she first got here. She'd hated Felix too. She'd been such a cow when they'd taken her bowling to welcome her. Every time it was her turn, she'd just let the ball thump to the floor. The other two had carried on, ignoring her. Felix had scored a strike and tried

352

to high-five her. Indigo had thumped him. And then she'd tried to thump Keely.

And Keely had still kept her. She'd knock on Indigo's door every morning to ask her if she wanted tea. Every night, it was hot chocolate. And Keely would sit on the end of Indigo's bed and listen. That was even better than the hot chocolate.

Indigo leaned her back against the sink. It wasn't just Bailey that killed the rage, it was Keely. It had always been Keely. That's why Indigo had to do this. Now she knew for sure. The mad thing that made her dad kill her mum. It was just a matter of time before it turned on Keely.

But . . . her dad had being doing drugs, hadn't he? Maybe it was different. Indigo could wait. She could go into her room, turn Blondie up loud and hang on until Keely got home. Keely would listen.

Indigo snapped her phone on to the charger and plugged it in next to the kettle. A text buzzed through straight away. Keely had sent it an hour ago. A bloke she'd gone on a date with last week had turned up at the shop with flowers for her. He was taking her for a meal in a restaurant up in one of the City towers. Keely sent a photo of the flowers, an enormous bush of pink roses. She hoped Indigo had a good evening. Kisses. Lots of them.

Keely deserved this. There hadn't been anyone for years.

Indigo closed her eyes. Keely disappeared. Indigo was

surrounded by guitars. *His* hands were guiding her fingers on the Yamaha. His breath was on the back of her neck. They were in his room, wrapped round each other under the duvet. She was studying his face as he slept, the tiny, pale scar above his right eyelid, the dots of stubble she hadn't noticed until she stroked his chin, his dark, eyebrows that he must secretly pluck or they'd meet in the middle. He was coming awake, smiling up at her. Then his face changed as he saw the pillow she was holding in her hands, pushing down, down until his breath stopped.

Her eyes snapped open.

The thing knew. It was warning her. The more you loved, the stronger it became.

She picked up her phone. It only took a few seconds to send the text to Bailey. The phone clattered against the kettle as she dropped it on to the counter. She plucked Keely's Man U mug off the dryer. It was tea-stained inside. Indigo launched the mug high and watched as it shattered against the wall.

Where was it? Where was the mad thing? If she had to do this by herself, the hole would stretch so wide there'd be nothing of her left.

Dad was humming, a tuneless noise over the music on the CD. It had started after Dad phoned Mum back. The call ended and all the lightness and smiles that followed Dad out of Ivygables disappeared. Bailey must have disappeared too, because Dad was flat-out ignoring him.

They passed the Seventh-Day Adventists church and waited to turn right. Bailey's phone buzzed. Hopefully, Austin had got Indigo's address out of Soraya. He glanced at the screen. His heart jumped. Thank, God!

He almost turned to Dad. He almost said the words, 'It's her!'

He checked the message preview: **Your perfect mum hates me because . . .**

What?

He clicked on the text. He read it, and again, slowly. The words didn't change

Your perfect mum hates me because she's a liar!! Ask her about Dan, the speech therapist in Medway. She looked like she was enjoying that kiss and they couldn't keep their hands off each other.

Mum? Dan? Who the hell was Dan? Bailey glanced over at Dad. He was concentrating on the road.

Bailey pressed 'Call'. It rang once and was disconnected.

'Dad?'

The humming stopped.

'What's going on?'

Dad swore as a bus accelerated past them to stop just down the road. 'What the hell is wrong with these people?'

'Dad, I asked you something!'

355

'When we're home. Nearly there.'

'Dad, has Mum . . . is there a problem?'

'She's stressed. Just like I am now.'

'So stressed you can't even manage a holiday together. If you're going to split up, maybe you should just do it.'

'Thank you for the relationship advice, Bailey.'

'Isn't that what people do? When one of them has an affair?'

Dad released the handbrake and swung into their road.

'Well, isn't it, Dad?'

'Jesus, Bailey. Haven't you learned that sometimes it's best to keep your mouth shut?'

Mum was waiting by the front door, the hall light on behind her. She watched as Dad parked up. At last, the handbrake crunched into place. Bailey whipped off his seatbelt and jumped out.

He said, 'Happy now, Mum?'

'Bailey?'

'All that stuff about watching out for me, going on like Indigo was too mucked up for me. But all along, you were just thinking about yourself, weren't you? Indigo told me!'

Mum didn't move from the doorway. 'What did she tell you, Bailey?' Her voice was quiet, like she was trying to calm the class.

'She told me about Dan, in Medway. She told me how

she saw you together. That's why you came back from Paris early, wasn't it? In case she told me!"

'Enough, Bailey.' Dad's voice was quiet behind him.

Bailey spun round. 'No, Dad! It's not enough! You knew, didn't you? You two ganged up on her!'

Dad's hand was on Bailey's shoulder. 'Let's go inside. The street doesn't need to hear this.'

'You embarrassed, then, Dad?' Bailey shook himself free. Mum was in front of him and Dad behind, like they really wanted to trap him in their lies. 'You don't want everyone to hear how Mum was having her thing with some bloke?'

A look passed between his parents, missing Bailey out.

'Let's go in.' Dad tried to propel Bailey through the door. Mum flattened herself against the wall to make the room. She was split in half, part-bright light, part-shadow.

Bailey pulled himself tall, so he could look Dad in the eye. 'Aren't you ashamed, Dad? You're always going on about how kids like Indigo are treated. Then you treat her like shit.'

'You don't need to swear, Bailey.' Mum, like he was a nine-year-old having a tantrum.

'Is that it, Mum? Is that the best you can do? Then both of you can just fuck off.'

Silence, like hearts stopped. Then Mum's breathing, the hum of traffic on the main road, Dad pushing Bailey inside and shutting the door. Bailey's feet on the stairs racing up

357

to his room, door shut, headphones on so the music had nowhere to escape.

Dad had followed him. He must have knocked, but the sound was hidden in the music. He came and sat down on the floor next to Bailey and waited. Bailey muted Axl Rose and slipped off the headphones. His head felt cold and empty.

He said, 'Is that a social-worker trick?'

Dad didn't smile. 'What?'

'Not saying anything.'

'Sometimes it's hard to know what to say. Though if you want to apologise for swearing at us, that would be welcome.'

'I . . .' No, there'd be no 'sorry'. Not until his parents said it first. He reached for his headphones.

Dad said, 'It wasn't Mum.'

'You hate Indigo too? I suppose you were just better at hiding it, Dad.'

'For God's sake! Nobody hates Indigo!' Dad lowered his voice. 'Our concerns were genuine. We wanted you to be together for the right reasons.'

The door twitched open. There was a quiet meow as Shuu padded in. She sauntered over to Dad and settled on his lap.

'What are the right reasons, Dad? You stuck with Mum after she did what she did. Why?'

358

'Mum didn't have an affair, Bailey.'

'Of course, Indigo was lying, wasn't she?'

'No, she wasn't. And will you stop being so bloody self-righteous? You broke promises. You let us down.'

'It's not the same.'

'Really?' Shuu buried her head in Dad's jumper as he scratched her neck. 'It's none of your business, but I'll tell you what Indigo saw. Dan was a speech therapist at the school and, yes, Dan was doing everything he could to persuade Mum to leave me for him. They kissed a few times and that was it.'

'And you didn't mind.'

'Yes! Of course I did!'

'So why didn't you stop it?'

Shuu shifted on Dad's lap, her tail swishing across his knees.

'Because, it was me. I was the one having an affair.'

'What?'

'Her name was Maura. She was another social worker. It lasted for four months until Maura ended it.'

'Or you'd have carried on?'

The only light in the room came from the hallway, a thin, bright wedge from where the bedroom door hadn't closed properly. Bailey wanted to kick it shut so he didn't have to look at Dad at all. Shuu jumped off Dad's lap and shimmied under Bailey's bed. Bailey could hear her scratching at the sheet music that had accumulated there.

'It was nine years ago, Bailey. Me and Viv sorted it out. I'm only telling you because you owe your mum an apology. A big one.'

'As big as yours?'

'Jesus, Bailey! I'd forgotten how judgemental teenagers can be! Do you really think you know everything about everything?'

The wedge of light widened. Mum's bare feet. Bailey couldn't look up.

She said, 'Ed? I think you need to check your phone. It's been going non-stop.'

The light shrunk again. Dad pushed himself up to standing and followed her.

Dad. And a social worker called Maura. It must have been around the time that Dad started taking Bailey out on Sundays, to the Horniman and the zoo and the cinema. It was to give Mum a rest, Dad said. Maybe they just didn't want to be around each other. Dad, with his sad little voice, talking about sleeping on the sofa. Dad, trying to cook up something special for Mum. Dad, who'd let Mum down.

Bailey's phone rang. He dug it out of his pocket. Austin.

'Man! Big Bang's gone off, d'you hear?'

'What the hell are you on about?'

'Soraya just heard. Indigo went mad and mashed up her foster mum's house. Police called and everything.'

'You got Indigo's address?'

'Yeah. I'll text it over.'

Bailey tried Indigo's number again. One ring, then nothing.

'Bailey?' Mum was in the doorway holding up the car keys. 'We heard. I'll give you a lift.'

The Eric Walrond estate was a large maze of red brick blocks caught between three main roads. Mum was driving, Dad next to her. They'd had to fuss about adjusting the seats so Bailey's legs could fit in the back. It was a long time since he'd sat there. It was always just him and Mum or him and Dad. Now it was the three of them, the car sealing in the silence.

Rehanna from Ivygables had been true to her word, letting Dad know as soon as she had news. Indigo's foster mum had called them after Indigo used the emergency cab account. It had taken her from Ivygables to Bailey's house.

Mum turned into Indigo's estate. 'Did you say Malmesbury House?'

Bailey checked Austin's message. 'Yes.'

Mum parked up next to some bins. 'Okay. It's that one.'

Indigo's flat was on the ground floor of a block of maisonettes. There was a little fenced-off section in front with pots of herbs and a trough full of plastic windmills. A gnome in a Man U football strip sat on a windowsill.

A party had kicked off in a flat upstairs, music and voices filtering down from the balcony.

Mum knocked on the door. It was opened straight away, by a tall, skinny guy who was probably about Indigo's age.

He said, 'Who are you?'

Dad moved to Mum's side, a wall of parents between Bailey and Indigo's home.

'My name's Ed,' Dad said.

Bailey stepped around Mum. 'Are you Felix? I'm Bailey. I don't know if Indigo . . .'

Felix glared at him. 'You've done some good work here, Bailey.'

Mum tensed. 'I don't think—'

'Who is it?' A woman's voice from inside the flat.

Felix called back in. 'The idiot who told her to meet the tramp.'

Mum stiffened again, but kept quiet. Felix was gripping the door like he wished Bailey's face was just a bit closer when he slammed it shut.

A woman pushed past him. She was a bit darker than Dad and at least half a foot shorter. Her hair was pinned up and long silver earrings dangled against her cheeks. 'There is no one to blame for this.'

Felix sucked his teeth and spun back into the flat.

The woman almost smiled. 'I didn't teach him that. When he lived here, he had manners.'

Mum held out her hand. 'I'm Viv, Bailey's mum.'

'I'm Keely.' She accepted Mum's handshake. 'I'm . . . I . . . I was Indigo's foster mum.'

Bailey said, 'Was?'

Felix shouted from inside. 'She's gone! Thanks to you!'

Jesus! 'She's run away?'

Mum put her hand on Bailey's shoulder, almost like she was trying to hold him in place. Keely blinked and wiped her face with the kitchen towel balled up in her hand.

'No, she hasn't run away. '

'What happened?'

Mum's nails dug through Bailey's sweatshirt into his skin. 'Not now, Bailey.'

'It's okay,' Keely said. 'I'm still trying to get my head round it myself. The neighbours called the police. They thought someone had broken in and was smashing the place up.'

She opened the door wider and moved away. The hallway floor was thick with broken crockery, knives, forks, a chopping board that had landed on its edge against a wall.

'They told me from the beginning,' Keely said. 'I knew she had anger issues. What teenager doesn't? I did.' She nudged half a shattered Man U mug with her toe. 'She learned to hold it down, though. There'd be little glimmers now and again, but it would usually blow over. I was so proud of her.'

'I'm so sorry,' Dad said. 'She was so lucky to find you. I know Bailey didn't mean to interfere.'

Because Bailey can't talk for himself, can he, Dad? But what could he say?

'I'm sorry.' Another one, even though a sackful of 'sorries' wasn't going to make this right.

Keely shook her head. 'You haven't got anything to be sorry for. Please, come in. But be careful.'

Mum first, then Dad, Bailey last, closing the door, trying not to stand on the fragments from Keely's kitchen.

'You thought you were doing a good thing,' Keely said. 'The one sister she had a chance to know properly cut her off, did you know that?'

'No,' Bailey said. 'Indigo said they were supposed to meet, but her sister cancelled.'

'Her name's Primrose,' Keely said. 'She's seven years older. Indigo didn't see her much, but they used to chat on Skype. Then Primrose and her family decided they'd move to Australia. It shouldn't have made much difference, but Primrose wanted a completely fresh start. Indigo wasn't part of that start.' Keely stepped back. Something crunched beneath her feet. 'And her grandma died earlier this year.'

'That's hard,' Mum said.

'She left a letter to be posted after she died,' Keely said. 'It was supposed to come to me, but it seems Indigo got there first.'

She disappeared into a room, leaving them standing there. Mum and Dad's faces were talking to each other without words.

Keely returned with a folded sheet of paper. She handed it to Dad. Dad read it and passed it on to Mum. Mum offered it back to Keely. Keely shook her head. 'Bailey?'

Bailey smiled gratefully. The note was short, the writing getting looser and more scattered towards the end.

My beautiful Indigo,

Yeah. She was.

Time is short. This morning I woke up in a strange room, but they said I have lived here for many months now. It won't be long before it's all gone. Even when the words are taken from me, I know you will still be in my heart.

Bailey glanced over at Dad. He seemed to be lost within himself. Mum's hand was on Dad's back.

I want my spirit to rest in peace.
Forgive your father. Find him. Forgive him.
Mahalia told me. Not H. Just me.
love love love
Your nanna

Bailey frowned. '"*Forgive your father*." Why would she say that? He killed her daughter!'

'She said she wants her spirit to rest in peace,' Mum said quietly. 'She felt that it was time to let go of her anger.'

'But "*Find him. Mahalia told me*." Don't you get it? She's trying to say something else about Indigo's dad. H, that's Horatio, Indigo's granddad. He didn't know, either.'

Dad plucked the letter out of Bailey's hand. 'Just before your nan died, she didn't recognise me. I had to pretend to be a nurse or she'd scream any time I went near her. All she wanted was my father. It was like she refused to remember his funeral at all. The letter makes it look like there's a big mystery. But, imagine trying to remember who you are, where you are, every day, then trying to write it down. I know what you're thinking, Bailey. But it's just . . . you should see some of the notes your nan wrote to me before she passed away.'

He gave the letter back to Keely. She folded it in half, and half again.

She said, 'Maybe it's telling secrets and maybe it isn't. But when Indigo needed me, I was out with some guy. My phone was off.'

Mum said, 'My phone spends most of its time on silent. We can't be available all the time.'

Keely tried to fold the letter again, but the paper was too stiff. 'By the time I picked up the message, an emergency social worker had collected her from the police station. I couldn't understand it. Why now? And then I checked the taxi account. From somewhere called Ivygables to a street in Hackney.'

'Our house,' Mum said, quietly.

Keely looked at her. 'Why would she go there?'

'She was looking for me,' Bailey said. 'I wasn't there, neither.'

Keely sighed. 'I phoned Ivygables. They told me she'd been there looking for someone. And then the woman said you'd been there and gave me your number. But I think I wrote it down wrong. I begged the social worker to let me see Indigo, you know. I begged her, but Indigo doesn't want to. They've asked me—'

The words came out in hiccups and suddenly Keely was crying, hard crying, as if her whole body was going to dissolve. Mum picked her way through the carnage and put an arm around her while Dad moved round to the other side, patting her back like she was a tambourine. Bailey looked down at the floor, littered with fallout from Indigo's rage. Her thing.

'They've asked me to pack her things. She's moving away for good.'

For good?

Keely was trying to talk. 'It's all my fault. I shouldn't have gone out. I should have been here. I wish she'd let me

367

see her.'

For good? 'Dad? Where will they take her?'

'They'll look for an emergency foster placement,' Dad said. 'If not, she may be in a residential home for tonight. There's a couple over in Ilford that usually have places.'

'And then?'

'I honestly don't know,' Dad said. 'She's coming up to eighteen. Maybe she'll go into some sort of semi-independent accommodation. She'll be okay. Don't worry.'

'Don't worry?' Felix stormed out of the room at the end of the hallway. Two of him could fit in Dad, but he looked ready to take Dad on.

Keely was shaking her head. 'No, Felix.'

'It's just typical social-worker bollocks!' Felix glared at Bailey. 'Do you know what "semi-independent accommodation" means? Some stinking hole in the arse end of Croydon, near no one you know or want to know. You up for it, Bailey? Going to give up your nice cosy house for that next year?'

Dad's hand dropped to his side. His mouth moved like he was trying out answers. Mum slid round and kissed Dad on the cheek.

'It's okay, Ed,' she said. 'You take Bailey home. I'll give Keely a hand clearing up.'

Keely started to protest.

Mum scanned the rubble. 'At least let me help you take

368

the edge off it, or you'll only be waking up to face it tomorrow.'

'No.' Keely bent down and picked up a couple of forks. 'I'll be okay.'

'I knew Indigo when she was little.' Mum gathered up a fish slice and a wooden spoon. 'She wanted to be a fashion designer. She used to draw pages and pages of dresses.'

Keely laughed. 'Really? I can believe that.'

Dad nodded towards Mum. 'I'll go, then.'

Mum nodded back.

'Come on.' Dad nudged Bailey.

'No, Dad. We need to—'

'No, Bailey. We don't.'

Dad closed the door behind them. The party on the second floor was really hotting up. A black cab stopped opposite. A woman got out, Indigo's height, in a short sparkly dress and heels. She swept past Bailey, into the flats, trailing perfume behind her. It was sweeter than Indigo's perfume, more sickly.

Dad was holding the car door open for him.

Bailey said, 'She's gone. But I can still find her, can't I?'

'Maybe. But perhaps she doesn't want to be found.'

21

Indigo was stuck in her own heart. In, out, in, out. It was making her skin thump. It was pushing hot air through her head, turning the darkness grey-orange. It was like looking through the bottom of a dirty glass.

The social worker opened the car door. 'We're here.'

She'd told Indigo her name at the police station, but Indigo had let it float away. She'd told Indigo where they were going, but that had floated away too. She was holding a red overnight bag that Indigo hadn't seen before. Maybe there were special ones for times like this, because it wasn't the bright blue one that Keely bought when the three of them had gone on that summer trip to Dorset.

Keely. Jesus. She must have walked into the flat and seen . . .

The social worker said, 'We'll pick up the rest of your belongings tomorrow.'

What belongings? Her bed? Her wardrobe? The mirror on the back of the door? None of that was hers.

'You'll survive for tonight, won't you?'

No.

'This way.'

She was on a street of terraced houses, all murky in the street light. They were walking towards two houses that had been knocked together, the front gardens paved over to make a car park. The windows on the ground floor were covered in security grilles.

'There's a back garden,' the social worker said.

'I don't care.'

The social worker sighed. 'I thought you might want to know more about where you're staying.'

Know what? Indigo knew it already. There'd be another bed and another wardrobe that hundreds of kids had used before her. Someone long ago had chosen them, not Indigo. Keely had let her— Indigo breathed in hard. She needed more than air to stop it hurting.

The manager was waiting for them, talking away as she led them inside. Indigo followed them through a small communal area. A girl in a giraffe onesie was slumped in front of the telly and another girl, maybe a bit younger, was perched on the arm of a sofa painting her nails. Two boys were hammering the crap out of an Xbox. They all turned to look at Indigo. One of the Xbox boys – the little git couldn't be more than twelve – grabbed his balls and licked his lips. Indigo gave him the finger. Up and hard. He needed to understand right off.

Beside her, the social worker sighed again and nudged Indigo into the manager's office. More talking. Indigo was supposed to join in, but the lump in her throat kept the words down. Let the social worker tell the story the way she wanted to. Even though she hadn't been there at the time.

Indigo closed her eyes. The grey-orange inside her head was sliding away, leaving spaces for the pictures to flash through.

The tramp with the beer can and the wet patches on his trousers.

Bailey's stupid mum and the expression on her face.

The Man U mug, falling, smashing.

The picture. Torn into pieces on the bed. Did Keely find it?

Bailey. Curled into each other, her head buried in his neck.

The manager stood up. 'Let's go to your room.'

All the kids were watching her, waiting for that moment when her blankface slipped. Idiots. She was an old hand at this. She gave them a sweeping look and followed the manager into the hallway and upstairs.

'It's a couple of nights at most,' the social worker said.

Indigo had heard that before. She closed the door on the manager, the social worker, the support worker, the lot of them. And that little git who'd been playing Xbox, she'd seen him all right, lurking at the top of the stairs. He'd better not give her any trouble. None at all.

The red bag was on the bed. She unzipped it and emptied everything out. Leggings, t-shirts, underwear, her washbag. They must have picked it up from Keely. She'd even remembered to pack Indigo's charger. On top of it was the bottle of Gaultier perfume with a sticky note in Keely's handwriting.

It smells better on you than me. Let me know you're all right. Keely xxxx
P.S. I found a little crocodile under your pillow. I've packed it with your washbag in case it's important.

Indigo picked up the perfume carefully. If she held it too hard, it might pass through her like a ghost. She caught a whiff of the scent. Outside the bedroom door, whispers, scuffling, a bang where one of the little bastards must have kicked it. She unzipped the washbag and tipped out the little crocodile. It lay on her pillow, its teeth bright against the dark blue pillowcase. She twisted the top off the perfume and sprayed it across the bed, swept the clothes on to the floor and lay down on top of the duvet, burying her nose into the thin cotton.

She had done it. She had done what she was supposed to do. She'd been sent away from Keely. Keely was safe.

She closed her eyes and brushed the crocodile towards her. It slid between her cheek and the pillow, the ridges on its back, the smooth snout etching themselves into her skin.

All those years ago in Medway, she'd made hand sculptures with Viv. They'd stirred up a bowl of liquid plaster of Paris and poured it into a rubber kitchen glove. When it was set, they'd peeled off the glove. Some of the other kids broke off fingers when they eased off the mould, but Indigo's was perfect.

Viv. She'd taught Indigo more than she realised. When you pour the filling into an empty space, don't leave any gaps. That's what makes it weak. That's what makes it break.

22

The new girl in Indigo's seat was called Comfort. She'd come from a sixth form near Highgate. Apparently they asked her to leave after she posted a photo of her form tutor's bum crack on Tumblr. Or that's what Carly was going on about. Carly's cousin, Malisha, went to the same college and all the students got serious grief about it. It wasn't just Comfort, though. There'd been other girls involved, but Lacey was a bloody little snitch and—

Shut up! Just SHUT UP! It was deliberate, just to wind Bailey up. But when he turned round, the girls on the table behind were in their tight group. Bailey might as well be invisible. And Indigo might as well not have existed. Even Levy, who'd apparently split from Mona again, was leaning towards Comfort with a smile. Any minute soon, a tentacle would slip out of his sleeve and dive down the top of her shirt.

Austin poked him. 'What d'you reckon? You gonna give it a go?'

'Leave it.'

Another finger jab in Bailey's arm. 'You seen her skirt? It's tiny, man!' He looked thoughtful. 'Indigo's legs were good, though. But she hadn't got enough . . .' He swept his hand past his chest.

'You going to be a knobhead all your life?'

'Touchy!' Austin wiggled his fingers. 'Maybe if there was a bit more touchy, she wouldn't have run off.'

'Is that what Soraya says? "More touchy, Austin"? Or has she given up on you and found a proper man?'

Austin's face changed. 'Not funny, man.'

'I reckon it is.'

Austin turned his back on him and started talking to Harbir. Comfort giggled. Under the table, Levy was nudging her feet with his top range Air Force.

Godalming came in and glanced around the class. 'Okay, *1984*. Which, of course, you've all read.'

Yeah, Bailey had read it. Dad had given it to him when he was twelve, muttering something about media conspiracies and social workers.

'So.' Godalming held the book up. 'Is Doublespeak still relevant today?'

Yes, Mr Godalming, it's called telling lies.

Where the hell was Indigo? She must have changed her number. All he had were little pieces of her – the hair he'd found under his pillow. Her t-shirt, the one she took off in his music room, balled up next to his music books. The pictures they'd taken at Covent Garden.

Dad had made him promise. If he told Bailey what he

knew, Bailey had to swear to leave Keely alone. Indigo had spent a few nights in one of the residential homes in Ilford. Then she was passed on to a 'specialist foster carer' in Brent. If Dad knew any more, he wasn't saying.

Last Saturday, Bailey had taken the train to Willesden Junction and spent the afternoon switching from bus to bus, peering out of the windows. He'd gasped out loud when he saw a girl coming out of the clothes shop – DMs, high ponytail, mini skirt, everything. He'd jumped off the bus at the next stop and sprinted back. It was a woman in her early thirties. She'd almost had a heart attack when Bailey ran up and stopped right in front of her.

He'd even logged on to the Blondie discussion forums to see if she was there. Anyone with anything to say seemed to be Dad's age. Soraya, Jade, no one knew where she was. And no one seemed to care, either.

Bailey had to find her. He wanted to feel her head resting against his chest, feel her fingers in his hair. And he had to show her what came through his letterbox this morning.

The English lesson dragged on. *What's the significance of the cage full of rats?* Carly said something about war and literally facing your fears. Godalming looked like an open safe full of money had suddenly appeared at his feet.

Finally, the bell rang for the end. Austin shoved his books into his bag and stormed off. That was the problem with Austin. He could give it but he couldn't take it.

'Bailey?'

'Sir?'

Godalming paused, scanning the classroom for lingerers. Mona and Levy were having another argument by the door. Ayesha was still at her table, speed-texting.

Godalming called over. 'Put it away, Ayesha.'

Ayesha rolled her eyes and slunk out of the room.

'And, you two,' Godalming said. 'Take it somewhere else.'

Levy smirked back at him and slithered off, followed by Mona.

Godalming lowered his voice, even though it was just the two of them now. 'I was wondering if you'd seen Indigo.'

Bailey felt his cheeks redden. 'No, sir.'

'Oh. A pity. I heard she's not coming back. I just wanted to be sure.'

'I don't know, sir.'

'Okay. Never mind.'

There was an hour and a half to kill before physics. The old routine – meet Austin, eat chicken, talk crap – had trailed away. Bailey walked through the common room. Comfort was there with a couple of other girls, chatting like she'd been here since nursery. No one was hanging round the vending machine singing stupid Abba songs at her.

Bailey had to get out. He cut through the quadrangle and went out the back way. On the main road, Rooster

C's was taken over by St Ecclestia girls. He walked round to Wings 'n' Tings. Jammed. He turned the corner into the park.

'Yo!' Austin was sitting on a swing. 'You owe me an apology!'

Bailey searched for the joke in Austin's face, but it wasn't there. 'You serious?'

Austin stood up and came towards him. 'Yeah, I'm serious, man. You didn't need to bring Soraya into this.'

'You've been bad-mouthing Indigo from the beginning. If you give out, you have to take back.'

Austin screwed up his face. 'Give out what? Indigo was mental! Anyone could see that! Except you. Indigo and Soraya.' He smirked. 'Those names shouldn't even be sharing the same breath, man.'

Austin should have ducked. It wasn't like Bailey was an expert fighter. And Austin, with his fast mouth, enough people had taken a lunge at him before. But he didn't duck and Bailey's knuckles clicked against his cheek. God! Bailey had just done that? This was stupid. He'd step back. He'd make a joke.

Austin's fist caught Bailey under the chin. His teeth clamped down on his lip. Blood. It was like there was a camera in Bailey's head, replaying the action, a second out of sync – Bailey shoving his mate back against the swing frame; Austin's head clanging against the metal; Austin

379

banging his fists against Bailey's shoulders. And there was shouting. Not his voice, not Austin's . . .

Soraya. 'What the fuck, Bailey?'

He let go. Austin staggered away.

'What's wrong with you?' Soraya said. 'You're acting like a nutcase, man!'

'That's 'cause he is a nutcase.' Austin was brushing himself down. There were dots of red on his collar and blood dribbled from his nose. 'That stupid nutcase girl. He caught it from her.'

'Ah.' Soraya's face softened. 'Indigo was all right.'

'No,' Austin said. 'She was not.'

'So that was it,' Soraya said. 'You were running off your mouth about her. Bailey was just defending her.'

Austin grunted. Soraya came and put her arms around Bailey, though, somehow, she was barely touching him.

'He needs to learn from you, hun, doesn't he?' she said. 'You were gonna take on my dad too.'

Austin scowled at them. Bailey could have laughed, but it felt like his face would cave in. His own teeth had caused him more grief than Austin's fist.

Soraya side-eyed Austin. 'Bailey's got proper upbringing. He's never gonna talk nastiness about a girl.'

It was just as well Soraya wasn't holding Bailey properly or she'd have felt him tense. He hadn't exactly talked nastiness about Soraya, but there'd been some disrespect.

380

Austin was right. Bailey should have left her out of it.

Austin's eyes narrowed. He opened his mouth. Bailey waited for him to start talking and Soraya to add her slap to the mix.

Austin said, 'Can you grab my bag, Sor? I think my shoulder's broken.'

'You'd be rolling around in pain if it was.' Soraya let go of Bailey and went and retrieved the bag. 'Dad's gone to a warehouse near Colchester today. Come back to mine and clean up.'

Austin winked.

Soraya rolled her eyes. 'Clean up. That's all.' She hoisted Austin's bag over her shoulder next to her own. 'You going to be all right, Bay?'

Bailey lifted his hand.

'Cool.' She gave Bailey a little wave. Austin looked straight ahead.

The ache in Bailey's hands was working its way up his arms. He wiped his mouth. Blood and spit slicked across his palm. He sank down on the swing where Austin had been. They hadn't had a fight since they were ten. But he'd just punched Austin. In the face. And Austin had upper cut Bailey's jaw. If there'd really been a film of it, they'd look like a couple of sock puppets being moved about by a drunk bloke. They'd still hit each other, though. And Bailey had really wanted that first punch to hurt.

He took out his phone. Nothing new in the Blondie forums. No new notifications that could be her. Her old number still wasn't recognised. Where was she? Maybe there was someone else now. Someone who didn't stick their nose into her secrets. If she walked into his path right this second and he had to pretend to forget all the things he knew, could he? If that meant being with her, maybe.

He pulled the official-looking envelope out of his bag. Thank God he'd got to it before Dad did. How would he explain why he had a copy of Indigo's parents' marriage certificate or why he'd circled one name in pencil?

Bailey had tapped the name into Google. It had all started to make sense. But there were still questions to ask.

Nelson's Motor Repairs' forecourt was empty, but the double doors were open. Bass was booming out from the back, hardcore dub from a pirate station. Someone had switched the tinny radio for something a bit more megawatt.

'Hello?' Bailey had to yell over the beats.

'What?' Rif, the sulky mechanic, sauntered out from the office.

'Where's Horatio?'

'Not here.'

'Where is he?'

Rif shrugged. He must have been one of those kids in

class who'd roll his eyes at the teacher and look around waiting for everyone to laugh.

Bailey said, 'I need to speak to him.'

Rif shrugged again. 'Yeah?'

Bailey imagined it. Grabbing a handful of those stained overalls. Rif's head against the swing poles instead of Austin's.

Bailey took a deep breath and stepped back. 'Got a number for him?'

'Yeah, but I ain't giving it to no total stranger, am I?'

The MC on the radio was shouting his call-outs. The bass kicked in again, making the air rattle.

'I am not a total stranger,' Bailey said. 'You were here when I came in last time.'

'Can't remember.'

'Okay,' Bailey said. 'You know that picture he's got in his office? That's his dead daughter and her baby.'

Rif's mouth fell open. *Yeah, wondering why Horatio didn't confide in you?*

'Well, his granddaughter needs his help. And you can be the one who tells him why he didn't get called.'

Thoughts were trying to form in Rif's mind. Bailey almost expected to see his head start bulging.

'If I get bollocked, I'm going to come and find you, right?'

Of course he was.

'He lives in Miner Street. I don't know the number but there's loads of old cars outside.'

As Bailey left, Rif must have jacked up the volume. *Rewind, rewind, rewind, rewind.*

Yeah. Rewind.

Rif was right. Horatio's house stood out. A London cab rusted in the driveway and a van was parked in the front where a garden should be. Another two cars were slowly disintegrating on the pavement close by. It was like Horatio had moved his forecourt to the road outside his house. If his neighbours were anything like Bailey's, they'd hate him.

The curtains were drawn, but there was a bag of rubbish by the bin. Bailey knocked on the door and waited. After a few seconds, a chain jangled, disconnecting from the bolt and the door opened.

Horatio was smaller. In the garage, there'd been a toughness beneath the overalls, but in his sweatpants and jumper he looked like he had lost parts of himself. Beyond Horatio, a carpeted hallway led to stairs on the right and rooms off to the left. The front door wobbled as Horatio steadied himself, wincing as he tried to stand straight.

Bailey said, 'Are you okay?'

Horatio gave him a cold look. 'You didn't turn up at my doorstep to ask after my health.'

'No.'

'Is this about my granddaughter?'

Bailey nodded.

'I told you, I can't help you.' Horatio started to close the door.

Bailey held out his hands to stop it. 'Yes, you can. I tried to help her but I got it all wrong. Indigo really needs you now.'

Horatio's eyes narrowed. 'What did you do to her?'

'I . . . I gave her the picture. The one I showed you. I thought she should have it.'

Silence.

'Please, Mr Bankes. Please, can I come in?'

Horatio sighed and moved away from the door. 'This way.'

Bailey followed him down the hallway into the kitchen opposite the stairs. The walls were white, like Bailey's kitchen, but that was the only thing that was the same. Bailey's kitchen was a constant witness to Dad's cooking experiments. There were boxes full of spices, a pasta machine clamped to the work surface, a poster about different types of mushrooms. Horatio had the basics. Kettle, small fridge, microwave, cooker.

Horatio picked up the kettle. 'So you want me to clear up your mess.'

'I want to find Indigo.'

'I told you. I haven't seen her since she was a baby.'

'But you could find out where she was. You could ask her foster mum.'

'I have no reason to do that.'

'I think I have a reason. There's something she needs to know.'

The kettle thudded down on to the counter. 'Are you the expert, Bailey? On what people should know and what they shouldn't know?'

Bailey's face was heating up. 'I didn't mean it like that. Sorry. It's just that . . .'

'Go into the front room. I'll bring the tea.'

The front room was small, with faded floral wallpaper. The door knocked against an armchair stuck in the corner next to the window. A sofa was pushed against the wall opposite. A big picture hung on the wall – young Horatio and his wife on their wedding day. He looked like he was trying to smile at the camera and his wife at the same time. His wife was just staring at him – *love, love, love.* There was a dresser against the far wall, like the one Nan used to have. Nan's cupboards were loaded with the matching dinner sets she'd pick up at charity shops and her shelves were crammed with photos of Dad and Uncle Len from when they were toddlers, through to their weddings, along with random photos of family from Trinidad.

Horatio's shelves were stacked with magazines and a load of brightly covered books that could be photo albums.

Nothing must have moved for a while because Bailey could write Muse's whole back catalogue in the dust.

Horatio came in with the two mugs. 'You want sugar?'

'No, thank you.'

Bailey took his tea. Horatio lowered himself into the armchair, took a sip from his own mug and placed it on the windowsill.

Horatio said, 'Sit down, then.'

Bailey sat on the sofa. Was he supposed to start? Horatio was staring at the wedding photo on the wall. His chair was dead opposite it.

He seemed to force his attention back to Bailey. 'I'm waiting for you to talk.'

Right. Start. 'I . . . I was on the bus and these girls were giving Indigo grief. A homeless-looking guy got on and started shouting at them.'

Horatio leaned forward. 'What did he look like?'

Ill. Drunk, Falling apart beneath his stained clothes. 'I think he's about the same age as my dad.'

'How old's that?'

'Fifty-four.'

'And then what?'

'He followed me and we ended up in a café and he gave me the photo. He said he wanted to—'

'I know what he wanted because you came to my garage and told me. That should have been the end of it, Bailey.'

'Yes . . . but—'

'That man kidnapped her.' Horatio's voice rose. 'My wife never forgave herself.'

He knew.

Horatio was staring at his wedding picture again. 'He came here, you know.'

'Who?'

'Your homeless man. He came to me first, telling me how sorry he was about Olive's passing.' Horatio's voice rose. 'I told him what he could do. How dare he?'

'He came here?'

Horatio was watching him closely. 'I thought you were an expert. About what I should know.'

'No, sorry. It's just, I found out—'

'He's Indigo's uncle.'

The hot mug was burning Bailey's knuckles. He looked round for somewhere to put it, but the side table was piled with motoring magazines. He took a sip of tea. It was bitter and strong. He let the mug cradle in the palm of his hand.

Horatio said, 'Olive knew him, you know. That's what hurts me the most. He betrayed her, Bailey, but it was worse. She didn't tell me. I found it written down after she died. She used to write me letters, in case she forgot it. But she never remembered to post them. He used to come to the park. He wouldn't talk to her, but it was like they were playing a game, both of them pretending they were

388

strangers. He'd just sit and watch Indigo play. One day Olive was distracted when another child fell. When she looked round, he and Indigo were gone.'

'Did she tell the police?'

'She described the man, but he phoned the police himself and told them where to find the child.'

'Why didn't the police charge him?'

Horatio sat back. 'Olive changed her mind and told them that she gave him permission. Now I know she was already ill.'

'Do you think she really did give—'

'Do I think *what*, Bailey?'

'Did she give . . . sorry. Nothing.'

'Good. Then there is nothing else to say.' Horatio started pushing himself up. His face creased with the pain.

Bailey said, 'Would you like to know how Indigo is now?'

'It's too late.'

'You don't have to see her, but I can tell you. The last time I saw her, we went to the Horniman Museum.'

Horatio sighed and dropped back into the chair, rubbing his knee. He seemed to have shrunk even smaller.

'The Horniman?' It was the first time Horatio had smiled. 'I used to take her up there in her buggy. She hated the animal room. It always made her howl.'

'She still doesn't like it.'

'Does she remember me?'

'I don't know, but why should she? It's like everyone forgets about her. Even her sister, Primrose, dropped her.'

'Primrose?'

'She's moved to Australia and told Indigo she doesn't want any more contact with her. There's no one.'

'That's not true. Social services—'

'Indigo smashed up her foster mum's flat. It was like she wanted to be sent away. It's like she doesn't want to give anyone a chance any more.'

Another gulp of tea. Bailey licked the burn from his lips.

'Is it true, Mr Bankes? Is there really no one?'

23

Did Marcia think Indigo was an idiot, or something? She'd gone on and on with her stupid instructions until Indigo was ready to yell in her face.

No! I'm not going to leave the house until the delivery man has come!

Yes! I realise how important this is. You keep going on about it!

Because it **was** going to be such a bloody tragedy if Isolde didn't get her chemistry set in time for her thirteenth birthday.

Seriously, why the hell did Isolde need a chemistry set in the first place? She was the sort of demon kid who'd brew up a bucket of poison and dump it in the water system without breaking a sweat. Why did Marcia talk to Indigo like she was getting ready to throw a firework into a room and run, but had such a soft spot for the devil child?

Well, if Marcia thought Indigo was hanging about in this freezing hallway, she had another think coming. The delivery man'd just better bang the knocker hard enough for Indigo to hear it upstairs. It was taking time to get used to the sounds in this house. Though Indigo was going to get the hell out of here before it all got too normal.

Indigo sat down on the edge of the bed. Marcia had changed the duvet cover again. Indigo didn't get it. Poppies all over her curtains and across the bed was too much. All that red made it look like a bad accident. Keely wouldn't have forced this on her.

And that's why Indigo had done the right thing. Keely deserved better. Though Keely didn't seem to be getting the message.

Indigo slid off the bed and on to the floor. She pulled out her case from under the bed, tapped in the combo for the Isolde-proof lock and unzipped it. The brown padded envelope was under her knickers.

Keely had been clever giving it to Wade. He must have told her that he'd asked Indigo to keep an eye on the flat while him and Felix were largeing it up in Barcelona. She'd have checked when he was dropping off the keys and given him something extra. And Wade was sneaky. He'd shoved the envelope into Indigo's hand along with the keys and disappeared quickly.

Indigo tipped the picture out of the envelope. It must have taken Keely ages to match up the torn bits. It was only when Indigo looked closely she noticed the faint, thin lines like scars across her mum's nose and her own chubby cheeks. Keely had stuck the picture on to card and she must have taken it to a proper framer's. It wasn't a pound-shop clip frame.

The letterbox banged. Yeah, you could definitely hear it from up here. Indigo dropped the picture on the bed. The doorbell rang. More bangs. The delivery man must have had serious grief from Marcia to be this hardcore.

'For God's sake, I'm coming!'

She ran downstairs and opened the door. It was an old mixed-race guy holding a plastic bag.

She said, 'Is that it? Don't they put no box round it? It's supposed to be dangerous chemicals.'

The delivery guy didn't say anything. He probably didn't speak English. You didn't need it to drive a van. He could stop staring at her, though. That was creepy.

She held out her hands, 'Can I have it, then!'

'You don't know me, Indigo.'

Of course she didn't bloody know him. Was she expected to be mates with every delivery driver in London? He was still having a good look at her, so she was going to stare right back. He must be in his sixties, shiny head, not much hair, wrinkly forehead. His eyes were light brown, almost the same colour as her own.

Maybe that's what was making Indigo feel odd – his eyes. It must just be a weird coincidence. She'd Googled her eye colour once. Apparently, it was called amber and was common in owls, but not so common in people.

He was just one of those people. Like her.

'Forget it!' She went to close the door.

'Wait.' He thrust the bag at her. 'Take it. It's yours.'

She looked at it. His long fingers still holding on, nails rimmed in something black, like oil. She snatched the bag from him and opened it. It was a photo album. He was already walking away slowly, like there was glass in his shoe. She wanted to call out to him, but what should she say? *Who the hell are you?* What if he was a creepo and he'd lived in one of those flats opposite Keely's, taking secret pictures of her?

No, a stalker wouldn't just walk off and leave her with the evidence, would they?

He'd gone. Indigo slammed the door shut and ran back upstairs. She sat on the bed and took out the album. The cover was made of red plasticky stuff that was supposed to look like leather. She flipped it open. The first picture was an old school photo. The girl in it was probably about ten, her forehead creased in a frown, her mouth forcing a smile. She was giving the photographer a serious side-eye. Someone had written the girl's name in silver pen on the bottom corner of the picture. Mahalia.

Mahalia? Like her mother? Why the hell would he have a picture of her mother? Maybe it was a social-services delivery or Keely had sent it, but there was nothing to say where it had come from.

Indigo rolled back the protective sheet, peeled the photo

394

off the page and laid it next to the patched up picture Keely had sent with Wade. She looked from the woman holding the baby to the child in the school uniform. The sharpness in the chin, the curve in the eyebrows, it was the same in both. And when Indigo looked in the mirror, it was in her face too.

Indigo tried to flick to the next page of the album. Her fingers weren't working properly. She tried again. Two pages of babies, like some kind of baby sales catalogue. A fat baby standing up in a cot, a big, yellow dummy hiding half its face. A different baby with the same-looking face, in a bouncy recliner. Another baby in a bright red sleepsuit, lying in a Moses basket. A name was written on a label below this photo in curly letters. 'Violet'. Indigo's baby sister? If it was, she wouldn't have been 'Violet' for long. Indigo knew the way it worked when a baby was adopted. Violet would have been given a new name and would now belong to someone else. Maybe when she was older, she'd find out that she was the end of a rainbow.

Indigo's family, stuck in time under plastic pages. Dropped off by an old man with eyes like hers and oil under his nails. An old man who had pages full of her mum, her sisters, her brother. Not just an old man. Her granddad.

She banged the cover shut and brushed the album on to the floor.

And now he was hammering the letterbox again. Her

stomach flipped. He must have thought she was an easy win. All he had to do was show her an album full of babies and she'd be happy. It didn't matter. He was the same as JJ, marching in and trying to ruin her life. He'd had his chance. He was fourteen years too late.

She stomped downstairs and flung open the door. It was a short Indian guy in a hi-vis waistcoat. He handed her a package addressed to Marcia.

'Name, please.'

'Indigo.'

He tapped it into his electronic reader and left. The street was empty. Good. She closed the door and dumped the parcel on the radiator shelf. Now the stupid chemistry set had come, she was going to sort out her things to take to Felix's. Marcia could moan to social services as much as she wanted, but Indigo was still going to go. It was going to be the best, lounging around in her PJs and sitting wherever she wanted without glares from Marcia because she was in her beloved hubby's chair. The photo album was going to stay right where she left it. It would give Isolde something to look at when she snooped in Indigo's room.

She stepped back and skidded on a piece of paper. It was folded in half, and there was her name again, written in capitals on the front. She opened it up, spreading it across the chemistry set. The letters kept fading, like they'd been written leaning against something soft. Maybe he'd stopped halfway down the street to rest the paper against his knee.

Dear Indigo,
   Sorry if I frightened you. I am going to the café next to the Co-op. If you would like to meet me, I will be there.
   Horatio (your grandfather)

Her grandfather. Her mum's dad. The one who'd got rid of her when she needed him the most. Dropping her a note through the door like everything was all right. It damn well wasn't.

She thumped back upstairs. At least when Marcia wasn't there, no one complained about her being too noisy. The album had fallen face up on the carpet, pages splayed open. No more baby photos. No photos at all. But there was a gift tag, shiny white card with black writing and a trail of dark blue ribbon. She kneeled down over it.

Happy birthday, my beautiful Indigo,
love Mummy.

Indigo flipped the page over. A lock of hair, darker and curlier than her own. She stroked the bump in the plastic cover. Was it Teal's? Primrose's? Maybe even Violet's, but it looked thicker than baby hair. She turned another page. A

397

recipe for pancakes written in pink felt tip, dotted with splashes of grease. And then it was back to photos again. Children, different ages, different school uniforms. She squinted at one. That was Primrose! And then . . . God! Indigo herself. Just when she'd hit reception class. She'd loved that red jumper, and she was gutted when she'd had to leave the school. And there she was again, a couple of years later, in a grey blazer, scowling. Year Seven, hair up and she'd just got her second lot of piercings. Both her ears were bright red. She'd hated that photographer; he'd been so full of himself, but she'd managed to force out a smile while frowning at the same time. She turned page after page, quickly, until the end. The final page was empty, but the plastic was loose and wrinkly, as if something had been taken out.

Indigo flicked back to a photo of a toddler in flowery dungarees wearing a grin that was going to split her face. Someone had built a sofa fort, just like the one she'd put up for Nial at Mischa's. Two high-backed dining chairs were parked either end of a sofa with a big, tartan blanket draped over them. A cuddly owl was perched on a cushion, amber eyes peering over the kid's shoulder.

There should have been two owls. The memory was flickering alive, like the film on slow stream again. But one owl is a prisoner inside the fort. And laughter, as the blanket dips lower and lower, heavy on Indigo's head.

And suddenly, everything changes. She's screaming, but her mouth is filling with thick fibres, her nose too. There's darkness and her own breath making her skin damp and the screams caught inside her until she's going to burst. Black-stained fingers lift her free. She rests her cheek on the overalls, he strokes her back until she stops crying. Then, together, they rescue the buried owls and build the fort again.

Fort builder. Overalls. Horatio, her granddad. He was in the café down the road, waiting.

Horatio's back was to the window. As a kid, grown-ups were always so big. Then Indigo grew up too. Maybe that's why he seemed so much smaller now.

Indigo took a deep breath and pushed open the café door. A couple of workmen were sitting opposite each other, chewing sandwiches. All the other tables were taken by people on their own. Horatio looked round as the door opened, standing up as she slid into the booth opposite him. He slowly sat back down.

'Sorry,' he said. 'My knees aren't good.'

She nodded.

He said, 'I didn't think you'd come.'

'I didn't think I would, either. Thank you for the photos and stuff.'

'They're yours. We saved them. Me and your grandma.'

The waitress came and planted herself by their table.

Horatio – her granddad – said, 'You want something?'

'Hot chocolate, please.'

The waitress turned her notepad to Horatio.

He said, 'I'm fine, thank you.'

Back to Indigo. 'Any food?'

'No. Thanks.'

At last, the waitress took herself away. Horatio was staring at his fingers, picking at the oil stuck under his nails. Maybe he knew she needed to look at him, the grandfather she used to live with but whose face was lost in her memory.

She said, 'You built a fort and when it all fell in, you rescued me.'

'We built many forts.'

'And then you abandoned me.'

His fingers moved on to his mug and spoon, stirring.

'Olive, your grandmother, was ill. It happened so quickly. Though now I know there were signs before and we both pretended it was nothing. She told me she walked to the shop at the end of our road and suddenly couldn't remember anything. The shop, the street, where we lived, nothing. She was going to call the police, but she'd left her phone at home and she said she wasn't sure if she'd remember the number. She sat down at the bus stop and waited until it passed. She didn't go to the doctor that time and I didn't try to persuade her. We didn't want to know. Soon she needed more and more help. I almost lost the garage because I couldn't leave her. In the end, it was too much. We found the right place for her.'

'But you abandoned me. Completely abandoned me. You didn't have to do that.'

Indigo's words seemed much louder than the pop music from the radio behind the counter. Horatio's gaze stayed steady.

'I am so sorry, Indigo. So sorry.'

'Here.' The waitress placed a tall glass of hot chocolate in front of Indigo. It was topped with a swirl of cream and candy sprinkles.

Indigo said, 'Why have you come back now?'

'Olive died. The twenty-first of February. Did you hear?'

'Yes. The social worker told me.'

'You were always in her heart. When she was ill, she'd talk about you all the time, looking at the pictures. She wanted you to have them.'

'Thank you. But you could have brought me these months ago. You could have sent them through social services. But you're here now. You know about JJ, don't you? Is that why you came?'

The teaspoon clanked in the mug, then he dropped it on to the paper napkin on the table.

He said, 'Olive used to take you to the sand pit in the park. It was one of your favourite places. Mahalia bought you a wooden ark for your fourth birthday with a set of animals – elephants, crocodiles, zebras, two by two, two by two.' He smiled. 'You made little caves and tunnels in the sand and you poured in water to make a lake and got all vexed when it sank away.'

Her bright green crocodile, buried in the damp, dark sand, snout up, ready to snap at the animals coming for water. Its weight in her hand as she walked away from the sand pit.

Horatio seemed to be telling the story to himself. 'One day, another child fell over and started bawling. Olive couldn't see who this child belonged to, so she asked some people nearby. When she turned back, you were gone.'

'It was my uncle. He took me, didn't he?'

Horatio nodded.

Indigo kept her voice even. 'And he took me to my mother?'

'Yes. She asked him to.'

'She asked him? Why didn't you just take me?'

He sighed. 'Mahalia could come to our house any time to see you, as long as me or Olive were there. But the places she lived, they weren't good for children. Nor were some of the people there. She told us she'd cleaned up, but she'd told us that so many times before.'

'*Was* she clean?'

Horatio rubbed his eyes. 'Yes. Though we only found

out afterwards. Nothing for three months, which is why the drugs took her so badly. That's why they think she had a seizure. But she had tried. She had tried for you, and the baby that came afterwards. Your sister, Violet.

Horatio picked up his mug and drank his tea.

Indigo, her brother, her five sisters . . . her mum didn't get to keep a single one of them. She felt tears prickling and blinked them away.

She said, 'Didn't you try and help her?'

The mug thumped down. 'Of course we did! She wouldn't let us. She thought we were on the side of the social workers because we wouldn't let her see you alone.'

Indigo's mouth was dry, like it was trying to make her stop talking.

'She kept asking us,' Horatio said. 'And we kept saying no. That's why she asked that man to take you.'

Indigo spooned some of the hot chocolate into her mouth. The sprinkles were greasy with cream, sticking between her cheeks and gums.

Horatio's fingers were twisting round each other. 'But after that, I still don't understand. I don't understand why Mahalia's husband . . .'

His name's Toby Scott. He's my father.

'I don't, I can't understand why he did it. Mahalia wouldn't have hurt anyone. There was nothing she could do. She was helpless and . . . I can't understand.'

I can.

Indigo pushed the hot chocolate away. 'I can.'

Horatio leaned forward, frowning. 'Sorry?'

She swallowed. Sprinkles were stuck under her top lip. 'I can understand. It was something in him. Something mad. He couldn't help it. I've got it too.'

'No, Indigo. They said the drugs he took—'

'It doesn't matter what they say. I know it. It's a mad thing. It comes out of you and you can't help it. My dad had it. I do too. That's why . . .'

'That's why what, Indigo?'

She'd never looked into eyes the same colour as hers before. 'That's why I can't be with people. In case I do what he did.'

'Oh, Indigo.'

She sat back. Short breaths. It stopped her from crying. She'd had enough practice.

'Indigo, I met someone who wants to be with you.'

'I can't go back to Keely's.'

Horatio leaned forward. Indigo caught a hint of his aftershave. 'You know a tall boy? He has a complexion like mine. Hair like Michael Jackson before he went white. '

She managed a smile. 'Bailey.'

Horatio nodded. 'Bailey. He told me I should find you.' His hand disappeared from the table. 'Your grandma made the photo album, a long time ago. She hoped that one day she'd give it to you herself. I took this out because I wanted to give it to you. I wanted to make sure you saw it.'

He slid a sheet of paper across the table to her. It looked like an article photocopied from a newspaper. The greys of the print hadn't copied well. She looked up at Horatio.

He said, 'It's about Toby Scott.'

Her chest tightened. She looked at him. 'Why the hell do I want to read about him?'

'Please, Indigo. It might help you.'

She squinted at the blurred letters. It was about a fight. Some men had ambushed another one and beat him up badly. The men had just been given long sentences for the assault.

She said, 'Was that my dad who got beaten up?'

'He was in hospital for several months.'

'Good.'

'Please, Indigo. Read all of it.'

She hunched over the paper. The date had been underlined in pencil. It was a couple of years before Indigo was born. Toby Scott had just left the pub when he was attacked. It seems like the men were searching for Toby's brother, Vincent, who owed them for a drug debt, but they were happy to make do with Toby. They'd treated him like a football, kicking him from one to the other. They'd left him with a ruptured spleen, ruptured testicles, a broken cheekbone.

405

Horatio said, 'It affected him in other ways too. He started drinking more, taking drugs.'

Indigo shrugged, 'Are you making excuses for him?'

'No, I'm not. But . . . it took me a while to understand why Olive left this for you. In the end, she couldn't remember. And she may have been mistaken. But now, I believe the injuries meant he couldn't have children.'

Breathe.

He's not . . .

Breathe.

'He's not . . .'

He's not my dad? But there's no talking when there's no breath.

'Indigo?'

Lying on the floor, mouth and nose pressed against the carpet. She can't move, the cushions and blanket from the collapsed fort are too heavy. If she opens her eyes, the darkness is even thicker. Her name is echoing from above her. A hand is taking hers, pulling her out. Black oil lines as his fingers closed round hers.

'Indigo, do you understand?'

'Yes,' she sniffed. 'Toby Scott couldn't be my father.'

'It means that whatever made him hurt your mum, it's nothing to do with you. There's nothing in you but Indigo. Just Indigo. Our beautiful granddaughter.'

Just Indigo. Just her.

Indigo pushed a deep breath out. The waitress must have passed by. She'd taken the mess of cold hot chocolate and cream and left extra paper napkins. Horatio took one and handed it to her. She wiped her face.

She said, 'I'm sorry about Grandma. She left a letter for me that came in the post after she died. She loved all of us so much, didn't she?'

Horatio blinked hard and nodded.

'And did she make pancakes for me?'

Another nod.

'I wish I could remember her. What was she like?' This time she reached across the table until her fingers touched his. 'Please tell me.'

'She . . . she was beautiful too.'

24

Mum was at the table, reading a book. It was a change from the usual tower of exercise books piled beside her plate. She turned a page and took a sip of her wine. Bailey laid out the serving spoon and a fish slice. The clunk made Mum look up.

She said, 'What's on the menu tonight?'

'Something with courgettes and tomatoes.'

'Oh. Sounds nice.'

Yeah. If you liked courgettes and tomatoes. Luckily, Bailey had checked the snacks cupboard earlier. It was well stocked. He went back down to the kitchen, where Dad was manoeuvring a giant glass dish out of the oven. Courgettes for the next three days, at least. Great.

Bailey glanced at his phone, lined up in a row between Dad's iPad and his parents' mobiles. Since Mum had banned screens at meal times, they were all probably fit enough to finish a marathon from running up and down to check their messages. Or maybe it was just him. In the last couple of weeks, Mum and Dad were having conversations that didn't end in shouting, grabbing their hardware and stalking off to different rooms.

Dad kneed the oven door shut and headed towards the stairs. 'Can you bring the salad?'

'Sure.'

Bailey picked up his phone; a new message from Austin. Soraya must be training to work for the United Nations because she'd managed to get him and Austin talking again. Bailey wondered if Soraya knew how many times Bailey'd had to apologise for what he said about her. Though, respect to Austin, he'd kept quiet about it. They didn't talk about Indigo. Maybe Austin didn't trust his mouth.

Bailey replaced his phone and picked up the bowl of salad. So, they were having lettuce with their courgette and tomato. Even duck and strawberry jam would be better. He pulled the salad tongs out of the utensils jar and went upstairs.

Dad was standing by his record collection. 'Your mum and me were having a disagreement.'

Seriously? Peacetime didn't last long.

Dad held up a record. 'Viv, here, reckons the best bass line ever is "Under Pressure". I mean, come on! If you're going to have Queen, it's got to be "Another One Bites the Dust". Everyone knows that.'

Bailey laid the salad and tongs on the table. 'It doesn't mean it's good just because everyone knows it.'

'Exactly!' Mum said. 'That's my argument.' She fished a piece of lettuce out of the salad bowl. 'Even I could probably

409

do "Another One Bites the Dust" and I can't play the guitar. And I didn't say "Under Pressure" was my top choice. The Stranglers' "Peaches". That's up there.'

'All completely wrong.' Dad dropped the record on to the player and lined up the needle. 'Because of this.'

Reggae. Yeah, a good bass line, but – it was reggae. It was meant to have one.

Unfortunate Dad-skanking was happening in the corner. Mum seemed to be conducting him with her lettuce leaf.

'Toots' "Pressure Drop",' she said. 'Wins any argument.'

No, it didn't. They needed to hear Muse's 'Hysteria'. Chris Wolstenholme worked a bass line with his head and not just his fingers.

'You can't compare genres,' Bailey said.

Dad came and sat down. He sank the fish slice into the baked courgette. 'Okay, maestro. Assuming that reggae bass is superior to all, what comes next?'

Mum and Dad turned to him.

He said, 'Muse. You know that.'

Dad sighed. 'Prove it.'

Oh, yeah. Bailey could do that. They'd better make themselves comfortable, because this could be a long night.

Indigo had run out of things to look at. She'd had a poke around Wade and Felix's wardrobe – nothing exciting – and their bathroom cabinet – much more exciting. She'd found Felix's stash of Ikea candles, lit a few in the sitting room and watched a TV talent show with the flames flickering around her. It was great. It was like being a villain in her lair, yelling insults at the contestants.

Her phone sat next to her on the sofa. She'd written the message. One little tap of the 'Send' button, that's all she had to do.

Would he come?

She was going to be positive. She was going to press 'Send'.

So why was she still sitting here with her phone in her hand? She laid it face down on the sofa. Then put a cushion on top of it. Then another cushion on top of that.

Maybe she should rewrite it. Her words were hanging around in draft, waiting for their instructions to whizz over to him. But she'd been writing the sodding thing for the last hour and half. No. Not again.

She turned the telly off and zapped Wade's hi-fi with the remote control. Grace Jones. She needed strong and powerful. She needed 'don't give a damn'. She needed to send that message now.

Okay. She would. In a minute.

So, she had to have a plan if – when – he came. She didn't have to tidy up, at least. Wade and Felix's cleaner had been here when Indigo arrived this afternoon. She was a small South American woman who'd almost had a heart attack when Indigo let herself in. After that, they'd got on pretty well. Indigo might blow out the candles, though. He might think they were a bit cheesy. When he came. When she'd sent the message asking him to come.

It was nearly ten o' clock. Was he really going to come over now? Well, she was never going to find out unless she sent the bloody text, would she? She knocked off the cushions, flipped over her phone, tapped it and . . . there it went. Tiny bits of letters high-speeding it to Hackney. Gone.

She waited. The screen darkened as the phone flicked on to standby. Right.

Bailey was with someone else, wasn't he? Jade hadn't been properly sure that he didn't have another girl, not a hundred per cent. He could even have made a link-up on the train coming back from seeing her granddad, someone who could guitar jam with him and who . . . who was easier to be with.

Shit. Her face was getting hot, cheeks, forehead, behind her eyes. If – when – Bailey came, she wasn't going to be bawling into Wade and Felix's posh cushions. And Bailey was going to come. He wasn't going to let her down.

Her phone screen winked. A message. Yes! No. It was Felix. For God's sake. He and Wade were just going out for the night and wanted to make sure everything was fine. No, Felix, she hadn't invited all the Holloway Road ravers to shake the miserable woman upstairs out of her bed with electro-dance. Indigo snapped a selfie sitting in the middle of the empty room and sent it to him.

Her phone went dark again.

This was good. It gave her time to think clearly. Indigo had asked Bailey to come and talk, so that's what she had to do. Talk. She'd tell him about her granddad coming to see her and she'd say thank you. She'd show him the photo album with the article flattened under the plastic sheet, right at the back.

She picked up her phone. Nothing.

The microwave beef curry she'd eaten earlier felt like it was having a dance-off with Grace Jones. She slid the phone down the back of the sofa, pointed the remote and jacked up the music. Indigo should be able to hear Grace from the bathroom. And Bailey was going to come. So she'd better make a start on her hair.

Dad laid the three albums out, side by side, on the floor. Chic versus The Jam versus Muse.

Dad said, 'The rules are, you're allowed one track from each album. You have one minute to make your case.' Dad tapped Chic. 'Though, can I say, Bernard Edwards needs no words. Just open your ears to "Good Times" and listen.'

'Can people be disqualified for being pompous?' Mum pushed her chair back. 'Come on, Bailey, help me take the dishes down.'

Courgette up. Courgette down. It didn't taste too bad. But the snacks cupboard was still calling.

Mum said, 'You load the plates, I'll bring the rest of the stuff.'

Bailey opened the door of the dishwasher and started stacking. Upstairs, music started, bass turned up to 'Vibrate'. Mum might be a little while; he could hear her laughing. Dirty plates sorted, he checked his phone. A text from a number he didn't recognise, probably another load of scammers telling him he was due compensation for an accident he'd never had. Except scammers didn't tell you they were called Indigo. They didn't want you to come round. They didn't want to see you right now.

Indigo. Forget butterflies in his stomach. This was like an angry kid had run through Trafalgar Square screaming at the pigeons. And meanwhile, his smile muscles were fighting to stretch themselves round to the back of his head.

'Bailey?' Mum was behind him. She gave him a curious look. 'Is everything okay?'

'It's Indigo. She's sent me a text.'

'Oh.' Mum squeezed behind him to add the serving bowls to his plates. 'Is she all right?'

'Yes. She wants me to go over.'

'Indigo wants you to go over? Where?'

'She's flat-sitting for Felix in Holloway Road.'

'It's a bit late.'

'She sent the text half an hour ago.'

Dad's steps thundering down the stairs. 'Come on, you two! Or have you admitted defeat?' He looked from Bailey to Mum. 'Ah. Have I interrupted something?'

Mum said, 'It's Indigo. She wants to see Bailey.'

'Does she?' There was a smile in Dad's voice. 'That's good.'

Bailey knocked out a message back. He should call her, but not with Mum and Dad exchanging parent looks across the kitchen.

I was upstairs. Missed you. Then he deleted the first three words and sent it.

Mum was saying, 'She wants him to go round now.'

'Okay,' Dad said.

'"Okay"!' Mum's voice had an edge. 'Are you sure about that?'

'Yes,' Dad said quietly. 'I am.' He took Mum's hand. 'Weren't you about to make your case for The Jam?'

Mum was resisting him.

'Come on,' he said. 'At least we won't have to listen to any more Muse.'

Mum sighed. 'Be careful, Bailey. Let me know when you're there. Just so I know you're safe. And tell her . . .' Mum shrugged. 'You'll think of something.'

415

Holloway Road was two rows of shops split by a wide river of traffic. At nearly eleven o'clock at night it was as busy as daytime, with kebab shops, student bars and mini-cab firms, all servicing the local nightlife. Wade and Felix lived in a street behind a boarded-up petrol station. The Street View pic showed a terraced house with a white plaster front and a grey door. Their flat was in the basement, though, with a separate entrance down some steps.

Do not ring the top bell! The old Irish woman who lives there's gonna call the police!

When Bailey had read that, it had turned into Indigo's voice inside his head.

Bailey opened the small gate and walked down the steps. The door opened before he'd even reached it. Indigo was standing there, waiting for him. He moved closer and laughed out loud.

She said, 'Do you like it?'

He said, 'Yeah! It's the best colour in the world.'

Because the heap of hair piled into a loose beehive on top of her head was now bright red.

They were face to face, almost eyelash to eyelash, Indigo taller on the inside step. Her eyes dark copper. He breathed her in and caught the perfume she'd been wearing in Covent Garden.

He said, 'I missed you.'

She smiled. 'I know. You've sent me about hundred messages.'

'Sorry.'

'I know.' She took his hand. 'So am I. You coming in, then?'

She closed the door behind him and clicked the latch in the place. No going out until morning. His heart bumped, like it needed to remind him to keep on breathing. He took off his jacket and hung it on a wall hook. He'd planned it on the bus, all the things they needed to talk about. He'd even made a list on his phone in case he forgot, but . . . his arms reached round her and she was holding him too, her hands slipping beneath his jacket, beneath his t-shirt. Muscles were supposed to have memory, but did skin? His body instantly remembered her. She released him and took his hand again, leading him into the sitting room. Wooden floorboards, a big squashy sofa, a fireplace lit with candles. And music too. Grace Jones's 'Vie En Rose'. They sank into the sofa, his arms wrapped around her, kissing her forehead, her nose bridge, her lips. He moved a curl of hair to kiss her neck.

She said, 'D'you really like the colour?'

'It's gorgeous.'

'So's Wade's bathroom now.'

She eased away from him, just enough to make his arm strain.

She said, 'Don't you think we should talk first?'

Yes. He did. Well, sort of did. That's why she'd invited him. That's why he'd made all those notes on his phone. He shuffled closer to her, the sofa cushion bending to tip her towards him. She curled her feet under and laid her head on his shoulder. He buried his face in her hair, his world turned scarlet. She shook her head, like she was trying to dislodge him.

'Okay,' he said. 'You're right. Let's talk.'

She took a big breath. 'I want to say thank you.'

He stroked the damp hair tucked behind her ear. Her ear was tipped with red too. 'Thank you for your thank you, but you don't owe me anything.'

'I do, Bailey.' She lifted her head and shifted sideways, cross-legged, facing him. 'My granddad came to find me. Do you want me to pretend you'd nothing to do with that?'

'He really wanted to. He'd just convinced himself you wouldn't want to see him.'

'He was nearly right.'

'I'm sorry.'

'What for?'

'If I hadn't stuck my nose in . . . if I'd just told JJ to bugger off, you'd still be with Keely.'

She picked up his hand and kissed his fingertips. It felt like a rubber band stretched tight and split apart at the bottom of his stomach.

'No,' she said. 'I wouldn't. I'm glad you stuck your nose in. I stuck mine in too, though, didn't I?'

'When?'

'Your mum. I shouldn't have told you.'

'It's been stressing them out for years.'

'And I made things crappier.' She buried her bright red head in her hands. 'Sorry.' Muffled.

'It was Dad who was having the affair, Indigo.' A small sentence, still hard to say.

Her head shot up. 'Your dad?'

Bailey laughed. 'That was, kind of, my reaction.'

'Did your mum know?'

'Yeah. I think it was supposed to be old history, but she was still pretty pissed off about it.'

She wrapped her fingers in his. 'How do you feel about it?'

He shrugged. 'I haven't really thought about that.' Because when he did, he wanted to yell at Dad for pretending to be someone he wasn't. And Mum too, for letting Dad get away with it. Indigo was looking at him, eyes flickering brown and gold in the candle light.

He said, 'You made it come out in the open. Properly open. They had to talk about it.'

'That's good,' she said.

'Indigo?'

'Huh?'

He reached out and rested his hand on her knee. 'There's something else.'

Her face was hard to read. 'I think I know.'

'You know?'

'Sort of. Why JJ came back.'

'It's because—'

Her hand clapped down on his mouth. 'Don't.'

The music had stopped. Now it was just the distant sirens speeding along Holloway Road. And she was crying. That wasn't supposed to happen. He leaned towards her, but she moved away.

'I'd always thought I got it from my dad.' Words between breaths. She lifted the edge of her t-shirt – his t-shirt, the Guns N' Roses one he'd lent her. As she wiped her eyes with it, he caught a glimpse of her skin, a hint of neon-pink bra. 'I was sure it was from him.'

'What was?'

'The thing. I thought if he had it, I had it too. I was scared I'd hurt everyone. Keely, you, Felix.'

'But you didn't hurt anyone.'

'I bashed up Keely's flat, Bailey. I made her send me away.'

'You did it because you didn't want to hurt her.'

Indigo didn't reply.

'Indigo? How many times has it happened in the last few months?'

Still silence.

'Indigo?'

'Once.' A whisper.

'Just once.'

'Yes.' A tiny smile. 'Just once.'

He held out his arms and they were facing each other, sliding down against the fat cushions. Their legs interlocked, Indigo's face against his chest, he held her while she cried.

Bailey opened his eyes. The candles had burned down and street light sliced through a gap in the curtain, across the floor. Holloway moonlight.

She whispered, 'Are you awake?'

'Yes.'

She kissed him on the lips. He kissed her back. Her fingers traced a line over his t-shirt, from his belly button, across his chest, tickling the skin beneath his chin. His head filled with sliding guitar strings and percussion, four-four time with an echo, banging against his ribs. Her hands were busy, beneath his t-shirt now. She bent forward and kissed him in the hollow where his ribs met.

She said, 'Felix will never let me back here if we mash up their sofa.'

'Did you tell him I was coming over?'

'He guessed. And he's not planning to come home early, neither.'

Indigo swung off the sofa and stood up, holding out her hand. He took it.

She said, 'Are you okay?'

Before he could answer, she rolled her – his – t-shirt up and over her head. She raised her eyebrows. He took his off too. He reached for her.

She said, 'In here first.'

She led him into the bathroom, just opposite the sitting room. The bath and sink had turned several shades of red, though he wasn't sure that Wade and Felix would call it 'gorgeous'. Indigo opened a mirror-fronted bathroom cabinet.

She said, 'Take your choice.'

It was a treasure box of condoms. He felt himself blushing, grabbed the nearest packet and pushed it into his trouser pocket. Indigo was standing in the doorway, elbow on the doorframe. It was hard to ignore her hi-vis bra.

She cleared her throat. 'All sorted?'

'For the next ten years, by the looks of it.'

She grinned. 'Come on, then.'

He grinned back and followed the bra into the bedroom. Indigo closed the door, cutting off the bathroom light, casting the room in shadows, her bra now just a hint of pink. Bailey sat down on the bed, pulling her on to his lap. Her arms were around his neck as he kissed the side of her lips, her cheek, her earlobe. Her hands were making random partings in his hair, smoothing it down, teasing it back up. His scalp was tingling, as if his follicles had opened up to sing a song.

Indigo shifted round until she was facing him. He unhooked her bra, sliding the straps off her shoulders until it fell away from her. He wanted to look at her, fill his brain with the shapes and shadows of her body, but she pushed him backwards until he was lying down and she was on top of him. Her breasts pressed into his chest. God. The smell of her hair, the slick of moisture on her lips . . . He had to think about something else. Something different. Shuu coughing up fur balls. That spot that burst on Austin's chin. This couldn't happen too quickly.

Indigo stroked his face. 'Okay?'

He kissed the tip of her nose. 'Yes. You?'

'Very.' She rooted into his pocket and laid the condom packet in his hand. 'Maybe you'd better do this now, in case you forget later.'

He said, 'We don't have to. Not if you don't want it.'

She said, 'I've had a lot of time to think about it, Bailey. You wouldn't be here now if I didn't want this to happen.'

She rolled on to her back, lifting her hips high as she peeled away her leggings. His trousers came off, quick, easy.

Indigo sat up and shuffled back until she was sitting on the pillows. She lifted the duvet.

'Let's get warm.'

Yes, let's! Warm. Warmer. Feeling their way beneath the weight of the duvet. A nipple, the slope of a breast, a nub of spine, the soft skin on her stomach. Knickers, pants, eased down, kicked off and away. He turned on his side and managed to get the condom on, first time.

She was stroking his back, his thighs, between his thighs . . . *Shuu heaving it all out in the garden! Giant spot, pulsing with pus!*

Bailey turned back, leaning over her. His eyes had adjusted to the light; he could see her face clearly. Eyes watching him. Lips damp from kissing him.

He said, 'It's you first.'

She half-raised her head. 'What?'

He stroked the hair off her forehead, the other hand trailing down between her legs. She closed her eyes and he rested his cheek against her hair. Later, he would keep his eyes open, seeing Indigo beneath him, soft, beautiful, her.

25

Indigo had cramp, but she didn't want to move. She'd been lying on her side, looking at him, for ages. This was starting to become a habit. She could see the hint of stubble. It was obvious now she knew it was there. The duvet was bunched up halfway down the bed, so if Bailey opened his eyes now, he'd be staring at her left boob.

And he did open his eyes. 'Morning. What time is it?'

'Too early.'

'Thought so.' His head moved towards her like he was going to kiss her.

She laughed, pushing him away. 'No way! Dragon breath!'

He breathed into his hand and sniffed. 'Smelled worse.'

'Yeah! From other dragons!'

Suddenly, his face changed and he jumped out of bed, a flash of bum cheek and wiggle disappearing out of the door. What the hell? Indigo didn't look that bad, did she? He came back in, staring at his phone.

'I promised Mum I'd text her last night, to let her know I got here safe.' He sat on the edge of the bed. 'Look! One, two three . . . nine messages over two hours. Oh, God, and Dad too!'

She moved so she could hug him from behind, resting her chin on his shoulder. Half of his hair was flat, the other poked up in peaks. She had to stop herself from making it all level.

She said, 'What did your dad say?'

'He's calmed down Mum, but can I please let her know first thing that I'm all right.'

She watched him tap in the words. **I'm fine, Mum.** Then. **So's Indigo.**

She said, 'Sure you don't want to send a picture too?'

He laughed. 'Best not.' He dropped the phone on to the floor. 'Fancy some breakfast?'

'Not yet.'

He gathered up the duvet and pulled it back over them. 'Me, neither.'

The clock on the DVD player said that it was nearly midday. Indigo had to admit that it was her fault. It was her who'd suggested dragging the duvet out on to the squashy sofa so they could watch TV. Her heart had blipped when the remote found *Heir Hunters*, but she didn't say anything when Bailey flicked past it. She didn't need it any more. She'd been found.

They'd settled on a David Attenborough nature programme, squished together, with Bailey propped up behind her with his elbow on the sofa arm. Indigo closed her eyes. Sir David's voice and the music was enough.

This was as much as she'd ever wanted. It was more than she'd ever thought she'd get. She should just relax into it, hold back the fidgets.

Bailey's little finger tickled her belly button.

'Oi!' She swatted his hand away. 'Get off!'

'I was just checking you're awake.'

'Yeah. I am.' She wriggled round to face him. The sofa *was* enormous until you tried to fit two people and a double duvet on it. 'I think we should go out.'

'Out? Where?'

His mouth said the words, but he was looking over her shoulder at the programme.

She grabbed a handful of duvet and squeezed. 'I want to see my dad.'

His eyes snapped back to her. 'Your dad?'

'That's what you wanted to tell me last night, wasn't it? About him.'

'You know.'

'My granddad told me.'

Bailey's eyes widened. 'He knew about it too?'

She crumpled the ball of duvet tighter. 'Yeah. Everyone knew except for me, didn't they?'

'Social services?'

'Maybe not everyone.' She let the duvet spring out of her hand. 'Toby Scott's name's on my birth certificate. They were hardly going to ask for a paternity test.'

'Did Horatio tell you what happened?'

She smiled. 'It still seems weird that you're on first name terms with my granddad.'

'Sorry, I shouldn't have interfered.'

He did look sorry too, like he really took the word seriously.

She stroked his cheek. 'No. You shouldn't have. But it doesn't mean things would have turned out any better if you hadn't. My granddad said that my other dad . . . my real dad . . . Vincent . . .' God. It still couldn't fit in her head. The homeless alkie was her dad. 'He was a bit of a drughead. He owed some dealers some money, and when they couldn't find him they took it out on Toby. He was—'

'The good one.'

His voice lapped over hers.

'That's what JJ – Vincent – told me,' Bailey said. 'Toby was the good one.'

She had another handful of duvet. She could feel her nails digging into her palm through the layers. 'After that, Toby couldn't have children, so I could never have been his. My mum told my grandma everything. She'd known Vincent for ages. Toby was in hospital for ages after he was beaten up. Vincent was really upset and somehow him and my mum got close. I know it sounds really bad, but mum trusted all the wrong people. That's what my granddad said. Vincent wanted to do more for me, but he couldn't get it together. So he used to come to the park, so he could see me.'

'When did your granddad know?'

'My grandma wrote him letters. Almost every day. She'd send them to be posted then forget and write another one. But then Vincent came to the garage and gave him the truth. Granddad thought he was protecting me, until you turned up.'

'Sor—'

'Don't say sorry again!' She slipped her knees between his. 'How did you work it out?'

'I suppose I should have thought about it earlier. Why would the guy who kidnapped you suddenly turn up out of the blue all worried about you? But I didn't have a clue. Then he said he was your uncle. I thought about telling you then . . . but it was like I was digging myself deeper and deeper.'

'What changed your mind?'

'You remember when I told you that he collapsed?'

Yes. When all she'd had on her mind was Mona and Levy bad-eyeing her outside the station.

'I thought he was going to die. It seemed so important to him. But I wanted to check that he really was Toby's brother before I told you. I didn't know his real name, but I got a copy of Toby and Mahalia's marriage certificate . . .'

'Bloody hell, Bailey!'

His eyes flicked away from her. 'Yeah. Now I'm telling you, it all sounds a bit extra. But it really mattered at the time.'

'Yes,' she said. 'I know. I'm just glad you didn't give me my parents' marriage certificate in the middle of a museum . . . what did you want it for, anyway?'

'The woman at the archives said that her brother was a witness at her wedding.'

'And . . .'

'Vincent Gardener Scott was Mahalia and Toby's witness. I still didn't know for sure if he was JJ, but once I had his proper name, it was easier. JJ had told me he'd been done for stealing slug pellets. There was a small bit about it in a local newspaper. Vincent Scott walked into a garden centre and grabbed a shovel in one hand and the pellets in another. The staff had been keeping an eye on him. They said he didn't look like a likely gardener. He didn't even make it to the door.'

'Yeah,' she said. 'He doesn't look like a gardener.'

Why the hell did she want to cry again? She breathed in and focused on Bailey's chest. She was going to count every curly hair on it and then his stubble and then, if her own chest still hurt, she'd peer up his nose and count every hair there. In the background, Sir David told them about penguins and whales.

She tried to smile it out, but the tears hadn't finished yet. 'So instead of Toby Scott, I get the drunk tramp. So what? Nothing's changed. It's still there.' She poked her stomach, gently in case her fingers went straight through. 'The big hole's still there and even though the thing's gone, it's just heavy and dark. And when I fall in, it feels that I can't get out.'

He kissed her neck, his lips close to her ear. 'When I was little, I used to get nightmares and crawl between my parents in bed.' He laughed. 'Maybe that's why I'm an only child. I'd find it hard to forget my dreams, so Mum and I used to take turns thinking up good things.'

She twisted in his arms. 'Bailey, I don't think . . .'

'What would they be, Indigo? If you were full of good things instead.'

'It doesn't work like that, Bailey.'

But what if it *was* different? What if you picked up a donut and you took a big bite and your teeth sank through the powdery icing sugar and the dough and you found . . . it didn't have to be sweet and nice. Anything would be better than the hole.

He said, 'I used to imagine I had a cloud inside me. When I was upset, it would lift me out of school and up into the sky. What about you?'

'Sand.'

'What?'

431

'Wet sand. The sort you stick your toes into and wriggle around.'

'So your good thing is sand?'

'Yeah. Sand.'

Indigo was impressed. Bailey made a decent breakfast. Pancakes with maple syrup and blueberries. And then he whizzed up banana smoothies in Wade's super-posh blender. Showers, then time to sort out their hair, side by side, battling for space in the bathroom mirror. He showed her the afro pick he always carried in his back pocket. There were so many little things about him, all waiting for her to discover, including the fact that his hair was way more work than hers. All that fluffing and patting. Blimey. By the time he was done, she'd cleaned up all the red dye splashes from the sink and tiles.

Finally, they left the flat, old school, hand in hand, like all the girls Indigo used to take the piss out of. *What? D'you think he's gonna run away or something?* No. She glanced up at him. Bailey wasn't going to run away. She just wanted to feel him next to her. And if it was just their hands, that would do.

They passed a chicken and pizza place. Bailey glanced inside.

'You still hungry?' she said.

'No. It's just . . . I met JJ somewhere like that once.'

She said, 'I'm glad you did it.'

'I'm kind of glad too. Well, now I am.'

The bus was full of Arsenal fans. As soon as it emptied out, they climbed up to the top deck, Indigo first, Bailey so close behind her she could feel him breathe.

She said, 'Front?'

'Of course.'

There wasn't much leg space. Bailey's thighs were rubbing against hers, moving together as the bus started and stopped.

Bailey kissed her cheek. 'Just let me know what you want me to do, right?'

'I don't think I even know what I want to do.'

He put his arm around her and she rested her head on his shoulder. Why couldn't the road loop round and take them back to Felix's flat?

Bailey wanted to hold her, both shoulders, turning her round to make her face him. He wanted to tell her that it was going to be all right. But he couldn't make her that promise. It was unfair.

The bus rumbled on, Sunday-afternoon London stretching out in front of them. It was like looking down at a film called *The Road To Camden*. A taxi U-turned to pick up a fare as a bus sped past the empty stop opposite. An old lady pulled a trolley across a zebra crossing. As they passed a skateboard park, a young kid shot off a curve and landed with a turn. Her mates all applauded.

She said, 'We're here.'

Bailey strained to remember it. Greyish brick houses, a mix of cars, a newsagent. That looked like the side street Dad turned into for the hostel.

He said, 'Are you ready?'

She gave him a curious look. 'No. But I don't think I'll ever be. Not for this.'

She ran down the stairs and he followed. On the pavement, he slid his fingers between hers. He wished he could summon up a ball of strength, make it snake through his body, buzz along his arms through his fingers to Indigo.

Yes. That was definitely the street to the hostel.

He said, 'Shall we cross over?'

'Just a sec. Wait here.'

She dashed into the newsagents, the door bleeping as she disappeared. She came out a couple of minutes later carrying a blue plastic bag. She held it open so he could see inside – three cans of Coke. He went to take one, but she swung the bag away.

'Later.'

She took Bailey's hand again. Maybe she'd swigged back a couple of cans of Red Bull in the shop, because she was filled with a new energy, pulling him across the road. She didn't need his strength. She seemed to be giving him hers.

She said, 'I think we should try the park first.'

'Okay.'

Okay? JJ could be so smashed he didn't recognise her again. Or shouting at things that only he could see, like some of the old people in Nan's care home.

The park was on the right. A few kids were kicking a ball across the tufty grass and close to the playground, a man sat on a bench. He was huddled into himself, a grey beanie pulled down over his head.

Bailey and Indigo stopped walking at the same time. He wrapped his arms around her. 'What do you want me to do?'

She put the bag of drinks on the ground. Her fingers glided up the back of Bailey's neck and through his hair.

She said, 'I want you to stay here.'

'What?'

'Just at first. I'll call you when I'm ready.'

Are you sure? ARE YOU SURE?

Bailey nodded.

She walked away from him, a quick, sure walk. He wanted to run after her, bring her back to him, before JJ even noticed. But she must have called out something because JJ looked around. Then he stood up, steadying himself slightly on the bench. Was he drunk already? Or just weak and ill? He held out his hand. Indigo took it and they sat down together. Indigo opened the bag and offered it to her father. He took out one can; she took another. JJ opened his and sipped.

He'd told Bailey that Toby was the good one. And maybe that's how it was at first, the two of them with no family of their own. They'd had to look out for each other, though it was Toby, the youngest, who was doing the looking out, taking the beating for his brother's drug debts. Knowing that he'd never have children of his own. And then he had his chance. Marrying Mahalia, offering a proper family home for Vincent's child while Vincent was inside again. Did Vincent agree that his brother's name went on Indigo's birth certificate? Maybe that's what he was telling Indigo now.

They both turned to look at Bailey. He knew what Indigo wanted him to do. She wanted him to sit down next to her, so close they'd touch. She'd offer him a Coke and he'd hold her hand. And he'd listen as Indigo and her father told each other their stories. Old stories. New stories.

That poem from school was stuck in his head, now. The one that made Indigo sink into her chair. The one that made Saskia and Mona start their stupid songs. Maybe now Indigo understood. She had always been loved.

You were
the fishes red gill to me
the flame tree's spread to me
the crab's leg/the fried plantain smell
replenishing replenishing

Go to your wide futures, you said

Acknowledgements

The obvious thanks – my parents, for my inspiration to tell stories and win arguments. To Josephine – my plot sounding-board, my modern-teen language and etiquette advisor, my guitar hero and Muse expert. Thanks for your thoughts on *that* scene. Oh, and for sending me pics of Jackie Chan with puppies when I'm feeling down. To Patrick for knowing everybody. To Aunty P and Linda for encouraging me to love books from an early age and for the libraries – Whitehawk, Haywards Heath and in my schools, that fed the hunger. Likewise, those wonderful teachers, from the ones who read Roald Dahl to us at primary school to the secondary school teachers who widened my reading horizons. (Mr Jones and Mrs Sykes (aka Miss Clarke) – do you realise how chuffed I was that you got in touch?)

For the razor-sharp critique from Nathalie Abi-Ezzi, Katherine Davey, Jenny Downham, Anna Owen and Elly Shepherd. You continue to stop me embarrassing myself.

A big thank you to the booksellers for your massive support so far, including Waterstones, Letterbox Library, Pages of Hackney, Write Blend in Liverpool and One Tree Bookshop in Petersfield. A big-up to the bloggers – Chouett,

Charlie Morris, Jim Dean, Little Luna and Tea Party Princess, among many, who have been outrageously generous with their support. Likewise other children's and YA writers. Good grief, you are so welcoming. Cressida Cowell, Juno Dawson, Jane Elson, Candy Gourlay, Liz Kessler, Tanya Landman, Anthony McGowan, Teri Terry – just a few who have offered warmth, encouragement and advice. David Almond – we have never met, but you generously allowed me to inhabit *Island*.

The Lost and Founders – Kathryn Evans, Eugene Lambert, Olivia Levez, Sue Wallman. For chats about second-book wobbles and for bubbles in the Premier Inn in Liverpool. And the rest of the SCBWI network for friendship and expertise. (Tania Tay, you rock!)

Catherine Johnson – you are, and always will be, my role model. Alex Wheatle and Malorie Blackman, you have opened doors. I hope so many more will step through.

And thank you, Grace Nichols, for the kind use of your wonderful poem. It is at the heart of this book.

Hachette folk, past and present – Anne, Jen, Kat, Nina, Sarah, Lauren and so many more – I'm so happy you kept me on. A special call-out to Michelle Rochford, cover designer extraordinaire, and Emma Goldhawk, who will happily debate a hyphen with me as well as help me shape a mass of ideas into something we can both be proud of.

For my friends who will ensure my head remains in

proportion to the rest of my body – Carolyn, Flo, Liz G., Miranda, Natalie, Odina, Sheryl. Lisa – thanks for getting the word out in NZ! Lucy – still having to read my stuff after forty-five years. (And your mum!) And Pauline – thank you for the guidance on haircare and the . . . um . . . other details.

For the girl below me at school who inspired Bailey. I do remember your name, but it's not fair to mention it here. To all the people who shared their tales of bereavement and loss, in private and in books. Thank you. It makes people like me feel less alone. I am also so grateful for people with experience of the care system, good and bad, some I have met personally, others who have published their accounts. I hope I have done you justice.

Finally, to Caroline, Felicity and Megan at Caroline Sheldon Literary Agency for – well, that would be another whole page!

Discussion Points

💔 *'It was easy for the thing to wake up, scrabbling and hooking her insides, heaving itself through her.'*
Indigo calls her anger 'the thing'. Why do you think she does this?

💔 Bailey and Indigo come from very different families. What does the word 'family' mean to you? Can you think of families that aren't like yours? What do you like about these families?

💔 Grief is a theme that runs through *Indigo Donut*. Have you helped someone who is grieving, or have you experienced grief in your own life? How did you handle either situation? Do you think grief applies to circumstances beyond someone dying?

💔 Would you have forgiven JJ for what he did? Why? And if not, why not?

❤️ Indigo's icon is Debbie Harry. She dresses like her and loves her music, but she also identifies with Debbie as she was also in foster care. Do you have any icons you admire? How are you influenced by them?

❤️ Both Bailey and Indigo like to match their musical choices to their mood. Do you do this too? Can you think of any go-to songs that match certain emotions?